TIANA
GIFT OF THE MOON

Women of the Northland Series
Volume II

Pinkie Paranya

All rights reserved. This is a work of fiction. No part of this book may be reproduced in whole or in part in any form or format existing or to be developed without the express written permission of the publisher.

TIANA
Gift of the Moon

Copyright © 2004 by Pinkie Paranya

ISBN: 1 59025 020 6
First Edition

Cover Art by Bob Paulson

Published by SANDS Publishing, LLC P.O. Box 92, Alpine, CA 91903
Visit our Website: www.sandspublishing.com
Printed in the USA   0 9 8 7 6 5 4 3 2 1

Thank you to the readers of *RAVEN WOMAN*, the first book in the series *Women of the Northland*. You have been so supportive and positive in your comments.

An especially big thank you to my friends Hal Smith who reads my work and provides excellent feedback, Gloria and Johnnie Vickers who never say no when I need them, and Erika Weichmann, a lovely person inside and out. Bobbie Black, a true friend, what would I do without you? I treasure your friendships.

Again, to Elizabeth Klungness and Sandra Smith, thanks for your editing and computer expertise and to my sister Donna Garrett for her love and support.

Last but certainly not least, a big thank you to Sandy Scoville and Diana Saenger of SANDS Publishing for your patience, foresight and attention to detail. You've been a pleasure to work with.

PROLOGUE

Tiana, daughter of the woodland people, you have been chosen to be the next Raven Woman.

"Who . . . who is speaking to me?" Tiana sat cross-legged with eyes closed, hugging her body with arms wrapped around her chest. She thought of her earlier visions of the Raven Mother. Tiana took shallow breaths, her heart tripped hard in her breast, afraid to move else the voice might leave. But in the quiet, the voice continued.

I am Oolik, daughter of Umiak, the first Raven Woman chosen by Tulunixeraq, the Raven Mother.

Should she answer? Would that destroy the vision? But if it did, she knew she would have no answers to the long ago visions of her people. Tiana feared to speak, but also feared that if she remained silent, Oolik would disappear. "Many stories have been passed down of you and your mother, of how courageous and strong you were. And how you made the mountain passes safe for all travelers," Tiana said.

My mother and I lived a good, long life together. When it was time for me to leave, it was with my mother's blessing. The wolf and the raven accompanied me on my journey. We traveled across many mountains and over tundra.

"Legends tell us you reunited with your mother's people."

I had a loving family with many daughters of my own, but none were chosen as Raven Women. The mystical Raven Belt has been passed down through many uncounted winters, over vast expanses of the Northland, until it has reached you, the next Raven Woman. Some of their stories have been lost in the mists of time, but the carved squares in the belt tell the story of each one. And now the belt belongs to you.

Tiana wished with all her heart she could see her, this Inuit ancestor of so long ago. She tried to form an image on her closed eyelids of Oolik standing in front of her. If she opened her eyes, she knew the voice would melt away like the snow piled against the sides of the tent.

I must go back. You will have many trials and suffer many ordeals throughout your lifetime, but being Raven Woman is an honor and privilege not given to many. You need to be strong — to earn the right to wear the Raven Belt so that you may pass it on to future descendants. Your reward will come with the ability to change your destiny and that of your daughter.

When would she have a daughter? What would she and her daughter create for the people to better their lives as did Umiak and Oolik? Would they create legends to be told after everyone she knew had left this earth and gone to the other side? It was too much for a young maiden just-turned-woman to understand, and her head slumped forward in sleep.

TIANA

 **ONE**

Northern Canada and Alaska A.D.600

"HE comes! The giant sun-touched bear walked through our camp last night leaving his signs behind," Quaanta, a man who seldom showed his feelings, shouted. He bent his head to peer into the tent at the two women and the astonished girl sitting before him.

Grandmother spoke into the sudden silence, the first to recover from the shock of seeing her daughter's mate in such a state. "It is an omen, a sign from the spirits. Surely it foretells the end of our hunger."

Tiana shook her head. A child of nine summers understood that to slay a grizzly was forbidden under any circumstances, even if the tribe starved to death.

Quaanta withdrew his head and shoulders from the tent flap, still unable to contain his exhilaration. "The shaman has called a meeting in the *kaslim*, the big tent."

Grandmother, her daughter Akiia, and Tiana sat in silence after Quaanta left. Finally they dressed in their outer furs, with no words coming forth, so great were their apprehensions.

Outside the bite of the northern wind sweeping down from the nearby mountains chilled Tiana to the bone, in spite of her jacket made of badger skins and the wolverine cover for her head. She looked around the camp at the snow swirling and sifting through the village of caribou and moose-hide tents. Most of the tents were conical shaped to prevent snow piling up and offered a small opening to crawl in and out of. Some of the tents put up by less skilled families had snow piled high on the sides, now hardened in the brittle cold of the forest. Wind shrieked between the willows and pines in a never-ending cacophony of discord. The tribe had named this *the winter of the big snows* which Quaanta, her father, said was the reason the game had disappeared.

The shaman of the tribe, however, warned that someone had angered the spirits.

Inside the large tent, the two women and Tiana sat in their accustomed place. "Mother, I am sleepy." Tiana rubbed her eyes and looked petulantly up at the woman. They rested on soft caribou skins and yet the slender girl did not have protection against the hard earth beneath the furs, and her bones hurt. They sat packed shoulder to shoulder with the adults of her tribe. Tiana was the only child permitted except for babes held close in their mothers' arms. The air was stale and heavy inside the room packed with kinsmen dressed in furs and hides to keep off the sharp night air.

The little girl had interrupted her mother's concentration, but Akiia was patient. "Hsst! Tiana, you must not speak out! You are nearly grown and were brought here to observe and learn. You, too, will be shaman when it is time. The vision of the Raven Mother came to you, and you shared it with us all. You must pay attention and watch every movement the shaman makes, for it all has a meaning. Memorize his chants. It is only in this manner you will learn to summon the spirits you will need later." The girl let out a submissive sigh, which did not deceive her mother, not even a little.

"Ayya-yayyay-ayya-yayyay . . ." Tiana watched the villagers crowded inside the large caribou skin tent belonging to the shaman, a man who seemed as ageless and ancient as the pine trees surrounding the encampment. In Tiana's visions, which foretold that one day she would be Raven Woman and a shaman, she understood the terrible responsibility. At first she was loath to tell others of her future, even her own family.

The shaman, who never allowed his name to be spoken, formed the center of their lives. He held complete control over every aspect of the tribe – including their mating, births, deaths and illnesses. The shaman was the invisible sinew around the tribe that held it together. But even at Tiana's young age, she knew his power did not come without cost. When the season of the cold came and many children and old ones perished, the shaman took the blame. When animals did not appear to the hunters and the tribe went with empty bellies, he must find a person who had violated a taboo, or accept the grief of the people as his burden. For he was the caretaker, the guardian, the one who guided them.

In the tent the shaman held the group enthralled while he performed his magical rites. He pranced through burning coals showing no signs of distress. He made voices, deeper and stronger than his own, emanate from behind the crowd and when they turned to look, no one was there. But the people waited in anticipation for his visit to the moon. They had heard a grizzly near the camp during the night and seen paw prints. A powerful spell must be put on the bear's spirit, to make it amenable to being slain by the hunters.

Tiana was not too young to know that in normal times these giant beasts were taboo for eating. Their tribe was known as the Bear Tribe and the grizzly was their totem. Now, though, some of the old ways had to be set aside. She'd known many of the elders and some of the more delicate youngsters who had already died from lack of food. This was the worst season for hunger in anyone's memory. She shivered at the thought of the tribe eating the taboo animal. Only a powerful spell from the shaman could expiate this terrible happening.

Tiana's gaze fastened on the familiar figure of her mentor. When she visited him each afternoon, she sat in her designated place on a special bear skin by the door flap and never moved from there. He was a kind man, but strict. She knew that, before the oldest person's memory, no one recalled when this shaman came to the tribe or remembered if he had a name. He had just always been there. Tall and thin, he kept himself clean, his hair trimmed and tied back with a strip of dried rabbit skin at the nape of his neck like the other males of the tribe. He never let another touch his deerskins, fearing this might disturb his mystical skills. He kept his tent clean and the dirt floor swept to protect him against harmful spirits which may be hiding in his belongings.

The shaman's voice droned on. The heel of his palm pounding the flat drum with a soft, monotonous tone that echoed the peoples' heart beats. It caused heads to nod and jerk, nod and jerk as they fell into a gentle sleep and then woke again and again. Each time they slept longer. Finally the light of the flickering lamp went out, and silent darkness enveloped them all. Only the spirits could hear his voice in concert with the wind.

Tiana closed her eyes. The shaman had taught her how to concentrate to stay awake, unlike the others. This time was important to a shaman.

An enthrallment of everyone's thoughts allowed a tranquility within a shaman's domain to accept visions, dreams and visitations from *outsiders*. A scene of her father and the hunters imprinted itself on the inside of her eyelids. Gazing in rapt attention, the sight unfolded in front of her. She had not had many visions, but those which came were powerful and true.

In the vision, Quaanta, his name meaning *the hunter who never fails to bring food to his family*, searched for the grizzly with the men of the village. In spite of the shaman's special séance to insure the success of the hunt, she could feel they did not go with joy in their hearts. None of the group, not even the bravest hunter, would deliberately search out one of the spiritually dangerous bears except for dire need.

The hunters stalked through the woods, carefully treading in one another's snow-steps, her father in the lead. The bear must not be made offended by so many men tracking him. It was proper that only a lone hunter armed solely with his knife and lance challenge a grizzly to the death. Never for food, but sometimes to prove his manhood.

She heard the crisp crunch of the snow under their boots and the soft whisper of the wind following stealthily through the pines. Her small body felt the tension of the men as they crept forward. The sensation was so strong it almost pulled her from the vision but she renewed her concentration, knowing this was important to all.

Suddenly her gaze jumped over the hunters to a clearing ahead of them. Her mouth dried, and her heart leaped in her chest. The massive animal stood upright, swaying as if he could see through the trees to the approaching men. She *knew* he could see them, and was calmly waiting. The bear was not the golden brown she expected to see, but pure white, with dark markings like shadows around his eyes.

The White One! A powerful omen. She'd heard stories passed down from the elders of the white bear that came into their village and conversed with the people in their own tongue. They were very

TIANA

hungry and were prepared to slay the creature, but the bear offered an exchange that gave the people food to survive the long winter. That was how the tribe received its name and totem. Since then, no one had seen a white bear in many generations.

The hunters might not know it was the White One until too late. They must not harm this bear. Tiana knew she must offer a chant to prevent harm to the bear and her people. Ignoring the chills sweeping up and down her arms and the dryness in her throat, her chant began in a whisper and grew louder as she went on.

"Father Bear, your golden fur has turned white,
your beauty wondrous to behold.
Oh powerful and great one, with the body
and heart of a giant
Do not take notice of my father and my kinsmen
advancing through the forest.
Let them pass."

Pausing in her song, hearing the indrawn breaths of those closest around her, she dared not lose her concentration. In her mind's eye she focused on the far away scene. Her voice took on the vibrancy of an adult, the woman whose destiny she was to fulfill.

"O great spirit of the forest, hear me,
Tiana, daughter of the woodland,
gift of the moon,
I offer a promise of the future.
One day I will be Raven Woman.
From that day forward
we will be as brother and sister.
Take what you will as an offering, but
do not permit yourself
to be the cause of misfortune
for our people,
should they break the taboo
and slay you."

Her eyelids fluttered when the bear's roar of challenge rang in her ears and echoed through her slender body. Inside the tent, no one spoke until Tiana began to stir again, rubbing her eyes as if she had been asleep. The people opened their eyes, some looked dazed and still half asleep while others stretched arms in the air and yawned loudly.

Tiana's indoor clothing of scraped rabbit skin was drenched with sweat, her trembling hands clutched the Raven Belt, her fingers tracing over the carvings in the ivory squares.

How did the Raven Belt come to her from its hanging place in their tent? The puzzled looks on the faces of her mother and grandmother showed they too had not seen her leave to bring back the belt. She rose from her seated position to be heard, and told them of her vision.

The dark-eyed stares of the people almost drove her to her knees, but she held to her mother's shoulder to steady herself. The shaman nodded but remained silent, as if considering her words. Quaanta unfolded his long legs and stood, along with the hunters who had been ready to leave at daybreak. When none of the hunters spoke, Quaanta asked, "Are you certain it was a white bear?" At Tiana's nod, he asked, "When will this happen?" thrusting his strong voice into the sea of whispers surrounding them.

She swallowed with a dry throat, not knowing how to answer her father at first. Quaanta's dark brows had grown nearly together across his forehead, giving him a look of perpetual bad temper. Her father could be kind and gentle to his family, yet stern and unyielding toward others. The tribe had no special leader, but they all looked to Quaanta for guidance. Tiana shook her head. "I do not know, Father. The vision is gone. If you slay the beast or are slain by him, it will be the same. Our people will be cursed by the taboo to suffer greater hardships than they have ever known, and it will continue through the smallest child's lifetime."

The grandmother and the mother looked at each other and shivered.

Quaanta beckoned for the hunters to follow him and stepped past Tiana, his chin tilted up, not deigning to speak to the females of his family. Tiana knew she had embarrassed him, and he would wait

TIANA

no longer to begin their hunt. Several of the older men seemed reluctant to leave with him, but seeing the younger hunters following in Quanta's lead soon changed their minds, and the men moved quietly out of the large tent, their heads high.

As soon as the last hunter left the tent, the people rushed to their feet and ran outside, eyes averted from the painful sight of the men slinking off into the forest without the usual joyous celebration and singing of praises for the animals they were about to hunt. Tiana knew it was her vision that caused the break in custom, and it hurt that she stood alone in this.

Akiia turned to Tiana and took her hands, putting them to her cheeks. "You are so young, not yet versed in the way of the shaman. Are you so certain of your dreams, my child? This could cause damage in our family that cannot be healed."

The shaman walked up to them, glaring at Akiia until she dropped her daughter's hands. He had never spoken to them before about Tiana, yet the tribe knew she was special in his eyes.

"Tiana, *gift of the moon*, is young in summers, but her thinking is not young and never has been. When little girls play in the dirt and leaves with images of small people carved from wood, Tiana sits aside from them, separate. Her eyes are always full of thought, her hands mold likenesses of small animals from mud and bits of dried vegetation, as I have taught her. She brings her offerings to me, and I place them in the sacred fire within my dwelling. When they harden, I give them to the people as charms to ward off sickness and untimely death. This serves as part of her discipline as an apprentice to the shaman." For a time all was silent.

He waved his arms, producing a heavy smoke around his body and when it cleared he had disappeared. The villagers left for their own abodes without speaking, unusual after an event in the meeting tent.

Tiana was certain her vision was true, in spite of the brief moment of anxiety.

Back inside their own shelter, Tiana looked at her mother and grandmother. Her heart felt bursting with love for them. She often wondered if she might be a disappointment to her mother, who perhaps longed for a daughter more like other daughters. But she had never been like the others and never would be. Girls and boys her own age avoided her, politely keeping their distance. Possibly that was the reason her mother wished for more children.

Her mother answered her unspoken question as if Tiana had said the words out loud, so close were they in thought. "Two babes died stillborn before you and one after. I met with the shaman to obtain his blessings for my fertility, yet there came no other brothers or sisters."

Tiana knew this and felt saddened for her mother.

Akiia brought a hot bowl of broth and knelt in front of Tiana, wiping her daughter's forehead with her cold palm. She smiled into her eyes. Behind the smile, Tiana saw the negation of her own previous thoughts. Her mother was not disappointed in her and did not wish to exchange her daughter for any other children, the look said. Tiana pretended to sip the fragrant liquid. As soon as the women turned away, she poured the contents back into the pot. Her stomach gnawed with painful hunger pangs, but this cauldron of broth might have to feed many people. Whatever they cooked or whatever Quaanta and Grandfather killed, they always shared with everyone in the group, for were they not all kin?

"Try to rest, it will do no good to worry," Grandmother said. "What will be will be, and only Tiana can judge if her words to the bear will be helpful to the hunters. Her destiny was decided long before her birth." The three rolled up in their caribou hide coverings, as close as they could get to the warm rocks of the fireplace, and slept.

Tiana awakened after a dreamless night and knew fresh soft snow had fallen during the night by the hushed sound outside their tent. Grandmother sat nearby, humming to herself and sewing on new garments for summer, weaving in dyed porcupine quills for decoration in the top part of the garment. Part of Tiana's work lay in gathering moss and fungus to make the dye which she shared with the tribe as dying for porcupine quills and for her artwork also.

She arose, greeted her mother and grandmother, and used the clay pot that sat back in the dark side of their tent. No one spoke of the meeting in the *kaslim* the night before. Later, Tiana sat near her grandmother on the caribou furs to help her sew. She pulled a piece of loose fur up to cover their bare feet.

"Tiana, your stitch is not tight. You will never sew well," Grandmother scolded with a gentle voice.

"I know, Grandmother. I will try to do better." Tiana hoped her voice sounded more repentant than she truly was. She didn't like to sew.

"It could be she is not meant to sew clothing," Akiia suggested, touching the thick, black hair that lay in a cloud around her daughter's face. After her first bleeding time and she became a woman, she would wear her hair in two braids as did the unmarried women. Akiia patted her own hair, the thick single braid looped around her head in a circle. Grandmother's hair was nearly too thin to make a braid anymore.

"Even shaman must live on this land," Grandmother said mildly, her dark eyes sharp and clear. "They must wear clothing and stay warm and eat to exist. Therefore we cannot know what Tiana needs to have knowledge of during her lifetime."

Grandmother seldom lectured, not like her husband who was full of advice and sulked when he thought his admonishments were ignored. "We live with you as do the other elders in the tribe live with their children, but we still have our own thoughts."

Tiana enjoyed the old ones living so close within their abode. During the summer months when they packed up their possessions and moved across the land to hunt, the old ones had their own shelter nearby. It was too warm then for so many bodies in one tent. "The shaman invites you to talk with him more often as you grow older," Grandmother commented. "He knows you are capable of learning and some day may become shaman of this tribe when the old one goes."

Tiana made a face.

"I understand what you are feeling, Daughter," Grandmother patted her knee. "It is not easy to be different from other children, but it is nothing you can change. One day you will grow inside your heart as you are growing within your skin and you will know a kinship with the Raven Woman and your destiny. Then you will never feel the pain of separation again. This may be part of the discipline required from you."

Tiana never spoke about what the shaman taught her, and she was certain her family, though curious, did not wish to be involved in shaman doings. She thought of her grandmother's wise counsel and vowed to look forward to the visitations rather than dread the time spent with him teaching her.

"Are you hungry?" Akiia asked, already knowing the answer.

"The long nights of cold are nearly past. We will survive until the first green shoots of plants appear under foot," Grandmother pronounced. "And then surely, the caribou, the musk ox and the wild birds will return."

Akiia walked to the center of the tent and knelt in front of the fire pit dug in the ground. The women had covered the sides and bottom of the pit with the tough, stretched lining from a caribou's stomach. This made a leak-proof shell to fill with water. Akiia lifted hot stones from the fireplace with a scoop made of moose antler, and dropped them carefully into the water.

Tiana watched as the stones sizzled and a great gust of steam shot up, clinging to the ceiling like some live thing before it dissipated into soft drops of liquid on the dirt floor. She thought of the large, skinny rabbit caught in her trap. The boiling stones would cook the rabbit quickly. She could hardly wait. In the past she recalled filled pots and drying racks covered with strips of game, but not this season.

"Ayiie, you may be right, Daughter." The old woman took Tiana's face between her withered hands, and smiled a toothless smile before releasing her. "Becoming a shaman is not easy for a woman. Although in my lifetime I've heard of medicine women, but it is not the same."

"No, I will not be a medicine woman. A shaman is different, I do not know how it differs but it may be that a shaman has a spirit within that not many own."

The mother and grandmother nodded in agreement.

"Grandmother, please tell me again about the Raven Women and how they chose me to be one of them." Tiana left the unfinished shirt in her lap, forgotten.

The old woman looked into the upturned face, seeing

TIANA

anticipation in the velvet-black eyes of the girl. She sighed, remembering how Quaanta, her daughter's husband, had chosen the name Tiana, meaning *gift of the moon*. It had been a bright, round moon that shone down on the birthing, truly a magical night.

"Nothing is for certain, little one," Grandmother chided. "First you must be judged worthy. Neither I nor your mother wished to become shaman, nor were we chosen. The magical Raven Belt has been passed down through many lifetimes. When I was yet a girl, I had a dream – and in my dream you, daughter of my daughter, were Raven Woman. Dreams never lie. Yet your father does not wish you to be a shaman," she reminded.

Tiana and her mother nodded solemnly and looked up at the belt hanging at the entrance to the abode. She stood to touch the belt and when her elders nodded in accord, she took it down and sat in her place, rubbing her fingers over the carved squares. She caressed the soft cold ivory which began to warm in her hands. Intricate ivory swivels were also carved, separating the squares with a strong ivory clasp. How had these early ancestors acquired the skills to make this miraculous creation? Many of the squares had been carved by past Raven Women and many were blank, waiting.

"I tried the belt when I was young, and your mother also," the old woman mused. "But in my dreams I saw it was not fitting. We were not the ones destined to wear it."

"And the story of the first Raven Women?" Tiana prompted with her usual impatience. Umiak's carving was of a solitary figure sitting cross-legged on the ice, a huge glacier at her back. Oolik's carving was more graceful, of three women walking on the ice with a wolf by their side. When it was her turn, what would she carve? She was skilled at painting on rocks and skins. Perhaps that was her gift as a shaman and the legacy she would leave on the belt.

Akiia and her mother smiled over the girl's head. What could it harm to speak of the Raven Women past? The rabbit would be done to falling apart by the time the males of the family returned. They did not have much to do until then, and they needed to keep their thoughts from the hunters.

"My grandmother told me and her grandmother told her, and so it has been since the beginning of time," the old woman began. When she closed her eyes, Tiana watched in fascination as blue veins in the thin eyelids seemed to move about under her skin as she spoke.

The boiling rabbit was forgotten, the howling wind and piercing cold all faded, and the story unfolded itself from the layers of the grandmother's memory.

"The first Raven Woman was Tulunixiraq who lives forever deep within a magical glacier. She is the Raven Mother. Then came Umiak and Oolik. Their names sound peculiar and harsh-sounding to our ears, for they were of a different clan. They came from the land of the frozen waters, where people ate only raw flesh and lived in houses shaped like ours only made of ice. Perhaps it is still thus."

Grandmother opened her eyes, and Tiana knew the old woman no longer saw the cozy scene with her daughter and granddaughter. It was as if her grandmother's voice conjured up the image of strange people dressed in clothing so different from anything their own people wore and speaking in a somehow familiar but different tongue.

"Umiak and her daughter, Oolik, journeyed from the land of the ice to find their woodland descendants as the Raven Mother desired them to do. Umiak learned to survive alone, with a child and a grandmother to take care of."

"In her lifetime, she destroyed the leader of the terrible clan that had preyed on travelers for as long as the oldest person can remember. They vanished, never to return," Tiana added, the only time she interrupted. When her grandmother continued the story, Tiana listened, entranced by the sing-song voice of the old woman and knowing sometimes old ones went into trances much like what happened at the shaman's séances. Everything they spoke was said to come from the spirit world because they were old and so close to returning to it.

"A descendant of Oolik – Nikvik – flew to our people on the backs of two giant Ravens. She brought with her the belt and permitted herself to be captured by our bravest hunter, so that her blood mixed with ours." The old woman wiped her thin hand across her face in weariness. "A grandmother hopes to live enough seasons more to see Tiana wear the belt."

The fire crackled and snapped in the silence, while the old

TIANA

woman's voice faded off to a whisper. No one spoke for a long time, their thoughts continuing to wrap around Oolik, the magical belt and the women of the Raven.

Akiia broke the silence. "Our people knew the legend, that there have been no male children to survive with the Raven Women. It is only the superior hunter, unafraid to father a line of females, who will take a Raven Woman as his mate. Perhaps it is because of this legend that your father despises shaman so and forbids you to become one."

As Akiia talked, the worried expression left her face. Tiana knew she remembered back to the days of her courtship, a wondrous story she told to her daughter many times over the years. Quaanta and his band were passing through the forest as Akiia and the other women from her tribe fished in the river. From the time he first saw Akiia, he left his own people, as was proper, and hunted and worked for her family until they decided he had earned her as a mate.

"When will my time come, Mother?" Tiana asked. She never tired of hearing the story, though she knew the answers by now.

"When you make a shelter in the forest for your first bleeding time," Akiia answered with fond patience. "We ask the shaman to put the marks of beauty on your chin with charcoal and if it is right, you will make a mind journey. Then the belt of the Raven Woman will be yours to wear. While you are alone in the shelter, thoughts from the spirit world may enter to become a part of your own thoughts. You must be receptive to them. They decide what manner of shaman helper spirit is yours."

These were the very words the shaman had used not long ago. Tiana wondered if he spoke through her mother and grandmother, who were very wise. Long before this vision, back when she was a child crawling on the ground, she recalled nights when she closed her eyes before sleep and sometimes within a dream, the huge grizzly appeared, always snarling and snapping angrily. It frightened her so that often she stayed awake a long time, postponing sleep. What did it mean? Was that a prophesy of how she would end her life – devoured by a huge bear?

She stared into the steam rising from the stew cooking. Normally she would be begging for pieces or a sip of the broth. Everyone said the child's belly was never full since the time of her birth. Now the delicious odors barely penetrated her thoughts. Something bothered her, clawing for attention.

The hunters did not return that day nor the next. The two women and the girl no longer tried to hide their worry. But no matter how hard she concentrated, Tiana could not bring forth another vision. Long into each night, they listened to the drumbeats and chants of the shaman inside his tent. He never stopped to sleep or partake of nourishment, for the sounds continued, without pause.

Tiana's head pounded as if the drum were inside, her scalp prickled from agitation, and yet she tried to hold it inside so as not to cause more apprehension to cloud the small space. She was helpless to do anything but wait.

TIANA

 **TWO**

SUDDEN complete silence filled the camp. The shaman's voice and drum stilled. At almost the same time commotion surfaced at the edge of the clearing, waking Tiana from her doze. She was alone in the tent. Where was everyone? She kicked away the covers and leaped to her feet to run toward the uproar.

Cries and lamentations rent the peace of the forest when the crowd flowed through the camp. The hunters paused, her father in the forefront. He did not appear to be hurt, and for that Tiana breathed a sigh of relief. They dragged behind them sleds fashioned from large beaver skins sewn together and frozen flat, piled with furs. Her heart jumped to her throat; she couldn't swallow. Had they killed the white bear? Tiana saw her mother and grandmother reach the men. To her dismay, Grandmother threw herself down on the first sled. Tiana pushed people aside to get to her mother and grasped her hand.

At the foot of the crowd, Grandmother lay on top of the frozen form of her mate, Tiana's grandfather. The second sled held another body; a hunter whose family already keened and cried.

"Tiana, help me." Akiia knelt on the snow and took firm hold of the old woman's shaking shoulders. "Old Mother, come with me. You must leave now and let the shaman prepare your husband for his journey to the other side of the earth."

Tiana knelt and took one of her grandmother's hands in hers. She fought to keep tears from her eyes. "He is no longer in his body, Grandmother, but may be looking upon us from the spirit woods." She spared a look over her shoulder toward the forest as if expecting to see her grandfather standing there watching them mourn over his body.

At first the old woman's thin frame tightened in refusal, but gradually the combined persistence of Tiana and Akiia won over. Grandmother stood on trembling legs. Her dark eyes were shiny with tears, her wrinkled face folded in upon itself with the effort not to cry any more. She held her chin high with pride.

Tiana looked up into her father's stern, impassive profile which might have been carved from the side of a stone mountain. Before they had returned to camp he and the hunters had marked their faces and upper torsos with charcoal, creating fearsome masks. Their hair, usually tied back at the nape of their necks with thongs made of deer skin, flared loose about their faces in disarray. They would stand guard to frighten away evil spirits while the shaman prepared the bodies.

The shaman beckoned to Tiana. She turned away, not wanting to obey. It was the first time he'd called on her for a death ritual. Part of her took pride in the honor, while part of her grieved that one of the men lying so still was her own dear grandfather. Even if he would be joyous in the hunting ground he journeyed to, she would miss him so.

She lifted her shoulders and followed the shaman into the tent with the bodies. New clothing for the dead, especially made for this time, lay in separate piles near the inside edge of the shaman's tent. Only with a steady effort did Tiana keep her eyes clear from the tears that wanted to spill out over the bodies. It wasn't the first time she'd seen a dead person, but this was her doing. An answer to her prayer to the bear spirit. She looked at the shaman and felt a wave of shame for the relief that he worked on the men's faces. Their eyes were closed peacefully, yet she did not wish to look upon their vulnerability.

Her fingers touched the stiff, unyielding deerskins the men wore. Blood smeared over their chest and leg coverings. When she gently cut the deerskins off with the special ritual knife the shaman handed her, nothing prepared her for the injuries on her grandfather. Part of his chest looked crushed and caved in where sharp hooves had run over his fragile body. She paused, feeling his last minutes of fear and pain wash over her, causing her legs to tremble and her hand to

TIANA

shake. The sudden kinship with her grandfather's spirit gradually turned into a gentleness like fog coming out of the woods in the morning. He told her that he was happy to be free and young again and understood her prayer to the bear to save the tribe and her father.

She turned to see the shaman watching her. He knew she communed with *someone on the other side* and did not speak or interrupt. Taking a deep breath, she bent to cut off the remaining garments. After nearly finishing her task, she paused and let her long hair fall as a veil down the side of her face to obscure her vision. She watched the shaman wash away the blood from the wounds and cover the men's faces with a special mixture of herbs found beneath certain trees. All the while he chanted low and monotonous words that Tiana did not entirely understand – words of death, of departure, of encouragement for the two spirits seeking a new place to stay. After using a special white coating made by peeling thin bark carefully away from the trunk of a birch tree and soaking it until it was pliable, he pressed that on the men's faces, then covered it all with a special moss that insured the hunters would be made whole again on the other side.

Tiana's hands shook when she tried to fit the new clothing on stiff, resisting bodies. The shaman spared a gentle touch to her shoulder and moved to help her.

Outside, she knew the men were putting together the body coverings. From semi-dried reeds and river grass, the women had woven sleeping pallets which were kept rolled up and stored to be used when a member of the tribe died. The men wound braided *babiche*, sinew made from moose hide, in and out of the side openings until they formed two rolled containers in which to slip the bodies. The dead would be put out in the sacred grounds together, since they died together, fortunate not to have to make the long journey alone.

Tiana tried not to look into the face of her grandfather, feeling it disrespectful to witness his weakness. He would not have approved. Her grandfather had been grim and austere. Not everyone liked him as she had.

When she had finished helping the shaman dress the men, she went outside to listen to some of the clan reminiscing about the old days and how her grandfather had come to win his jovial, charming wife – her grandmother. It was proper to speak of the dead, to let them know they would always be remembered.

Tiana recalled her grandfather sometimes scolding her mother as he might scold a child – not a woman old enough to have a daughter of her own. Tiana alone knew his love, the affection he'd been incapable of sharing with others, including Akiia.

Tears poured from Tiana's eyes and froze on her cheeks with her silent cry. She would miss him so. Unlike her own father, her grandfather was proud that she would be a Raven Woman one day and exulted in the idea that as a powerful shaman, she could enrich the lives of her people in many ways. His last words came back to haunt her.

"Granddaughter, *gift of the moon,* I see sadness in the back of your eyes which troubles me. In the legend of the Raven Women, each has the task of bringing together the tribes of the Northland. This signifies you must go away from us, away from the woodlands to the bare ice land. How will you do this?"

Tiana remembered hugging the thin, bony old one and feeling her warmth seep into his icy skin. "I do not know, Grandfather. When it is time, then it will come to me as it has to all Raven Women. It is not meant to be easy, but I was a Raven Woman born, you know that. From adversity comes strength."

He'd patted her back clumsily, and she'd felt as if she could break his frail body in two if she hugged too tightly. His hands touching her face had felt like crisp dry leaves fallen from the trees.

"Girl, you will decorate the wrappings of the body when they are encased later." The shaman spoke directly to her for the first time since they came together to work on the bodies. His voice shook her from the past. She nodded, not knowing how to answer.

When the hunters brought the bodies outside to be put in the containers, Tiana held her grandmother's frail hand in hers. She knew they must leave for a time to insure the dead connect with those who had gone before and not be tempted to stay in their bodies. At this special time it was possible that any spirit could manifest itself to be seen and recognized as a soul from the other side. Since she had already communicated with her grandfather, she didn't think this

TIANA

would happen, but no one in the tribe with the exception of the shaman, was comfortable with this idea, and it was clear they all wished to be elsewhere.

Tiana swallowed behind a tight throat, knowing the little girl inside her was lost forever and that from this time forward she was on the direct path to becoming a shaman.

When the shaman pronounced the time proper, chosen hunters would carry the wrapped bodies out to the forest to the special sacred ground.

Grandmother and Akiia held Tiana's hands and walked to their dwelling. When Quaanta returned to their hut, Akiia helped him remove his outer clothing and gave them to Tiana to beat out the damp snow with a stick. In spite of the cold, she held the garment close to her face, inhaling the scent of her father. Akiia smiled and took it from her to hang on a special rack near the fire. Then grandmother, mother and daughter sat down to listen, waiting patiently for Quaanta to finish eating the rabbit stew.

While she waited, Tiana sat cross-legged on the floor on soft skin pelts and held a large square of scraped antelope hide. She brought her little clay pots closer and carefully dipped her raven feather into melted beaver tallow, made up for her especially by the shaman, then charcoal and then into separate little pots of different berry juices pounded into liquid for color. She had red, blue and white to work with. Eventually she would find other colors when she went out in the woods to examine the plants. She was just learning to recognize plants that made colors and felt grateful that the shaman knew of her ability to paint and left it up to her to find her way with the colors. It was an honor that this was the first time the shaman had bid her decorate the coverings for the dead.

"We followed the great bear, walking properly in one set of tracks." Quaanta rubbed the wrinkle of tiredness embedded in his forehead.

Tiana watched the expression on her father's face and then closed her eyes to enter the scene as he described it. Would it be the same one she had envisioned?

"We sensed the bear was close. Hunters spread out through the trees to prevent the animal's escape. We heard a loud roar. The sound shook the snow from the tallest branches of the trees. Without warning, a herd of musk-ox thundered through the brush, straight toward us. Some of the men near me yelled in surprise and joy at the unexpected gift of food. The noise startled the beasts so they charged straight toward the old one standing apart from the others. The hunter knelt near by, removing a stone from his boot. The two men never saw the herd that ran over them." Quaanta directed this to his wife's mother, who keened softly enough that she could hear his speech.

Tiana recognized the exchange the bear-spirit made when she begged him not to allow himself to be killed or to slay Quaanta. This was the bargain the giant bear had struck with her; to spare her father and the rest of the band in exchange for one old man, well-used by time, and another hunter to keep him company on his passage to the other side. For this gift, he would cause the herd of animals to be offered as much needed food.

Quaanta and the two women watched Tiana who had opened her eyes from the inward journey and began painting again. She painted graceful arcs that signified moving from one life to another. Circles both large and small meant entering eternity where the dead either returned as spirits to live on the outside of the tribe's normal living to watch over them, or to stay in the other life and hunt and fish with dead comrades. She didn't know if they had a choice; she must ask the shaman. He was always patient with her questions and seemed pleased by them. Engrossed in her work, she moved the Raven feather over the worked hide, imbedding the colors.

"Daughter, do not blame yourself. Grandfather and the hunter sacrificed themselves for the good of the people." Akiia spoke without first making certain her husband had finished his story; a rudeness that startled him out of his sorrow.

"Remember, she had a vision of the white bear." Akiia said. Her mother reached inside Tiana's head to retrieve the bargain her daughter made with the White one. It had been a part of her song in the meeting tent. "In her vision she touched the bear's spirit. He told her the people would be destroyed if you and the hunters dared break the taboo and attempted to slay him. In return the bear sent the musk-ox and asked for Grandfather and one brave hunter to make

TIANA

the journey with him to another place, far away from here."

They all knew this, Tiana realized, having been present at her vision in the shaman tent, but it needed to be said again.

Quaanta's long, shapely mouth twisted, and his nostrils flared when he spoke. "It is well, my daughter, that you watched out for our people. Grandfather will be proud to join the hunter on the journey made by the bear-spirit." He placed his large hand on Tiana's shoulder. Although the pressure was great, she managed not to flinch. Tiana sighed with relief to see he was no longer angered by this vision as he had been when it first came to her. "You are strong, with much to give to our people, though your gift is tempered by a sorrow that makes me angry." He stood. "For now I want no more talk of visions. Men and women have gone to bring back the animals we have slain. We will feast tonight, to help Grandfather go joyfully to meet his adventures on the other side."

He released Tiana's shoulder and touched his fingers to Akiia's cheek. "Woman, you have given me a great treasure with this child we call *gift of the moon*. Even if I do not approve of her spirit world and though you were never able to give me a son, I am blessed."

That night and all the next day, the people in the camp moved about silently, as if paying respect to the dead lying in their midst. Even the children were subdued with their playing and stayed out from under their elders' feet. It was a different quiet than before, when the villagers had worried about starvation, dispirited and with empty, grumbling bellies. The shaman sang songs and drummed in fixed monotony as the women put the dead men's prized possessions with the bodies in the containers.

Even in the summer, the permafrost was too close to the surface to dig a large hole. The shaman and Tiana watched in a mind journey as the men walked away, singing a low, soft chant while they carried the bodies far away from the village. In the middle of the forest, she saw them pile stones around the sides and over the tops of the bark containers. On the way back to the village, they hid their footprints by dragging a branch behind them on the path and dispersed in different directions, to confuse any watching spirits and prevent mischievous ones from following them back to the village.

———

During the ensuing days, women went to work butchering the meat. Girls were put to slicing the flesh in strips to dry on the willow racks in the center of camp. Every tent contained a boiling pot with meat bubbling away. Most everyone by now, including babes held by their mothers, felt stuffed to repletion with chunks of raw liver and intestines filled with tender, musty-sweet, half-digested vegetation.

Despite the sorrow over the two deaths, vibrancy thrummed through camp; a renewed conviction that they would survive the severe winter without hunger. The people began to look forward to the coming season of plenty. Word of Tiana's intervention with the white grizzly spread. People brought gifts of scraped hides for amulets and pieces of musk-ox horn for her paintings. Sadly, she felt more isolated than before. It was clear to her that although the community was grateful, it was wary of her powers.

The shaman never came to their tent, knowing Quaanta would not welcome him in spite of reluctantly permitting Tiana more leeway with her shamanism. Tiana sneaked bowls of cooked food to his lodge. If her father knew, he appeared unaffected by the feelings in the camp, but continued to visit the campfires of his friends, where he and the other hunters played gambling games. Sometimes the shouts of their uninhibited, exuberant wrestling matches sounded throughout the woods when they played like overgrown children, their half-naked torsos sweating in the warm afternoon sun.

Since Tiana had helped the shaman in her first ritual, she was allowed to take down the Raven Woman belt as often as she liked, to look at and touch. She never did this in the presence of her father.

It was not proper to wear the belt yet, but she had need of its solace and comfort, for she felt alone even in the presence of her beloved family. Tiana knew she would always be different and apart from the others — a source of pain to her father. A voice within warned her someday she would have to go against him because her feet were set in a path, and she could not go back.

TIANA

 **THREE**

AFTER what her family and the tribe later referred to as the *winter of grandfather*, two summers sped by quickly for Tiana. They had been blessed with so much game, the tribe had not had to split up to hunt and then to assemble again in the winter for support during the cold months. Tiana knew no one, not even grandmother, had ever seen a winter as harsh as the one where they came so close to starvation.

Often women brought their children to Tiana to have her touch their round, full cheeks in a blessing. Three came to their tent door and a woman spoke, "Our children have not suffered hunger since your intervention with the White Bear Spirit."

Tiana was moved by their speech. The little children looked up with solemn black eyes and it was true, their cheeks looked round and full as chipmunks saving nuts in their mouths. She placed a hand on each shiny dark head and smiled. "We are a good tribe, and each of us has done much for one another's survival. Our shaman, too, has worked on our behalf."

As spring came upon the land, the rivers and streams thawed with swiftly running water. The hunters in the tribe had readied for caribou and deer hunting by ferocious games of competition, dancing, running, leaping, wrestling and for five turns of the sun were not allowed to eat or sleep. When this came to an end, every able-bodied hunter was prepared to leave camp knowing possibly two full moons would pass before they would return.

Before the hunter's journey, Tiana took long walks with the shaman. He pointed out medicinal herbs and plants in the meadows and thriving around the roots of trees. Once they sat for hours staring high up at an eagle's nest, concentrating hard until Tiana could see each stick individually that the eagle had used for the nest, and she could count the feathers the eagle had lost at the edge of the nest.

"We do not heal bodies only," the shaman told her. "When sick people come to us for help, we must work at healing their souls also. For to heal one part and not the other is useless. Many times an evil spirit enters a human and makes him ill. We must discover where the evil spirit came from if possible and why it has come to abide with him."

Will I be able to do all this as well as the shaman? Tiana wondered. It seemed impossible. Where would she find the sickness? In a woman's leg? Under the dark hair of a hunter? Where did sickness hide? She hadn't attended many séances for sick kinsmen, they seemed all healthy and strong.

Tiana thought of the food taboos she must honor. Never could she partake of owl, for that was the spirit helper of the shaman. She didn't know her spirit helper yet, that would come later. She fervently hoped it wouldn't be the grizzly. Lately her dreams of the giant bear had changed from the benevolent White One to a huge beast with fur the color of the sun and a deep, penetrating growl that never failed to wake her in a sweat. "Must I have a helper spirit that is fearsome?" She didn't want to look into the shaman's eyes, certain her question was not proper.

The shaman shook his head, his eyes spoke to her even when he did not say words. He'd warned her that the spirits played tricks on a shaman, and the helper spirit, especially a spirit guide, was not a choice. "We will speak of that later," he said. "Now is not a good time."

During the walks they found items to include in amulets the shaman showed her how to make to give to people for protection. They used parts of dried squirrels and lemmings, fur from different wood creatures, and many feathers, as well as plants and flowers later dried. Once they found a bird nest that had dropped from the tree and little dried skeletons of baby birds were still in the nest.

"Daughter, this is a splendid find. The mother bird has gifted us with this sacrifice. It is a magnificent talisman to ward off evil spirits from our tribe." He allowed her to carry it home, which felt to her

TIANA

like a turning point when the shaman no longer looked at her as a troublesome child, but entrusted her with an important magical charm.

The idea of tattoos had been bothering her for quite some time, but she didn't want to appear disrespectful and question him. What if she asked and he said yes? She shivered. The decoration must hurt, and she already felt the needles pierce her skin.

She finally got the courage to ask him one day as they sat out in front of his tent. "Will I wear tattoos on my chin such as yours?"

He studied her a long while until she began to feel uncomfortable. His eyes could pierce like a shaft from a hunter's lance. Finally he shook his head.

"I do not think it is appropriate. Male shaman do it, some females have it done, but you will be a strong and powerful woman one day, with no need to show superiority by decorations on your face."

Tiana couldn't help her big sigh of relief, and noticed the shaman look away to hide his smile. She had seen the tattoos done and it must be very painful, even if the shaman did create a spell to take away the pain. An older woman skilled in the procedure would drag a needle and fine sinew through the soot of an oil lamp and then pull it in and out through the surface skin of a young person in long lines from the bottom of the lower lip to the tip of the chin. Sometimes there were many rows and the recipient sat patiently without a murmur, eyes straight ahead. Although in passing years it did present a comely appearance, Tiana did not want it done to her. And certainly Quaanta would not have permitted it.

Finally it was time for the hunters to depart. At first when the shaman left, Tiana panicked. What if something happened to the families in her care while he was absent? But the respect and honor shown her by the older women soon allayed that fear and she became comfortable with the new responsibility.

Tiana especially enjoyed being a part of the women's work when the hunters were gone. Sometimes she merely observed them while they waited impatiently for the day of the first salmon run. They worked on seines made of the inner bark of willow trees and strong nets from sinew. They set the boys to sharpening deer antlers to use as harpoons to spear the salmon as they swam by. Often she went with the girls into the forest to gather acorns from oak groves along the river bank. At night around the campfire, the women, children and old ones left behind removed the shells. She helped the women grind the nuts between special rocks into fine dust. First they had to be soaked in water to remove the bitter taste and then covered with fresh water. They cooked the pulverized dust in a tightly woven pot to make soups and stews. Tiana didn't like making pemmican, pounding the smoked and dried strips of caribou along with the marrow from inside their bones. It made a good food for hunters and those who went on journeys and kept well all summer. In the absence of the old shaman, when she wasn't helping directly, her presence offered a blessing to the procedure.

In the gradually warming afternoons, boys played rough and tumble hunting games through the forest and dashed between tents shouting and yelling until their mothers came out to shoo them away.

Tiana often observed the girls her age playing together. At times the girls reluctantly accepted her, but the special treatment of the shaman and the retelling by their parents of the White Bear story made them wary, and they kept their distance. Tiana had painted strong, vibrant designs on her deerskin shifts and on the sides of her family tent. One of the girls asked her to paint her deerskin dress and after that they permitted her to join them when she wished.

Sometimes on a warm afternoon, six or seven girls gathered to play a special game. They drew a large circle, each doing her share of smoothing the dirt with knives and scrapers.

When Tiana was asked to join them, she used a large raven feather to smooth her portion of the clear ground. After the play area was neatened to everyone's satisfaction, the girls took turns telling stories about the figures they drew in the dirt. Some girls had carved story sticks to draw with, and again Tiana used her raven feather. Tiana's mother and grandmother had played this same game when they were children. Nothing had changed. The girls told of imaginary visitors, of simple family incidents that moved them. Tiana recognized it as a time for communicating and learning between the young girls, soon-to-be-women.

When her story telling time came, she tried to not frighten them

TIANA

by shaman doings. She told her story of how Quaanta and the mother wolf came to an agreement one sunny afternoon in the woods. She smiled to recall the incident, and decided playing with the girls sometimes was not so bad at all. At first Tiana felt warmed by their acceptance, but their giggles, laughter and silliness soon palled and she took long walks alone in the forest, trying to find her special spirit helper.

One morning the quiet air was split apart by a shriek.

"Ayii! They come!" Two old women serving as lookouts shouted from the crest of a green hill just beyond the camp. The first salmon of the season swam up the stream toward the women who trembled with eagerness and waited.

Tiana dropped her side of the net she was holding for Akiia to mend and leaped to her feet to join the boys and girls running toward the water yelling and laughing. She stood entranced at the wondrous sight of hundreds of fish, their bodies flashing back sunlight at every flick of their tails, swimming toward their camp. It seemed to her as if the river was on fire.

At the signal from the lookouts, three women ran to push a lightweight bark canoe into the water. When they reached the opposite shore, one played out the sinew net while the other managed the craft in the swiftly moving water. On shore, their partners worked feverishly to hold the long wooden stretcher taut, with the net attached, to make a barrier across the stream. The other women dispersed along the shoreline.

Each knew where her duty and responsibility lay. If anyone shirked her work, or lost fish through carelessness or clumsiness, the group talked it over later around the campfires, ridiculing the unfortunate person until she became heartily sick of it. There were few slothful ones among the women.

While they worked, an old man who could not go with the hunters kept watch above the scene. Luckily the old man's eyesight was still good. The women and children depended upon it for their lives. Attacks by other bands of roving Indians were not unusual, for the tribe of Quaanta was well known for its beautiful, hard working women. Once the summer before, the group had to run and hide in the forest until intruders went away.

No able-bodied man ever stayed behind in camp in spite of the danger to their women and children. Not only was it important to slay caribou for the coming winter months, it was common knowledge that the salmon were attracted to women. If even one hunter stayed in camp, the fish would be offended and not come into the nets.

Suddenly a frantic burst of churning, fighting masses of fish exploded against the nets. The women in the canoe at the far shore jumped out, shoved the craft up out of the water, and pulled their end of the net shoreward. As the women held tightly to the pulsing, tugging net, some plunged shoulder-deep into the frigid water to reach down and grasp the weighted bottom. They pulled it toward the top of the floating net, painstakingly dragging it slowly toward shore.

This left only the young girls, who splashed into the water's edge to grasp the salmon by the tails and toss them as far as they could toward the beach. Once the flopping fish struck land, several older women dispatched them with clubs so the slippery ones could not flip back into the water.

"Ayyah!" Tiana shouted as she tossed a large salmon, which landed back in the stream with a loud splash.

"Tiana! Do not take time to give the fish a bath. We are supposed to be catching them," a girl standing next to her teased.

Firm hands grabbed at Tiana's ankles and jerked, the penalty for being the first one to lose a fish. She fell over backwards in the cold water, splashing her arms and yelling. The older women paused to watch and laugh at the antics of the young girls.

Akiia smiled at Grandmother, it was good to see Tiana play.

The girls and women worked in the crisp sunshine of the warm spring day, not feeling the numbing cold of the water slapping against brown thighs, only the exhilaration of the back-breaking work. They did not stop until they tossed the last salmon ashore. Then they collapsed in noisy confusion on the beach, chests heaving, faces flushed from the effort.

It had been an excellent haul, and some shot looks toward Tiana as if wondering whether their good fortune was tied to this wisp of a girl. She did not acknowledge the looks, for pride had no part in a

TIANA

shaman's life. A shaman was put on earth for the good of the people. If the salmon wished to give themselves up to the women of Quaanta, who could say their reasons?

The women allowed themselves only a short respite before the real work of fishing began. First they divided the catch equally among the families. Each household had a pit ready outside the tent, lined with leafed-out willow branches and twigs. The family's portion was laid in the pit, fish heads pointed toward the inside to prevent the fish-spirit from desiring to be free.

In acknowledgment for being the eldest woman, Grandmother was given the first fish. She held it up in the air by its tail and with surprising strength, swung it around her head. "I offer our thanksgiving to the fish people," she cried out, her voice barely cracking with the effort.

Accepting this fish from her mother, Akiia knelt by her pit holding a sharp little jade-chipped knife in her hand. With quick, sure strokes, she severed the head and threw it with the intestines into a huge woven willow basket. Later they would boil it down to extract the rich oil. Bright orange flesh of the salmon slid off the shiny green blade of Akiia's knife, mixing with the sharp brightness of blood as she deftly freed the strips of meat from the backbone.

While she did this, Grandmother and Tiana knelt alongside and grasped the slippery meat, chopping it into short pieces, each one still attached to the skin. When she had enough ahead, Tiana rose and began to hang up the filleted segments and the clusters of fat roe on the drying rack.

"I have finished, Mother. I want to go to the river to wash off the blood." Tiana looked at her soiled dress and held out her bloody arms. "How is it that I am more soiled than you and grandmother?"

"You work too quickly, Child. A steady pace is better than the way you do it."

Tiana smiled, knowing her mother was right, but she was unable to do anything slowly. She ran down to the stream to wash her blood-spattered body, and knelt by the edge, pausing briefly to stare at her image reflected in the water. Her long black hair hung over her shoulders in a riotous disarray. She'd be glad when her mother or grandmother could braid it for her in long, thick braids. The short rabbit skin shift she wore did nothing to hide her slender thighs, and the beginning of the woman she would soon become. She lifted her work-weary arms toward the sky, exulting in the beautiful, bounteous day; a silent 'thank you' to her helping spirit, wherever it was.

When she finished washing, Tiana decided to check her traps along the shore. There was always the danger of raiding wolverines stealing from the traps if they were left too long. Boys in the camp usually had this task, but since Tiana was 'different', she was permitted whatever freedom she wanted. In her traps she found two muskrats and a beaver. The beaver was too heavy for her to carry so she would ask one of the boys to come back for it.

Time blurred into weary, slogging drudgery of fishing, preparation, and harvesting the bounty of their woodland traps. The women, children and a few old people worked side by side, without complaints or grumbling, thinking of the dark nights when they would be secure. This season of the snow no one need be left behind when they moved again.

The fish quit running one morning. Everyone began to relax, to take a much needed rest and await the men. They must conserve their energy for when the hunters came back with meat and hides to flense. The task of butchering, scraping skins and making new clothing fell to the domain of the women.

Still, the women were not idle. The boys and girls gathered willow roots, alder bark fern stems and bear grass for the women to weave flat-bottomed, water tight containers for cooking. They also wove deep, conical shaped containers for gathering and storing dried foods. Nets had to be replaced almost every season.

Tiana was not always welcome to help the women. Her movements were too quick and impatient and often times she ruined more than she helped. Her mother explained that this judgment was not made with unkindness, for not everyone was destined to work at the same pace.

"The hunters return! The hunters return!" Someone shouted and pointed to the men emerging from the forest and heading their way.

Tiana was anxious to see her father and to learn if the hunt had

TIANA

been successful. The thought of boiled meat and cracked marrow bones made her mouth water.

"Father!" Tiana ran up and stopped just in front of him, as was proper for a daughter who was almost a woman. Akiia watched nearby as father and daughter touched hands briefly. Quaanta's eyes echoed the affection between them as they looked at each other in the midst of the confusion. Hunting gear spread scattered in the middle of the camp where the hunters left it while men, women and children all talked at the same time with no one listening. Tiana sighed with relief, thinking of how tired she was of eating fish. The piles of bloody caribou chunks looked wonderful. Even now some of the women were dragging their share toward their tents.

"You had a victorious hunt," she said.

Quaanta nodded. "Yes, Daughter. We tracked long and found the large herd, and then in our canoes we drove the caribou into the water. They gave themselves freely for our needs and we were grateful. It will be a good winter."

Tiana frowned at his satisfaction. It was not good to tempt the lurking spirits by showing contentment. She hated to spoil his homecoming and perhaps start a quarrel with her father, so she said nothing.

The pelts lay piled on the ground, heads still attached, glassy eyes staring. Later the heads would be removed from the pelts in a ceremony, taken to a special place in the woods, and left so the departed caribou would be at peace in the afterlife and ever grateful to those who made use of their bodies for sustenance.

"We must have a celebration. To thank our brothers, the caribou," Akiia stepped up as if she knew Tiana might want to say something and anger Quaanta.

Quaanta stood tall and wide-shouldered, his face tanned to a rich russet, the color of the underwings of a hawk. Her father always reminded Tiana of the hawk. His nose arched in the middle, his mouth was curved with long lips which drew straight when he was angry. His eyes were dark and penetrating. It was fitting that he held the vibrant hawk as his totem.

He shook his head at his wife. "It would be more sensible to return to our cache before wolves and bears find it. The women and old people have plenty of work now. The time for celebration can come later." His stern expression dissolved as his eyes crinkled and he laughed. "Come, I am surrounded by women, yet is nothing prepared for a hunter to eat? Must I beat each of you?" Tiana joined in the laughter, keeping up with his long strides by skipping ahead to their tent. She had been saving some especially nice, plump berries preserved in caribou tallow just for him. Life was good.

In the coming days, the women won out. The hunters stayed to rest, eating to repletion, playing gambling games and wrestling like young boys showing off, while the women watched with sewing on their laps.

Tiana had less repose than any of the others. At night while they rested, she went to the tent of the shaman to learn more of what he had to teach her about his mystical world. She had mixed feelings about the old man. He prophesied at the time of her birth that she would be a great seer when she became a woman. Sometimes Tiana thought he might have forgotten his prophesy when he became silent and non-communicative. Then again he could be patient and careful with her feelings as much as her dear grandfather had been. The drum he used did not seem so big to her now that she had grown used to holding it, but he did not permit her to make sounds from it yet.

Women brought him prepared fish cooked over the campfire or boiled with greens found in the woods. He could not have remained behind while they caught fish, for although a shaman, he was also a man.

The shaman and the young girl spent much of their time in silent meditation, permitting their thoughts to roam at will. At first Tiana had a difficult time concentrating. She soon learned that by sitting perfectly still and closing her eyes, pictures sped across her eyelids as in a dream.

"You must always remember, once you embark on the life of a shaman there is no going back. We are put here to protect our kinsmen against hidden forces and changes in life. Because we are shaman we have the ability to shake the earth, walk on clouds, make ourselves invisible, go into the sky to talk to the moon person and raise the dead if we think someone might have departed before his

TIANA

time. It is a heavy responsibility."

"You told me once that we will have the ability to fly, to visit the sun and moon and to retrieve lost souls." This sounded frightening and yet appealed to her imagination.

"This is true. When your time comes, you may just want to fly for the joyous exercise of your powers. That is good. You must not be too full of yourself, too taken with your powers so that you fear to be excited by life."

They talked about her ancestors – Umiak and Oolik and the Inuit woman Nikvik, who joined a woodlands clan to bring the Raven line to the people.

"Have you given more thought to your spirit guide?" The shaman asked her one afternoon.

Truthfully she hoped the idea would just come to her in meditation. "It may be that the white bear shares my dreams. I spoke to him when the hunters sought to slay him. Must I have a helper spirit that is frightening? I would prefer a fox or a beaver or even a wolf."

"You have made songs for the bear." The shaman reminded her, his eyes were bright when he peered at her from under dark, bushy brows. "He listened, did he not and gave you what you asked?"

"Yes. Although I did not wish for my grandfather's death." It still saddened her that her grandmother was without a mate now, and she understood the grief the old woman felt because she, too, missed her grandfather so much. When her grandmother had that far away look in her eyes, Tiana knew she was recalling the old days with her husband. Tiana longed to touch her softly wrinkled hands and comfort her, but knew the way of the people. They bore their grief alone within their hearts, and nothing outside could warm the coldness within. That no one blamed her for his death was such a relief to her that she would be eternally grateful to whichever spirit caused this forgiveness in the tribe.

"We do not choose our helper spirit or our spirit guide, they choose us. A helper spirit lives so that it may become part of our lives. That often becomes a burden because when we ask for a favor, it does not always come as we wish. Their thinking is not like ours. Therefore, be careful what you wish for – although you did well this time, it was a fair exchange. The tribe would be lost without Quaanta."

Tiana knew this, her family understood it, and she should not have been surprised that others recognized her father's quiet strength also. He was a leader, although their tribe never had a recognized chieftain.

"You may never encounter such a rare white bear again in your lifetime. Or he may stay with you from now on. There is *inua*, or a spirit occupant, in everything put on this earth. You may find a helper spirit in a certain rock or stone, a tree or water, it need not be an animal although those are more common to a shaman. Often inuas serve as observers to tell us who broke a taboo in the village so that this person can be healed of an affliction or punished for a transgression."

"A shaman's life is complicated," she said.

"That is what you must learn. We do not have to hunt or fish to earn our keep, but the people call upon us to create good will between the tribe and the animals they hunt. In good times we hold a position of respect. In times of poor hunting and faced with starvation, the people are quick to blame us for our lack of magic or whisper in their tents that the shaman must surely have offended someone important."

"I have heard the old stories that some of the Raven Women were medicine woman and not shaman."

"We have heard that story. Often tribes had medicine women, usually very old ones well past their prime. Female shamen are few. It is said they receive the duty as you have, from the time of birth."

"Grandmother and Akiia have always told me my birthing was special. That was when my mother had the only vision of her lifetime. In her vision she saw a young woman with wings of a raven, riding on top of a running bear. It was a very troubling dream and the next night, when she gave birth to me, it troubled her even more.

"She told us how the moon was full and when she looked up into the round orb, my mother saw the same figures on the face of the moon. When she told Quaanta, he scoffed at her fears and said they would name his daughter Tiana, gift of the moon."

"Yes, that is how it happened, I was there. I made a journey to

TIANA

the moon, and he told me you would be named for him."

As Tiana walked back to her tent, she thought on the lonely life she would have as a shaman. Would any strong hunter take her to bed? Would she always know what to do when a kinsman came to her with an injury or with a harmful spirit imbedded in his head? The shaman was the oldest one in the tribe. Though it was known that shaman lived well beyond others, he was still ready to depart this life any time. She didn't feel ready to assume his responsibilities and yet, in spite of misgivings and her father's hostility toward her calling, Tiana looked forward to stepping into the path of the Raven Women.

One afternoon Tiana walked through the woods to check on her traps when shouts of boys playing reverberated through the forest, interrupting her thoughts. She stood, holding a dead rabbit by its ears, as the sudden outburst of noise disturbed a flock of ravens. The large birds surged out of the trees, wings beating the air amid raucous cries of outrage. Tiana's eagerness evaporated as she watched the birds fly away.

Was this an omen of misfortune?

She knew she was too inexperienced to read the signs properly. She walked back with a heavy heart. Should she ask her father? Would he think she was filled with her own importance, laugh at her and not believe her? It might be better, she decided, to wait and speak to the shaman about this. Having put the responsibility of what she saw on another's shoulders, she set aside her feelings of apprehension and raced toward the village.

Pinkie Paranya

TIANA

FOUR

IT would now be a long journey back to the hoard of meat for the hunters, but they had rested well. Although they had left two men at the temporary camp to prevent wolves and other animals from molesting their cache, everyone was anxious for them to leave and get back to the meat. A few of the younger boys and some of the wives went along, there being no need to hurry their return for they all had enough to do to keep busy. Those who stayed behind butchered and sliced the meat and put some to dry on the racks. They buried wrapped bundles in the ground, just above the permafrost. It would keep well unless the weather turned unseasonably warm.

Quaanta chose to go back with the hunters, and the other men agreed it would be good to get away from watching the women work. He asked Tiana to come with him. She felt tempted, but one look at the huge pile of meat to cut up was enough to tell her this would be pure selfishness on her part. Her mother needed her.

Beyond that, something gnawed at the inside of her memory that she was unable to shake away with her usual sunny nature. She struggled with the vision until she recalled the sighting of the ravens.

As soon as her chores were finished, Tiana rushed to tell the shaman about the ravens in the woods.

"Do you remember how many there were?" he asked.

"Six – no I think five." She frowned, breaking off in confusion. He would be disgusted with her, it was important that a shaman notice and remember details.

His dark eyes regarded her for a long moment, and then a wide mouth broke into a toothless grin. "Do not worry so, Daughter. You have done well – for a beginner. It must have been six ravens. Five would mean the spirits are angry with us and that cannot be. Our women have caught many fish. Our brave hunters journey to bring back enough caribou to last the time of the cold moons. No enemy has attacked us to carry away slaves. Who can be angry with us? It must have been six ravens."

The conversation should have set Tiana's mind at ease, but it did not. She wanted to tell her father about the birds, but she was afraid. Her father was loving and patient with his family, but the idea that his beloved daughter would one day become a shaman was a constant source of dissension between the members of the little family. He vowed he would never permit it as long as he was alive to prevent it.

Several days had passed since the hunters left the camp. Gradually the vague uneasiness left Tiana. She had been working hard cutting meat, her arms bloody up past her elbows. Her hair had crept out of its restraining tie, fluttering against her face and sticking to her sweaty neck.

"My daughter, why do you not cool off in the river? The work will be here when you return. Perhaps some of the other girls wish to go with you."

"I feel the need to think upon something important. May I take the Raven belt this one time?"

Akiia looked at Grandmother, and they nodded in accord.

Tiana went inside and reached up. The belt seemed to glow with warmth, as if it wanted her to take it. Tiana turned the ivory over and over in her hand, as always, admiring the workmanship and strength in this object that had been passed down to span many, many lifetimes of old people, starting before her tribe even began on the land. The swivels that held each segment were carved also. None of her people were skilled in such work. Some of the carvings had been made with a knife and depicted wolves, ravens, and glaciers while others were outlined with black liquid to stand out beautifully on the yellowed ivory squares. Not for the first time Tiana wondered what she would carve on her segment when the time came. She touched Umiak's carving of one fur-wrapped Inuit sitting alone in the

TIANA

desolation of an ice field, and then moved her fingers over the finer carving of Oolik's three silhouetted women with a wolf at their side.

She lifted her garment and fastened the belt underneath, next to her skin. Outside, she straightened her tired back and turned a grateful smile toward her mother. "I will go to the river and rest. And you? Will you and Grandmother also rest?" They watched the old woman make long, sure slices in the red meat.

The last of it, finally.

The older women agreed to take a respite from the work, so Tiana felt no guilt walking through the village to the edge of the woods. She passed several girls who might have gone with her, but she did not ask anyone. She had an overwhelming need to be alone, away from giggles and laughter and teasing. She waved and returned their good-natured shouts of greeting, but hurried on.

The thickly growing, sweet-smelling trees and bushes closed in on all sides and above her head as she entered the forest. When the darkened silence descended upon her, her tension eased, her body relaxed; the sounds of the busy camp no longer intruded in her thoughts. She plunged ahead on the narrow path, brushing aside low branches. Reaching the place where the stream widened, she walked barefoot on the round, hard pebbles lying on the shoreline.

Tiana removed the Raven belt and laid it on a pile of leaves. She let her soft rabbit skin shift fall to the ground on top of the belt. She stood poised, slender and straight, letting the sifting, shimmering rays of the sun play across her golden body. Then the child within her surfaced. With a whoop of glee she dove into the frigid water, enduring the shock all at once. The icy jolt hit her, taking her breath away, but she recovered quickly. Flipping her hair out of her face, she swam in long, sure strokes across the stream.

Time slipped away as she enjoyed her solitude until she noticed the shadows growing longer across the water. The hush of the forest deepened. Just as she was about to paddle to shore, she heard a sharp snap of a twig nearby.

Tiana froze, much as a rabbit does, hoping to go unnoticed. Her heart rose in her throat, choking her. Her legs felt as if they would not hold her up in the icy water.

Four strangers emerged stealthily from the brush.

The men looked straight at her.

"Are you alone, girl?" One of the men spoke, moving out of the trees.

She nodded. Perhaps her ability to understand them meant that they were not her father's enemies.

The one who spoke appeared younger than the rest, though not a boy, and she saw that one of his legs was twisted. He waded in toward her, and she backed away, treading water. He laughed, his teeth a slash of white against the dark tan of his face.

"We may not harm you. Do not run away." It was meant as a joke. They knew she could never outrun them, even if she had been free of the tugging, binding water that swirled around her bare legs. The young man reached out to grab her. She raked her nails across his cheek and tread water trying to back away from him. The Raven belt, she had to get to it before they found it.

"Ho, Namanet! You have captured a wolf pup." One of the men shouted encouragement while the others laughed.

The one called Namanet narrowed his eyes and regarded her warily as he dipped water on his hand and wiped away the blood from his cheek. In one swift motion, he reached out and captured both of her small wrists in a tight grasp, easily avoiding her kick in the water. He pulled her toward him, twisting her arm.

The threat of what he could do to her arm stopped her flailing legs, as he must have known it would. "Are there others? Where is your camp?" he demanded.

"Bring her out! Bring her out! Let us see what the wolf cub looks like," one of the men shouted. The man holding her dragged her toward shore. When her feet touched bottom, he let her go.

Tiana stood facing them, trembling from the icy air on her body. At first she felt no shame in her nakedness. Everybody swam in the stream, most without their deerskins. Something in the four intruder's eyes caused her to feel a difference now, as if they looked at something about her body she had never seen before.

The young man called Namanet motioned for her to pick up her shift. She slipped it over her head and in one swift motion grabbed up her belt as he repeated his question. With trembling fingers, she held the belt behind her.

TIANA

"Answer, girl! Where is your camp? How many are you?"

What was she to do? If she told them of the camp and led them there, perhaps the women and old men could overpower these four. But if the surprise was too great, they could easily capture many of the women and children for slaves and kill the old ones.

"What people are you? Where is your village?" she asked.

One of the older men lashed out with his hand, slapping her across the face. She felt an explosion of light in her head and the taste of blood in her mouth.

"Do you dare question us, wolf cub? We ask what we wish to know!"

Tiana saw Namanet step toward her as if in defense, but he seemed to think better of it and moved back again. His eyes pleaded with her to answer the questions.

"My people live in a large village over there." She pointed away from the village in another direction. "We have many powerful hunters in our camp. If you wish to make war, they will be grateful. They may not slay you, only make you our slaves for the balance of your miserable lives." If they had wanted to kill her, they would have done it at first. Now she had hopes that they would consider her too inconsequential to bother with.

Tiana decided not to take the chance of leading them to her people. Better to sacrifice herself and save the camp full of old ones, women and children. If they took her with them, later she would escape. Her fingers moved over the Raven belt, searching out the familiar scratches and carvings. Touching it, she felt a strong conviction of not being alone. She tried to hold her arms steady but they trembled at the abnormal position of being behind her back. When a school of large fish splashed in the middle of the river, all the men turned away to look and Tiana swiftly pulled her shift up, hooked the belt around her middle and smoothed the deerskin down again so the belt was covered and lying next to her skin.

The men spoke together briefly. She let her breath out slowly when the three older ones turned and disappeared back into the forest, heading away from her camp. Namanet took hold of her hand.

"We are not prepared to fight, although we are not afraid." When he saw she did not laugh at him, his expression softened a little. "I saw you first, in the water. You belong to me as my captive. I must tie you – the others will make jokes if I do not." He sounded apologetic. "The older hunters do not like captives. If you try to escape or if you make trouble, they will slit your throat and leave you. Which way do you choose?"

The young man and Tiana stared at one another for a long moment in the silent forest. She was surprised at his eyes, they were not brown, but gray like the sky on a rainy day.

"I will not make trouble for you – now. I promise no more. It is the duty of a captive to escape her captors," she pointed out with calm dignity. She did not fear this man, although there was no doubt in her mind that the others would have preferred to kill her and have done with it.

Namanet regarded her solemnly, then pushed his palm against the middle of her back to start her in the direction he wished to go. There was nothing for her to do but move forward.

It took some time for the crippled boy and the girl to catch up to the men who walked in a steady, monotonous pace that ate up the miles through the woods. Darkness came, and with it the night creatures. Close to the path, Tiana heard the sounds of life and death which barely intruded on her weariness. She sensed, rather than saw, the great owls swoop down on their prey, and the shrill cry of terror and pain that always followed. In the distance, the howl of wolves split the close blackness that surrounded them. There was no moon, but the men seemed to know where they were going.

By now Tiana's legs felt as if they did not belong to her. Her bare feet were scratched and punctured by stones and debris from the woods. Her stomach growled and complained from hunger, but she did not protest. The man who slapped her continued to grumble about bringing her along. She was still in danger of having her throat cut and being left along the trail.

She lifted her head to let the soft rainfall soak into her face. The rain made the air colder but she needed to stay alert and awake. Shivering, she tried to hide it from Namanet, but he saw. Grumbling, he unrolled a deerskin he carried alongside his pack and wrapped it around her shoulders, brushing away her mumbled words of gratitude.

TIANA

Finally, just before Tiana thought she would have to give up and let them drag her, the men stopped and leaned against the trees to rest. They each took a piece of dried meat from the small hide bags they carried around their necks and began to chew, ignoring her presence as if she were not there.

"Here, girl. Eat." Namanet finally seemed to notice her and walked forward to offer a piece of jerky from his supply.

Pride stiffened her neck and she stared at the food, tempted to spit on it. Common sense won, and she nodded. Namanet untied her wrists from behind her. The smooth ivory belt felt warm against her skin, and she was grateful that she'd had time to hide it. It wouldn't do for them to see the belt as a valuable prize and take it from her.

"What will you do with the skinny one?" One of the men teased Namanet.

"Ayiie! It will be a long time before she becomes a woman fit to warm a man's sleeping robes," one of the others commented. He reached out and pinched Tiana's upper arm. She grimaced with the pain, but made no outcry.

"She may be just fine for a crippled boy," the one who slapped her spoke.

Tiana sensed Namanet's indrawn breath at the contemptuous remark. If someone had spoken so to her father, the person would have two mouths to speak from by this time, his throat cut from ear to ear. The young man surprised her by not responding to the taunt.

She had noticed during their journey that Namanet walked with a limp, but she supposed he had hurt his foot on their journey. Indeed, she could almost sympathize. Her own bare feet were cut and bruised beyond feeling by now. If he truly was a cripple and a coward, as he seemed to be, perhaps it would not be as hard to escape as she feared.

Tiana chewed the smoky-tasting meat and considered her chances. The men seemed to forget about her, talking among themselves. Namanet had re-tied her wrists in front with a loose knot, enabling her to kneel down and scoop up water to ease her thirst. She could have slipped out of her bonds easily, but when she started to pull at them, warmth from the Raven belt next to her skin seeped into her body – a warning. Even if it were possible to escape now, it would serve no purpose. They had traveled far from her village, changing directions many times. What hope had she of finding her way back alone? Instinct told her the belt warned to stay.

"We are near our village," one of the men said.

"Good, it has been a long journey, and I am weary. I need good food and a wife to warm my back in the sleeping robes."

"I too am weary of the journey," Namanet declared. He looked at Tiana to see if she mocked him.

"You would not be so weary if you did not drag the wolf club every step of the way. We had to wait until the moon arose last night before you caught up with us. I say leave her here."

"No! She is my prize. I will not leave her behind." Namanet's voice rose, causing birds to fly startled out of the treetops.

Tiana felt shamed for him. The men had just been teasing him. Surely they would not abandon her this close to their village. It was clear that Namanet did not laugh much if at all. This made her sad for him, in spite of wanting so badly to hate him.

Sometime during the night the three older men left them behind and Tiana and Namanet awoke to a silent forest.

"Do you know the way to your village? It appears your friends have abandoned us." She didn't laugh at him, but he seemed to take it so.

"You are an ignorant girl. I do know the way to the village. It is not far." He walked closer to Tiana and knelt, picking up her feet to examine them. By now they were so numb with cold and injuries they had no feeling, but she wouldn't tell him that.

Tiana thought of kicking him in the stomach, but the kindness in his eyes overcame her anger. Closing her eyes with weariness, Tiana recalled the ravens of dark omen. If the shaman stood before her now, she might tell him they both were wrong. It had to have been five ravens, not six, and must signify someone's spirit was angry with the tribe.

Namanet picked her up and carried her the remaining distance to his village.

TIANA

 **FIVE**

TIANA awoke to the familiar sounds of a busy camp. She opened her eyes cautiously. By the shadowy outline she knew she was in a tent – alone. Someone had placed a hollowed bowl of bark near her containing some brown liquid. She reached out and grabbed it with trembling hands, for she was hungry and thirsty.

"Ayiie! So the child awakens. It has been two sleeps, and I was becoming worried about her."

Tiana looked up to see a woman enter the tent with Namanet not far behind. She struggled to gain her feet, but the woman motioned her to be still. Something about her commanded respect at once, and Tiana found herself obeying.

The woman laughed, showing good white teeth with only a few missing. "What a fine son I have. Look what a gift he brings his old mother." She turned and cuffed Namanet good-naturedly with her fist against the side of his head. He ducked and returned her laughter.

"Mother, she is skinny, true, but I believe she can be taught to work for you. Look." He grabbed up one of Tiana's hands, turning it palm up to show the calluses. "See, the girl has seen hard work. She is no child as you say. She may have seen ten summers."

"Perhaps. Perhaps not. Anyway, she is mine. You gave her to me. Child or not, stay away from her. Even the beasts of the forest do not rut with their half-grown," she warned.

Namanet snorted in derision. "I would sooner mate with a wolverine. She scarred my face." He rubbed his hand ruefully over his cheek.

Tiana listened with amazement. Her captors were not unlike her own kinsmen. They spoke the same language and appeared to have many of the same customs. She frowned, wanting to hate them.

"My father is a powerful warrior. When he comes for me, he will kill all of you."

Namanet regarded her with smoke-colored eyes fringed by thick, black lashes. The beautiful eyes were startling in a strong, masculine face. She had never seen eyes but black or dark brown. His eyes must have set him apart from the others – as did his limp.

"Your people think you lie at the bottom of the river by now – that you drowned while swimming alone. We covered our trail, and the rain washed away anything left to speak of us."

"Did you see her village?" the mother asked.

Namanet shook his head. "No, she said there were many warriors, and by then we were weary from our long journey. We had searched many full moons for the 'eaters of raw fish' who call themselves Inuit. My companions wanted to capture some of their women and children, but we did not find them. They must have returned to their land of ice. Yet they had been seen below the tree line."

Tiana listened, certain he spoke of the people who were a part of her ancestry, the people of Umiak and Oolik. If so, she was happy the warriors did not find them.

"I am called Kania," the woman shook Tiana's arm gently to get her wandering attention. "My son is a brave warrior, and . . ."

Tiana interrupted. "Brave warrior? He is a coward to make war on a young girl! He would not dare search out my village and do battle with my father!" She smiled inwardly at their startled expressions, knowing she had mother and son unsettled.

Namanet gestured as if he wanted to slap her face, but one glance from his mother held him in place.

"My son is a gift. No children had come to my husband and me after long years together." Kania's smooth, brown face creased with a grimace of troubled remembrance.

Tiana tried not to care, but could not help but feel for the woman's torment. Didn't her own mother fail to produce a child until it was time for her only daughter to be born? Thinking of Grandmother, Akiia and her father distressed Tiana, and she

TIANA

concentrated on Kania's next words.

"I promised the shaman that if he allowed us to be blessed with a child, he could have anything he desired from us. After I became big with child, my man was slain by wolves in a hunting journey. I went to the birthing place when I was already old and thought to be useless. A huge wolf came to me in the birthing lodge and demanded my boy. I refused to give him up and the animal twisted Namanet's leg for spite and changed my son's eyes to the color of a wolf's fur."

Tiana was moved by the look of love exchanged between the mother and son.

"Namanet is considered by the tribe to be a good talisman. He is special, although some of the men taunt him. He is not a coward."

"Why did he bring me here? For what purpose?" Tiana didn't bother to hide the bitterness in her voice.

Kania smiled gently and reached a hand to touch Tiana's cheek. "Everything that happens in our life is to a purpose. You were sent to us for a special reason even if we do not know it yet."

Tiana regarded the mother and son. She felt disarmed by their mutual devotion. She had never seen this before. Among her people, fathers took over the raising of their sons as soon as they stopped sucking at the teat. After this, the mother never again hugged her son or showed affection in any way, for fear of turning out an inferior hunter.

Tiana suspected there was no giant wolf at the birthing, in spite of the unusual color of his eyes. It could have happened in Kania's dreams or she could have made it up to keep the elders from killing her son. A crippled baby was usually dashed against a tree, or left in the snow in wintertime. If done before the baby was given a soul name, it was not regarded as a real person and would not return for revenge. The people could not afford a weakness among them. In that, she was certain these people were no different from her kinsmen.

In one time of snow in Tiana's earliest memory, three elderly women were left behind as her starving tribe journeyed to find food. She remembered looking back, held close in her mother's arms, as the tribe moved ahead, chanting and moaning. The ones left behind remained stoically silent, watching the retreating group with dark, inscrutable eyes. As little as she was, Tiana had a quick vision of shadowy shapes emerging into the clearing after they moved away. She shivered to dispel the terrible memory.

"My father will come for me and make war with your people," Tiana repeated her warning. "I am destined to become a shaman in our village."

Both mother and son looked disconcerted. Kania recovered quickly. "So. I am right in believing my son is guided by the spirits. Our shaman, Ikgat, is old. Long ago someone must have put a curse on him to make him hated and feared by our people. You were brought to take his place." Her voice was firm with determination.

Namanet and Tiana's startled gaze collided across the short space. They looked quickly away.

Tiana touched the belt that lay around her waist beneath her garment. No one knew of the belt, it was safe. Was that an omen of the future?

Namanet's mother reminded Tiana of a she-wolf her father had come across in the woods once as the women and children picked berries. The she-wolf, too, had been willing to fight to the death to save one pup. Her babies tumbled and played all around the mouth of the den nestled in the side of a small hill, nearly hidden from view. Quaanta had grabbed up a pup, thinking to take it back and tame it.

The she-wolf dashed out of the den and, taking no notice of the ring of observers around her abode, lashed out at Quaanta. Her yellow-gold eyes caught fire from the slanting rays of the sun, which blanketed the spring afternoon. In a moment, her father had thrust the snarling, spitting pup into a berry bag. He swirled to face the wolf, his knife ready.

If Tiana closed her eyes, she could still see it in her memory. Her father, crouched and powerful, his glinting knife echoing the baleful glare of the wolf. They circled one another warily until the wolf made a dash for his legs. By then the pups had all run to safety, deep in the bowels of the hill. This caused the mother to lose some of her fighting edge and she became more cautious.

Tiana remembered hoping her father would not be hurt, but she did not wish the wolf harmed either. No one noticed as Tiana dragged the squirming pup back toward the bushes and then

TIANA

cautiously opened the bag. She had to hold her hand over her mouth to keep from laughing. The pup was covered from nose to rear with squashed blueberries. She opened the bag wider. Like a streak of purple fur, the pup leaped out and headed toward the mouth of the den and safety.

As the little body scurried past, both Quaanta and the mother wolf stopped in surprise, watching the furry rump vanish into the brush covering the den entrance. The mother wolf followed, disappearing as if by magic.

Quaanta turned to his waiting family, sliding the knife into the sheath of his belt. It was not difficult to find the culprit. Everyone stared at Tiana, a child of six summers, standing with the empty bag clutched in her hand. She tightened her shoulders and held her head stiffly erect, waiting to receive his wrath.

She smiled now at the remembrance of her father's laughter, a big sound in the silent woods. It was then she understood. He had no desire to kill the she-wolf, but it had become a matter of ritual between the two. He could not back down once it had started.

Tiana dragged herself back to the present by the touch of a garment which Kania draped across her bare legs.

"I made this for you while you slept. You are too big to wear the one you have on. Only small girls wear their skins short as yours."

Tiana was surprised. Her shift was ordinary dress among her clan for a girl of her summers. How many other customs of this tribe would she find different? Would the shaman be friendly to an outsider? From what Kania said, he was fearsome and not loved by the people as was the shaman in her village. Did they fish? Did the men hunt? Some things must be the same as what she knew. She slipped the rabbit skin over her head, and then wriggled out of the old one while staying covered. Both Namanet and Kania laughed at her modesty, but the mother's expression showed approval.

"I thank you for your work. It fits well," Tiana said stiffly. One part of her wanted to shout and rail at these people who had disrupted her life, while another part of her felt full of curiosity and a strange sense of order – as if this was destined to happen. She had thought to escape the first chance she had. They couldn't watch her day and night. They didn't seem inclined to tie her up, for which she was thankful. But if this was her destiny to be here, the belt would let her know. She felt secure in that.

Kania knelt by her fur pallet and took Tiana's hand in hers. "Today you will rest. Tomorrow I need help drying fish. Must I keep you tied or will you stay?" Kania's words almost echoed Tiana's thoughts.

Tiana looked at mother and son, wondering how she should answer.

"Mother, the girl told me it was her duty to try and escape when she could," Namanet protested.

"Silence, my son. You are just afraid she might run away and make you look foolish. The men are going to mock you, no matter what you do. When will you understand this and refuse to let it hurt you?"

Tiana made an instant decision. When she spoke, the belt around her waist exuded warmth, as if showing approval. "I will stay with you for now. You have been kind to me, perhaps more kind than my people would have been, had they captured you. If, in the moons to come, I discover my helping spirit and it tells me I must return to my people – then I will do it or die trying."

"Honorable and truthful words," Kania said. "What are you called?"

Tiana thought a long moment. If she gave her name to these people, they might have the power to take her spirit away. But if she told the truth, word might get back to her father so he could come for her.

"My name is Tiana, it means gift of the moon." It was as if the name-surrender sealed her fate.

At first the three hunters who were with Namanet when they captured her taunted and teased him about the "wolf pup" he'd dragged home. Both Kania and Tiana heard them outside in the clearing.

"Can you not stop them?" Tiana asked. She didn't like Namanet, but it was not fair that they torment him so much.

Kania shook her head. "No, Child. It would only make it worse for him if I interfered. Sometimes we must be patient and wait. My

TIANA

son will prove himself one day, and they will leave him be."

In the small tent, Namanet was curt toward Tiana, but there were times she caught him staring at her in a strange way, as if he wanted to look inside her head. Instead of angering her, it made her like him a little more. He had to be a very lonely man. She'd not seen him with a woman. At his age he should be with his own family.

At times in the night when Kania and Namanet were asleep, tears fell from Tiana's eyes and she cried silently, remembering her father, mother and old grandmother. Did they think her dead? Did they miss her as much as she longed to see their dear faces? She missed the old shaman too. He had been strict and demanding, but kind. If it had not been for the belt imparting the feeling that she was where she was supposed to be, the torment would have made her angry and sullen. But gradually, Tiana watched the time of *almost summer* pass by, following up a long winter in the village where she now lived. Her thoughts of her first family had become comforting and a pleasant memory that was no longer painful to dwell upon. Tiana would have felt almost content had it not been for Ikgat.

"The shaman is unpopular with the people, " Kania confided in her one afternoon as they sat in their tent doing chores. Tiana stirred the cooking pot from time to time and Kania sewed on summer deerskin wear. "In his old age and infirmity he has grown spiteful and petty. He puffs up at any grievance, real or imagined, turning it into grand proportions. The unfortunate person who dares disagree with him or treats him with anything less than complete servility finds himself subject to terrible intimidation."

Namanet had entered the tent and sat near the fire, grabbing up a vessel to scoop broth into. "Yes, I and the others have seen him in such an intense rage that he writhes upon the ground in front of his tent, foaming at the mouth and snapping his jaws together. When this happens no one dares approach him. We all stood quietly around the fire, waiting to learn which of us had angered him."

"Are you fearful he can hear within your tent and know you speak ill of him?" Tiana wasn't frightened for herself but she didn't want anything to happen to her new family. The old shaman in her village claimed the ability to hear inside other's tents, but maybe this shaman was different, with other qualities. She hoped so.

Tiana felt Ikgat especially singled her as a focus for his malevolence. Both Kania and Namanet spoke of it often in hushed, worried tones. They agreed that he sensed Tiana's unwillingness to bend to his whims, a stubbornness that came with the certainty of her Raven Woman destiny.

At a healing ritual in the big tent, she witnessed the shaman's power over people. She'd never seen the old shaman back in her first village perform such a procedure. After they had all gathered in the tent and the shaman prepared them for the healing by intoning chants and a monotonous beat of his drum, he motioned the sick one to lie on the ground which had been covered with pine straw. With a strap made from caribou sinew, he placed it under the man's head while mumbling to himself about the person's infirmity, which in this case was a severe stomach ache. If the shaman could hold up the head until he finished a special spirit song, his answers would be one thing, and if the head became too heavy to hold up, he'd receive another answer.

"This man has broken taboos toward the owl. It is my belief he has slain one for his family to eat."

The man managed to protest in spite of his head being held in one position.

"Do you wish to be healed of the ache within your belly?" Ikgat spoke in a loud, deep voice unlike his own.

The man subsided with closed eyes.

"You may have done this deed without knowing of it. Someone, an enemy to our tribe, might have put this idea in you and you were unable to refuse. Now it festers in your belly like a discarded carcass filled with worms." He turned to the men and women packed inside the tent, watching. "Each of you in turn must excuse him for his violations."

Everyone knew what to do. One woman stepped forward. "Dull Knife needed food for his family, could that have been it?"

A tall man from the back of the crowd pushed forward. "Dull Knife is to be forgiven because he has grown old and his memory does not always serve. He perhaps forgot the owl was a totem and not to be slain." Murmurs of agreement came from the people. One

TIANA

by one they all stepped forward with excuses, some so thin Tiana wondered why no one laughed, but the group watched the shaman's hands manipulate the strap around the man's head as if waiting for the head to fall off.

When all had spoken except Tiana, they turned toward her with expectancy in their eyes. The shaman wanted to ignore her, she was sure of that, but could not. Everyone had to speak.

Having no idea what to say, she knelt by the sick one and put her hand gently on his head. He was burning up with heat. She pulled up his shirt and felt his stomach. The skin stretched taut over the bloat and felt hot also.

She took a deep breath. "I would carry him to the river and put him down in the cool water. His body is too hot. Then I would make a poultice of mashed berries and mushrooms and boiled pine cones and place it over his chest." This is what the shaman in her first village would have done, and she'd seen it help.

The people gasped and stepped back as if in fear of Ikgat's wrath.

"Stupid girl!" he shrieked, spittle flying from his lips. "You are only permitted to excuse this man as the others have. After the demons have heard the excuses, I will make them leave his body. Only then will he be freed from his demons."

Tiana refused to look away from his baleful glare beneath the thick, bushy eyebrows. Out of the corner of her eye she saw Namanet shift his weight first on one foot, plainly hesitating while Kania pushed with her hand in the middle of his back. He bent his head to listen to his mother's whisper and they both stepped forward, offering their support. Tiana was so proud of them, this new family of hers. She gained more courage and, separated by the prone figure of Dull Knife, stared eye to eye at the shaman until Ikgat turned away, facing the people.

"We as a tribe have excused our friend and companion." He raised his arms upward, waving his hands to depict flying birds. "The demons be gone from this man, fly away with the sparrow hawk and deliver them to his enemy so that he may become powerless to create such problems ever again in anyone from our village."

The people intoned the "Ay yah yah" that was always a standard closing of the ceremony, and they began to file out of the tent, leaving Ikgat alone with his supplicant.

Tiana never saw the man again. One night late she heard a commotion with drums and sad, dirge-like singing, but Kania told her not to go outside. Tiana was convinced the man died from the shaman's ministrations and since this was not something he wanted to admit, his loyal helpers took the dead man away into the forest.

"Mother Kania, will you fish today?" Tiana drew her long, slender legs up under her calf-length tunic to warm them. The air was cool outside their tent. The sun disappeared behind a bank of silver clouds.

"Why do you ask, child? We have fished every day since the salmon chose to come to us."

The girl remembered the fishing in her father's village and a tiny, jagged edge of sorrow stung her soul. Several seasons of the cold had come and gone since she came to this place. By now most all accepted her. With Kania and Namanet she could not want for a more affectionate, caring family life although she knew what it must have cost them both to take her side against the shaman and some of their own kinsmen.

Yet, though some of the keen edge of remembrance was lost, sometimes it came back all at once, catching her when she least expected it. When this happened, she took solace in the warmth coming from her belt – knowing it was her destiny to live this life.

As in the beginning of every hunting season in Quaanta's camp, the men made ready to go in search of caribou, leaving the women, children and old people to fish. Tiana hoped that Ikgat would go with the men, but he made it clear he stayed to guard against any mischief made in the absence of the hunters. He looked directly at Tiana when he spoke.

She longed to tell him that he was just too old and lazy to hunt knowing his food would be killed and cooked for him. As if he read her thoughts, he strode over to Kania's tent to face Tiana.

"Wolf pup, you do not fool me as you do the others. You are waiting your chance to cause trouble, and I am watching you."

Tiana felt his warm spittle strike her face. She took a deep breath, her blood singing through her body, cold sweat breaking out all over her so that she feared he might see it come through her deerskins.

The hunters had left at the first light of dawn and only a group of curious old men, women and children had gathered around the two, keeping a respectful distance. They gasped at Tiana's boldness and waited for the shaman to do something terrible to the young girl.

Kania came up close behind Tiana to offer support. Tiana saw her hands tremble as she clasped them in front of her, trying to hold them still. Tiana absorbed the older woman's fear and a sadness overcame her at the choice her new family had to make on her account. Then anger came to her because of what the shaman put them through.

"I cause no trouble. I did not ask to be brought to this tribe. But now I have a family, and the people have accepted me. So should you. My Raven spirit is as strong as your owl."

He inhaled sharply, his narrow, black eyes smoldered and his thick, bushy eyebrows crashed together on his forehead. They stared at each other long and silently. The shaman was the first to walk away, his robes flapping around his skinny body, his left arm shaking his walking stick in the air.

Tiana felt as if she'd come through a battle. Her legs trembled, and the blood in her temples pounded so she could no longer hear. Looking around the gathered tribe, she saw smiling approval. If only she did not have a terrible foreboding resting over her heart. Ever since arising from her sleeping robes at sun up, Tiana's dream of a snarling bear with wide mouth and gnashing rows of sharp teeth gave her a premonition of impending disaster that nothing seemed to assuage. That was probably why she found the courage to stand up to the shaman.

"I think it will be a bad day for fishing." She spoke to Kania and looked up into the darkening sky. "See how the clouds thicken and roll. There is a spirit who does not wish us to fish today."

Kania smiled at her adopted daughter in loving amusement. She felt so much gratitude toward her son for bringing this one into her home. The girl had made a few small predictions which came true. Yet custom decreed that a boy could not become a shaman until his first large animal kill, and a girl had to have completed her first bleeding. It was not yet her daughter's time. Kania felt a knot in her stomach, apprehensive at the shaman's unrelenting hostility toward the girl. Today was the perfect example. He had proclaimed this day to be the best fishing of all.

And Tiana said it did not bode well for them to fish today.

Kania wished Namanet were home. He would know what to do. The boy was becoming overbearing lately, even taking to swaggering in his walk to cover up his limp. Kania wondered if it had anything to do with the burgeoning beauty of this girl who had come to stay with them. She frowned at the unwelcome idea.

"I dare not tell them of your warning, Daughter. No one will listen to me. They will think you wish to spite. We might offend the fish if they come and we do not partake of their generosity. What if they decide not to swim up the river again – ever?"

"I do not know, Mother Kania, but it is only a feeling – a warning of some shadowy danger." Words seemed to fail her, and she tried again. "I believe someone will be harmed if you go today."

Kania tilted the girl's chin and looked into her eyes. "Are you certain? The women will be very angry if I tell them this, and Ikgat too. He pronounced this to be a good day."

Tiana looked at the older woman, and then away, not knowing how to convince her. She knew she had not yet developed the blind courage of certainty which she hoped would come later, when she became shaman. She might prevent a calamity by staying close to Kania, to try and be of help if something did happen.

Later that day everyone trooped out to the river. The wind whipped the water to foamy breakers as the net women tried to launch their bark canoes. The others lined the shore shouting encouragement, waiting for their turn to participate. Fish churned and roiled in the white water, causing even more short, choppy waves.

Tiana watched as a light craft bobbed and tossed in the water, dangerously close to barely submerged rocks in the river. She saw Sarnat, heavy with child, stand up in the boat to toss her net. A collective gasp broke from the throats of the onlookers as the woman teetered for a long moment in the rocking canoe. It flipped over

TIANA

suddenly, capsizing in the swirling water.

Tiana knew no one in the camp could swim. Although everyone in her first village swam like otters, she had given up practicing here. Swimming was an unknown skill to these people. Ikgat had decreed swimming to be a mystery better left to the water spirits.

Without hesitation, Tiana ran into the icy stream and dove into the melee of the tossing boat and white water. One terrified woman clung to the side, shrieking and screaming. The other, Sarnat, was nowhere to be seen. Tiana dove beneath the surface. Eyes wide, she probed the murky depths, searching for the missing woman. Once, twice, and again, she had to come up for air because her capacity for staying under water had diminished through lack of practice. She continued to dive and break to the surface, sputtering and choking.

Just when she thought she must give up, a scrap of deerskin close to the rocks caught her glance and she swam toward it. Sarnat had snagged on a submerged rock, her eyes closed as in sleep. Had she already joined the spirits? Tiana worked feverishly, tearing at the rocks, her fingers numb with the cold until she managed to pry the woman loose and drag her upward, holding her head up and treading water. Tiana's legs and arms felt so tired she didn't know how long she could hold Sarnat up.

She closed her eyes, waiting for help from her Raven Spirit, when hands pulled at the body she clutched so hard in her arms and other hands grabbed onto her arms and began to drag her toward shore.

As soon as Tiana reached a shallow place where more of the women waded out, she lay half in, half out of the water, barely noticing the icy wind rushing over her wet body. She watched the women pull the limp form of Sarnat up on the sand. Sarnat's face was pale, except for the long cut on her forehead and bruise on the temple where she had struck against the rocks. The icy water had sealed the wound temporarily, but now it began to bleed. Her round stomach started to move up and down with the effort to gain air into her lungs. The women held her upright to help her vomit up the water.

Kania pulled Tiana close and wrapped her shivering body in a caribou skin blanket. Her fingers where she had scraped them on the rocks to free Sarnat began to bleed from innumerable cuts and scratches. Tiana felt the respect reflected toward her by the glances of the women, but she was too tired to care. They must have decided to overlook her strangeness in knowing how to travel through the water like a fish. Had she not saved young Sarnat's life?

Suddenly Sarnat doubled up, drawing her knees to her stomach. The scream of agony that tore from her throat sent chills up Tiana's spine. The women jumped back, startled out of their momentary happiness at seeing Sarnat alive.

TIANA

 SIX

THE shaman strode into their midst. His black eyes sparkled with self-righteous fury, his thin lips flattened against his teeth in outrage.

Tiana watched, her heart thudding in her chest as the crowd parted, leaving him plenty of space when he moved toward the stricken Sarnat. Blood gushed from between her legs, staining the sandy beach beneath her body. Her face contorted with pain.

Ikgat raised his dried owl's foot charm and shrieked in a frenzy, pointing towards Tiana. "This one must be destroyed. Sarnat's terrible misfortune is surely caused by the demon-maker." He jumped around in his frenzy, first on one foot and then another. The crowd swayed back each time he leaped close.

Tiana, still wet and cold, stood alone, frightened by his bellowing outburst.

Kania pushed forward to stand by the terrified girl. "My daughter saved Sarnat's life!" Her voice rang out above the shaman's ravings. Silence greeted her words, wrapping the onlookers in a cocoon of disbelief. Few had ever spoken up to the shaman and lived to tell it.

When Kania held their shocked attention, she continued. "Tiana warned me before we went out. She did not wish me to go. It was not a good day for fishing she said. I ignored her, preferring to believe who proclaimed it an excellent day. If Tiana had not gone into the water after Sarnat, the woman would be with the spirits even now."

The crowd murmured in agreement. Tiana could hear Ikgat

gnashing his teeth. He was losing his hold on the crowd.

"Look!" he shrieked. Just at that unfortunate moment, the baby issued from Sarnat, stillborn.

In one voice, everyone wailed fear and sorrow. Kania whispered to Tiana, "She wanted this child so badly. She has lost several before, and the shaman promised this one would come into the world alive."

Tiana felt the ground sway beneath her feet. She held on to Kania's arm, breathing deeply as she watched the women clean Sarnat and stand her on her feet. Should she advise them to wrap the tiny dead child and the afterbirth separately in fresh green rushes to bury in different parts of the forest as was the custom in her first tribe?

Raising her voice above the murmuring of the women, she spoke, telling them what they must do. "This will keep the evil spirits from joining them together to make a monster baby come alive. I have heard many old people in my other village who had witnessed just such a calamity in their lifetimes. It is told that on dark, moonless nights, when wind rustles through the tops of the trees, a new child walks on the land, searching for a mother, trailing the bloody afterbirth behind him. On such nights even brave hunters stayed inside."

The women and the shaman stood petrified in one place, staring first at Tiana and then at the dead baby, as if listening to her words over and over until they made sense to them.

The shaman knelt in front of the infant and beckoned toward the women who already held rushes and long grasses to wrap the body in. "It may serve us well if we do this. A mere girl should not be able to tell us how to prepare the dead, yet there is a truth in her words, and if her tribe behaved in this manner, it could be true."

Tiana moved a little distance from Kania. This was not the time to show weakness. The people believed her when she had just spoken, they were wrapping the baby separately as she had said to do. If she showed any weakness, the shaman would feel free to punish her and her family now for what he considered her meddling. Her fingers reached to feel the outlines of the Raven belt. She tilted her chin and looked directly at Ikgat.

"I do speak the truth. And the Raven spirits came to me in the night and warned me there would be misfortune on this day. I, a girl from another place, did not wish to oppose you, so I said nothing. Only to my mother."

"In this matter you lie!" Ikgat shrieked.

It was clear to Tiana that he had given in about burying the baby and the afterbirth separately, but that was the only concession he would make.

Red spittle bubbled at the corners of his mouth, for he had bitten his tongue and the sides of his cheeks. Tiana knew the ploy from her days with her shaman friend in the old village. She was not impressed, as were the others.

"I speak the truth." She began to improvise quickly, knowing her life depended upon what she said now. While the tribe had been listening to the shaman rave on and on, Kania whispered that Sarnat had no people here, she had been captured as a young girl. There was no need to be concerned about reprisal from anyone but the husband. When he returned from the hunt and discovered that his child was stillborn, he would be ready to listen to anything Ikgat had to say against her.

"I warned . . ." and then Tiana stopped abruptly. If she continued to speak of warning Kania, they might all turn and blame her mother. "I will prove to you I speak the truth." Suddenly she knew what she had to do. "I do not say that Ikgat lies, only that we saw different visions. Tie my hands and feet and take me to the center of the river. Throw me into the water. If I do not rise again, you will be certain I lied."

"No!" Kania took Tiana by the shoulders and shook her. "I will not permit it! My daughter warned me this would happen. She saved Sarnat's life. You should be grateful."

Everyone, including the stricken Sarnat, stood as if carved of wood, watching the seemingly unequal duel between the girl and the powerful shaman.

"Do you allow me to prove myself blameless?" Tiana's eyes flashed a challenge to Igkat and his followers. She waited for thunder from the sky to knock her down for her daring. Had she pushed too far in testing her Raven spirit and the spirit guide which hadn't chosen her yet? When nothing happened, Tiana felt almost disappointed.

"Stupid girl," he said with a sneer, grabbing up sinew from a pile on the beach and striding toward her. Kania stepped in front in a protective gesture that moved Tiana more than anything her second mother could have done. No one opposed the shaman. The girl took Kania's work-worn hands in her own and rubbed her fingers lightly over Kania's misshapen, gnarled joints.

"Mother of mine, do not mistrust me now. I need you to believe in me."

They looked deeply into each other's eyes for a long moment before the older woman nodded and moved away.

The shaman tied Tiana's hands behind her back. She trembled at his touch, hating the feel of his whispery, scratchy hands on her arms. They felt like leaves from a winter tree, curled up, crisp and dying. The thought of his dying, as he must soon in old age, gave her courage. She stood straight as he manipulated the ties roughly.

Closing her eyes, she concentrated on what must be done. If only the memory of what she had learned summers ago in her old village served her. Children always enjoyed playing this game of tying each other up and taking turns leaping into the river to see who could get loose the quickest. There was a trick to holding her hands and wrists just so, to leave a little slack.

Tiana held her arms and hands rigid until they were on the verge of trembling with the strain, but she dared not let the others see. When they threw her in the water, she must loosen her bonds in a very short time. If she had not allowed enough free space to manipulate the ties – if her muscles had grown stiff and she could no longer squeeze her hands into the narrow pliancy required – she would never survive.

She looked up at the sky. The clouds had moved on, leaving the sun to trickle through the branches of huge pines casting oddly shaped shadows across the faces surrounding her. Perhaps this would be the last time she could look at the sky or the gentle, kind face of Kania. Tiana suddenly remembered Namanet, and nearly lost her balance. She glanced into the shaman's eyes and saw triumph. Did he perceive her tremor as terror of him and of what he was about to do?

The thought of never seeing Namanet again tore through Tiana's

TIANA

insides like a wild wind, leaving her weak and numb. She did not spare more time to question this sudden feeling of bereavement; what she had to do demanded her complete concentration if she was to survive. If only she might touch her belt. She closed her eyes and conjured up the shape and feel of it around her waist. This gave her strength to stand stiffly erect while the shaman jerked one last time on her arms to be certain they were held tight.

For the first time since she offered herself to the river, Tiana felt a shiver of fear when the shaman knelt and tied a large rock to her ankle. She hadn't counted on that happening.

She conjured up the vision of her belt and felt its warmth seep into her skin. Her eyes narrowed as she looked at him under her lashes. He must not discover that her helping power came from her belt, he might take it from her.

He commanded two friends of Sarnat to row Tiana out into the middle of the river. They seemed glad to comply. Apparently they now believed as the shaman desired, that Tiana had put a curse on the baby. They shoved and pushed her into the bottom of the boat. As soon as the tossing, bouncing craft neared the chosen place, they rolled her out over the edge.

Just as Tiana splashed into the water, she heard the pitiful cry of Kania echo in her ears, and she sank to the bottom like a stone.

She pulled against her restraints at first in involuntary panic. Before she could do irreparable damage to the sinew she had so carefully maneuvered just right, the Raven belt sent out waves of warmth, forming a cocoon of sanctuary around her.

Willing her hands to suppleness, she folded her palms and fingers together, to twist through the ties. Time sped by. Soon she grew lightheaded. Her body felt squeezed, as if the bonds were wrapped around her chest and not her wrists and feet. The shaman must have guessed her intentions to keep a slack in the sinew, for it stayed tight against her arms. The more she struggled, the tighter it became.

Was this how it would end for her? What would happen to the Raven Woman line? It would be unforgivable for her to perish when her ancestors had braved their abandonment and all their adversities to survive and pass the belt down to her. What of her unborn daughter? She would be a Raven Woman, of that Tiana felt certain. Had her arrogance and temper pushed her to do this?

She jerked up her head to look at a sudden movement in the water. Through the gloom appeared the outline of a woman of imposing proportions. A giantess wrapped in a reddish coat of strange fur. The woman wore a black headband of Raven feathers.

As the vision appeared, Tiana stopped struggling and calmness descended upon her. She knew she was looking upon the ancient Raven Mother, Tulunixiraq.

No words were exchanged, but as Tiana relaxed, the sinew loosened and fell away. When an irresistible urge to surface came over her, part of her wished to stay below the water – to continue to absorb the comforting substance of the Raven Woman. Her chest no longer hurt, she stopped needing air.

Go now. We will meet again. Soon.

No sound came from the Raven Mother's mouth, yet Tiana heard the words plainly. She undid the fastening of the rock on her ankle. Reluctantly she closed her eyes and kicked to propel herself to the surface.

When Tiana's head broke through the surface of the water, she heard cries and shrieks of excited women and children. One voice sounded above the others. Namanet called her name and waded toward her in great strides.

She reached up to grasp his hand. Suddenly her legs felt so weak she could barely stand in the shallow water. He scooped her up and held her close for a long moment before he walked toward shore with her in his arms. He held her so tight she didn't know when her heartbeats and his divided.

Tiana's first thought was happiness at seeing his face again, but her next feeling was a stabbing fear. When she saw Kania's worried frown mixed with relief at her appearance, Tiana knew his mother had tried to warn him. Had he seen the girl Sarnat and her dead baby? If a man saw such a sight as a woman giving birth or having just done so, he could lose his prowess as a hunter from that time on. It was a very serious taboo, yet he chanced it for her.

Namanet set Tiana down, reluctant to let her go. Kania rushed to her side; three of them faced a very bewildered and confused

TIANA

shaman.

"You see. I did not lie." Tiana spoke with unwavering boldness into the sudden hush tearing through the silence which surrounded them. She held up her arms to show him there were no more ties. "Hear me now. I am Raven Woman and a shaman." It was time to reveal the Raven belt. It could make her vulnerable to a magic spell by the shaman but it also could offer protection since he might be fearful of using a spell against her knowing about the belt.

She reached up under the deerskin robe Kania had wrapped around her and removed the ivory belt, holding it aloft. "I wear the mystical Raven Belt which has been passed down to Raven Women from the beginning of our time."

The crowd fell back, their black eyes wide, their stupefied expressions in the sudden silence told her more than if anyone might have ventured words.

Ikgat appeared stunned, staring up at the belt dangling in her hand. His thin lips worked but nothing came out. The villagers turned to look at the shaman with open curiosity. Tiana thought he seemed to shrink before their eyes.

She wavered, taking pity, all the while knowing that was unwise. "It is not forbidden for a village to have more than one shaman. One need not hold dominion over the other. I am young and have much to learn from one so wise in years and experience." She hated the conciliatory sound of her voice, but thought it best to make peace – to keep Kania and Namanet safe from any spells Ikgat might put on them to get even with her.

The shaman gaped in open-mouthed astonishment. She knew he expected denouncement at the very least, perhaps even banishment if the people turned on him. Obviously some malevolent spirit was to blame for Sarnat's misfortune, and he had not been able to stop it. He turned away and walked slowly toward the village. Some followed, others stayed behind.

Clearly lines had been drawn. Tiana wondered if she'd made a serious mistake in forgiving him.

That evening the little family of three sat around their fire while Kania told her son of the day's happenings. Namanet explained how it was that he had returned to the village without the other hunters.

"I felt something call to me. None of the others would come back with me, so I came alone."

"It must have been my thoughts of you," Tiana admitted, looking into his wolf-gray eyes. She remembered feeling sorry for leaving him behind when she thought she might die.

No one asked to know how Tiana escaped the water, nor did she expect them to. This was shaman's doings, after all. But Tiana did tell them of the experience with the Raven Mother in the water, and what it meant to her; explaining more about her mystical belt of ivory and allowing her family to touch it.

"You wore the belt when we captured you?" Namanet asked.

"Yes. It told me to stay with you." Tiana felt a new awareness, a new shy uncertainty toward Namanet and sensed his feelings were much the same. Always they had shared a casual relationship, like an older brother toward a somewhat annoying little sister. Now a subtle change came between them that had Tiana puzzled and not a little upset. She wanted everything to stay the way it was before.

Namanet no longer teased and made disparaging remarks. When he spoke to Tiana his voice was filled with care and concern. His bold glances challenged her to – to what?

Tiana knew Kania had noticed the change too for she took Tiana aside and advised her to begin putting away what she would need to take with her to the shelter for her time of womanhood which would surely come soon.

"This, my daughter, is to wear over your head as our custom dictates." She handed Tiana a softly worked white rabbit pelt. Around the irregular edges she had painstakingly sewn a binding with tiny stitches of red dyed sinew.

"Oh, Mother Kania, it is so beautiful," Tiana exclaimed, tears threatening to spill out at this woman's generous spirit. She lifted it to put it on her head but Kania brushed her hands away.

"No, it will mean a bad omen, you must only wear it in the shelter."

Tiana held it to her breast. "And after? I may keep it?"

Kania shook her head. "No, child. It must be buried with all of your bedding and moss you use." Her eyes sparkled. "But I have made another, identical, that you might wish to use underneath your

TIANA

drum when you are allowed to use it."

Tiana rushed forward and hugged her. When did she have time to do this? All day long Kania worked along with the women drying fish or preparing deerskins and fur for garments and cooking their meals. She smoothed Kania's roughened hands between hers and brought them to her lips. Kania laid her head against Tiana's shoulder and they stood together for a long moment.

In the sunny days that followed, Tiana felt that Ikgat was biding his time, waiting as a wolverine waits to pounce on an animal in a trap. If she had hoped to win him over by her generosity at the river, she'd failed. One look at his stern, unmoving expression told her everything. Her gesture had only provoked him into fuming resentment. Yet now, instead of challenging her openly, she had to fear his furtive, secretive scheming.

Kania warned her Ikgat had convinced both Sarnat and her husband that Tiana was to blame for the loss of her baby, for hadn't he, the shaman, promised this one would live?

Many of her traps had been destroyed and animals removed. She felt certain it was the shaman's doings. He never deliberately came near her but when they met in the camp, he walked as far away from her as possible so that he didn't have to look into her eyes. There were many times when she felt someone watched her, but when she looked quickly around, saw nothing. Was he sending his spirits to spy on her? Kania wouldn't let her go down to the water alone any more which was hard for her. She had enjoyed her solitude.

In the warm nights, most of the people slept outdoors around a communal fire, however Tiana preferred the solitude of her tent. One morning she awoke, and rolling over in her bedding, felt something touch her skin. She leaped up and shook her robes, unmindful of the commotion caused by her sudden eruption. A scream died in her throat as she looked down on what appeared to be a tiny dead baby covered with blood. When the object fell to the ground she recognized it as a weasel.

Sightless holes stared at her from where two bright eyes used to be. Its sharp little teeth expressed a mocking grin, its pale red tongue hung out in a grotesque manner. Someone had skinned it carefully.

The thin, denuded body was spattered with dried blood, an obscene caricature of a once beautiful animal.

Tiana had not realized anyone heard her cry of distress until Kania stood close by her side. They looked down in shocked revulsion at the thing on her bedding. A weasel was taboo to slay and eat, even in times of starvation. As the owl was the spirit helper of the shaman and taboo for him to slay, so the weasel was the spirit-animal of this little band of people and was regarded with much respect.

"Only one person would dare provoke the wrath of the spirit world by this desecration," Kania spoke at last. She knelt and scooped up the corners of the hide Tiana had been sleeping on. "I must wrap up the remains in this and bury it in the woods. You cannot know where, lest your powers be harmed."

Uneasily, Tiana awaited Kania's return.

"You won't tell Namanet, will you?" Tiana asked. He was already angry with Ikgat for stirring up trouble against them. He would surely seek vengeance if he knew about this terrible night.

Kania closed her eyes as if thinking about Tiana's words and then shook her head. "Perhaps not. But this trouble will not stop until Ikgat is dead. Namanet can kill him for you."

Tiana was moved to think they would do that for her. They must know that the spirit of a shaman who died seeking revenge could prove as unwelcome as leaving him alive to do his meanness.

The men had returned bringing much game, geese and ducks from their hunting. While the days continued warm, the signs of approaching cold weather crept through the air on the chill, damp nights. Only younger men and boys now slept outdoors on the ground.

One morning Tiana awoke and felt a dampness around her thighs and under her shift. Her first instinct was embarrassment. They would make fun of her. She had wet her robes like a baby during the night. Her hand touched the wetness. When she looked down it was bloody. It was her time! If Namanet came indoors now, he would suffer damage to his hunting prowess or his manhood. She called softly over to Kania to tell her to warn her son.

Kania understood at once. "Close your eyes tight," she

TIANA

commanded. "Do not look at anything in the village as I lead you through, or the people will be cursed." Tiana stood obediently waiting with closed eyes, while Kania put up a willow branch across the flap of their tent to bar anyone, especially Namanet, from entering an unclean abode until she returned to cleanse it. The robes Tiana lay on must be washed and aired in the sun for many sleeps, the dirt on the floor must be swept up and new pine straw put down.

"Mother Kania, please walk me by the place of Ikgat. I wish to stare at him and bring him as much harm as possible."

Kania laughed. "Good idea, Daughter. But he could have a charm to reflect your curse back onto yourself. I would not take the chance."

Once inside her new shelter, Tiana kept her eyes closed until Kania backed out. She knew for the next five sleeps she must be left alone, according to their custom. She could neither see nor hear anyone. She was required to wear the white rabbit skin over her head until dark. That way her eyes might not accidentally behold a villager or an animal. For the next five sleeps, Kania would leave a small portion of dried fish at her door sometime in the night. It was all she was allowed to eat during her seclusion. The small bowl of water Tiana found in front of her shelter she knew must last her until the next night. Kania had remembered to place a hollow reed beside it so she could sip slowly to make the water last.

The days and nights blended into one long darkness but Tiana turned her thoughts inward, to the Raven Mother, the past, and the inevitability of her becoming a shaman.

With so much time to think, her spirit cried out her fading sorrow for her lost people. She loved Kania, but how did her father, mother and grandmother fare? Were they alive and well? Did they miss her? She bowed her head and let the tears fall, knowing no one was near to hear her sobs. A feathery rustle touched against her cheeks as if someone had made a caressing gesture. She looked up through eyes dimmed by tears and saw the tall, majestic figure of the Raven Mother centered in a soft green fog.

Do not mourn for that which you cannot have. You have more than fourteen seasons of life and you are a woman grown. You cannot be a child again. Your father, Quaanta, would not have permitted you to become shaman and Raven

Woman. He is a good man, a brave hunter, and I wished no harm to come to him before his time. Therefore I found this new place for you. Nothing or no one is as important as the line of Raven Women. It is your destiny from birth. I, and the others, live through each new Raven Woman.

"But Ikgat is powerful . . ." tentatively Tiana reached out to touch the nebulous form, sensing it was beginning to fade.

No one can harm you but yourself. If you know you are Raven Woman and your daughter will be also, then your fate is secure. You have only to believe in this and be strong.

Tiana's eyelids closed against her will, she dozed and woke, dozed and woke. Many hours went by without remembering to eat the scant fare permitted her. One thought fed upon another, providing a feast that filled every portion of her being. She knew this was a time for renewal . . . of rebirth.

TIANA

 **SEVEN**

WHEN Kania came to bring her from her isolation, Tiana stood for a long moment, looked at the sky and soaked up the warm rays of the sun. It was so wonderful to see light again and to hear voices. She walked toward the village and saw people standing around in front of their abodes; she could almost feel the smiles on their faces and the welcome in their eyes. It was so good to be back, so good to see Kania again.

In her absence, Kania had made a new garment sewn from supple rabbit skin trimmed with soft Raven feathers around the neckline and hem. The older woman had buried all the clothing Tiana had previously worn, along with the moss used to keep her clean while in the shelter.

Tiana tried on the garments. "What a splendid surprise! Look, they fit so well, you are truly gifted, Mother Kania." She put her arm around Kania's shoulder, bending down to hug the shorter woman. She loved her new mother so much, now she could admit it without feeling guilt for having loved two mothers. What was past was past, the Raven Mother had explained that during her seclusion.

Tiana was surprised that some of the people had left gifts for her. Special food treats prepared to whet her appetite after her semi-fast – slices of raw musk-ox tongue in its own jell, ptarmigan plucked and fermenting along with their eggs in a special caribou hide bag.

Sarnat surprised her by coming to their tent and asking to enter. Inside she sat gracefully down on the furs, looking uncertain. "The shaman wishes we had not started another baby," she rubbed her full belly. "He said it was a bad time for me."

Tiana knelt in front of her and put her hands first on Sarnat's cheeks and then one hand on her stomach. "You do not have to tell him I said so, but you will birth a healthy boy child this time."

Both Kania and Tiana held Sarnat while the young woman sobbed between her smiles. When she could speak again, she pulled an object out of her woman's pack they all carried.

"Will you accept this for your new status as a woman? I made it two full moons ago, waiting for your time to come."

Tiana took the beautifully worked pouch of softest deerskin trimmed with tiny smooth red stones from the river's edge. This gift made it hard for Tiana to swallow, so moved was she.

Sarnat refused a bowl of soup and soon left the tent.

"The people love you," Kania stated when they were alone again.

"Mother Kania, I do not wish to be the cause of separating the tribe in two sides." The people's consideration moved her deeply, for it meant not all were against her. And yet she felt saddened that she might be the cause of a divided camp. A divided tribe could not survive long with hardships and hunger to contend with. They all needed to work together as one family. She had hopes that would come in time if the shaman gave in only just a little.

"What will be will be, daughter. This has been too much for my poor head to hold. You are too thin. Eat." Kania sat down to work on her son's winter outfit of musk-ox fur trousers and jacket of caribou skin.

"Thank you, Mother." Tiana's voice choked with the rush of feeling for this woman who had become so dear to her. She deliberately left off her usual 'Mother Kania' and knew it did not go unnoticed. She still missed her first mother and her grandmother and especially her father. Even without the Raven Woman's explanation of why it had to be thus, she could not have helped loving this family.

Neither Namanet nor Kania asked about her visions while alone in the shelter. They knew she would tell them if she wanted them to know.

"You must walk in the village with care," Kania warned. "Ikgat was not idle in your absence. He has stirred up much trouble for you."

"I should have slain him. I had the chance when we were out

TIANA

hunting." Namanet met Tiana's look for the first time since her return.

He had a different air about him. She was not certain she liked it. He no longer had a shy, sometimes sullen way she was used to seeing. He was more sure of himself now, more blustery and bold. Kania told her she thought the men no longer tormented him so badly since he had made a few good kills.

"Ayii, my son. Do not be arrogant. Even foolish children do not joke about harming a shaman. The helping spirits of Ikgat may be listening." Kania turned to Tiana. "The men have been telling him what a beautiful sister he has. He does not enjoy their bantering."

"She is not my sister!" Namanet exploded. "She is not of our blood and everyone knows this."

Kania's face showed as much shock as Tiana felt. They looked down at the ground to spare any embarrassment Namanet might feel at his unseemly outburst.

To change the anxiety she felt in the enclosed area, Tiana smiled and patted Kania's cheek. "Namanet is just jealous of the attention paid me when I rescued Sarnat and spoke up to Ikgat. We all know Namanet wants to be the center of attention."

Namanet leaped to his feet and threw a fat pillow of duck feathers at her. She ducked and they laughed. It was true. Even if it meant the men tormented or teased him, Namanet wanted to be noticed.

"My son will get over it when he realizes you do not seek recognition."

"Do not speak of me as if I am not standing here," Namanet pretended outrage. He knelt on the blanket where Tiana sat.

"I made these for you." Namanet held out his palms, his bluster gone, his manner shy and diffident, as if she might refuse to accept his gift. Tiana looked at the exquisite pair of earrings, fashioned from the downy inside feathers of a Raven and two long outer ones.

"Namanet, how splendid! You are so gifted. Just like your mother." She had no idea he had so much patience and imagination.

He nodded, pleased at her admiration. He was short for a man, his twisted leg making him seem even shorter. Tiana had not noticed before, since his upper torso was well muscled, more so than most young men his age. She only saw it now that he pulled her to her feet, holding the earrings for her to put on.

"Just like a man to be so unnoticing." Kania laughed. "See, my son, she does not have openings in her ears."

Tiana had observed that baby girls had needles poked through their earlobes and dangling rings inserted to stretch the skin. A long earlobe in a woman was sexually stimulating to the men, Kania had confided. In Tiana's first family, they did not pierce ears until after a girl became a woman.

"Will you fix my ears for me, Mother, so that I can wear Namanet's magnificent gift?"

Kania nodded happily. Her eyes reflected love for both of them.

"My totem will be very strong indeed, when I wear them." Tiana praised him while caressing the earrings with her fingers. A painstakingly delicate braid of sinew threaded through the light, soft feathers of the down, along with the stronger, more iridescent black outer feathers which would hang down almost to her shoulders. "How did you both come upon the feathers for my garment and earrings?"

"Yii yii – just like a woman, always asking questions. I could lie and say I shot a bird, but everyone knows this would desecrate your spirit helper. I hunted in the forest one morning and there, as if piled up especially for me, I discovered the feathers. I knew who they were for, and brought them back to camp. I gave some to Mother for her use and thought a long time before something told me to put them together in strings for your ears. Does that satisfy your curiosity, girl?"

Tiana was astonished at Namanet's bold speech. He had never addressed her in such an informal manner since bringing her home as a gift to his mother. She found it quite disturbing, although Kania seemed not to notice.

As the days passed, Tiana was constantly reminded of her new status in the camp. Her raven earrings dangled against her cheeks. The new, calf-length dress Kania made for her fit perfectly, accenting her slender curves. She felt good about everything in her new life except for her worry about Ikgat.

Ever since her entrance into the village, when the people

TIANA

discovered it was her destiny to be shaman, Tiana knew there would come a time she must challenge his authority. Many were on her side, she could tell by the many secret gifts given to her after her emergence from the shelter.

Kania told her Sarnat's husband believed she had saved the woman's life, even if the shaman had won over the ungrateful parents of the couple.

Each day Tiana gathered a steadily increasing crowd of women and children around her at the riverbank to show them how to hold their breaths under water and kick their feet as they dove for the bottom. Every salmon season claimed at least one life from drowning. As inducement for the older women to learn to swim or at least float, she brought up reeds from the muddy bottom and taught them to make baskets, more pliable and stronger than those made with tree bark and moss.

Many were grateful for this, but Tiana didn't want to be the cause of dividing the people between those who put their trust in Ikgat and those who liked and trusted her.

There was another problem she must face other than that of the shaman. Her entry into womanhood had not gone unnoticed by the young warriors. She peeked out of the tent to see would-be suitors strutting back and forth before their abode, sometimes bringing presents of food and furs. They showed off, staging mock-fights and wrestling like noisy, boisterous children, wanting her attention yet uncertain of how it would be accepted. Tiana ignored them all. Namanet sulked and pouted, and Kania looked worried.

To ease her mind, Kania suggested Namanet might treasure a *cover that stops arrows* if Tiana made him one.

"What is this you speak of? I would like to surprise Namanet with something I made to repay him for his kindness for these." She ran her fingers down the long feathers against her cheek.

The next morning Kania and Tiana set out alone at daybreak. "We must find a special bark from a tree way in the center of the forest, a tree who never sees the sun." She led the way, and they walked for a long time before Kania put up her hand and pointed. "There." Her voice was filled with satisfaction.

"It looks like any tree to me," Tiana protested, disappointed after all the walking.

"Come, we must thank brother tree to ensure the garment will be strong and withstand the longest arrow or the hardest thrust deer horn or even the claws of an angry bear." She took Tiana's hand and pulled her forward where they knelt in front of the tree.

"As shaman, you must make the song," she said.

Tiana hesitated only a moment while she studied the straight, tall tree nestled in among taller brother trees, hidden from the sky.

> *"Brother tree, we have no wish to slay you.*
> *We are beholden to you for the generous*
> *gift from your body, the bark which is your skin,*
> *for which we need fashion a shield for a warrior,*
> *for a brave hunter to wear to protect a brave hunter*
> *even as the spirits have protected you."*

Satisfied with Tiana's song, Kania took out her sharp woman's knife and began slicing gently along the middle of the tree, working downward. She motioned Tiana away. "This takes many seasons of practice, my child. Allow me to do this much for my son so you can make his shield." She peeled the bark in a thin strip, around and around without cutting it off until she reached a point where she thought she had enough.

"Quick, Tiana, bring me some of that damp moss from beneath that crimson flowered bush." She pointed her head in the direction she wanted Tiana to look, but did not take her hands away from the tree trunk.

Tiana swept up the moss which felt cool and soft in her arms and rushed to Kania's side.

"See, the tree weeps," she touched her finger to the trunk where the bark had been stripped away. "But your song will enable brother tree to understand he will heal and in the end we meant no harm to him." She laid the long strip of bark down carefully on the forest floor and gestured for Tiana to help her pack the moss all around the tree trunk. It stuck in place and when they were done, they stood back to see if the moss would stay. When it did, Kania rolled the bark up and stashed it in the deerskin bag she had brought along.

TIANA

When they walked back toward the village, the sun soared overhead, and Tiana felt a blessing of warmth soaking into their skin after being in the cool gloom for so long.

In days to come Tiana could only work on the vest when Namanet was not around or Kania said he would guess what she was doing. She made fine little stitches with her bone needle, in and out in and out with fine sinew that Kania had stretched and pulled especially for her task.

Finally it was finished and Kania pronounced it well done.

"Mother, I have never been able to sew before," Tiana rubbed her hand over the strong yet delicate garment in wonder.

"Perhaps it is because you are now a woman and not a child," Kania said.

Or perhaps it is for a very special person who has grown very dear to me, Tiana wanted to add but thought she had best keep those thoughts to herself.

Namanet came in that night and when Tiana presented him with the bark vest, he stared at it for a long time, then looked up at her from where he was seated. "I have never been given such a splendid, useful gift," he pronounced. He leaped to his feet and tore off his shirt.

Tiana admired the way the fire from the cooking pit played colors across his bare chest. He could be very handsome and she didn't understand why none of the young women in the camp had not seen this in him. He fastened the vest which came up to his collarbone and down to his flat stomach, reaching behind in the back to fasten the sinew ties. Then he did a dance around the small space, trying to avoid the cooking pots and the fire pit and landed in a heap practically on top of his mother and Tiana. They all began laughing, and Tiana felt so loved and so much a part of this family.

Only two mornings later, Kania and Tiana emerged from their tent and heard loud wailing and crying. They soon discovered what caused all the uproar. The traps had all been sprung during the night and the animals were either gone or killed and mutilated beyond the use for furs.

Ikgat suddenly bounded into the midst of the crowd, stopping at the clearing in front of Kania's tent. He beat his skinny chest, shrieking and screaming. "She caused this calamity!" He pointed to Tiana as the spittle collected at the corners of his mouth, and he bared pointed yellow teeth.

Kania had told Tiana that many of the older people swore Ikgat had filed his teeth to appear more fearsome, when he first became shaman, but no one remembered exactly when or if it happened. She wondered if he had been born this way, to show his power from the very beginning because when Ikgat became angry or went through one of his fits of ecstasy, he resembled the snarling, snapping wolf who was one of his helper-powers.

"It was her! She caused the snares and traps of the women to empty. The spirits have become angry, offended that we continue to permit her to stay with us."

Tiana looked around uneasily for Namanet, and remembered that he had gone out hunting early and would probably not return for hours. Kania moved forward, ready to defend her family.

Tiana stepped in front of her, gently pushing her back. "It is time for me, Mother. You have come to my aid too often. I am a woman now and must fend for myself." Tiana arched her neck and moved her head slightly to feel of the raven earrings against her cheek which gave her the courage she needed. The downy-soft feathers caressed her skin, then lower on her neck and shoulders they turned to stiffer, scratchy quills which seemed to arouse all the perceptive awareness within her. She straightened her back and went to meet her adversary.

"Ikgat, you are mistaken. What proof have you that I molested these traps?" Tiana felt as if her insides might shake apart. No one — not even another shaman — talked to someone so powerful in such an offensive manner. She had done it before when Sarnat was almost dead, but hadn't come up against him in many full moons. What spells might he cast upon her and her family or what additional mischief might he make against them?

He stood facing her, arms akimbo with his palms on the belt of his dirt and blood-encrusted tunic. "My helper-spirit saw you walk across the blood and bones of the caribou our hunters brought back

TIANA

to their lodges," he accused.

"You lie!" Tiana blurted out.

A crowd had gathered, curious and wary. After Ikgat's accusation they looked at each another, hardly daring to breathe. A woman never committed this offense. The game would all leave and never permit themselves to be slain again. Everyone would starve.

"Oooh! Ayiii!" The people spoke as in one voice.

Ikgat's mouth worked and no words issued forth, so stunned was he by her audacity. But not for long. He drew his dignity around him like a winter wrap and stared at his audience, never deigning to look again in her direction. The crowd fell back slowly under his baleful glare. No one spoke. He made a sudden gesture with his hands. A cloud of smoke enveloped him, and when it cleared he was no longer in their presence.

One by one the people dispersed, all the while looking back at the two women standing alone.

"Oh, Mother. I spoke in ill-considered haste. What will I do now?" Tiana felt close to tears, her inexperience making her wish to be a child again. It had been a much simpler time then, just a few sleeps ago. Why did a girl becoming a woman have to bring about such changes in a life? The young men playing around the tent, Namanet always sulking and brooding without reason, and now this.

Kania sensed Tiana was ready to cry. "Tsst! My daughter, you must not show weakness," she whispered in Tiana's ear. "The people will be on you like a pack of wolves and tear you apart if you display fear or despair now." She took Tiana's arm and turned her back toward the tent. "Come, it is time to consult your own helper-spirits."

"But I have only the Raven spirit. No other spirits have shown themselves to me although I was certain I would learn from them in my isolation."

"Then it was not time for the spirits to show themselves. Now may be the proper time."

Once inside the dim haven of their shelter, Kania pushed Tiana toward her sleeping furs. "Sit on your robes. I will prepare a special tea made only for shaman. I learned of it from my mother who lived with one many years before she died."

Tiana drank the strong-smelling brew and tried to fight against the drowsy, helpless feeling overpowering her until she dropped off into a deep sleep. In her dreams she saw the people, her only kinsmen now since her capture. They surged toward her with Ikgat in front, their loud voices raised in anger. Some carried caribou leg bones, others displayed knives and jade axes. Tiana felt a surge of fear for Kania and Namanet who stood by her side. Just as the first of the tribe nearly reached her, the dream broke into fragments like weak ice shattering on the lake. Something else floated into her consciousness.

She stood alone in the forest, recognizing the place where the women fished. Apprehension shrouded the air and something indefinable bothered her. A low growl came from behind, raising the hairs on the back of her neck. But when she could not turn around to see what was behind her, a calmness settled over her and she no longer felt threatened by the low growl. It was a warning. She looked at the trees ringing the shore and caught a slight movement through the brush. Crouching and holding her breath, Tiana waited a long time for the next movement. Why were strangers stalking an empty clearing?

In a moment she had her answer, for another layer of her dream became populated by the women, children and elders who always fished without the men. They were busy, shouting and laughing, oblivious to the skulking figures watching behind the screen of trees.

Gradually the two layers of her dream came together – the intruders in the forest – her people in the clearing. The strange hunters had been watching the women and now waited for them to return so they could capture slaves!

She opened her mouth to shout an alarm. Most of the hunters were back in the village, they would hear and come running. Something stayed her as she stared at the figures in the forest. There was a disturbing familiarity about their dress – the way the men pulled their hair back in two separate long strands, not clubbed together at the back of the neck.

When the leader strode into the clearing she looked into the eyes of Quaanta, her father!

Tiana awoke. Sweat drenched her body and soaked through her shift. She rubbed her palms against the Raven belt which she wore

TIANA

day and night, seeking solace in the smooth, warm ivory. She sat up and looked around, not certain of what to expect, for the dream felt so real. The only sound in the tent came from the soft plopping of the meat stew as it cooked gently in the sunken container.

"Raven Mother, I beseech you. What is a poor, ignorant girl to do? Did I dream or was it a promise of something that must come? Where do my loyalties lie? I do not wish my father and cousins to be slain or captured. Do I want to be the cause of my birth-mother's grief? First I became lost to her, now it may be Quaanta, her husband, who will not return." She leaned her chin on her knees and rocked gently back and forth, trying to calm the tripping of her heart.

Tiana ran her fingers over the downy Raven feathers at her ears, trailing them the length of the silky black quills which touched her shoulders. Kania would surely be killed. She was much too old to be of any value as a slave. Namanet would defend them with his life but he would be no match for a surprise attack. His crippled leg always made him awkward and slow, especially when he became excited or nervous. He would die too.

She reached for the partially completed drum. Now that she had become a woman and learning the ways of a shaman, she was permitted to make her own drum for ceremonies and mystical dances. Ikgat would not allow her to perform as long as he was alive, but she could still make chants in the woods, in solitude.

Tapping lightly with her fingertips, and then louder with the heel of her palm alternating with her knuckles, she moved her hands back and forth, back and forth. The hypnotic rhythm gradually took shape, soaking into the skin walls of the tent.

> "*Ayya, ayya . . . Raven Mother, hear my despair.*
> *Only you who are a part of me,*
> *only you know my thoughts.*
> *My spirit fills to bursting*
> *with sorrow for the people I love.*
> *Both my new family and my old.*
> *Raven Mother, your daughter beseeches you.*
> *Help me find a way to prevent*
> *this from happening.*"

Her voice drifted into the soft 'Ayya, ayya' of the spirit prayer, and her eyes closed. Again she felt her body fly back into the forest. This time the women and children did not splash in the river. The morning air lay still and heavy as death. Nothing moved.

Tiana was outside her body, watching herself, when suddenly men emerged from the forest, advancing toward her.

She recognized her father by the stiff-necked, prideful way he walked. Otherwise she might not have known him. Quaanta's hair was white. He had aged in the winters of her absence.

The vision vanished as shouting and singing outside the tent woke her; the excited, festive uproar of the hunters preparing themselves for the long journey in search of caribou. Joyous confusion echoed throughout the forest. This would be the last hunt until the beginning of warm days.

Tiana leaped to her feet and dashed outside. Kania and Namanet stood to one side, along with the women, children and old ones. She forgot her own vision and fears as the anguish of Namanet's embarrassment struck her. For a short time the men had seemed to show Namanet a little more respect since he brought home as much game as the other hunters when they went out. But now they had gone back to their old ways. When the hunters prepared to leave they put Namanet through the same twisted mockery. They called upon one another, bantering and yelling companionable insults as they grouped in the center of the circle of tents, until every hunter's name had been called but Namanet's.

Finally one of the men mentioned his name, as if some oversight had occurred. The men began giggling and snickering like small children over a huge joke. Tiana had witnessed this so many times before. She felt Namanet's broken pride and shame as if it were her own. She hated to think how badly Kania must feel for her son.

She stepped out, standing alone, one small figure between the discards and the hunters. "Wait! Do not go! Something might happen to the ones you leave behind." She had not thought ahead of how to tell these people of her vision but it must be done. These were her people now. Quaanta no longer held a close place in her heart, only in her memory.

Ikgat ran toward her, shaking his dried leg of owl in her face.

TIANA

"Do not listen to the she-wolf, daughter of the spirits who causes mischief among us." His lips turned up in a hideous grimace. His sharpened teeth reminded Tiana of the mutilated weasel hid in her sleeping robes. His breath blew fetid, a sickening miasma as it joined with the smell of his rancid, unwashed body.

She stood her ground, not moving back. She turned just enough to let the shaman and the onlookers know she pointedly dismissed him from her notice.

"I have had a dream. A terrible dream. Strangers approach through the forest to steal the children and young girls. The others will be slain."

"Enough! Do not listen to her!" Ikgat jumped back and forth, beside himself with rage at her defiant insolence.

She knew his thoughts as if he had spoken. It was bad enough for a mere girl to turn her face away, but to contradict his words was beyond reason.

"This is the last hunt of the season, and we always go to thank the animals that have given themselves to us and to accept their last offerings before winter. She is spoiling that."

"Oooh! Ayii!" The people murmured. Even the hunters were stunned by his mounting frenzy.

"She is trying to protect the crippled one, her brother," Ikgat shouted. "She does not wish him to go hunting with the men." His little squirrel eyes narrowed as he sensed a weak spot and near victory. The tension of the situation began to evaporate as snickering broke out here and there among the hunters first and then spread to the others.

Tiana realized she had lost when the hunters shouldered their packs and silently turned toward the forest. Namanet hit his fist against his chest to let her know he wore the bark vest and nothing could happen to him, but his eyes were troubled, before he, too, slid away to follow the men. Her only consolation came when she saw Ikgat leave with them.

"Daughter, do not despair. You must tell me of your dreams. Perhaps we can reason with the women, now that the men have gone." Kania took Tiana's arm and guided her into the tent. "You look dazed and defenseless, we must not allow the people to see that."

"I have made more trouble for Namanet," Tiana wept.

Kania pushed Tiana down on the robes and sat beside her. "Trouble is never a stranger to my son. It has been thus, ever since I gave him life. Everyone thought me an old woman, past my time, yet I bore him. But the boy was cursed. His father was always a stubborn man, as is Namanet. He insisted on hunting alone and we believe he became lost and a pack of wolves attacked him. The men found his body the same day Namanet was born. The wolf came back to tell me and gave Namanet the color of his eyes."

She kneaded her fingers into the soft fur, as if to stop the remembered pain. "Ikgat wished to dash my baby's head against the tree when he saw the twisted leg, yet I would not let him. Namanet has many things against him, but he is a good son, a loyal son. He will try to talk to the men while they are away. He believes in your visions, as do I."

"But what will happen to us?" Tiana cried out in apprehension. "My – the men – will come and . . ."

Kania interrupted. "These warriors that you speak of – they are not strangers to you."

It was not a question, and Tiana was amazed at this woman's quick perception. It was as if Kania were truly her mother now, enough to know her secret thoughts. "I saw my father leading his hunters. They do not come for me. They do not know I am alive. Hunger might stalk their village. It could be that many of their children and girls to make wives for the hunters have died. The men are not dressed for battle. They will come to steal our children."

The expression on the older woman's face showed she understood what Tiana had gone through, torn apart by two loyalties. "You are truly my daughter. The spirits were kind when they brought you and Namanet to me. Do you know when this is to happen?"

Tiana dipped the long bone from the caribou leg into the steaming liquid, stirring the contents as if needing time to think. "No. Only that it will be as we fish and are unprepared to fight."

"Then we must not be unprepared. We must tell the others over and over until they begin to listen. They will believe eventually, without the influence of Ikgat."

TIANA

"I do not know how much time we have. Perhaps my father plans to attack when the sun rises."

"You must compose yourself so that you can speak with your helper-spirits. I will circulate among the women, trying to get them to listen." She patted Tiana on the shoulder and left.

"My spirit guide did not disclose itself in my dreams," Tiana whispered to Kania's retreating back. But this may not have been true. In spite of her not wishing it with all her heart, the warning growl of the golden bear had come to her twice.

Tiana closed her eyes and let the silence wash over her. There was nothing to do now but wait.

Pinkie Paranya

TIANA

 **EIGHT**

EACH morning Tiana awoke, her nights had been filled with dreams. The scene of danger continued to return no matter how late she stayed up to watch the fire and talk with Kania. The ominous premonition never left her.

She had received the warning. It was up to her to resolve it. With heavy heart she joined the somber, silent women as they trooped together through the now-menacing forest toward the fishing stream.

Kania had harangued them day and night until most were ready to stay in the village, knowing there was some safety in numbers. When days passed and nothing happened, it was hard to keep everyone centered within the camp.

If Quaanta's men did not know the hunters had gone, they would never attack the main camp. That must be why she pictured them stalking through the trees, hoping to surprise the women before the hunters could arrive to help them.

This particular morning the sun did not shine. The mood of near-winter hovered in the air. Some leaves had already turned colors on the trees, and some lay curled and dried on the ground.

Tiana's sense of depression refused to dissipate. Her legs did not want to move forward. She asked Kania to call the people together in the middle of the camp.

"I am certain this is the morning of our danger. If you go to the river now, you may all be captured or die." Tiana spoke loudly, her forceful voice shattering the silence of the encroaching woods.

Everyone stopped walking to look at her. A few of the old women grumbled, and as if in one accord, turned back toward the village. They did not wish to fish anyway. The work was too hard for them, their bent backs told the story. Gradually, one by one, the younger women followed, dragging their children with them.

Only Kania, Tiana and the six who were serving-women to the shaman remained.

"You do not frighten us," the oldest of the women spoke. "Ikgat will be furious when he returns. He surely will place a curse on those who are too lazy to fish."

Tiana watched Ikgat's helpers turn and walk determinedly toward the river, nets clutched in their hands. She knew they feared the shaman's wrath more than any prophecy of hers.

"Please, Kania, return to the village with the others," Tiana urged.

Kania shook her head, her long, thick braids swaying against her back. "No. I cannot. I go with you."

"I do not know what I must face. We may all be slain."

"Then so be it. I have faith in your Raven spirit, even if you do not," she chided gently.

Tiana reacted with a rush of shame. Her Raven belt would protect her. Her time had not come to journey to the spirit world of the dead. But what of Kania and the others? In spite of her worry, she smiled at Kania's stubbornness. Once the older woman made up her mind, no one could change it.

"If that is your decision, then come with me." The two followed in the steps of the women who went ahead of them up the trail. By the time they reached the fishing place the others had waded into the water, to retrieve the fish from the traps they had built days before.

Tiana sensed their unease. They stopped in their work now and again to stare into the quiet forest, but still refused to leave.

She motioned for Kania to stay near her. The older woman sat upon a large rock, waiting.

For a long time the scene was unchanged as Tiana waited in restless apprehension. Suddenly the hair on her arms and the back of her neck rose and a breath of air blew against her feather earrings as in a warning.

The intruders had arrived.

Tiana stayed back, hidden by the shade of the trees covering her. She didn't think the men across the river saw her. She held up her

TIANA

Raven belt, clutched in her fingers and spoke softly, barely above a whisper. "Close your eyes, women of the owl, and rest your thoughts before you continue your work. Feel the soothing warmth of the sun soak into your closed eyelids. You are strong to stand still but you will sleep." Would she be able to soothe them into complete unknowingness? It seemed as if the stubborn women would resist and then they closed their eyes, standing still as if they'd been carved of stone, motionless at the water's edge.

She moved out into the pale sunlight trickling through the leaves above her. "Quaanta, leader of brave warriors. The shade of your beloved daughter stands before you." Until just that moment, Tiana had no idea of how to proceed. It was as if the belt emanated strength and wisdom through her arm into her very soul.

For long moments nothing happened. Finally a figure emerged from the shadows. She recognized her father. They stared at one another for a long moment. From the corner of her eye she saw the women, thigh-deep in river water and frozen in time.

"Daughter, is that truly you?" Quaanta held up his hand to shield the shifting sun from his eyes.

"It is me and yet it is not me," she replied. "You see before you a shaman of the Raven Women who lives a life that is different from the old one." She skirted carefully around the truth. Lies were offensive to all spirits and she dare not lie even to save her own life and that of the others.

"Then you are indeed of the spirit world," Quaanta's question colored his voice. "Your mother and I have long mourned your death. We knew the water spirits had claimed you."

Tiana knew his thoughts even before he spoke. She felt his struggle against believing in what he had always hated, her shamanism. He also didn't understand how she could have survived in the water and still be alive. That was even harder for him to believe. She watched the changes in his expression and with a saddened heart, saw acceptance there finally.

He motioned for the men behind him to come out of hiding. What matter that they were seen? He could not make war against the spirit of his daughter. The old women in the water were of no use to his band.

"Do you protect these people against your father?" He made one last try.

Tiana's eyes showed her pity, but she kept her voice strong and even as she replied. "I do not have to protect them. Their warriors are brave and strong and number many. Perhaps I am here to protect my beloved father." She held her breath. It could go either way now. If Quaanta chose to take offense at her offer of protection, he might attack the village just to prove his manliness. But if he decided not to question a spirit, then he would leave, never to return.

The silence around Tiana swelled until it became thick and oppressive, hard to breathe. Even the birds in the trees stilled their chattering, as if overwhelmed by what took place beneath them.

Tiana swallowed as her father raised his hand in a gesture of homage that went to her heart.

Then he was gone.

For a little while, time froze in place as the women stood still, unable to move. Tiana allowed them to open their eyes just long enough to see the retreating backs of the strangers disappear. Slowly breaking free of their hypnotic lethargy, they seemed to understand immediately that they had been in peril and ran toward Tiana, words of praise and thanksgiving breaking from their lips.

Only Kania, who was part of Tiana's heart now, must sense what this deception of her father had cost. To trick such a man, a great and fearless hunter like her father, gave offense to everything Tiana believed in. She wanted to run to him as if she were still a child and hug him to her, telling him she was alive and well, to ease his and Akiia's sorrow, but she had made her choice. She loved Kania as a mother and could not stand by and see her slain and her adopted village smashed apart with its women and children stolen.

This decision would help Quaanta cease his unknowing of what happened to his only child. He would return and tell her mother and the others what he saw and heard. It would comfort them.

Kania folded Tiana into her arms and held her close, murmuring to her as if she were a small child, while Tiana let go of the long-suppressed tears. Comforted by Kania's understanding and caring, she wiped her face and the wetness away to look at the women who stood back from the water, laughing and chattering. How much did

TIANA

they witness? How much did they hear? It would go ill with her and her family if anyone but Kania knew about Quaanta. Was she good enough at spell making to remove their thoughts while they waited in the water? Only time would tell.

They walked back to the village. Tiana felt anxious when later, the same women came to her tent and demanded to see her. A welcome relief washed over her, she relaxed and smiled at them when she saw they had prepared delicacies to give her. Some of the women promised her new garments to show their appreciation. That meant they did not know about her father.

Kania went outside to talk with the women, leaving Tiana alone, as if she understood Tiana's need for solitude.

"Oh Raven Mother. Come to console your shameless daughter who has dishonored a brave hunter."

Tiana sank to the floor of hides and crossed her ankles in the time-honored way of shaman. Her head bent forward and she touched the floor with her forehead, her eyes closed. The inside of the tent disintegrated into nothingness as her spirit fled her body and traveled into the air, searching for something – a release – an expiation.

Daughter of the Raven – do not grieve that you are unable to live in two worlds. You must be strong and stand fast in the path you have chosen. The first time, when you were stolen away from your tribe, was my decision. This is yours. Remember, you have not the power or ability to shame a brave man. He has accepted you as Raven Woman, something he was unable to do while you lived as his daughter. He is proud to be Quaanta, father of the Raven Woman. Your birth mother will understand, and she too will be proud. I have provided you with a last choice, to go back or forward. A woman of the Raven must be steadfast and certain for the mind journeys which are to come to her. You have done well, daughter. I am satisfied.

Tiana's eyes remained closed, yet she saw the form of Tulunixiraq as if she stood before her. A puff of warm air brushed the earrings against her cheeks in a comforting, caressing movement. The Raven belt she still clutched in her hand nearly burned her fingers.

Tiana opened her eyes and slipped the belt around her waist where it felt warm and soothing. She must go tell Kania that all was well, and her daughter had come back to her.

When the hunters returned there were many mouths to recount the wondrous happenings in their absence. Ikgat found himself ignored or worse, ridiculed for his inability to foresee the future. Now everyone remembered the first time that Tiana had warned them about the fateful day which resulted in the loss of Sarnat's unborn child.

Tiana walked with Kania and Namanet toward the *kaslim*, the meeting tent. The tribe wanted to give thanksgiving for the bounty which would carry them through the long winter, so the shaman had called a meeting. She supposed it could also be to express his continued dominance of the clan. Tiana decided she would show the old man no mercy this time, for she realized that this was her weakness as a woman and a shaman. No rabbit showed its underbelly to a fox twice, and never again would she.

The shaman addressed the people packed in a circle inside the tent. Tiana watched as he first walked through smoldering coals in the center of the circled villagers. He stepped away and raised his arms, shaking his drum and totem of dried owl's leg. A voice came from the other side of the closed tent flap. A deep, penetrating voice. "Your shaman gives thanks to the caribou spirits, to the fish people, to Brother Moon and Sister Sun who have provided us with a bountiful supply of food to last through the snow time." The people, slightly moving from side to side, murmured their approval.

"I will make a journey to Brother Moon, to tell him of our gratefulness." The shaman said this in his own thin voice. He faced the men and women watching him so intently and spoke to them in a quiet, steady voice, soothing them, lulling them into sleep.

Tiana felt the air around her thicken with everyone's breathing and the fire that burned in one end of the tent letting in just enough smoke to cause eyes to water and blink.

She held her Raven belt in her hand, pressing an especially sharp edge of ivory to her palm so that she would not fall into a stupor like the others. The shaman seemed satisfied that they were all nodding. Beneath her partially closed eyelashes, she saw him glance in her direction once before stepping inside the little circle of glowing coals.

TIANA

He gestured downward, toward his feet, and a huge puff of gray smoke arose to engulf him. When it slowly sifted away, he was no longer visible.

This was powerful magic, more than what Tiana had witnessed coming from the shaman in her first village. But perhaps it was because this shaman made use of both good and evil spirits.

She rested, waiting for Ikgat to return, and closed her eyes for what she thought only the time it would take to stir a pot of stew. When she opened them again the shaman was back in the center of the tent, staring in her direction.

Shaking herself from an enveloping lethargy, she stood up to face him. The people did not stir, he had not yet brought them back to life.

Before she could allow fear to shake her thoughts, she spoke into the silence. "I am a shaman and Raven Woman. I need prove myself no more – to you or anyone else." She stared at Ikgat. "The village is small. We have no need of two shaman. Stay if you please, but never encroach upon my magic again." She tilted her chin in a haughty gesture of dismissal.

The tribe awoke as one and listened to what she knew they would always later describe as the war between shamans. They looked upward, as if waiting for the sky to open up and fall upon their shoulders.

Tiana continued, "The Raven Mother brought me here for a purpose. I have been the one who predicted events which came true, and if it had not been for my interference against your wishes, the tribe would have lost many of our women and children. Do you deny this?"

Ikgat looked down for a long moment without speaking. Tiana felt the crowd holding its breath. She was young, inexperienced, it could go either way.

"Perhaps you speak the truth and perhaps not," his voice left an unspoken challenge. "The people have known me and my magic and healing since the oldest member's birth. I cannot leave off in my ministrations to them. I am bound by my shaman spirits to aid where I can. But you speak the truth when you say you have warned us of events which would have been disastrous to us as a tribe. Therefore, if we share the responsibility for the welfare of our people, that would not be amiss with me."

The crowd as one leaped to its feet and shouted words of approval.

Tiana felt relieved, knowing she lacked the experience to care for an entire tribe's grievances and illnesses alone from sunrise to sunset through each turn of the moon. Yet if she imagined she had won a battle, when she looked into the malignant glare of Ikgat before he stalked away, she knew it had not finished, but was just postponed.

One by one, the people left the tent until only she, Kania and Namanet were left. They too left, closed the tent flap behind them and walked to their abode.

When they entered and sat for their meal, Namanet began to pace back and forth in front of the fire. Tiana wondered what troubled him and settled down to watch, wanting to take her mind from the remnants of her battle with the shaman.

"I should have stayed with you! Those men who make war on women might have killed you both!" Namanet strode back and forth across the floor of the tent, filling it with his presence so the two women crouched on their sleeping furs, well out of the way of his agitated pacing.

Tiana tried to repress a smile by pressing the back of her hand against her lips. It had not been so many winters ago that Namanet had captured her in such a manner, and at the time she had accused him of the same behavior.

"Namanet, brother, do not distress yourself. It was meant to be this way." Neither she nor Kania would ever speak of what had taken place. The women in the river were dimly aware that strangers had threatened them, but did not know it had been her father leading them.

When Namanet finally subsided into grumbling, the three ate their evening meal together, and that was the end of it.

Weeks after Tiana's confrontation with Quaanta, Tiana expressed irritation when Kania refused to let her go out into the woods alone. "The hunter promised he would not return."

"Just the same, daughter, I have asked Namanet to go with you

TIANA

in your search for wild, delicious mushrooms."

Tiana did not attempt to hide her annoyance. These people had not known of the delicately flavored mushrooms hidden next to certain trees, nearly buried under the covering of loamy soil. She closed her eyes and imagined the rich clotting smell of decayed vegetation assailing her nostrils.

Mushroom hunting had come to mean a time of solitude, of enjoying her own company away from the demands and uproar of the camp. Now Kania insisted upon Namanet going with her.

"Only for one turn of the full moon or perhaps two," Kania pacified her. "When we are certain your fa . . . the hunters keep their word and do not return, you may again go alone."

Tiana guessed that Kania feared her father had not believed in her spiritual body and might come back to claim her. She knew better, but how to convince Kania? It was an impossible task, once her mother set her mind to something. Tiana gave in with as much grace as she could muster.

The next morning she awoke to a sense of adventure. She and Namanet had never spent any time alone together. She pulled out her Raven belt from underneath her furs and then decided to leave it behind this once. Hunting mushrooms could get messy and the connections that moved between the ivory squares might become packed with earth. Kania came to the tent opening to smile her goodbye, and Tiana and Namanet set out, with a great deal of grumbling on his part, to gather mushrooms. As they walked along, the well-worn path gradually diminished, and she used her instincts to find the way. So far she had discovered only one place in the entire forest where she had been able to locate the delicious mushrooms.

"Will you go with the men to trade when the time of snow comes?" Tiana asked.

Namanet shook his head. He walked in front of her, pushing the low branches aside. He did not always remember to hold them and she skipped lightly behind him so as not to be caught by the sharp twigs when they snapped back in place.

"No, we will not trade with the 'eaters of raw meat'. We have plenty and we do not enjoy their food. Only the good, warm leggings our women sew of the seal and white bear skins make the journey worthwhile."

Kania had told Tiana that in times of harsh winters, when the late fall caribou hunting had been poor, the men sometimes journeyed beyond the forest to the land of the ice that never melted. Once there, they traded caribou skins and especially wood. Kania told of the strange people prizing wood above all else. Tiana also knew from stories in her first village that no forests grew in this mysterious land, or so went the stories the returning hunters told. Tiana privately thought they made it up, just to impress the women and children. What manner of humans could live without trees?

A conviction deep inside her gradually formed. A conviction that these strangers of the ice and snow held a vital importance in her future. She longed to hear more about them but Namanet brushed away her questions impatiently. For the most part, ice people were enemies – strangers who sometimes ventured too close to the tree line and battled fiercely to avoid capture. Namanet would not wish to admit that his tribe actually feared the ice warriors and usually avoided them.

The morning passed quickly while Tiana found scattered mushroom deposits and stuffed the hide bag with the delicacies. Namanet didn't offer to help. He regarded this as woman's trivial work and seemed content to sit and munch on dried meat brought for their meal.

"Ayiie! That is enough to feed everyone in our village," he finally protested through a yawn. "Let us stop and eat."

"Eat?" She laughed. "That is all the fearless hunter has done since he left the village."

He glared, but she could tell his heart was not in it. He probably felt the same warm lethargy steal over his body as she did.

The noonday sun sifted down through the canopy of lacy leaves above their heads. The air felt still and close in a late summer burst of hot weather. Tiana, sticky and tired, was glad to stop and rest.

Namanet flopped down on soft grass and motioned for her to put out the food.

"You! Why do you need to eat more? That is all you have done!" She threw a handful of mushrooms at him. The clinging soft loam struck him in the face and upper torso.

TIANA

"Waugh! How dare you throw offal at a fierce hunter?"

She was startled. Had she hurt his feelings? He was normally a gentle person, but because of the relentless teasing and jibes he received from the men, he could be very sensitive. He had been known to sulk for days over an imagined slight or slur, and there had been times Tiana had witnessed when even Kania became the object of his petulance. She mulled this over in her mind because mother and son always had seemed to be so close.

"I meant no harm, I was only . . ." She broke off as a wide smile appeared on his lips. He could be quite handsome when he was not angry, she decided. The idea seemed strange, and somehow foolish. One did not think of a brother as handsome.

Made bolder by his smile, she plucked another handful of mushrooms from her bag and threw them directly in his face. "There! Shame on you for teasing me." She laughed as the soft loam spattered his bare chest again.

"Woman, now you have gone too far!" He brushed off the dirt and made a grab for her. She pulled away, turning to run through the woods. Tiana heard his crashing steps behind her and wondered if this time her ill-considered boldness had taken her too far. Even a sister was not allowed to assume privileges with the hunter of the family.

She thought of hiding behind a bush, as a rabbit would, waiting until his anger passed, but discarded the idea. If he was such a good hunter, as he always claimed to be, he could find her easily. It sounded as if he were gaining on her even now. Her heart pounded as she tried to run faster. Of course he could not catch her. She managed a giggle at her unreasoning fear. He had a crippled leg, something she rarely thought of now. He could not run as fast as she.

Perhaps she should stop and apologize rather than add insult by out-running him. She slowed her pace, ready to turn around and face him. Her blood pounded inside her head and ears so she could not tell how far he was behind her.

Something grabbed her shoulder. Her chest tightened, her heart felt like a closed, shriveled ball in her chest, the terror was so great. Her mind flashed backward, reliving her capture so many moons ago.

Pinkie Paranya

TIANA

 **NINE**

NAMANET spun her around hard. His warm breath touched her face and he held her arms so she could not struggle. He pushed her down to the soft, leafy ground and rubbed his cheek against her neck, so that she too was covered with soft loam. Her struggles were useless against his strength when he began to pull away her tunic.

"What are you doing?" Her voice bordered on hysteria. She had been keyed up to a nervous edge by the chase. Now everything began to take on an aura of unreality, as if her spirit was trapped in a séance, unable to return to its rightful position in her body.

He straddled her hips and brandished the knife he'd pulled from its sheath. Terror froze her for a moment, and then she struggled with a renewed strength of fear. Tremors shook her body, and she felt the wetness of cold sweat behind her knees. Was he going to kill her?

Her renewed fight meant little to him and before she could cry out, she felt the release of her garment as the sharp knife sliced through the leather bindings. She tried to twist away, but his weight pressed too heavy across her body.

Holding both her slim wrists in his big hand, Namanet bent his head and rubbed his cheeks against the softness of her breasts, his breath warm against her nipples. The shock of his actions caused her to pause in her struggles and then, though she knew it was no use, she gave one last surge of energy, trying to loosen his hold before sinking back in resigned helplessness, sensing it was too late to stop him.

Beneath his hands, calloused and rough though they were, she felt his restraint as he moved his lips across her skin. He tried to be gentle as he explored her body. His chest heaved, his smoke-gray eyes were heavy lidded with wordless passion.

Tiana had never seen a man up close like this, although the sight of people mating was not new to her. In both her first village and this one, the entire family slept in one tent. Many times she had heard Quaanta and her mother thresh around under their blankets late at night or early mornings and occasionally cry out. No one spoke of this.

Namanet dragged down her leggings and she renewed her struggles, but her ankles tangled in the soft deerskin.

He pushed his leg between hers, separating them and parting her thighs against her will. Her body arched at the sudden burst of pain that shot through her as he penetrated her soft flesh.

When the edge of the sharp hurt began to wear away gradually, another feeling invaded her body. A warmth welled up from below her stomach and seeped into her blood, infusing her, gorging her breasts until they felt ready to burst open.

He sensed the change in her and paused a moment to look into her face. Then he hugged her tight and began to caress her all over again, this time with care and patience. They lost all sense of time as they discovered each other to the fullest, satisfying their passion over and over again until finally he rolled away from her, spent and exhausted.

They lay close together in the silent forest. Only the birds trilled occasionally. Now and again, a rabbit or a small animal crunched past through the drying leaves, unaware of their presence.

Tiana closed her eyes and thought about what had just taken place. She wondered why she hadn't called on her Raven belt and then remembered she hadn't brought it with her. It was the first time the belt was out of her thoughts. Was this meant to happen, then? That was something else to wonder about. Or had they done the unpardonable? Surely brother and sister did not know one another in this manner. It was forbidden by a taboo so ancient and inflexible that in her lifetime she had never heard of anyone breaking it.

Once her grandmother had told her the story of the sun and moon who were brother and sister and loved each other with a forbidden passion. They were punished forever by having to live

TIANA

apart except for one or two times a season when Brother Moon reluctantly refused to set until his sister's light began to show through the trees.

And yet she had no birth brother or sister and neither had Namanet. They were not truly kinsmen.

"You are beautiful. Like an otter swimming in the dark lake. Your skin is so soft and smooth and smells of wood smoke." He leaned toward her, touching his lips to her breast. Little puffs of his warm breath caressed her nipples like the softest feathers until she trembled with fresh, awakened desire.

She smoothed the straight, black curve of hair from his forehead and felt a surge of love well up inside her until she thought she would scream out. She clamped her lips together in denial. Her voice came soft, blending with the muted sounds of the forest.

"Namanet, we must never do this again."

He made no answer. His moving hand, leaving trails of white-hot tendrils across her body, jerked slightly, the only sign that he heard her.

"Do you hear me, my brother?" She reached for his face and cupped it between her two hands, staring intently into his gray eyes, beautiful - like the smoke from a hundred campfires against the blue sky.

He jerked away from her. "Do not speak of such to me! We are not brother and sister. What put such a silly idea into your ignorant woman's thoughts?"

"Your mother calls me daughter, does she not? I have been cared for with love and consideration. We have shared meals and a tent together since you brought me here three summers ago. Does that not make us kin?"

"Of course not, stupid woman!" He rolled away and stood up in one fluid motion, only teetering a little on his crippled leg until he regained his balance. "I captured you as a gift to my mother. Always have I thought of you as a mere child until you came from your woman shelter. Since then I have looked on you with different eyes and different thoughts. When the strange hunters came and might have slain you, or taken you away from me, I realized then we should be together. Always." He knelt at her side and took her arms in his strong hands. "Deny, if you can, what you feel for me now. Forget you are a shaman for once. You are woman! I wish to protect you, keep you safe from harm as a man takes care of his woman."

Tiana swallowed, throat dry. "I – I have certain feelings for you also. But what will the others think? What about your mother and Ikgat and the people of our village? They will not approve."

"My mother will rejoice. As for the others, what care we? You are a strong shaman, and Ikgat is no longer in power. No one can tell you how you must live. Anyway, we are *not* brother and sister!"

He covered her gently with her torn tunic. "Now rest quietly, as a bird sleeps in the tree, and then we will return to camp. I will stand watch over you."

She thought it would be impossible to sleep with the emotions churning inside her mind and body, but in a brief time she sank into exhausted slumber. When she awoke, it was nearly dusk. Namanet leaned against a huge tree, his back to her, looking out into the woods – standing watch as he had promised. Her gaze caressed his smooth, brown back and lingered over his wide, muscular shoulders.

"Oh! It is nearly dark, and Kania will worry about us." She leaped to her feet and adjusted her tunic to cover as much as possible while he watched. At first his greedy eyes made her self-conscious, but then the strange, warm feeling pervaded her senses. She arched her slim hips in a gracefully sensual movement that came to her as easily as breathing.

His words caught in his throat as he tried to speak. He drew her close, wrapping his arms around her. Underneath her loose shift his hands were warm against her skin.

"I do not want other hunters' eyes to feast on the beauty I have seen today," he said against her cheek. "You are my woman. I will share you with no man."

"I make no promises. We must speak with Kania first."

He made a noise deep in his throat, she was not certain if it was an acceptance or not.

They began the long walk home.

When they crept into the tent, darkness had descended upon the camp, and most everyone was inside. The nights had a new bite to them. The moon hid away in a tiny curved slit. No one wanted to be

TIANA

out on such a night.

Kania made no mention of Tiana's disheveled appearance and torn tunic as the two hurried into the tent. The only sign she noticed anything at all was the mother's sharp look toward Namanet. When he volunteered nothing, she ladled up a soapstone bowl of rabbit for him.

Back in the corner on her sleeping robes, Tiana hastily removed her torn, soiled garment and changed to another, leaving off her leggings, as most of the women did inside their own tents. She ran a dried bird claw through her hair to remove the twigs and leaves and then made new braids. When finished, she hurried to sit at her place near the steaming pot.

"Mmm. This smells delicious."

"I suppose so, since you have worked so hard to gather wild mushrooms for an old woman."

Suddenly Tiana remembered the bag lying on the ground beneath the tree they lay under. She and Namanet looked at each other for the first time since entering the hut. Their glances skidded away, but not before Kania's sharp eyes noticed.

"When you have finished eating, one of you, or both, will tell me what has come between you. I have seen it growing, and it troubles me."

Namanet set down his bowl and tried his manly scowl on his mother. It did not work. "Tiana and I wish to live together as husband and wife. We decided this today." His voice was over-loud with forced bravado, much as when the men teased him.

Kania laughed. "Look at the wolf-cub swagger!" She wiped her hand across her face in a gesture of helplessness. "This is not possible. The people will not approve. You may offend the animals of the forests. You have lived as brother and sister and . . ."

"No! This is untrue! We cannot be brother and sister. We do not both come from your blood."

Kania shook her head sadly. "No. But if a child is given to us from other parents, it is treated as part of the family, is it not? No one within the family is permitted to mate. You know that."

Namanet leaped to his feet, his face contorted with impotent rage. "We will go away from here! We can return to her people and stay with them, if you do not want us."

Tiana and Kania looked at one another with the same thought. He did not know it had been Quaanta who came to raid the women and children from the tribe. Nor did he know that Quaanta now thought of his daughter as a shade, residing in the world of the spirits. How could they explain this to Namanet when they had not confided in him in the beginning?

"And you, daughter? I must hear your words on this." Kania touched Tiana's cheek.

"I – I wish it also – Kania." No matter how disrespectful it felt, she could no longer continue to call her Mother. "I know it is against your people's custom, as it is against ours. Yet a part of me insists it can be no other way. We *need* to be together as husband and wife." Her gaze fell on the Raven belt lying on her sleeping robes. "I will sleep with this next to my heart tonight. My powers will tell me what I must do."

Kania turned toward her son. "And do you promise to abide by what her Raven spirit tells her?"

He looked at Tiana, the pain of desire clouding the pale smoke of his eyes. His full lips flattened in a desperate attempt at composure. Then he nodded. "Yes. I know, even for me, she would not go against the Raven." He stalked out into the dark night.

It took more than one sleep for Tiana to resolve the conflict raging within her. She loved Namanet fiercely. She always had, even if it hadn't been clear to her before becoming a woman. He had claimed her body and soul from the beginning, when he stole her away from her beloved family and yet showed care and concern for her. The Raven Mother said she was free to make choices. Then she would make a choice.

Namanet went hunting alone while Tiana sat and thought, fasting with only sips of water to cool her lips and throat. The Raven Woman did not appear, but Tiana dreamed of many things.

On the third morning Tiana awoke icy cold from the vision which had grown stronger and more painful each time it came to her – a dream of desolation and suffering. She saw herself out on an expanse of snow, the like of which she had never seen. White, white everywhere with a constant wind moaning through huge carved

TIANA

figures in the ice. She stood apart, watching the lone figure of herself standing in the midst of this bleakness, calling – calling for someone. She heard her own voice echoing across the penetrating cold until she put her hands over her ears to stop the echo. Even then, the mournful sound continued.

Tiana moaned, bathed in sweat. She saw Kania look at her with sympathy, but knew she would not attempt to comfort her, knowing often, with a shaman, the most need for isolation came at the awakening from a dream.

Finally Tiana spoke. "I am hungry. Might I have some soup?"

Kania brought it to her and the pangs of hunger calmed. "I have not received permission from my spirit power – neither has a denial come forth. Therefore, I believe I should go in the way my heart directs. I wish to be Namanet's woman, to belong even more to this family. If we had broken a serious taboo, I am certain my Raven spirit would have intervened."

Kania's face lit, as if from within. She ran to Tiana's side and embraced her. "Ayiee! My daughter, this makes me so happy for you and for my son. I have been torn apart these summers since he brought you here to me. Torn by the wish that you and he might mate, and yet afraid that it would be forbidden. It was even on my mind to give you to another family until your time of bleeding, but I could not bear to be apart from you. You are the daughter of my spirit. You are the children I bore who died without seeing the sunshine."

They held one another close until Kania pulled away.

"You have not chosen an easy way. Ikgat is sure to set many against us. Until this old man dies, we will not be free of him and his hate."

Tiana ran her fingers across the comforting texture of her ivory belt. "No, it will not be easy but I can do nothing else. Namanet and I must be together."

At first, when the people heard the news, Tiana saw their expressions of happiness for her. She had spoken to many of them and knew they felt the benefit of her more gentle works as a shaman. It was plain to see most hated Ikgat and his years of tyranny. A ceremony would have to come later, in the meeting tent. There everyone would be free to express thoughts and feelings.

Kania, Namanet and Tiana talked of it within their tent, whispering to be sure the shaman didn't have his ears inside their abode. "He will have something to hold against you both," Kania advised, sadness in her eyes. She took both of their hands in hers. "It will not be easy. He can turn many against you."

"None of us wish the tribe to be torn apart with arguments," Tiana answered. "I must speak to them today, before this feeling of dissension grows any stronger." She fastened her Raven belt around her waist.

"No! It is my place as husband. They must be made to understand we are not brother and sister, nor have we ever been."

"My beloved children," Kania put her hands on their shoulders. "I am oldest and have lived many more years among these people than you. It is my place to speak to Ikgat. I have no fear of his magic works. How can he harm me, an old woman? I will talk to him."

Tiana felt a tiny sting of shame at Namanet's obvious relief. He had always been deathly afraid of Ikgat. Kania explained once that his fear had come from working as a young boy for the shaman. He would never talk about it to his mother, or tell her what had frightened him so. But Kania told her that when his time of service was over, he never again went near Ikgat.

Kania stayed a long time in the shaman's tent. They waited.

Namanet sat in the way of men with his ankles tucked under one another, his back straight as the pole that held the center of their tent. Tiana stretched out on the robes, her head resting on his lap. He smoothed his palm over her sleek braid.

"Do not worry, little one. My mother will make him understand."

It was the first time Namanet had touched her since coming together in the forest. She had begun to fear he had changed his mind and started to give in to the pressure in the village. He nuzzled his chin against the back of her neck.

"I would like to get this behind us. I want to begin our family. We will have sons – many sons."

She rose up to look into his eyes. "First I must have a daughter, Namanet. It has been foretold by the Raven Mother."

TIANA

He scowled. The heavy brows crashing together over his forehead reminded her of rain clouds in a darkening storm-sky.

For the first time since the wonderful, strange feelings of passion entered her mind and body, she began to wonder if this was a wise decision. The legend of the Raven Mother foretold that sons were not permitted in the line. What would happen between her and this proud man when he discovered the truth?

She should have confided in him before this. Telling Kania was not enough, for obviously the mother had not repeated it to the son. Could she make him see that daughters also were important? When daughters took husbands, parents received sons. What could be more perfect?

"Perhaps – perhaps we are not meant to be together . . ." she formed the words unwillingly, not wishing to say them out loud.

"No! Never speak thus!" He rolled over and in one smooth motion swept away her flimsy, indoor shift. He pushed her back and straddled her body, not giving her a moment to respond, even if she had wanted to. He shoved aside his clothing and thrust into her unprotected softness, again and again.

This time she felt tearing pain. Her body had not warmed to his touch as before in the forest. She clamped her lips together and bore the hurt in silence. Her eyes closed tightly until he had finished, and she willed the tears back inside her eyes so he would not see. He lay exhausted beside her. She pulled away from him and sat up.

Namanet sat up too and took her hand in his. He turned the palm over and kissed it tenderly. "I did not mean . . ." Tears of anger and frustration made glistening paths down his cheeks. He had no words to offer in apology, but his eyes begged her forgiveness. She touched her cheek to his and he smoothed her hair with gentle fingers.

"Never take my body again as you have today, Namanet. I willingly give myself to you, but not as an animal rutting in the forest. If you ever do this to me again, we will not be together."

He nodded, his head bent in shame. They lay back down and he held her close until he fell asleep.

Tiana pushed gently away to observe him in his defenselessness. He looked like a little boy, with his lashes lying thick and black against his sun-browned skin. Without the open, wolfish eyes, Namanet seemed so vulnerable. He had always had to fight with the men in the tribe for everything he possessed. It was time he learned a better way. She would teach him. She sighed and lay down again beside him to await Kania's return.

When she awoke, she watched the mother and son before they noticed her. They spoke in hushed whispers. Namanet looked happy. Kania appeared drawn, her face a mask of distress, but the smile when she saw Tiana awake brightened her expression.

"He will leave us alone, my children. We need not worry about Ikgat taking vengeance against you. In time the people will forget his words."

"But how did you accomplish this wonderful feat?" Tiana wanted to know.

Kania shook her head and turned away to stir the cooking pot, something she usually did when wanting time to think. "It is of no significance. Do not trouble yourself about it."

But Tiana did feel troubled. For the first time since coming to this village, she sensed Kania hid something important. It left a cloud over their home that she knew even Namanet felt uneasy about.

For once, touching her belt did not ease her unrest.

TIANA

 **TEN**

DURING the warm summer months, Namanet and Tiana were seldom apart. They took bedding furs wrapped in rolls and camped out in the woods alone. They made love and laughed at each other, and she was able to tease and joke with him without him becoming angry or defensive. It was a whole new side to this man, and she told him so, many times.

They brought a canoe out onto the lake near the tribe's abandoned summer camp and spent long, leisurely afternoons drifting down the smooth water, with Tiana sitting on furs on the bottom of the boat, leaning between Namanet's strong legs. She trailed her hand in the warm water, while Sister Sun sifted down upon them as if giving her blessing.

"Namanet, this has been a good time for me, a renewal." She looked up at him. His eyes were slits as if he'd been dozing.

He touched her hair. "I know, *quinta,* my beloved. Because of me you lost your first family. I know how well you must have been loved and loved them in return."

She smiled at his use of the love word seldom spoken in his tribe. They were not people who hugged and kissed often. In her first tribe they had comforting words for goodbye and greetings of love and happiness to see a person. She'd tried to explain that to Kania and Namanet in the beginning and then gave up.

"I hated you for a long while," she admitted, rubbing his hand against her cheek. "At least I needed to hate you for disrupting my life. But you and your mother showed such a loving bond together, I wanted to be a part of that."

"You are. You were from the outset. You joined us as if you had always belonged with us." He rubbed his chin on the top of her head. They watched an eagle dive into the still water and come up with a flopping, wriggling fish.

"Perhaps brother eagle would collect our dinner for us instead of waiting for some lazy hunter to fish," she teased.

"Woman, you go too far!" He nuzzled his chin down into her neck, tickling her until she shrieked with laughter. Not until she gasped for air did he stop.

It was so good to be carefree for a time, not to worry about the shaman or the long winter coming up or what her helper spirit would be. She loved arguing with Namanet just to see him puff up with anger and then watch it dissipate when he realized she was teasing.

She reveled in their lovemaking, trying to do it in the canoe once, and they tipped themselves into the warm water. They came to the surface sputtering and laughing and when they swam to shore pulling the canoe, they loved each other right there on the soft leafy earth.

Eventually though, she thought it time to return, although he seemed reluctant.

"Soon the hunters will go out for winter food. You must be there to go with them."

He nodded. He knew she worried about the others teasing and taunting him, but it no longer had any effect on him. He wished she knew that.

When they returned, the villagers presented them with a generous feast. Tiana knew what a sacrifice they made, their stock of food was low until they hunted again. Her eyes filled with happy tears when each person came up to her and Namanet and welcomed them back as a couple. Much to her surprise, the shaman approached and offered her one of his favorite rattles as a gift.

Two turns of the seasons had passed since she and Namanet began living as husband and wife. Tiana stood at the tent flap and watched the snow swirl around the encampment. It was the first winter storm after the warm sun days. Sometimes she thought of the wonderful day in the forest hunting mushrooms that brought their feelings for each other out into the sunlight for all to see. The time

TIANA

when Namanet took her body by force also came back to haunt her, but less and less as time passed. He never treated her in such a manner again and for that she was grateful. She would have kept her promise and moved into her own shelter alone. The lazy summer days and nights they spent together on the lake also helped to dissipate much of that memory.

She patted her stomach, growing rounder with each turning of the full moon. First, when she suspected she was with child she didn't tell anyone, wanting to keep her very own special secret. It hadn't taken long for Kania to notice the truth though. She understood Namanet's impatience with the lack of babies playing on their hearth, but knew this was a girl child growing in her belly. Hadn't the Raven Mother promised?

One night Tiana and Kania sat on furs near the glowing fire, sewing in the light of the tallow lamp. "Soon we must abandon this *camp of the season of the warm sun* and move back to the main village of sod houses."

"Yes, Mother Kania." It was now proper for her to call her that again, since both she and Namanet continued to share their abode with her. "The leaves turn thin and brittle and change colors on the trees, yet the hunters had searched long and hard and seem cursed by some evil spirit."

Kania nodded. "They have managed to slay only a few musk ox and caribou – not nearly enough to last the village for this entire season of the cold."

Her brow furrowed with worry and Tiana longed to reach over and console her with a pat on her shoulder, but this tribe did not show affection as easily as did her first tribe. Tiana closed her eyes, stilling her fingers a moment from their task, while she thought of that life so long ago. It seemed to come to her now like fog sifting through an early dawn, and soon she would forget them altogether. And yet it was from that lineage that the Raven Woman came. This thought brought on a guilty twinge, and she opened her eyes and bent again to her sewing.

Tiana seldom set eyes on Ikgat. He stayed out of her end of the camp as much as possible. The villagers brought gossip to her and Kania about the old shaman, crippled and bent with pains in his bones, and how he blamed the early snowfall for the game vanishing from the forest. It could be the truth.

When he called a meeting in the tent for a healing, Tiana was relieved that he always considered her and asked her opinion. Many times tribe members had come to her in the night, asking for her cure over his. Sadly, it was not always within her ability or Ikgat's to help someone. When it was time for a kinsman to leave the group, Tiana helped them find peace. For this gift, she felt gratitude to her Raven spirit.

"We go to search out game tomorrow," Namanet said into the comfortable silence. Tiana and Namanet had welcomed Kania to continue to stay with them, but she preferred to spend nights in the little hut he had built for her nearby. During the day, Tiana enjoyed her company.

"But the hunters have been out to search for game and found little," Tiana said.

"That is true, but the shaman had a dream. He told us that we must find a lake. Around the lake will be many caribou and moose. We must drive them into the water and with men placed in canoes, we can slay them easily."

When the women made no reply, he spoke louder. "I want you to come with me."

Both Tiana and Kania looked startled at his sudden vehemence.

"That might not be a good idea," Kania said mildly. "Tiana appears as if she will have the child any time, although there should be many full moons to go before this happens."

Namanet had seemed restless since he volunteered to go with the hunters. As if he regretted his impulsive act. It was plain he didn't want to be away from Tiana, but she knew he dare not admit it. That would have been unmanly and a subject of great derision if any of the men found out.

"Do you think I might be of help on the journey?" Tiana asked. She didn't want to be away from Namanet either. Yet she could become a burden to the group if she had trouble keeping up.

"You are strong, stronger than any woman in the camp, even with the babe inside you. We may have need of a shaman on our journey." The words rushed out of his mouth in his fervor to explain

TIANA

why she needed to go.

Kania looked thoughtful. "That might be so. Ikgat is unwell and more quick-tempered than ever, but he would be here for us and you would have Tiana."

Tiana recalled the time she had told the old shaman that there was only a place for one shaman in the tribe, and she was the one. He seemed to diminish in stature and worth if not in ill temper. It might be good for him to regain a little respect. Tiana felt certain that he would never again be a threat to her.

"I would like to go, Mother. It will be a fine adventure, and I tire of resting and sewing."

The two women exchanged looks. Tiana couldn't help but notice that Namanet had become dependent on her company since their coming together. Now, when custom forbid their mating because of her large stomach, he couldn't seem to get enough of touching her. At night they lay close on the skins, his face pressed into her swelling bosom, murmuring words of endearment until they both fell asleep.

When both Kania and Tiana decided she could go, Namanet flew around the hut getting his equipment ready. Women seldom traveled with the hunters, but Tiana knew this was an unusual undertaking, hunting this late in the cold. Three women came to their tent to tell them they were going also, to keep the men's equipment in good repair and to make certain clothing and boots were patched and weather-tight. The little band expressed their gratitude that Tiana was coming along. Who knew when a shaman would be needed?

Early next morning Namanet and Tiana hugged Kania and left the camp with the others. Even though Tiana had forgotten her old tribe's word for goodbye, she felt sad to leave her alone. Kania's fingers were gnarled and twisted from long seasons of harvesting fish in the cold waters. Her back was bending forward, much like the old shaman's. Tiana knew it wouldn't be long before she would have to move in with them for all time. That was not an unpleasant idea.

On the trail, the women helped pull the sleds that contained the pots for cooking, extra firewood, and deer hides for tents which they would put up most nights. The men ranged far ahead, searching for any kind of game they could find, and returned with rabbits or birds Sometimes, if the weather held, they slept out under the protective coverings of tall pine trees, wrapped in their robes of fur. When they set up camp finally, Tiana was relieved. Her back hurt, and the burden she carried in her belly seemed to grow more every day that passed.

When the women awoke each morning, they sat out in front of a warm fire, sewing and cooking. Tiana helped, flensing out the puny amount of hides the hunters brought in. They made and set up makeshift drying racks in each campground as they moved along, lighting small fires beneath the meat and drying the flesh and hides while the men hunted in the long hours of daylight.

One early morning she sat alone in front of her and Namanet's tent before the other women had awakened, and watched the men leave. They had camped here the longest, and each day the men returned later and later, never finding the magic lake that Ikgat had told them about. Now the days began to grow shorter, as Brother Moon claimed more time from Sister Sun. Tiana knew the day would come soon when it would not be light at all, just barely, and they must give up hunting. She shifted the ivory belt to a more comfortable position. Even big with child, the belt adjusted miraculously to her growing figure.

Soon the other women joined her. "You have been sewing for many nights. Are you preparing winter clothing for Namanet?" one of the women teased.

Tiana laughed and tossed her single thick braid over her shoulder lest she make her hair a part of the garment. "No, it is for the small one who will come to stay with us. But I remember someone telling me that I would never sew properly, that my stitches were never tight enough." How her first family would have loved to see her baby. She doubted that her grandmother was still alive. Tiana held up a tiny jacket and hood nearly finished.

"You will need a soft deerskin covering the babe, they are so cold when they enter the world," one of the women said.

"I think Mother Kania is making one for us," Tiana said.

"And little robes – they need little robes to wrap in, like tiny little people." The women laughed at the older woman's comment.

TIANA

A shadow of anxiety passed over Tiana, and she put her hand across her face to hide the sudden emotion. Her companions would know by this polite gesture that she did not wish to share her thoughts.

What if the small person turned out to be a male child, as Namanet wished for? She caught her bottom lip between her teeth. Was it only a legend, made up as old people down through the ages, that a descendent of the Raven Women was not permitted a male child? Tiana had never confided this to anyone but Kania, and that had been a long time ago, when she first came to their village. She rubbed her hand along the soft ridges of the Raven belt and felt a warm tingling in her fingers.

"I was very young when my first mother showed me this belt, but I loved to listen to her and grandmother's stories about Umiak and her beautiful daughter Oolik – ancestors of a different clan."

The women stopped their tasks and looked at Tiana. One of the older ones spoke into the silence. "Yes, we have heard stories that encompass the entire Northland from the trees to the barren ice. We have heard about those things." She folded her lips over her toothless mouth as if in smug satisfaction to be able to tell the younger ones something important.

One of the other women said, "Can you tell us some of what you have heard?" She smiled at Tiana.

How good it felt to be a part of the women group. So many times she had been left out, as if they didn't know how to talk to her.

"Legend tells my ancestors came from the land of the ice and never-ending snow where trees were unknown, and only wolves, foxes and huge white bears lived. Once Oolik, daughter of Umiak, the first Raven Woman, visited me during a shaman's séance." They nodded in agreement, waiting for the story to evolve.

Ever since she began this hunting journey Tiana felt an eerie closeness to the ancient ones. "Perhaps it is time to make a séance, a magic seeing. It could help the hunters if I asked the spirits how the people might have offended the animals, and why we cannot find the lake. We could make restitution and obtain enough meat to save the village from hunger during the long, cold winter to come."

"Yes! Yes! You must do this." The women chattered together excitedly. It was then Tiana realized how depressing this journey was to everyone, not finding game.

When the hunters came back to camp, Tiana fed Namanet and then broached the subject of the séance. She assumed the women did the same with their men.

Namanet looked solemn, as if considering the idea. The fire crackled in the fire hole, and some of the smoke drifted up through the small opening in the top of the conical tent. Much of it stayed around their heads in a layer of pale haze.

"A good idea," he finally pronounced. "A visit to the spirits may tell us how we have offended them." He looked at her fondly. "You are tired?" His look and voice told much he would never say. It was unseemly to speak of the strong feelings he had for her and their unborn child at this time before the birth. Namanet sighed.

Tiana felt sad for him. He must reflect often upon the complications of living as the mate of a shaman. But still, she knew he was proud of her and of how much the people had come to respect and love her. She saw her reflection when she waded into still water and was aware that her appearance differed somewhat from the women of the tribe, now that she'd reached maturity. She was small boned and slender, but tall, with flat, high cheekbones and a slightly-curved nose like her father, Quaanta. At first she hated her different look, but later grew to realize that Namanet thought her the most gifted woman in the village. He'd often told her over and over how he gloried in her unusual beauty. Now he had become more reticent, as if in their becoming parents it was no longer proper to display feelings so openly. She missed that from him.

She intercepted his glance falling on her bulging stomach and the carved belt always encircling her middle. She wore the earrings he had made for her in celebration of her becoming a woman. The ornaments threaded through her lobes with tiny chains of carved links. The long silky Raven feathers draped gracefully along her neck, blending with the curls at the nape of her neck that had escaped from her braid.

"I had a dream of my ancestors today," Tiana said. "The *eaters of raw flesh* who called themselves Inuit."

TIANA

"I remember," Namanet said.

Kania had told her this clan was also a legend to the forest people. She said no one, not even Ikgat, was certain of exactly where this strange tribe lived. They were peaceful creatures, for the most part, passing across the tundra in the warm months, sometimes venturing close to the forest to trade sealskins and fish for food or deer hides.

The Inuit also collected wood. This made them even stranger. Why would anyone place value on parts of trees which were everywhere? Kania thought this unbelievable.

Tiana knew Namanet felt she and his mother may keep secrets from him. She wondered if she would ever be able to confide in him about the Raven Mother's edict that there be no male children. Kania forbid her to say a word, ever. He never questioned how Tiana knew this small person would be a girl child, but she could tell he wished very hard, sometimes out loud, that it be a son. It had become a matter of pride.

"Do you think it is time to make a place for your birthing?"

She smiled and shook her head. "Not yet. The time for a daughter has not come. Perhaps it will not be until we return to the village."

His face reflected skepticism. "It appears to me that you may be hiding the young of a musk-ox in your belly. Everyone gossips about how big you have grown."

Tiana laughed, delighted at his retort. Imagine giving birth to a musk-ox baby! Namanet was usually so glum and sulky lately. When he made the rare jest, it struck her more amusing than any of the people-who-tell-the laughing-stories.

She muttered a quick chant, just to be on the safe side. It was not good to make laughter at this time, and not unheard of for a woman to mother animals. Stories had been passed down through time.

"It also feels like a mountain to me. Perhaps in a séance I will be able to ask when the child will come forth."

That evening, when it grew dark and the moon stayed behind a thick cloud, all the hunters and their women gathered together in Namanet and Tiana's shelter. She had performed séances in the village before, but not since she became pregnant. She felt anxiety blend with anticipation. She was by far the youngest of the group, not many summers out of her girlhood. But they had always shown respect for her shaman status though some of the older in the tribe were loyal to Ikgat.

Tiana sat apart, and as soon as the little group quieted, her palm and fingers moved slowly on her drum. She stared long and hard at each person in turn, and her lips began to form a soft, monotonous chant. Her eyes stayed open, but they focused now on the smoke as it eddied in a whirling, dancing haze. The gray turned into pale green and ceased to burn her eyes. Looking through it was like seeing another place – another time.

"Tulunixiraq. Someone calls for the Raven Mother." Her voice came soft, fitting between the drumbeats. She knew the hunters and the women slept in their trance.

The sides of the small enclosure began to expand. The Raven feathers against Tiana's neck lifted so they were at right angles to her cheeks. The Raven belt tightened slightly across her middle, sending rays of warmth in all directions of her body.

I am Tulunixiraq, come to you again. You have remembered much about our heritage. The Raven belt has survived, as has our legend.

Tiana waited, not wishing to interrupt, but the Raven Mother seemed to be waiting for her to speak. "O Tulunixiraq, tell the others about the beginning. Tell them about the ancient ancestors of our line."

I chose Umiak, the first Raven Woman, to wear the magical belt. She was our beginning, and my choice was good.

Tiana peered closely, trying to see the Raven Mother, but there was only the soft, green mist with a nebulous, wavering form in the center. A line of chills sped along her bare arms, as if the damp, icy wind from the glacier crawled inside the tent. She had never seen a glacier, but the legend spoke of the Raven Mother's spirit living inside one.

"How may a human please the Raven Mother?"

The fog drifted closer, and Tiana saw the tall, stately form wrapped in the strange, auburn-colored fur. The same vision she had seen twice before, one which had come to her underwater when she

TIANA

nearly drowned, and again when she went to her solitary hut to become a woman.

Her fingers drummed gently with automatic cadence, to keep the sleepers in a trance.

Daughter of the Raven, you will know much anguish and desolation. In time to come, you may curse your birth. You must have the courage of your destiny. The others before you honored our line as you will do. Take strength from my words and remember them well. We will survive in all time to come – but only through you and your daughter.

Someone coughed, otherwise there was silence. Tiana closed her eyes, sensing that her communication with Tulunixiraq had finished. She continued to drift in and out of the dream she had had before. She was outside, with snowflakes falling thickly, covering everything. Never had she seen so much whiteness – it was everywhere. A crumpled form huddled over a small pile of stones, and she recognized herself. The form wept and tore at her hair. Was she always alone? Where were the others? As if in answer, a small, indistinct gathering stood off in the distance, watching in silence. Namanet was there; his face grim, eyes dark and unyielding. Why did he not offer comfort in her obvious grief?

The image faded, and she awoke.

Tiana broke the silence finally. "Did you see where I journeyed, Namanet? The Raven Mother let me know our daughter would be born." She flexed tired fingers and watched her husband. The others still slept, although several stirred restlessly.

Namanet frowned, rubbing his eyes. "A man saw nothing, but sounds of much wailing and weeping came to me inside my head." They looked at one another a long moment, and she realized how close they had grown, with him able to share part of her dream.

She had been weeping – but why? "Did your helper spirit tell you where we might find food?" he asked. By now the group had awakened, rubbing their eyes and yawning. They listened intently.

"No. I learned nothing about where the animals are hiding. It may mean we should return to our village."

Namanet leaped to his feet, his face contorted in anger. "No! We cannot return without more food. We were chosen as hunters who would find game. We will be ridiculed."

One of the older men spat on the ground. "We cannot leave off hunting yet. It is too early to give up. Perhaps if we had brought Ikgat."

Namanet spoke again, his voice loud, his eyes filled with hostility, this time turned toward the one who questioned his woman. "He could not come with us. We would have had to carry him on our backs. Tiana has done the work of three women, she has carried her load. She had a vision. It was not of game, but that may come later."

Tiana could tell the people were not angry with her, but disappointed that she hadn't seen a vision of plentiful game.

During the coming days, everyone gathered equipment and Tiana, along with the other women, packed away their dried meat. Turning her face up, she let the snow fall on her skin – big, soft drops that clung to everything. The usual north wind died to a low, whining voice echoing across the glaring white land. Silence deepened around them, as if they were the last survivors on the land. She echoed their underlying uneasiness, not knowing when the unusual storm would stop. The men barely spoke, and the women not at all, as they prepared to break camp.

Even after they were ready to go they waited several sleeps to see if the storm would let up. But the snow continued to fall.

"I wish to speak." Namanet sat with the men around the fire in his shelter. The women sat alongside the outer edge, their usually busy hands empty of work now. Everything had been packed away in tight bundles and strapped to the long sleds for the men to push or pull.

"Speak then," one of the men finally answered. They all looked at Namanet with undisguised expectancy.

"My woman saw something in a dream," he began. He stumbled with words at first, but plunged stubbornly on.

Tiana observed his self-importance grow as the group's interest centered on him. She cared for him more than anyone, but he could be small and petty at times, and she hated this about him.

"Tiana saw snow covering everything. There was much lamenting. Who can be certain of what this signifies? I know what I feel and think. It is surely a sign we had best return to the village quickly, without waiting longer for the storm to ease."

TIANA

"Ayah!" The men murmured and nodded their heads, agreeing to leave early the next morning.

All that night Tiana sat up, softly singing the shaman's songs and chanting to any of the spirits who listened. In the morning she opened the tent to a clear, brilliant sky with no snow clouds in sight.

The people smiled in relief, and she absorbed their wordless thoughts that it could be her magic which made the difference. In a very short time they were ready and began their trek, heading for home. The first day they broke trail through the thick, moist snow. Tiana listened to the groans and moans and mumbled complaints and she too, wished to shout out the hurt in her legs from dragging her feet through the heavy snow. Someone grumbled about leaving the large pieces of carved wood back in the village, which they used on their boots to walk on soft snow. No one had thought to bring them along.

"We should put on our snow eyes," she suggested, surprised that the men hadn't thought of it. She took out hers, a piece of thinly carved wood slitted to help look upon the stark whiteness without becoming blinded. How strange they all looked wearing the masks, like spirits from another place, and she knew she looked the same.

She walked with the women behind the men as they trudged onward in grim stoicism. No one suggested halting or even resting. If someone tired, he or she dropped to the side, chewed on a piece of dried meat and then caught up with the others after a brief rest.

Namanet and another man pulled the first sled and two others towed the second. The third sled contained most of the equipment. One man or two women alternately pulled it along.

Tiana did her part and more. Having a big belly was no reason to shirk her duty. She tired easily now, but otherwise retained her youthful endurance. She pulled extra times and carried the heaviest load, for the other two women were much older, and one especially puny. Tiana could not understand why Fat Beaver brought this skinny creature along. She was already a grandmother and his first wife. Tiana supposed he wished to show his youngest wife that he could not be bossed.

By nightfall they were too exhausted to care about small comforts, and didn't bother setting up their tents. The snow had not begun again, but worse, the weather began to warm slightly. With the warm Chinook wind, the snow beneath their feet clung in sticky lumps with every step they took. Tiana could barely raise her legs to walk now.

"Namanet, how much longer will it be before we see the village?" Tiana had finished making the tiny fire to melt snow water for their next day's travel. They munched on the dry meat and huddled beneath the meager protection of hides propped up with hunting lances.

He wasn't too successful trying not to show his concern, she noticed. He must be doubting his wisdom, not for the first time, of asking her to come with him on this tedious journey. Knowing her husband so well, he had probably already changed it in his head that she was the one who wanted to come. Namanet had a way of doing that, to escape self-blame and responsibility.

"I should have forbidden you to come with us. As if I could have stopped you once you decided to come!" He frowned and then laughter crinkled his eyes.

Some of her worry dissipated. Her husband was not one for laughing, especially at himself. Since they had become husband and wife, he had become a different person. More self-assured, less giving. Yet he was good to her. Other wives envied her good fortune. None of them had recognized the man inside the crippled boy. If only he was not so obsessed with having a male child.

"I wish we had found the caribou herd," she mourned. "You said you saw traces of them in the snow. Where did they go? It is hateful to return to the village – to face the long cold nights without enough food for everyone."

Namanet grunted in agreement. "We must not let them leave Kania behind if they set out the old people first."

"No! Without her courage, we would not be together. We will fight to keep her near us." The idea of life without Kania was impossible to consider. Namanet's mother always managed to keep up their spirits, no matter how poor the hunting. She even managed to cheer Tiana when she felt large and unappealing with her burden of child.

Tiana and the women waited while the men set up the tents,

knowing they would have to protect what meat they had from an encroaching wolf pack. All during the night the men took turns watching the sleds. Tiana awoke several times, listening to wolves howling and snarling as they ventured closer and closer to the huddled little group.

The small person inside Tiana began to stir restlessly. It would not be long until it demanded entry into their world. She had no vision of a future. Carrying the child must have blocked her powers.

That day they took time to set up tents, and the sky looked as if snow would fall during the night. "Will we reach the village soon?" she asked Namanet again.

He frowned and shrugged his shoulders. It was clear he did not know.

The next morning when Tiana awoke, the entire surface of the earth lay covered with softly sifting particles of ice. The dreaded white-darkness had descended upon them. Every hunter or traveler looked upon this fearful spectacle with dread. She could not see as far as the next tent, although they were pitched close together, touching sides.

Namanet squatted on his haunches and readied a long piece of sinew. He fastened it around his middle and motioned for her to hold the end. She watched until he disappeared. He would first find one tent and then another and then the sleds. From there, the men would tie sinew between everything so they could go back and forth holding to the rope to avoid becoming lost.

Just when she began to worry about him, Namanet shouldered his way back into their tent, bringing as much meat as he could carry.

"We had to remove the packs from the sleds. The wolves grow more courageous. Each of us took a portion to bring inside. We may have to use it to survive if the white-darkness stays long."

He looked so regretfully at the frozen chunks of meat on the ground that Tiana longed to comfort him, but he would not wish her to intrude on his anxiety. His forehead wrinkled in thought and she guessed what bothered him most. They were the hunters, the strongest men in the tribe, sent to bring back food for the people. They would be forever in disgrace if they were forced to eat the food belonging to the village.

Pinkie Paranya

Time passed slowly inside the small tents. It was impossible to tell day from night. Sometimes Namanet ventured outside to speak with the others but no one came to their shelter.

Tiana sat in one place now, as if rooted into the ground. She understood, even before Namanet told her as kindly as he could, that the others did not want her company. It was unlucky to have a woman give birth in front of a hunter, that was a bad omen that even a shaman could do little to expiate.

Namanet also showed his unease. She knew he could not stay near her much longer. Perhaps he should erect another shelter close by. Otherwise he might have to destroy their clothing and weapons.

While they pondered the dismal possibilities, they heard a shout. Jumping to his feet, Namanet looked out the narrow opening. The white blindness had lifted a little. Visibility extended from the ground to about the center of his chest for as far as he could see in the distance.

They saw the other tents and the ice-encrusted line going from shelter to shelter. Two of the hunters stood at the edge of the clearing, their snow masks already in place.

"We are prepared to begin our journey again. Does this please Namanet?"

They looked like eerie wisps of *wiivaksaat,* Tiana thought, peering under her husband's arm as his bulk blocked the opening of their tent. It occurred to her to wonder how she knew the Inuit word for *spirit from the other world.*

"Yes! It is time." Namanet began taking down their tent. The others ran back to their tents and shouted at the women to help get ready for the journey. The snow mist still surrounded them, only now it had risen into the air, leaving the ground free from the thick, white clots of ice particles.

Tiana closed her eyes and went within herself. Her lips moved, her eyelids flickered, while Namanet watched in uneasy silence. He stepped from foot to foot impatiently, but dared not intrude. She opened her eyes and touched the sleeve of Namanet's fur jacket. "I speak, not as a woman, but as a shaman. I asked to be shown a sign and saw two small birds plummet from the air, unable to fly in this terrible cold. This tells me that the whiteness will return. Soon." The

TIANA

air was bone-snapping cold, and so dry her skin felt drained of blood, like a thin, scraped hide.

Namanet looked at her and then at the impatiently-waiting men. "I have never seen birds fall from the sky with cold. None of the others want to chance staying in one place and being forced to eat what little game we will bring back to the village food supply."

"I know. The women told me their men would prefer becoming lost or frozen in their tracks to facing the humiliation and shame of returning without meat," she said.

Never resolute, Namanet wavered. She knew him well enough to know that one part of him felt gratified that they looked to him for leadership, while yet the other part objected at his burden of decision and responsibility. Tiana wondered if he knew the only reason they looked to him for leadership was out of respect for her as a shaman.

The idea must have crossed his mind too at the same time. The thought brought a scowl to his face, his eyes narrowed. "We go. Help me with the packs, woman." He signaled to the waiting men.

His broad back warned Tiana that immediate obedience was beyond question, especially with other hunters standing nearby. He was a good man in his way, she reflected. Only his childish pride made him small. She understood that his crippled leg gave him great pain during the long winter, becoming worse with each passing year. But it was more than mere physical pain. He could have borne that without complaint. Why did he not believe in himself as she believed in him? Why did he always feel it necessary to prove his worth? At first she thought of not obeying him. She was shaman, a woman in her own right, and had no need to walk behind him.

Tiana hesitated in her work, wondering if her argument would prevail against the will of the group. Should she speak up and perhaps forever wedge a barrier between herself and Namanet? The premonition had dissipated somewhat. Did the foreboding deceive her? Was it only worry and fear of the coming birthing that had unnerved her? The spirits had been known to play extravagant jokes on a woman big with child. Until after the birth, the mother's body and mind were thought to belong to the new visitor for a time, and no one could tell if the small intruder would be amiable or hostile.

It did not take long for the eager little band to form the line of moving sleds. Each person had a tie around his waist, attached to another, to prevent anyone from wandering off to be claimed by the fog spirits. They walked a steady pace, neither rushing nor dawdling.

Tiana found it an eerie sight. Everyone was visible from the chest down, while heads and shoulders were shrouded in the fine ice mist. Namanet suggested she sit on one of the sleds, but she steadfastly refused. It was hard enough to pull the sleds through the thick, soft snow, without her bulk to add to their weight.

She leaned into the back of a sled, pushing it forward. By turning her thoughts inward she was able to push away the tiredness that permeated her entire body. Her mind drifted along with the ice fog. The muscles in her legs no longer burned, and her belly did not tighten with hunger. She made a soft chant as she trudged along. When she finally opened her mind to the present, it came as a shock to see her ankles shrouded in the mist. It sifted up from the ground like some evil spirit, just as she had feared! When it met in the middle, they would be lost. She called to Namanet but he did not hear her. Someone must have told him she'd called out, for soon he trotted back to her place in the line.

"You are well?" he asked. "The village must be close."

Tiana pointed down to her boots. "Look. The white blindness rises. We will surely be lost if we continue."

Namanet shot her an uneasy look and then became angry at what he deemed her shaman interference. "Do not intrude in this, for it is my decision. Soon we will come to the village."

She continued in her place behind a sled. The men stayed as far from her as they could, knowing the powerful mischief of the magic dwelling in a woman about to give birth. It would not be long now. Her stomach bulged more than any woman's they had ever seen. Nikka, one of the wives, walked close to her, but she too seemed uneasy. She had offered to act as midwife on the trail if that proved necessary, but it was not a decision the woman felt happy with.

Tiana understood her thoughts as if Nikka had spoken aloud. She had never worked with a shaman before. What if the baby died? What if it was the wrong sex and angered Tiana? Would she put a curse on Nikka and her family?

Pain shot through Tiana's back and legs as she forced herself to

TIANA

move with the group. Her stomach felt bloated and tight, as if any time it might burst open and fling its contents onto the snow. Her time would soon be here, and her entire being called out for Kania. Through the haze of suffering she saw Kania's dear face. She gasped at the realness of the vision. Suddenly soothing hands caressed her and a feeling of relief overwhelmed the pain. It *was* Kania. Her husband's mother had come along with some of the villagers, to search for them.

Soon they would be home at last.

Pinkie Paranya

TIANA

 **ELEVEN**

TIANA heard the shouts of welcome ringing through the once silent white-encased forest before she saw the men greeting each other with hearty back thumps, loud talk and much wild gesturing.

"Mother! How good you look to me!" Tiana reached for the older woman and hugged her.

Kania took one long look at Tiana and without a word to Namanet, bundled her into the birthing lodge at the outskirts of the village.

What followed was like being inside the white blindness except Tiana no longer felt cold and alone. They hadn't had time to sing the birthing songs handed down from their ancient ancestors before the pains began, and Tiana was unable to utter a word. Kania did her best to sing away the demons who might be waiting outside. Dimly through waves of pain Tiana saw Kania, loving and concerned, kneeling at her side. She bore the pains with stoic detachment.

The labor persisted so long, she worried if she had offended any spirits that might wish to harm her baby. Had she committed some disrespect while on their journey? Had she ever touched her husband's bow and arrows? She felt certain she had not. Once when a hunter snared a wolf, she made a song to the wolf spirit to permit the group to eat the flesh of the forbidden animal.

Everyone knew it was unwise to use any part of brother wolf but his fur which they highly prized. They usually buried the body out of courtesy to the animal to avoid desecration. Tiana clutched the Raven belt as she crouched low over the birthing hole. Through a tearing of her insides and a blinding jolt of pain she heard Kania's voice.

"Daughter, you have done well. A girl child has come to you."

Tiana breathed a heavy sigh and then felt her stomach. Its roundness still stubbornly protruded over her knees as she squatted over the hole lined with soft moss. "Mother, something is not right. Should not my round belly go?"

They waited, not knowing what to do. Tiana's tired legs were trembling, ready to collapse. She would have liked to kneel but that was not proper. Sweat broke out across Tiana's forehead, and she tasted sour on her lips.

Kania knelt facing her, holding her shoulder with one hand and pushing hard on her belly with the other. "Wah! I wish one of the older women had come inside to help us. I have never encountered such a strange thing. No one wished to help at the birthing, since not even the oldest had ever been present at a female shaman's birthing."

Tiana was unprepared for the searing agony that now tore through her innards. She screamed. Kania clamped a hand over her mouth. The men must not hear.

"Daughter! Another small person comes!" Kania's voice cracked with alarm.

Tiana sucked in her breath, trying to pull it back inside her body. It was a dreadful mistake! She knew another child was destined for her sometime in the coming years but not now! She felt a final tearing anguish and then looked down in the hole at the male child lying there.

Kania hesitated only a moment before she scooped up the baby and disappeared with both of them, one in each arm. Tiana knew she was going out into the snow to cleanse them. This ritual served to make the small one strong for what it had to bear during a lifetime. Often the child turned pale and its spirit left and when this happened, it was meant to be. She smiled at the dual squalls of protest which rose louder and louder.

Kania brought the crying babes inside and laying them down, covered them with a wolf skin which lay readied. She gave Tiana wet moss to clean herself.

Afterwards, Tiana lay wearily on the bed of furs, suddenly shaking all over, although she did not feel cold.

"Mother, how can a woman give birth to two children at once, like a she-bear or a caribou? Is it because I am shaman? We have all

TIANA

seen two offspring the same size from these animals and marveled at it."

"No one in my memory – in our clan – ever heard of a woman making two small persons at one time. Could it be in your tribe this is normal?"

"I do not remember hearing of it. No one ever spoke of it." She looked at the babes lying close but not touching her. One of the babes kicked and screamed, face contorted in anger. The other lay still and silent, like a proper little one.

Kania wrapped the infants in soft deer skin and carrying one in each arm, gave one last look at Tiana before leaving the little enclosure.

It was a long time before Kania returned. Tiana became anxious. Had she shown the babies to Namanet? What would he think this strange event?

"Daughter, take one child so that I may wrap up the other." Kania shouldered her way past the fur flap on the small dwelling and entered the darkened space.

Tiana knew a lamp was not permitted the first night after the birth, nor was a fire allowed lest the birthing offend the fire spirits. Everything would have to be done quickly, before night came upon them. If she was lucky there might be a nearly full moon tonight and she could leave the tent flap open. Tiana held the one infant close and snuffled into its soft delicacy.

Kania stopped her, the expression on her face grim. "Do not do that!" she warned sharply.

Tiana was shocked. Kania never spoke harshly to anyone.

"What must I not do, Mother?"

The older woman shook her head. "Namanet – I spoke to Namanet . . ." she faltered, unable to continue.

Sorrow filled Kania's voice. Tiana knew her mother had been troubled for a long while, perhaps now it would come out. When had this odd behavior started? It seemed to her that Kania had changed from the time Namanet told her there would be a child. Tiana remembered how they had waited for signs of happiness after they told her. She recalled the strange, haunted expression on Kania's face before she hid it.

From that day on there had been sadness in the older woman not anyone or anything seemed to be able to reach. Tiana had assumed she worried that her birthing time might be difficult.

"Mother, share your thoughts with me. Why are you so tormented about the birth of my children? Surely in the time you have lived, you have heard of mothers giving birth to two little people in other tribes."

"I have heard this spoken of. In other clans it has been known to happen, but never once in ours for as long as the oldest person can remember."

"But what can be wrong? My spirit helpers gave me no feeling of ill will. The Raven belt did not warn me."

"It – it is a lean year. We cannot keep two extra mouths to feed."

Tiana shook her head. "No. That is not the reason. A mother can feed a child from her breast for many summers. I am shaman and Raven Woman . . ."

At the words, Kania burst into tears, rocking the baby in her arms and pressing her face into the tiny bundle so that it squirmed.

Tiana, alarmed, struggled to rise from her pallet. She had never seen this calm, self-controlled woman so distraught.

"Daughter – there are no words . . ." Kania wiped her wet face on the soft fur covering the child she held, refusing to meet Tiana's gaze.

Neither woman spoke for a long moment. Only the whimpering of the baby in Tiana's arms broke the silence.

Kania finally began to speak, haltingly as if she tore out each word from deep inside. "When you and Namanet wanted to become husband and wife, Ikgat aroused everyone against you. The people would have you both banned from the tribe or have slain you to avoid becoming wrapped inside the shaman's curse, for he threatened terrible consequences."

Tiana waited, still holding one infant close to her warm body. At first it trembled from the cold but now it warmed and instinctively searched for food. Since custom dictated that a new life not be nurtured for two sleeps after its birth except for little sips of water or thin broth, she had to withhold her breasts, which ached with pressure of needing to give suckle. The babe she held was the boy

TIANA

child. His hair, thin and black, lay in fine swatches around the outer circle of his head. He was tiny and wrinkled, like a little old man.

The one her mother held, the girl, had a full head of hair which stood up at all angles on her head. This baby arched her back, flinging her legs and arms straight out in angry protest. Her eyes looked out at Tiana in fury as she bellowed at the inhospitable world she had suddenly been thrust into.

The boy child lay still and unresisting, gurgling his quiet acceptance.

Tiana waited, still not speaking. Her chest felt as if a hunter had stabbed her with a lance. Something bad was coming from the mouth of Kania that would change all their lives. She wanted to run away, to leave before words were left hanging in the air that no one could take away ever again. Kania's head was bowed, her chin down, so that Tiana could not see her face.

"When my husband and I did not have children, I visited the shaman. He promised I would give birth, but a very terrible exchange would be made. I agreed. Before Namanet's birth a wolf killed his father. When you and Namanet wanted to be together, many were against it. I – I made a promise to Ikgat that you would give him your first son if he would make magic to permit your becoming husband and wife."

"You promised that old he-wolf our *son?*" Tiana's voice rose in near-hysteria.

"You said your Raven spirit would not permit you to keep a male child. I thought that meant you would never give birth to one. It was the only way I could persuade Ikgat to allow your marriage. Without that, you both would have been slain or cast out. I could not bear that." Kania raised her eyes finally to meet Tiana's. "When winters passed and you bore no children, I thought I had made a wise exchange. The shaman would receive nothing for his concession. I rejoiced in my cunning at out-thinking this shaman who hated you so."

Tiana buried her face in the soft skins wrapping the baby, while trying to shut out the sounds of Kania's sobbing.

Finally, with heavy heart, she stirred herself. "Mother, do not distress yourself more. You have suffered alone, caged inside your thoughts these many winters. Do not cry. It is true, I must not keep my son, but we would have found someone to keep him and love him."

Kania looked down at the angry specimen she held. "No, I think not. Namanet would not let him go. He wanted a son so badly. No one in the tribe would dare take your child. The people fear this is a bad omen. They are certain we will have a bad winter. The hunters did not bring enough back to last more than a turn of the moon. People are saying the misfortune is because a brother and a sister mated."

Something about the girl child distracted Tiana from Kania's grim pronouncement. "Mother, take the girl child closer to the opening so that the moon shines on her." Tiana got carefully to her feet and still holding the boy child, reached for one of the girl's flailing arms. On the inside of the delicate arm from her elbow to her wrist a graceful design curved, just a shade darker than the surrounding skin.

"Look! It is the mark of a Raven feather!" She touched her finger to her own earlobe and followed down the curving length to the tip of the Raven feather of her earring.

Kania peered closely, and looked at Tiana, puzzlement plain on her face. "Why is she marked? You have no marks from the Raven spirit." Gently she rubbed the mark, as if convinced it could not be real. It was real, and the baby pulled away.

"Did Namanet see them?"

Kania nodded. "Your husband looked at the small people." She hesitated before continuing. "I am afraid he was ashamed. He reminded me that women can mate with wolves. He wonders if this had happened while he was out hunting." She bent her head, looking sad to have to repeat her son's words. "Ikgat is telling everyone that if this has happened we must leave the babes in the snow. The wolf spirits would not permit humans to keep them."

Tiana felt a constriction in her chest, her heart thudded and she could not speak. "Namanet wishes to leave our babies in the snow?"

Kania shook her head. Her face seemed to have aged overnight; tired from her long ordeal of helping Tiana with the birthing and from the terrible secret she had kept for so long. "Perhaps one.

TIANA

Before the darkest of the cold season we will suffer much hunger. Many kinsmen may be left behind."

Tiana closed her eyes, letting the hot tears well up and spill out from beneath her eyelids. She didn't bother to brush them away and they coursed down her cheeks and fell upon the babe she held so tight. Namanet was within his rights to say who might join his family and who might not. She struggled to hold back the wail of terror and fear, knowing the babies and Kania would be frightened by her outburst. "Which – which one does he seek to abandon?"

"I did not speak to him of my promise to the shaman." Her dark eyes implored Tiana to understand. "He wishes to keep his son."

Tiana jiggled the little boy gently, without protest from the wrapped bundle. Little ones were so fragile, not like most newborn animals which quickly learned to walk and eat on their own. She thought of the cold enveloping the thin baby skin and working toward their insides to freeze them into death. This one was hungry, poor little one, but his hunger would have to wait. Decisions must be made. Important decisions.

"Perhaps we could give Ikgat the girl child. You are still young. You will have more," Kania offered tentatively.

Tiana cried out, eyes blazing. "Never! I will see them both delivered to the spirit world first! My daughter will be the Raven Woman one day and must survive. Because of Ikgat's hatred for me, my son would suffer a living death with him. There is also Namanet to consider. He would never permit his son to be given away to slavery, not even if he discovers his mother made a sacred promise."

Kania buried her sobs in the furs of the child she held. Her shoulders moved with her effort not to cry out loud.

"Will you leave the babe with me and let me speak to my spirits?" she asked Kania.

Unable to speak, her mother nodded and put the girl baby gently into Tiana's waiting arm.

When the tent flap closed, Tiana sat in darkness for a while, contemplating what had been done. Gradually her eyes became used to the gloom, and she reached fingers out to pull aside the tent opening so she could look at the babies.

She lay the boy down on the fur pallet and sat beside him, still holding the girl child. Tiana reached beneath the fur and pulled out her Raven belt. She thought it might have been improper to wear it during the birthing.

"Raven Mother, come to me in my time of distress. How can I make a decision to allow one to die and another to live? How can my husband think I might have mated with wolves? I have been a good wife, putting my life as a shaman and Raven Woman aside many times to accommodate his needs." Her voice rose in anguish, tears continued to fall and her throat constricted so that no sounds could come. The girl baby struggled and kicked in her arms until Tiana laid the Raven belt across her body. The baby reached for it and Tiana moved it closer to her cheek. The child stopped fretting and lay still.

She looked down at the boy, her son, lying still and asleep. She'd questioned her mother and grandmother once long ago as to why Raven Women were not permitted sons. Neither was certain but her grandmother supposed it had to do with man's taking on superiority when that had always been a woman's domain. Taking away sons would be her punishment for allowing it to happen.

These thoughts came to Tiana while she stood looking out into the moonlight and feeling the cold of the north wind penetrate her body. The girl did not protest but raised her face to the icy wind as if in challenge.

Was this her answer then, the only answer to come from the Raven Mother? She had comforted Tiana before and though the greenish haze holding her form did not appear now, Tiana felt a soothing warmth across her shoulders – enough to relax her body and allow her to take a deep breath again. She hadn't realized she'd been holding herself in tight as if she might splinter apart like an ice crystal dropping from the tree and hitting the rocks below.

She took up the little male child in her other arm and bent her head to snuffle their scent and feel their bodies against her wet face. The girl baby still touched the ivory belt.

Tiana moved toward the tent opening and called out. "Mother Kania, it is time."

Kania had stood close by, suffering the cold without complaint, waiting for her decision.

"It is difficult. I want both my babes but it is not meant to be

TIANA

so." Tiana held them close and then laid them both down on the furs at her feet. "Then so be it," she said barely above a whisper. "Take the boy child away. Put snow in his mouth so his spirit will depart quickly and he need not long endure the cold."

When Kania hesitated, she cried out, "Quickly! Take the boy before I change my mind. If no one in the clan will take him and claim him, the boy will suffer all his life." She motioned toward the bundle of wrapped fur. The girl baby still had the Raven belt wrapped around her tiny wrist and hand, clinging to it. She lay silent, no longer protesting, but her eyes never ceased looking at Tiana in that odd, old person way. It was as if she were trying to communicate – to tell her mother something of importance.

Tiana rocked back and forth from her toes to her heels, trying hard to contain her anguish. Could she do anything more? Could she have made a séance? A séance to make the Raven Mother come to her as she had before. Dare she perform one now? She knew that to a shaman, the birthing shelter was a particularly dangerous place to be. It allowed an opening in the spirit world where her powers could be overcome by an enemy spirit and taken away forever. No one could exist without one's spirit inside. How should she reconcile this with the custom that demanded a mother stay inside the birthing place four sleeps after a birth? So many thoughts. She pressed her palm against her forehead, feeling the heat of her emotions.

Kania reached for the girl baby. "So be it. If that is truly your decision. But Namanet must name her."

Tiana held the babe close, pressing her face into the warm little body. The child twined her fingers in the long Raven earrings and would not loosen her grip. She wanted to stay with her mother. She felt as if the baby was already a part of her, singing in her blood, living within her heart. "I have named her. From this day forward she will be known as Nikota, *woman of the people*."

Kania sucked in a deep breath, her voice trembled. "You cannot name her unless Namanet agrees. It is for the father to . . ."

"I named her so that Namanet *must* agree. One cannot give a name to a child and then throw it away without taking a chance that the spirits who watch over children will be offended."

"I know. The spirits may not be angry, but Namanet will be. I am afraid to take these babies back to him now."

"You cannot fear your own son," Tiana reproached her. Although it could be true, for Namanet had changed gradually since they had been living together as husband and wife. Perhaps the hunters were taunting him again.

Kania looked skeptical, but straightened her back and clutched the two children to her breast. "That is true, I cannot fear my own son. I will return soon – with Nikota."

Time passed slowly as Tiana lay waiting in the small, dark place. Usually if she had a moment alone she thought shaman thoughts, but something warned her to not approach this solace now. She busied her hands in work on a little cape for Nikota made of woven Raven feathers and trimmed with soft wolverine fur. When she thought of the tiny little boy lying out in the snow alone, tears streamed down her face and her throat closed tight in pain. At times she could barely breathe and had to stand, looking outside. The sinking moon sifted through the partially-opened hide doorway. Although it also brought in cold air, the pale shimmering light comforted.

Kania returned at dawn. Tiana looked at her empty arms and felt her heart push into her throat. It was impossible to breathe.

Kania shook her head in helpless distress, her expression so filled with concern and love that Tiana had to look away.

"Nikota? Where is my baby?"

"Gone." Kania held up her palms in a gesture of futility. "Both of them gone. Namanet heard my words that I repeated from you. I have never seen him so enraged before. He said – he said if you did not want the boy child, then you should not be permitted to have either. He said more small people may come to your lodging later – if he ever decides to forgive you for shaming him by first giving birth to two and then by not keeping his son."

"I told him the promise I had made to the shaman so long ago." She dipped her head and touched her fingers to her cheek. "He – he struck me." She looked into Tiana's eyes, her heartbreak so plain to see. She was past tears, as if they had dried up inside her.

Tiana waited. There was more to be heard, and her legs felt so weak they could hardly hold her, yet she had to hear it all.

TIANA

"He asked if I would leave him alone to commune with the babes and I – I thought that was proper. I waited in the empty meeting tent, but when he did not call out to me, I went into our abode. All his weapons and clothing were gone, along with the babies. I sat and waited, but he never returned."

Tiana grabbed Kania's shoulders, shaking the old woman until her braid whipped back and forth around her cheeks. "Why would he do this? Do you think he will be back?" Kania went limp in Tiana's strong grip. Her anguish was so complete that it was clear she wished to die without taking another breath.

"Do you say that I no longer have *any* babies?"

Kania stepped back, her eyes filled with alarm. "You look like your daughter, your face is like your daughter's when she cried, you are just alike. Perhaps Namanet was right. Perhaps the children were cursed."

"No! I will not accept this." Tiana pulled on her leggings and reached for her jacket.

"What are you doing? You cannot go outside! The people will be alarmed and very angry."

"I do not care! I want Nikota. I must save her from the snow spirits before they claim her. I have changed my thoughts about my son also. I will keep him and cherish him until the Raven tells me what to do."

"Daughter, going outside will do no good. You will be punished, and it will not help the children." As if she had not wanted to say the next words, she whispered, "Namanet took them away. I asked and someone said he loaded them on a sled and left the village. He refused to tell anyone where he was going or what he would do."

Tiana pushed Kania's gentle, restraining hands away. A scream of anguish tore from her throat, filling the little shelter and bouncing off the driftwood and mud walls.

Kania put her hands over her ears to protect herself from the shaman power of this woman who now seemed a stranger to her.

Raven Woman. Do not despair. I will not allow the Raven line to die. You must find your daughter. You will find your daughter.

Tiana's scream died in her throat.

Kania sank down weakly on her haunches, her arms raised

protectively over her head as if she too had heard the voice of Tulunixiraq.

In her distress, Tiana had thrown the Raven belt to the ground where it now lay. She bent to pick it up, shaking it in the air with impotent fury. "Why have you not helped me, Raven Mother? It is hard enough to lose a son. How can I bear to lose my daughter also? How can *you* bear it?"

The belt seared into her fingers and she wanted to cast it from her, but her fist would not open to release it. She picked up the tiny cape she'd been sewing for her daughter and closed her eyes tight. On the inside of her lids she saw only white at first, swirling white mists with spasms of pale sunlight filtering weakly through. It gradually cleared and in the center sat a small figure surrounded by bulky furs. She willed herself to venture closer and saw that tranquility encompassed her daughter. One of the fur objects turned, and Tiana saw that it was a person, a stranger with a round face, black eyes and an expression of warmth and love.

Suddenly Tiana felt torment drain away like snow melting from the side of a tent. Her body relaxed, and her eyes opened to see a delicate green mist lingering in the semi-gloom. A tall, stately form stood before her. The features of her face were shrouded in the green fog, but even so, Tiana knew her expression – that of loving compassion – so that it warmed her to her bones.

"What must a wretched woman do to find her daughter? Where could my husband take her? Perhaps the snow spirits claim her as we speak. And I do not wish my son to perish." The soft edges of the image shifted slightly, and the tiny cape in Tiana's lap seemed to rustle as if alive.

I cannot tell you where or how to find your daughter. You were chosen to carve the belt and you must prove worthy. This I can tell you. Your daughter Nikota is not one of the lost and wandering ones. She has not died. You will make the journey to me before you will find her.

"Wait! I must learn more! My son?" The Raven Mother seemed to shake her head sadly and began to fade. Tiana reached to touch the form as it gradually melted away. It was as if time had frozen in place. When the green mist disappeared, she looked down at Kania. She too had frozen in one place, with her arms still held over her

TIANA

head in a protective gesture.

Tiana bent and pulled the old woman gently to her feet.

"Mother Kania, a daughter must go from here. Namanet has walked on my soul, and I have to find him before he destroys us both. Please help me."

Kania looked at her sorrow and pain deep within her eyes. "I will leave my people. I will go with you to search," she offered. "I do not wish to lose both a son and daughter."

Tiana felt moved beyond words to know this woman would exile herself from the people, her only kinsmen, perhaps forever. It was the most terrible punishment ever meted out in council, and happened rarely. Yet Kania, who was not even her birth mother, was willing to do this. Tiana's eyes filled with tears. "No, Mother, you must stay here. He might reconsider and return with the babies."

Tiana saw weary resignation on Kania's face.

"I have loved you as my own. Come back to us." The two women embraced, their tears blending against each other's cheeks as they clung tightly for a long moment.

Tiana felt sadness that would take a long time to heal. She had lived in this village half of her life. She did not wish to leave Kania and the security of the tribe. Yet, somehow she knew that even in his rage and despair, Namanet would return one day to be with his mother and care for her in her old age, but she felt certain she would never see any of them again.

Even through her sadness at leaving Kania, part of her became impatient to begin searching for Nikota.

She must find her – and soon.

Pinkie Paranya

TIANA

 **TWELVE**

PAIN shot through Tiana's aching legs when she stretched them out from their cramped position where she tried to rest on the sled. Tonight marked the fourth sleep away from home. Namanet's trail had grown fainter with each new sun, and she begrudged time wasted resting. Her full breasts ached from the milk inside them, and she shivered in the thin, icy air. Her tiny, fragile babies! Would Namanet protect them from the cold or had he already laid them out to perish? She hated Namanet so much at that moment that the heat from her anger helped to warm her insides. She clutched the slate-tipped lance tightly in her mittened hand and wished Namanet stood before her so she could run it through his body.

She pulled the fur covering up closer around her neck in a futile attempt to stave off fear as the sound of howling wolves broke through the solemn stillness of her white world. Should she stay here and make a fire against the side of that rock outcropping? She hated to stop but didn't like to travel in the dark. Even with a full moon she could miss Namanet on another trail close by. But the wolves were never this close before and last night the grizzly growled in her sleep. Was it a warning? Of what? To stop or travel faster?

The wolf cries had echoed each night, closer and closer. Each day she looked backward at their shadowy shapes, always following her, ever at a cautious distance. She knew from experience that soon the leader would grow bold by her inaction and try to rush her. What would she do? Women were never allowed to hunt, but even the men had to take special precautions when they killed a wolf. The animal had exceptional spiritual qualities.

She felt a little comfort knowing that the several hunting trips she'd made with Namanet might help her survive. Her thoughts filled with sorrow and confusion. Leaving Kania ripped a violent hole in her life, and though she hated Namanet for a time, she already missed him, too. If only her mother had not promised the shaman her first born son.

The next day, just before nightfall, Tiana found an abandoned fox den and pushed her legs backward inside to cover them from the falling snow. She draped a deerskin over her head which caused the stale, musty odor from the fox to rise up, clogging her nose and making her eyes sting and water. She carried some dry pieces of wood beneath skins and took out the fire starter in a pot to make a little fire in front of her so she could at least see if something approached her through the forest.

Her legs ached from walking all day, her back and neck hurt from always turning around to see what followed behind her. Yet she wanted the pains to continue without abating to keep the thoughts of her village and Mother Kania at a distance. It was no use. As soon as she made herself somewhat comfortable in the fox den, she lay looking out at the white expanse in front of her. The tree limbs dipped down with their heavy burden of snow. It had turned warmer when the snow began to fall, but that made it hard, slogging work to walk through the new softness.

Tears threatened at the corners of her eyes, and she squinted them tight, willing herself to be strong. She would miss some of those back in the camp and wished she could have said goodbye. But the tribe had no words for farewells, and the only time anyone left the tribe was in death. She hated sneaking out in the darkness of early morning, but for Kania's sake, she knew it would not help to confront Ikgat.

She hadn't thought of that possibility. What if the shaman and his wolf and owl helper spirits were pursuing her through the forest, spying on her even now? Terror pushed through her meandering thoughts; bile turned her mouth sour. She had to catch up with Namanet before someone stopped her or he laid the babies in the snow! He hadn't done it yet, she would have been able to sense it, she was certain of that. She forgot the snow falling and watched the flickering fire which threatened to go out because of the wetness in the air.

The Raven belt at her waist gave off no feeling except that of warmth. The Raven Mother expected her to take care of this, to show her mettle as a Raven Woman. She must find a way to keep both babies and return to the village, even if she had to slay the shaman herself to protect her family. Later, when the Raven Mother decreed it time, she would give her son to another family. She would at least see him every day that way. There were many in the village who would raise him with loving care as soon as they realized he was not cursed. As for Kania's sacred promise to Ikgat, if the old shaman was dead, he would not be able to extract his payment.

Warmed by what she thought might be solutions to her dilemma, she dozed fitfully. In her dreams she saw herself finding Namanet and stealing into his tent as he slept. She felt the rage and frustration and plunging her knife into his chest gave her a sensation of pleasure.

When she awoke, groggy and dazed, the burden of hatred toward Namanet had dissipated. He had done what he thought was right, had acted in his best judgment, which though flawed, was the only path he saw to take. The nagging fear mixed with hope of meeting Namanet on the trail never left her, day or night. What would happen when his familiar form came trotting toward her as he pushed his sled along – empty? How could she face him? It was not his rage that bothered her. Away from the other men, with no one to hear, she knew he would plead with her to return with him.

How would she answer? The villagers listened to him of late, but Kania said it was because they respected her Raven powers. They did not think well of Namanet, for he had become belligerently opinionated as he grew older. Far from improving his personality since they had begun living together as husband and wife, he had changed to a small, but potent tyrant. Kania claimed the transformation came about because at last he felt equal to the other men. Perhaps in time he would have returned to being the old, loving Namanet.

Tiana closed her eyes and snuggled down into the warm furs, remembering his gentleness. She missed his warm body against her, his strong arm thrown possessively across her hips as he often did in his sleep. Tears threatened, and she wiped at them, knowing they would freeze her lashes together and blind her.

Her reflections turned to Kania. Could she journey in her thoughts, to tell her not to worry? Perhaps not, since Namanet's mother was not shaman. She rubbed the Raven feather lying against her cheek.

How could she hope to find her babies in all this vast whiteness? The Raven Mother promised she would find her daughter and yet it depended upon her, Tiana, to prove worthy of the line. How big was this land she journeyed through and where to begin her search? Would she travel until she fell off the end and joined clouds high in the sky? She shivered at the prospect.

She struggled to her feet, her body stiff and achy from the damp cold. After taking care of her morning needs, she washed clean snow over her face and shook out her covering. She took a dried piece of meat from her pouch and chewed to relieve the hunger growling in her belly. She washed it down with melted snow water kept inside her wrappings to prevent it from freezing in the night.

"Soon I must build a larger fire when I stop at day's end, to melt snow to drink." She said the words out loud to hear a human voice. Though she spoke softly, the woods echoed her voice and snow fell from nearby trees. Several birds flew out from their places in the tall pines. She raised her head and craned her neck back to see the patch of sky above, but saw no ravens.

She packed her furs on the sled and knelt to examine the earth. At first she'd had no difficulty following the dim path of Namanet on the crusty, hard surface. This pass was well traveled both in the cold days and the warm, for it was near the resting place of the huge caribou herd who came to calve during the warm moons.

Starting out, pushing the sled and sometimes pulling it, she tried to keep the doubts away of the wisdom in her headlong flight. At least in the day she was not alone. Rabbits and ptarmigan darted everywhere around the ice-covered bushes, scurrying fearlessly close. "Chuck-chuck-chuck," such deep throaty odd sounds came from the stately birds. She would not starve when her dried meat gave out.

As if in a dream, the horizon filled with a moving line of fur-wrapped people, heading toward her. She stopped and listened, but

TIANA

heard no sound. It must be a hunting expedition, which always traveled silently. Should she hide in the brush like a rabbit or stand and wait, hoping to learn if they had seen Namanet? She knew it could be dangerous. Women never strayed away alone because they were fair game for tribes who captured slaves.

She straightened her back and tilted her chin up as the first sled pushed over the little rise. They must not think her afraid or anxious. She had to take the chance, to know if they had seen Namanet and her babies. While she waited, her heart thumped painfully against her ribs. She'd pulled her own sled to the side of the path, permitting them to pass.

"Hoo!" The man in front lifted his hand when he saw her. The others behind him stopped suddenly to see why he halted. The leader pointed toward Tiana and began to speak, using his mittened hands to punctuate his words. His accent sounded strange and harsh to her ears. She knew they were the outsiders from the frozen sea – the people of ancient Umiak and Oolik, the first Raven Women.

The stranger's expression was one of open friendliness and frank curiosity. The people looked like plump, exotic animals dressed in sealskin jackets and thick leggings. Their faces were round with fat cheeks, their skin the same light tan as her own.

Their sleds amazed her. Her own tribe sewed beaver pelts together and froze them to use as sleds to pull game and to take their belongings to a new place. In the summer they carried their possessions on cut logs wrapped together with sinew, which was very heavy. These people had a much better idea. Their sleds seemed to be fashioned of pale, gray pieces of wood with something smooth beneath them to make them pull along easily.

They stared at her, and she stared back. Never had they seen a woman traveling without a man to accompany her, their thoughts came through the air to her.

"Is a woman-who-walks-alone hungry?" The man spoke, a little too loudly, as if he was uneasy.

She shook her head politely. "No. I search for my family. Have you seen a man traveling alone with a beaver sled?"

They were too polite to ask why a woman need follow her husband, but their faces were filled with curiosity. They conferred together briefly then turned to her. "Many sleeps ago, we did see a stranger such as yourself. He was not alone but traveled with some of our clan from a different village."

"Did – did you see a – baby with him?" She spoke barely above a whisper. The man had to lean forward to hear her.

He turned back to the others to confirm his reply. "No one saw a small child. They were just people, walking together. The man was not of our people, therefore we noticed him."

It was Namanet! It had to be! Her throat dried, and she stammered out her next words. "Which direction did they go?"

"Wah! They go over the mountain pass, toward the home of the *aakluq*, the great bear with the sun-touched fur. A man thinks they begin their journey back to the ice."

Bears! She did not like the sound of it. Bears frightened her ever since her pact with the one who killed her grandfather. There was a promise made, a promise that one day she and brother bear would meet. She rubbed her jacket arms to rid herself of the sudden chill. It was a bad omen. "Thank you. Does anyone wish to trade dried fish and caribou for a bit of *muuktauq*?" She knew of the whale blubber most of them carried with them, a great delicacy for her people. Now she felt the need of fat in her system to ward off the penetrating cold.

The leader regarded her solemnly, then walked away. It was not until then that she realized they had understood each other though their language was different. It was best not to think overlong about such mysteries; as a shaman, she knew some things were not to be explained.

He came back with the whale skin wrapped in a thin parchment of hide. "We do not trade with women. We give this to you." He managed a shy smile, showing rows of large white teeth. "If a woman intends to go into the valley, the journey is long with many perils. We wish you well."

Tiana took the package and thanked him. The fat meat was very precious and might save her life. If only she had something to give in return. She thought of the arrow-stopping vest of Namanet's packed away in her sled. He had loved her long and tenderly the night she gave it to him as a gift. He valued it highly, thinking it his totem and never leaving on a hunt without it. She took it to punish him,

TIANA

knowing he would miss it when he returned to the village.

Before she could decide what more to say to them, the strangers moved along. Every face turned toward her, inquisitiveness strong in their dark eyes. She felt saddened as they trudged out of sight. She began to consider her plight more seriously. Had she enough food and weapons on her sled to carry her through the many changes of the moon? She'd brought a lance, a formidable weapon if used properly. She had not much experience with it, never having been allowed to practice throwing. She had her own weapons, the bird bolo, fishing hooks and rabbit snares.

At the last Kania had insisted she take one of Namanet's beautifully carved throwing boards and the small spear. Namanet had let Tiana practice with this. Being a shaman held its rewards. She took pride in her ability to bring down large, slow flying birds.

Tiana felt the small furry pocket strung on a lace of sinew around her neck. The fire starter was her own, given to her by Kania as a marriage gift. Just thinking about the small amount of meat on her pack made her hungry. She forced herself to push the sled toward the pass.

She believed Namanet still had the babies, otherwise he would surely have turned back toward the village and they would have met by now. Hope gave her the courage to go on. Hope that if he had not left the little ones in the snow, he still looked for someone to give them to. She must reach him first.

Pushing the light sled through the hard-packed snow, and following the trail was not too difficult. The birthing had weakened her, but Tiana felt a determination of purpose, and their previous journey searching for food gave her added strength. Darkness came earlier each day that she traveled north. She built a small fire at night to keep the wolves away and get a few hours sleep, but soon the pieces of dry tinder would be gone. There was not much chance of finding more under the deep snowdrifts. Luckily it was not hard to follow the path. It led from flat, nearly treeless land to rise gradually to an area with forests on each side. She was beginning to understand why the people of the north placed such desire in gathering wood down in the forest.

Though every inhaled breath filled her chest with sharp needles, and exhaustion claimed her well before daylight ended, she pushed forward. She lived each waking hour in torment, imagining her babies lying out on the snow. In one breath she cursed the day she met Namanet, and in the next, she sobbed with pity for the torment he must be going through alone.

One morning she awoke to a blowing snowstorm. There was nothing to do but pack up her sled and move ahead. If she stayed, the snow would soon cover everything.

Briefly, the temptation to sit down and just let it happen to her entered her thoughts. It would be so easy to give up and allow the soft, cushioning snow to envelop her. She touched one of her earrings and drew comfort from the hard quill running the length of the feather. The Raven Mother told her she would find her daughter and it must be so. She stiffened her back and walked faster.

At first she needed the shadowy greens of the pine trees on either side of her, or she would have lost her way almost from the day's beginning. The trail beneath her boots had long since been obliterated by snowfalls, yet she plunged on. Her body and mind were numbed from the constant, pounding waves of cold, her lack of sleep and inadequate food. Nagging fear drove her on and on, until it was as if she walked in her sleep.

Tiana awoke suddenly to the feeling of warmth and the taste of something good in her mouth. She sat up and coughed, choking on the warm liquid as it oozed down her throat. Was she now in the land of the far-travelers, the dead? Someone held her head and she craned her neck to see. A round smiling face looked down on her, the black eyes friendly and cheerful.

"Are you a person?" Tiana reached out a tentative hand to touch her.

The woman continued to smile. She spoke, but Tiana could not put the words together to form any sort of meaning. It was obvious the woman was one of the ice people, like the friendly ones who passed her on the trail and left her with the chunk of *muuktauq*. But they had understood each other. Now it was not the same.

The woman gave an outcry, and several people burst through the skin doorway. It was then Tiana noticed that she was inside a tent and was warm for the first time in many sleeps. When she struggled to rise, the woman pushed her gently back on the bed of furs.

"Woman-who-walks-alone, do not weaken yourself more. We offer no harm to you." A man knelt by her side, touching her hand with a gesture of compassion. His forehead wrinkled with concern, and even as she pulled her hand away she felt drawn to him. Tiana recognized the leader of the little band that had passed her not so long ago.

"I must continue my journey. I search for my family." She wanted to ask how it was they met again when they had been traveling in opposite directions, but she didn't have the strength to utter the words out loud.

The woman who had been pouring warm liquid down her throat exchanged an odd look with the man as they both stood.

"We know. You talk in your sleep." He put his hand on his woman's shoulder with a casual affection Tiana found embarrassing. Namanet would never do such a thing where others might see. He would have considered it unmanly.

She brushed away tears of helpless frustration. Every part of her body ached with weakness that left her exhausted if she barely moved. Her emotions churned and roiled in anxiety. She had no idea of how long she had lain asleep.

The man noticed her discomfort at once. His gruff voice broke the silence. "This is someone's wife called Igigik. She has been caring for you for many sleeps. A man called Kivisik found you out in the storm." He pointed his thumb into his chest to let her know that was his name and that he had found her. "For many sleeps we thought you had gone to join the spirits."

"Thank you. I am very grateful to you and to your wife. I cannot understand every word, although you speak plainly." It was true enough, his speech was quaint and old fashioned by her people's standards. He took a roundabout way to say the simplest words. After he had said something especially odd, Tiana managed a weak smile, and she caught her lip between her teeth to suppress it so they would not be offended.

"A man understands your speech also. A hunter lives as he can, on the trail, visiting others on his journeys. He must learn many people's speech." He spoke with simple dignity, not puffed up or bragging about his knowledge.

"Can you drink some more ptarmigan broth?" The woman asked shyly. Her words were slow and careful, to make sure Tiana understood.

Tiana shook her head. "Not now." She threw back the covers and saw that her body was wrapped in a soft doeskin. She had nothing on underneath. Her face showed concern, and the man tilted his head back and laughed.

"We did not steal your clothing. Do you not see your jacket and leggings on the rack? We have dried them in front of the fire to make them ready for you. You may have your clothing back when you wish. But perhaps a wife intends to hide them away to keep you from leaving before you are able to walk."

Tiana could see he was teasing, and tried to offer a corresponding smile. These people had saved her life. She owed them a great deal. She still did not know if they planned to keep her as a slave, but somehow she was not afraid. She would escape and return to the trail. They must be curious, yet they did not ask why a woman walked alone in the midst of a storm, searching for her family.

"I search for my husband," Tiana said again. "You told me he was in the company of people like you. Why did you turn back?"

The man and woman exchanged another look. Tiana sensed they hid something from her.

She sat up. Igigik had combed her long hair and re-braided it neatly. The Raven feather earrings scratched lightly against the side of her neck. "My belt! Where is my belt?" Her agitation was so intense the woman knelt to comfort her.

"Here. Your belt is here." Igigik motioned toward her husband who picked it off the top of her clothing and handed it to her. Tiana sighed and pressed the cool ivory to her cheek.

"We noticed your belt is very unusual. It does not look like any belt we have ever seen. It must have come from the land of ice where we live."

"I will tell you about it soon," Tiana assured her. "First I must learn of my husband, Namanet. I think you have seen him, or know about him and do not tell me." Her voice accused gently.

TIANA

"You are shaman?" the man asked. His dark eyes seemed to pierce her like a bird in flight. She wondered if being a shaman and a woman was forbidden in this clan.

"Yes, I am shaman. My helper spirit is that of the Raven Mother, Tulunixiraq."

"Ayiee!" The woman moved quickly away from her. The man frowned, his eyes pensive as he watched her. Then he nodded.

"*Tulugaak*, the raven trickster. He is in many of our legends. We have heard of the line of Raven Women. It is an ancient story which our people tell over and over until we know every word. But we thought the legend was our own."

Tiana smiled. "I know my earliest ancestors were named Umiak and Oolik. Is that how your legend begins?"

Kivisik beamed. "Yes! Umiak and her daughter were the first of the line."

"And were they of your people?" she asked.

He regarded her with a strange look of perception. "No. You are right. The legend has been passed down with us that Umiak came to us from a land far from ours, from the land of trees, but in time she became one of us. Was she from your clan then?"

"I believe so," Tiana answered.

"Do you have a spirit guide? A man believes most shamans claim one."

"I have not found it yet," she admitted.

"When it comes to you, we call it *tunarak*, a shaman's helper."

She said the word out loud. "That sounds like a powerful word. We do not have a special name for it. I will remember – when I find my spirit guide." They stayed silent a while, digesting all the new thoughts that had intruded into the small area. Finally Tiana spoke. "Please, tell me about my husband."

Kivisik ran fingers through his thick, coarse hair and looked uneasy. "No one can be certain the man we saw was the husband you speak of. He traveled with the sons of my father's brother. They live in a village two sleeps from ours on the ice. The man we saw was not tall, but he had a face such as yours. It was easy to see he was *itkiyyiq*."

"What does this mean?"

"It is our word for stranger. Those who mate with wolves. We know your people like to fight and steal slaves."

She watched Kivisik closely, yet could detect no contempt or disrespect in his expression. It was as he said, her clan was different, more war-like and aggressive than these calm, peaceful people.

"And what are your people called?"

He grinned. His teeth were large, square and unblemished in his pleasant face.

"We are *Inuit* – the people."

"Did you see a babe with my husband?" She held her breath, afraid to exhale for fear of chasing away good news.

He and the woman looked at each other. "Someone thinks we have spoken enough for now. You must rest. We came here to hunt the red fox. He is our totem, and we have need of his fur and tails in our village. We have trapped many. We were sure seeing you on the trail was a sign we should begin our journey to the ice, so we turned back. That is how we came upon you again. When we trap enough fox, we must return."

Tiana thought he might be changing the subject deliberately, so that he would not have to answer her. She tried once again to swing her legs off the fur and stand up. This time Kivisik took hold of her shoulder in a grip that made her wince.

"Sit. We will tell you what you wish to know. Perhaps the man – your husband – did not speak the truth."

Tiana looked up at him and waited, her eyes brimming with sorrow.

"This man, this stranger, left my kinsmen, telling them he was returning to his own village. A man cannot be certain but there was talk of a small one left with the Inuits. This is what we have heard."

"Did you see yourself?" Her heart beat within her chest so loud she felt smothered. He said child. One must have died, or Namanet was taking his son back with him.

Kivisik looked into her eyes. "No. A man only heard something. Women gossip, and a man sometimes listens."

She leaned her head back, closing her eyes to keep tears from coursing down her cheeks. He must not have heard right, it had to have been two babies but she would not say that. "How will my babe

TIANA

survive without mother's milk?"

Igigik spoke up, her voice soft with concern. "My husband's kinsman had a small one perish on the long journey. He was only two summers, and the mother had plenty of milk for the new visitor."

A stab of bitterness toward this mother who suckled her little ones when she could not coursed through Tiana's body, leaving her even weaker than before. Shame followed quickly behind. She should be grateful her babies would not starve.

"Where are your kinsmen now?"

"They return to their village," Kivisik answered. "They came here to search for the beaver, their helping spirit. The tails are big magic. To eat them makes a hunter strong and powerful."

"Then I must follow them." She attempted to rise again but his hand clamped upon her shoulder.

"Why do you not wish to return to your own village? It is a wife's place to be with her husband and his right to give away a child if he chooses."

Her eyes mirrored her unhappiness. "Never! He is no longer husband to Tiana. I search for my daughter, Nikota, the small person he gave away. Do you not understand? She will be the Raven Woman after I am gone."

She had decided from the beginning not to mention giving birth to two babies. It was very complicated, and she did not know if she could explain or if they would believe. If they believed, would they think her cursed? Was the child taken by the Inuit her daughter or her son? The boy had been born weaker, and the Raven Mother promised that the line would live on. She had to believe her daughter lived. Her joy on learning that one of her children was alive was tempered by the sad knowledge that the other must have weakened and died on the trail. Nikota had been the stronger of the two.

"We journey to our home on the ice. If you grow stronger and will not be a burden, you can come with us."

She listened to his meditations as if she had crawled inside his body and absorbed his thoughts. The blood of kinsmen was that of a sacred obligation. A man's first duty lay with his family which extended down through his cousins, his wife's people and even children born to friends with whom he had shared wives. If he took this woman-who-walks-alone to the village of his cousins he was sure to bring trouble. Perhaps they would refuse to give up the child.

Tiana realized what a generous offer he had made in spite of the group's serious misgivings.

The Raven Mother had said they would be together again someday. Nothing but this tenuous promise carried Tiana forward now. She smiled in weary gratitude at this man and his wife. For the first time since the birthing, a heavy sorrow shifted away. She began to breathe more freely.

She would find her daughter Nikota. There would be time to worry about the other problems later.

TIANA

THIRTEEN

TIANA'S body felt as if it might fall apart in little pieces. So sure this might happen, she looked down often and touched her mittens to her chest to make sure she was whole. Looking up at the sky which stayed dark and cloudy, she wondered when one day began and another ended. It warmed her bones a little to let go of the sharp edge of anxiety which had lived in her heart for so long, now that she had the hope of eventually catching up to her daughter.

During the day, Igigik forced her to eat little bites and made her walk outside the tent. She leaned against Igigik, walking only a few steps until her legs began to tremble and she had to stop and rest. What had happened to her? Her people were seldom ill. She'd watched the shaman burn pieces of their hair at first sign of any sickness and it always passed. She remembered performing many rituals for this purpose herself. A woman gave birth to a child and stayed inside the birthing place for four sleeps. Perhaps this was the problem. Had she offended the spirits by leaving too soon?

"A woman must make a song to appease for having angered the shades of small people." Tiana spoke softly to Kivisik and his wife as they ate their meal one late afternoon. It had become a habit to speak as these people did, never referring directly to oneself. They explained how speaking of I or using one's own name angered spirits with the lack of modesty and the spirits would do mischief.

Kivisik continued to chew the stringy caribou. He stabbed his knife in the thick stew hanging over the fire in a baleen pot and cut off a large piece with his knife, just at the edge of his lips.

"Yes. Then you may be well and can travel. Some of us would like to return to our village for the warm months. Our clan gathers together, and we enjoy much singing and telling of stories." He motioned for her to go on with what she intended to do.

Tiana removed the Raven belt and sat on furs, tucking her feet under her and pulling the deerskins over her legs. She unrolled the white rabbit skin she always carried with her and laid the Raven belt on the fur. The silence from within the tent as well as from the muffled snow outside settled around her shoulders in a comforting way. From around her neck, she loosened the ties holding the hide bag containing her fire starter and laid that next to her belt.

Last, she placed her drum on her lap and started a soft humming. Before closing her eyes, she spared a glance toward the two people who busied themselves eating, politely turning away from her preparations. They were strangers, a different clan, but she must include them in her magic if she was to live among them until she found her daughter.

She was *itsikomaq* now, an outcast from her people. No one in her village would wish her to return. She'd broken all the taboos of the birthing lodge, bore two babies instead of the proper one and, finally, opposed her husband and abandoned her family.

Her past was cut off for the second time in her life. She had to go forward. But before she dared move ahead to a new future, her shaman helpers must be soothed to assure they stayed loyal.

> *"Brother Moon, the snow glistens*
> *with your gift of light*
> *spread out across the whiteness."*

Her fingers began playing on the tight skin of her flat, round drum. Her voice rose and fell with the touch of palms and fingers on the drum as her singing grew louder. She noticed when the door flap opened and others from the group entered to sit quietly around the edge of the tent but it did not disturb her concentration. She knew the more who listened, the more power it gave a shaman.

> *"Sister Sun, let your pale hair*
> *fall across the land*
> *causing the animals to come to us*

TIANA

so that we might live.
Permit the caribou to birth their young –
to cover the land with their grace and
bring us fine hunting.
Do not be angry that on the occasion of a
small person's birthing a mother's
conduct was not proper.
A woman is also shaman and must obey
her spirit guides first."

"Aya-ya-ya. Aya-ya-ya." Beneath the smoothly flowing thoughts of her song, Tiana heard the people chanting softly in cadence with her drum. Her thoughts turned inward, and she lost herself in the magic as she went inside her village to search for Kania . . .

Namanet had returned and sat with Kania by their fire eating together. They spoke so softly, it was hard to make out their speech, but they appeared as old friends again.

Tiana sighed with relief. Namanet must have realized that his mother had only tried to help. He would not hold a grudge against her. Ikgat was so old and infirm that he would offer no retaliation against Namanet or Kania. He hated only her. Tiana's spirit ventured closer. Now she could see that Kania had chopped off her long, thick braid in her terrible guilt and grief.

Tiana accepted the shame that she had not cut her own hair.

She looked at Namanet a long time, wondering why she did not feel the affection and loss toward him that she felt for his mother. The answer came to her. She had given him up when he took her babies away.

Tiana drifted closer, reaching to touch the mother lightly on her shoulder. Kania's lined face, eyes filled with unbearable sorrow, faced Tiana. She cocked her head slightly in a gesture so familiar and bleak that Tiana felt pity flow white-hot inside her soul.

Then, as if she *knew* of Tiana's presence, Kania's lips formed a sad smile. Her eyes filled with love, looking long into her daughter's eyes. The bond between them was so strong, so intense, that Tiana feared she would be pulled from her body and become a real spirit.

Before this could happen, Kania broke the connection by

turning away.

Tiana knew then that although her mother might not understand completely, she accepted her daughter's sacrifice of leaving home and the people who cared for her to search for Nikota. If only she could tell Kania she was not lost and without hope. Tiana concentrated hard, holding on to the Raven belt. Kania turned back once again and looked into her eyes, the slight smile still upon her lips. She understood, and in her eyes acceptance mixed with the sadness of knowing they would never see one another again.

Tiana wrenched her thoughts away, bringing herself back to the present and into her own body again. When she opened her eyes, her palm and fingers still lightly played on the drum in her lap, and the people in the tent, eyes closed, swayed from side to side in rhythm to her soft chanting. She wiped the tears from her cheeks and began her song again.

*"Thank you O Tulunixiraq for showing
a Raven Woman the path she must travel.
Thank you for allowing my mother to know
I did not wish to leave her and my love
will always be twined with hers.
Provide these, my new friends, with
many indications
of your boundless generosity.
Entreat Sednah,
your sister Goddess of the Sea,
to share her abundance."*

Soon after her séance, Tiana regained strength, and the group resumed their journey. Tiana thought the Inuit seemed grateful for her company, especially the man, Kivisik. He had a lively curiosity and had never known an *itkiyyiq* to speak to before. That their word meant those who mate with wolves didn't make her uneasy. It could be the truth that her people were more quarrelsome and aggressive than this strong, quiet clan.

She proudly showed them the lance she brought with her. It was a source of amazement to them. They had never seen one carved of

TIANA

wood with an iron point.

"Where did your people obtain such a wondrous weapon?" Kivisik asked. The two women walked on either side of him while he pushed the sled. One of the group had volunteered to pull Tiana's small sled, and she was delighted to be free of it for a while.

"I do not know," she answered truthfully. She pushed back the hood of her caribou jacket. Her hair was short now, each side curving in and touching her cheeks, blending with the black of the long Raven feather earrings she wore. Kivisik had opposed her cutting off her long braid, but she was adamant. Her husband, mother and children had been lost in one day. She had much to mourn.

"We trade with other bands," Tiana began. Thinking back on some of her travels with Namanet was very painful, yet this friendly man asked her a sensible question. Where did she obtain this weapon? "Sometimes our hunters go great distances to find trading partners. If they meet someone who wants to trade from another clan, then, when each warm season returns, they take turns making a journey to visit one another. Each brings what he knows the other wishes to trade for."

"Wah! That is good. The Inuit do not do this, we only trade among our own kind."

This surprised Tiana. "How strange. Why?"

Kivisik's wife giggled politely behind her hand. "Our clans are known as Inuit – the people. We do not need others. We have many villages with kinsmen surrounding us. Some are good fishermen, some search for the giant whales, some journey to the tundra and the forests to find caribou. When we meet together, everyone shares everything." It was the most she had spoken at one time, and both Tiana and Kivisik looked at her in surprise. She ducked her head shyly and walked a little faster to get ahead of them.

The three traveled in silence for a time. Others in the group spoke only occasionally. Tiana decided they were not talkers. Not like her own people. The women back in her village chattered like crows around freshly killed food. She was unused to all the silence.

The tree limbs on both sides of the worn path hung with heavy burdens of snow. It was the coldest winter even the old people could recall. With her own eyes she had seen birds fall from the skies, the life frozen out of their small bodies, such as she had predicted to Namanet.

"You will need warmer clothing when we reach the land of the ice," Kivisik remarked. Igigik made Tiana wear her extra white bear skin parka. It was so much warmer than her caribou garment, but heavy for her weakened state.

"Perhaps a woman will not stay so long to need other clothing. Perhaps she will claim her girl-child and return to her own people." Tiana was unused to speaking in such a manner, but felt it a courtesy after Kivisik had explained why they did it. She wasn't prepared for Kivisik's heated reply.

The man stopped in his tracks, looking first at his wife and then back at Tiana. Finally he spoke. "This is foolishness coming from the woman-who-walks-alone, a woman with courage and strength to leave her family to look for her daughter. You may never find the child. She may be with the spirits even now. It is certain that you may not return to your village – ever. Understand this and take care of yourself. Do not live the balance of your days in dreams and wishes."

His wife nodded and touched his hand in a gesture of alliance. Having said his piece, he moved on, not waiting for the others to follow.

Tiana didn't want his words to matter, but still, she knew he spoke wisely and spoke the truth. She lifted her shoulders and decided to trust her spirits – especially the Raven spirit which she'd been neglecting lately.

Ahead of her, the Inuit reminded Tiana of white ptarmigan walking in line on the snow path. This comical idea caused her to smile. She hid it behind her palm so Kivisik would not assume she was laughing at him, as Namanet surely would have. Walking ahead of her, Tiana could observe him. His hair was longer than Tiana's and he tied it at the nape of his neck with a thin strip of fox hide. While some of the men wore a small ivory *labret* in their lower lip, Kivisik did not. Someday she would ask why when she learned how to do that without offending her host. She thought him handsome for a man from a strange clan. His nose was not long and sharply curved, a feature admired by her people. His cheekbones hid beneath a smooth layer of roundness giving his expression one of constant good-

TIANA

natured serenity. His eyes, black and opaque, remained unreadable.

When they stopped for a rest under the lee of rocks and tree branches, the wife took out some pemican and passed it around. Tiana thought it might be time for a few questions.

"Did you make this long journey just to obtain fox skins?"

"The *kavaktuq,* red fox is our totem," Kivisik said. "We took an abundance of game at the time of the cold moon and also in the warm sun's time. The shaman in our village counseled us to offer our gratitude by making a journey to bring back the meat and pelt of the fox. Then everyone could properly offer thanksgiving."

"And your kinsmen – the ones who have my child? They came for the beaver?"

"Yes. We were chosen to lead our groups." He beamed with pride. "Only once in a hunter's lifetime is he challenged to lead such a journey. The man you see before you was chosen, and he brought his woman and whaling partners."

"When will you cease hunting and travel to your home?"

The pure wistfulness of her question caused him to frown, and he looked at the ground with obvious embarrassment.

"We have not finished. We do not have enough skins yet, but must set traps for more, or our long journey will be for nothing."

Tiana flicked her tongue across her lips, which turned suddenly dry. "I thought – someone thought – that you were ready to return to your village now." With racing pulse, the weakness that was by now familiar threatened to overwhelm her. She leaped to her feet and leaned against the edge of the sled to steady herself. If their kinsmen reached their village long before these people, anything might happen to her daughter. The strange people might pass her along to another family, in another village. Nikota might die of the frightful cold. Her daughter needed the protection of the Raven.

Another thought intruded, one Tiana had been holding back. What if the baby Namanet left with the strangers turned out to be her son? Suppose her daughter had perished back on the snowy trail? Tiana bowed her head in sudden pain. Then she had disrupted her life for nothing. She must leave the boy where he was for his own protection.

She would have no one. She had to find the truth!

169

It appeared that Kivisik recognized her sudden consternation. His expression registered sympathy, but his mouth set in stubborn lines. "We are permitted to trap only this many foxes each day, otherwise they become offended and will not come to us." He took out five small, worn pieces of ivory from his pocket. They were about the length and width of a man's fingers and had carvings on them.

"This is signified by the shaman as *mitkosaaret,* meaning enough skins for a jacket. We must return with an acceptable amount to share with all the hunters. The tails serve as charms for the shaman."

As if in one accord, they all turned to their sleds and began walking again, while Tiana digested this new idea. How much longer would it take them to gather fox hides for their entire village? She had no idea of how large the community was, but she tried to imagine how many jackets might be needed to cover the backs of the men in her village. She held her mittened hands together to keep them from shaking.

Her secret hope that they would soon catch up to Kivisik's kinsmen faded fast. If she could have claimed Nikota and returned to her own people, they might be safe. Namanet's wrath had surely vanished now that he was back with his mother. He would be happy to see his wife and daughter again. The old shaman would be a problem, but the tribe liked her better as shaman and with the help of Kania and Namanet, Ikgat would have to let her be.

This hope dissipated much as the sun melted the snow along the edges of the small frozen ponds they passed.

That night the group camped near the shoreline of a lake shaded by huge trees. It was frozen over except for sections here and there in the sun.

"This will be a good place to stay a while," Kivisik pronounced as he untied the strips of sinew used to pull his sled when he did not push it. He looked back at the people who had stopped behind him.

Everyone broke into smiles, and words flew about the still forest until Tiana had to wonder how she ever thought these people silent. It was most unsettling to hear so many voices sounding at one time.

The sky, clear for a long time, turned a dull gray. The sun played tricks, hiding behind lemming clouds. Tiana thought of the legend Kivisik had told her about the lemmings.

TIANA

Once, long ago, before the oldest person's memory, the little brown furry rodents lived in the sky. Only then they were white as fresh snow and served as clouds. Lemmings were known for their *maqurauq*, mischief making, and this disturbed the older, more sedate Sun and Moon. Finally, in outraged indignation, Brother Moon broke the sky apart with undulating colors of the frighteningly beautiful northern lights display. This banished the tiny lemmings to the earth forevermore.

Tiana wondered who was right. She recalled her tribe's legend of the moon as a brave hunter, doomed to live a solitary life in the cold, lonely night, while his beautiful sister sun was condemned to live by day. She thought the Inuit legend more pleasant. Namanet would have considered it weak.

Tiana's nostrils flared as she caught the scent of the north wind. She knew the night would bring snow. This meant further delays, unless the men hunted while it snowed.

She thought at first Kivisik would set up a separate shelter for her, but both he and Igigik wanted her to lodge with them. Since he was the leader of the group, and his tent was larger than the others, there was plenty of space inside. Igigik expressed joy at having her company.

Kivisik's wife was older than Tiana, though not nearly as old as Kania. Her face was plump and unlined.

Tiana had never seen people face hardships and forced delays with such temperate grace. The men in her own clan never hesitated to voice their complaints at the smallest inconvenience. She had seen no Inuit man beat his wife, though among her people it was an everyday occurrence.

Her thoughts turned to Namanet who had not touched her in anger since that day so long ago when he attacked her in the tent and took her body so fiercely. Even if she could find her babe and return to the village, it came to her that she could no longer live with Namanet, he had forfeited the right to her attention and care.

That night the wind howled and whistled, buffeting the tight tent. Tiana and the couple stayed comfortably warm inside. The men had made ice deadfalls during the afternoon to trap foxes, and they would move out onto the frozen ground to harvest the bounty the next day.

Kivisik slept curled in his furs while Igigik and Tiana sewed by the flickering light of the small fire in the center.

"Will it annoy your man if we talk quietly?" Tiana clipped the fine sinew with her little knife made especially for sewing.

Igigik snickered behind her palm. "That one would not hear the opening of the ground when the glacier angers."

Tiana smiled. They were silent a while, a comfortable, companionable silence. The thought came that perhaps this agreeable person had been sent as the sister she'd never had, and to take the place of Kania, her lost mother. It remained a bittersweet idea to mull over as she hummed to herself.

"Do you have children back in your village?" Tiana was not certain if this question would be considered polite. Her old grandmother used to tell her that curiosity was as important to Tiana as breathing. Kania maintained that it only brought trouble.

Igigik smiled broadly. "Yes! An unworthy mother has this many." She drew four marks of different lengths on the ground in front of them. "Kivisik's mother is caring for them while we are away hunting." She bent her head to peer closely at a seam, and the light flickered on her black, shiny hair. She had finely traced tattoo marks on her chin, from the corners of her bottom lip to the edge of her jaw line.

"Do you not consider these marks beautiful?" She asked in the face of Tiana's frank appraisal.

"A stupid woman apologizes for such discourteous behavior. Sometimes our shaman makes such a mark on a boy or a girl if a mother or father ask it. I feared the shaman might cut off my nose for spite, so I did not permit him to touch me." She laughed at the expression on Igigik's face. "Our men do not wear ivory in their lip."

Igigik sucked in her breath and tried to hide her amazement. "How peculiar! Yet you put an opening in your ears to hold your Raven charms. To us that is strange. May an ignorant woman look closer?"

"Of course." Tiana obediently leaned forward so Igigik could push aside the downy soft feathers gracing the top of her earrings. The longer wing feathers lay against her cheek, blending with the

TIANA

curve of her hair. "Oh! A woman sees the openings at the end of your ear for the tiny chain. Can you do that for a new friend?"

"Will your husband be angry if you do not ask his permission?"

Igigik giggled. "What an idea! A wife's adornment is of no concern to a husband."

This was surprising. She had much to learn about these people who held such strange customs. That they laughed much and talked little was still the greatest mystery to her.

"Did your man tell you why I travel with you?"

Igigik raised her head from her sewing and stared into the fire. "He said your husband had given away your baby to our kinsman." She looked at the younger woman. Confusion filled her round, black eyes, but politeness suppressed her question.

Tiana wondered briefly if she dared trust this woman enough to unburden herself about giving birth to two babies at one time. Igigik, as a proper wife, would tell her husband, and when he told the others they would discard her as an unworthy person. She would perish without ever knowing what had become of her child.

"My husband, Namanet, is a good man. His temper is a legend among our people, though tempers are not uncommon with us. Not like the Inuit," Tiana added graciously. "He took offense at something I said inside the birthing lodge and ran away with Nikota. Perhaps he did not like it because I chose her name." It was a flimsy lie; surely Igigik would not accept it.

But her new friend only smiled and continued sewing. "We sometimes have those among us who have bad feelings toward others," she began shyly.

Tiana waited, knowing she would eventually finish her story. Above all else these new friends seemed to love stories, to hear and tell them.

"If the quarrelsome ones in our clan are too violent and no one trusts them – if their kinsmen will not be offended and start a feud – then someone kills them," Igigik said calmly.

Tiana thought that made sense, and yet the idea was foreign to her way of thinking. It was not something her people were likely to do; plan and carry out a killing for the good of the community. If a man in her clan killed someone in the heat of anger, everyone suffered for lifetimes of blood feuds between the families. Therefore killings were rare, although the men did fight between themselves.

"Do not worry that our customs are not alike," Igigik touched her arm lightly. "You will enjoy living with us. Your land of tall trees and caribou is plentiful with game, but our land is more beautiful. We have tall ice of many colors — some so clear you can see through to the other side. We have *naanuk*, the great white bear, and whales to slay in the warm days when Sister Sun returns to us."

"You miss your family." It was not a question.

"Yes," Igigik sighed. "It has been many turns of the full moon since a mother last saw her children. They will be grown and have babies of their own perhaps before a poor woman sees them again." She giggled self-consciously at her joke.

"I do not come to stay with you," Tiana said as gently as she could. "I journey only to find my daughter, Nikota."

Igigik's bright eyes shone. When she smiled her tattoos spread, in an oddly engaging manner, across her chin and up toward her cheeks. Then she turned serious. "Kivisik hopes that you do not mention your search to the others in our group. When we arrive at our village, we will talk of it then."

"But . . ." Tiana frowned, puzzled by her new friend's attitude. Something felt wrong.

"A foolish woman's husband tells her that if woman-who-walks-alone does not keep still about it, word could fly ahead. Our cousins might dispose of the child to avoid a confrontation."

That made sense, Tiana conceded. Still, something was not right. Igigik knew something else she was not telling. Tiana removed the Raven Belt from her waist and held it close against her cheek.

Its warmth suffused Tiana's face, and she felt the warning down to her feet, along with the fear that finding Nikota would not be the end of her ordeal.

TIANA

FOURTEEN

THE next sleeps blurred into one another as the storm continued. The Inuit seemed not to notice that the snowfall decreased along with the rising wind and the deepening cold. It was as if they allowed nothing to penetrate their barrier of constant good humor.

"Will we leave soon?" Tiana asked of Igigik. The women gathered in her larger tent, skinning fox and cutting up the meat in neat chunks.

This catching of foxes took longer than Tiana had expected. Once they caught the *mitkosaaret*, the hunters attached sewing needles and thread if females, knives if male, to each animal. Then they brought the carcasses back to the tents, cut off their heads to free the fox spirit and replaced the real weapons and sewing kits with tiny carved replicas. They put the heads out onto the snow with the offerings and songs chanted to the fox spirit. All this ceremony took time, valuable time that Tiana begrudged.

Igigik regarded her visitor with a smile. "Someone thinks there is enough after today – if our men are fortunate."

Tiana closed her eyes in silent thanksgiving. Wild imaginings of her daughter being carried ever forward, more and more out of reach, tortured her. The painful fullness of her milk-filled breasts had departed, making her more conscious than ever of her terrible loss.

The next morning, Kivisik came inside the tent to tell them they had enough foxes, and they made ready to continue their journey home.

"How do they feed my baby? Perhaps she is already of the shades, and I am making this journey for nothing." Tiana asked this as they packed their equipment to leave. She held the little raven-feathered vest she'd made for Nikota to her cheek She didn't have much to pack now, any provisions she'd brought with her had been shared with the Inuits, which left only her drum, the bark vest and tiny garments.

"It will go well with your daughter," Igigik assured her. "There are several women from Iliaauq's band who have brought their children along. Not like the people of Kivisik who had to leave theirs behind," she teased her husband.

"Paugh! It is time a man took another wife when the old one complains too much," Kivisik shot back in passing, giving Igigik a swat on her well-padded rear.

The small group traveled by day, stopping only when it became so dark they could no longer move through the tundra. Tiana, who felt so at home among the trees, thought it odd that the Inuit feared the forest at night. They were convinced that dark spirits lurked behind every tree and bush, waiting to capture their souls.

She no longer had to wonder why these people placed such value on worthless pieces of wood. In her village, wood was everywhere and more often times in the way of setting up a camp or finding a good fishing spot on the shore of a river. But if there was only ice and snow where the Inuit lived, they would surely need wood for sleds and weapons and would never use it for burning up in fires. She thought of the huge fires in her village to celebrate victories of the hunters or a special time when they wanted to feast. It seemed wasteful from the Inuit point of view.

Periods of daylight grew ever shorter as they progressed directly north. The men pulled the sleds loaded with frozen fox carcasses, long pieces of branches and parts of the thinner trees while the women pushed them over hummocks.

By now, some of the formal politeness of the Inuit began to rub off on her, and she refrained from satisfying her curiosity by asking questions about their taboos and customs which were different from hers. Some were alike, they would not slay a wolf unnecessarily. They feared something called a glacier, they used the word *sirmiseraq*. She had heard tales from old people in her tribe about traveling to a land where giant chunks of beautiful ice spread out in a smooth thick

TIANA

covering on the land. She mentioned the grizzly, so familiar in her dreams, but Kivisik said the bears slept in caves in the cold time.

One morning Tiana awoke abruptly to the complete absence of sound. It was an eerie feeling, as if her head was buried in furs. She looked around to see Kivisik and Igigik sitting by the fire, making repairs on their equipment and clothing. They made no attempt to pack for the morning travel.

Tiana jumped up from her sleeping furs, rubbing her eyes. "Forgive a lazy woman! It was so quiet a person thought it was still night." She smoothed down her hair and walked toward the tent flap, to go outdoors and relieve herself.

"No! Do not go out!" Igigik and Kivisik both cried together.

Tiana stopped, amazed at the sharpness of their voices, they who never shouted except in laughter.

"The sky fills with many colors. It signifies that Brother Moon and Sister Sun disagree. Their sky-words are harsh, and we dare not intrude." Kivisik barred Tiana's way so she could not step around him. Over his shoulder she saw a glimpse of the undulating aurora borealis.

She looked at the two earnest faces before her and wondered if this was the time to assure them that her people did not fear the colorful display, but considered it good luck to stay outside absorbing the rays of color. Tiana struggled with the question of differences. The Inuit were her people for at least as long as it took to find her daughter. There would be times to mold herself to their ways and times to let them know she was not always in agreement with their beliefs.

They waited for the morning to end. Usually the lights lasted no longer than it took the shadows to change from one side of the forest to the other. The women sewed while Kivisik whittled another loon charm from his little pile of wood saved just for that purpose. It would not be proper to work on his weapons – to sharpen or repair them – when the awesome light hovered in the air.

To amuse them, Tiana took out the dried colors from her pouch where she kept them rolled up in a thin deerskin. She painted pictures on shards of mud pottery and the inside walls of their tent. They seemed overwhelmed that she could make pictures from the charcoal of the lamp and mashed berries when she explained about the colors she applied. While she entertained them, from inside their tent they could not help but see the movement outside, the swishing, dancing shadows cast across their tent roof while the light cascaded as if thrown from the top of the sky directly down upon them. The three pretended to ignore the display.

When it was finally over, the group packed hurriedly and pushed on. Kivisik explained this was the day they had to struggle up the pass and then over to the other side. Now they must keep a lookout for Brother Bear. During the Cold Moon time the giant usually slept inside his shelter, but they could not always depend upon this.

As they walked, carrying their burdens up the wide pathway made by centuries of migrating caribou, Tiana chanted quietly. The Inuit were more curious than afraid of the possibility of a grizzly coming upon them.

She shivered inside her warm furs. She had never wished to be present when the hunters from her village brought back a bear carcass to be skinned out and never knowingly ate of their flesh. Since her pact with the White One, she knew something in the form of the fearsome bear lurked in the darkness of her soul – waiting. If it turned out to be her spirit guide, perhaps she had to earn that right.

It took the passing of two full moons to climb the gradual upward trail dividing the forest from the tundra. With every step the Inuit quickened their pace, their casual meandering left behind. They were anxious to get to the flatlands. Kivisik explained that after the passing full moons the closeness of the trees became suffocating.

"Friend, the land is strange to this woman." Tiana spoke to Kivisik as they rested. Across the landscape, large boulders piled one on another as if some giant hand had flung them all together. The trees had thinned out gradually. The travelers had crested the mountain pass and were on their way down. Tiana was so happy to be moving at such a rapid pace, she felt a contentment she thought lost forever.

In the distance, a giant glacier shimmered and glowed with a translucent blue-white reflecting off the pale winter sun. Tiana stood holding her breath, absorbing the beauty that filled her eyes. Finally Kivisik touched her shoulder.

TIANA

"It may be better not to look overlong in that direction," he said with a worried note in his voice.

Tiana reluctantly turned away from the glacier and looked at the concerned expressions of Kivisik and Igigik. "It is only ice," she said. They shook their heads and started up the sleds again. Though the trail led in that direction, the Inuit veered purposefully away, toward the vast expanse of open snow-covered ground.

"This land is beautiful, is it not?" Kivisik said, looking around in satisfaction, his mouth spread in a wide smile.

Tiana had to return the smile, thinking how unusual for the Inuit to speak out of something he thought wonderful. Whenever any of the group felt they spoke immodestly or in any sense bragged, they usually dipped their heads in embarrassment. Tiana found this amusing and so different. All men in her tribe loved to brag and showed off shamelessly in front of one another.

"Why do we not follow the trail of the caribou?" she asked.

Both Kivisik and his wife looked toward the glacier. "The *sermersiraq* is an abode of demons and those who die violently by another's hands," he said. "Some say shaman go there when they depart this life, although perhaps not all shaman," he added quickly, for fear of offending her.

"Surely your people also fear the dwelling place of hostile spirits?" Igigik wanted to know.

Tiana nodded. "Yes, we believe in the *ekoavik – the place where people are afraid*. It lies deep within the forest, always guarded by a great white bear."

"A white bear? Like our *naanuk*? He would never venture into the forest but must live on the ice."

She shook her head. "A woman does not think the white grizzly is like your white bear. This one is very rare, he passes through many generations of our people before he is seen again." She paused, afraid they would think her too bold. "A shaman saw one in her vision." She told them of the exchange she'd made between her grandfather and a hunter to spare her father.

By now others in the clan had crept forward to listen, their burdens set down and eyes wide in rapt attention. Some sat on the dry snowy ground, legs crossed, unmindful of any discomfort from the cold. When she finished speaking, the group sat mesmerized, the silence closing in behind her last words.

Kivisik looked worried.

She touched her chest, "This woman has never before seen a – a *sermersiraq*," she stumbled over their word for glacier. Their silence made her uneasy. Had she said too much to make them afraid of her or regretful that they were bringing her back to the village? She tried to lighten the feeling surrounding them. "A woman has traveled on hunting trips with a husband, but never saw this wonder. We would consider glaciers as beautiful as the lights that fly across the sky." There. She said it. Now let them think her completely strange. She could not go on pretending to be someone she was not.

No matter how long she stayed with them, she would be apart – woman-who-walks-alone. As Raven Woman she'd always been part of her tribe, yet separate. It no longer bothered her, she'd learned to accept it

Igigik and Kivisik drew in their breaths sharply, looked at each other and then back at Tiana. What manner of strange people did she come from? Their expressions plainly showed their confusion. As if he spoke out loud, Tiana knew Kivisik questioned, and not for the first time, his judgment in bringing her with them.

Would they abandon her along the trail some morning when they began a new day? Her mouth dried with the idea of being alone in a new land, but even so, a Raven Woman could not pretend to be someone she was not.

They lifted their burdens and moved the sleds forward again.

As they moved along pulling the heavily loaded sleds, the hard frozen tundra beneath their feet made the going much easier than in the slushy pass. Only rifts of pushed-up earth encountered in scattered places across their path impeded their way now. The wind blew ever constant, clearing the land of excess snow, chilling Tiana from inside out. No one in the group seemed to notice the dropping temperature.

On the third day of tundra walking, Igigik insisted Tiana use the extra seal skin outfit she had been saving for Kivisik. "No one will be offended by a female wearing man's clothing, since you are much taller than Inuit women."

TIANA

Tiana could not see the connection between her height and wearing men's clothing, but she said nothing. When she tried to get at the bottom of some of their reasoning, it only confused and embarrassed them.

"When we reach our village, a friend promises to show you how to skin a seal and make new trousers and jacket," Igigik promised.

Days and nights blended together, offering little in the way of variety or contrast. They journeyed only on days of a good moon, which meant they spent part of the time lying in their tents eating or ice fishing if they came onto a frozen lake. Once they left the forest, they slowed again to their customary leisurely pace.

That Tiana was in an obvious hurry seemed of little consequence to these usually sensitive people. She wanted to shout and rail at them when they stopped. She fretted and worried, tormented by something constantly nagging at her. Something she felt but did not *know*.

Just when they finally decided to move ahead again, one of the group might see a good place to camp. Like children, they would suddenly be diverted by their curiosity. What sort of fish inhabited this strange place, and were they amenable to being caught?

Tiana's tribe seldom fished in the winter, unless they had no caribou or moose left. They usually had plenty of dried salmon from the summer's catch and by winter's end all were heartily sick of it. Therefore she watched at first with great curiosity.

"We do not use barbs, which could tear the fish's tender mouth and make them so angry they would never surrender to us," Kivisik answered her questions patiently. He showed her the ivory sinker and explained how they attached sinew over a short stick notched at both ends. "First, when someone sees a good place to fish, we cut through the ice with this pole." He held a long staff tipped with a sharpened piece of glistening black rock.

"Eeeyah!" Igigik shouted with glee as she flopped a long fish over her shoulder, falling on her rear and hitting her husband directly in the face.

Tiana held her breath, waiting for the fury in Kivisik's expression. Instead he and others who were nearby began laughing until tears came down their tawny cheeks and froze half way to their chins. The fish gave several flips of its tail on the hard packed snow and then froze where it lay.

"It appears someone's wife has forgotten how to fish properly," Kivisik said when they hiccoughed their last giggle. He bent to help Igigik up from her sitting place.

"Would a new sister like to try?" she turned to ask Tiana.

"It may be that her aim will be better," Kivisik told the watching men and women who had gathered about them. "A man will remove himself from harm's way." He walked away laughing and men slapped him on the back as if the greatest joke had happened to him.

Tiana shook her head to the offer. No, she cared nothing about fishing. She fretted and found it hard to be idle, but the Inuit treated any sign of impatience on her part with mild regret.

Should she strike out on her own? It could not be so hard to find the other tribe. Perhaps they were walking ahead by one or two sleeps. One afternoon she decided to take her throwing board, bird darts and bola to do a little private hunting on her own. As an afterthought, she tied the lance onto the back of her parka. The Inuit made loops of sinew and carried their extra weapons this way. Tiana wondered why no one in her tribe had ever thought of that idea.

The succulent, rich seal meat which they ate almost every day became ordinary and tedious. Dried caribou did not taste much better. She longed for fresh, tender bird meat. If she continued on her way north, it could do no harm. She was strong and able to travel alone if she had to. Didn't the Inuit name her woman-who-walks-alone?

She did not tell anyone that she was leaving. These people had become her friends, but she would see them again later if they were parted now. Her first tribe had always touched hands politely and said the words for parting or mentioned their leaving, but these *eaters of raw meat* owned no words for greetings or leave-takings. When they chose to leave, they just disappeared.

Tiana meditated on the differences between her people and this clan. Before this, she had assumed all people lived in the forest and were just the same as her own. Now she knew different. Even the Inuit were not the same among themselves.

The tribe who took her daughter had the totem of the beaver and never partook of fox meat. They were also not good fishermen,

TIANA

or so said Kivisik. This might mean the beaver people would reach their village much sooner than Kivisik's little band. She did not know why this thought troubled her so, but it nagged at her constantly. Was the Raven trying to communicate a warning she did not yet understand?

She slung the weapons over her shoulder and set out to find some birds.

After walking a long time she reached a grove of twisted willows. The pale sun changed directions while her thoughts had been on her problems, not on the hunting. She stopped and looked around, knowing she had traveled much farther than intended.

Suddenly a white object darted in front of her, as if a large chunk of snow had abruptly grown legs and began to run. Instinctively she slung out her bola of tangled sinew and stone weights. The ptarmigan squawked and shrieked as she twisted its neck in one quick movement. Tiana examined her kill of the plump bird. Her mouth watered at the thought of burying it in hot coals until it cooked to falling apart.

But just one bird was not enough. She must catch more to share with the others, or at least enough for Kivisik and Igigik. Before long darkness settled down around the tundra. The moon had not yet risen. By now her bag held many fat ptarmigan and several owls speared with her bird dart.

Worry lines furrowed her brow. What had happened to her sense of direction? Her usual keen instincts failed her in this flat land with no appreciable landmarks.

She pondered about the many twists and turns taken in tracking the birds. As soon as the moon came up over the horizon she would know the way back to camp.

The wind whipped across the tundra, stabbing her face with horizontal barbs of hard snow. Tiana stopped in her tracks, terror blasting waves of fear over her body, chilling her to the bone. The white darkness had come upon the land, a blinding freezing air that sucked the life out of a person caught in it unaware. Soon she would not be able to see her hand in front of her eye. Without shelter she would perish.

Forcing her feet to move forward, she searched for a large

outcropping of rock to huddle beneath. A large, darkened spot loomed on the side of a hillock. She hurried toward what appeared to be a cave. Tiana stepped into the entrance, and at first the relief of being without the wind and sleet striking her face warmed her. But a moment later she reeled back, sensing danger, her nostrils flaring when the musty smell of decaying fish assaulting her. Bear! She looked out of the cave entrance into the frozen white that had crept upward until she could not see the sky.

She touched her mittened palms to her waist, as if she felt the belt beneath the layers of clothing. What should she do? Was the bear inside the bowels of the cave, sleeping? Would it stay asleep or would it smell her as food? She thought bears had to live in the forest, and yet it wasn't many sleeps since she'd left the woods. Perhaps a bear had become lost. If she went out, she'd be lost forever. The Inuit believed they could fall off the end of the earth if they ventured out in the white fog and who was she to say? It could be true.

Tiana made herself as small as possible and sat huddled just behind the lee of the entrance to the cave. Waking and dozing with only the occasional howl of a distant wolf to disturb the quiet, her body grew colder and colder. Finally, after sitting so still, a sensation of warmth crept from inside out toward her skin. It felt good, and she slept.

Awaking to the sound of a deep-throated growl almost in her ear, the smell of rotten fish enveloped her. Without moving, she knew the bear was behind her. She could feel his sharp teeth tearing at her scalp, feel his long black claws ripping through her clothing to her body. It was as if she felt all the pain he would cause her, and for a moment she gave in to her fate.

Her next instinct was to roll down the hill in a ball and try to out run him. The thick whiteness outside the cave had cleared somewhat while she slept. Or could she stay perfectly still and hope he ignored her?. The bear growled low in his chest, coming closer.

Heart pounding in her ears, blood surging through her veins in sporadic thrusts of fear, left her dizzy and trembling. This was the meeting she'd dreaded since her first seeing of the white bear.

She touched the bird bola with her mittened fingers and then set it down again. The weapon was too puny to use on a bear. Without

TIANA

moving abruptly, she reached her hand to where she had laid down the lance. She felt its cold hardness through her mittens.

Using the element of surprise, she leaped to her feet, grasping the lance and turning to face what she knew was her age-old adversary – the white bear of her dreams.

Only this was not a beautiful white creature, but a giant sun-touched grizzly, the largest she'd ever imagined. The animal retreated a few paces. The cave was not high enough for him to rear on his hind legs, for that she was grateful. She closed her eyes and began to chant.

> *"Brother bear, I wish you no harm.*
> *In the past a Raven Woman asked for*
> *your help – to spare hunters of her tribe.*
> *In exchange you took away a beloved*
> *grandfather and a hunter to keep*
> *him company on his long journey.*
> *Now I ask again, that you leave me in*
> *peace, a woman who mourns for*
> *lost children*
> *and must search for the*
> *daughter who will be Raven Woman one day."*

She held the lance downward in a non-threatening way and waited. The bear never took his eyes away from her. His mouth showed rows of yellowish teeth. She was close enough now to see his drool as he stared at her. Her imagination let her feel his hot breath on her neck, feel his teeth rip into her flesh and feel her life blood ebb out one agonizing bite at a time. He did not appear to have listened to her chant.

Remembering the birds she'd caught, she bent cautiously to pick up the sealskin bag and pulled out a frozen carcass. "Here, giant of the tundra. Accept my offering."

The ptarmigan fell at the animal's front paws. He snuffled it with his nose and then looked up at her again. His little narrow black eyes seemed to devour her, sucking away her strength.

"No! I must live to find my daughter. You will not feast on my blood today! I am the hunter, I will not be hunted." She held the lance outward and ran toward him. Startled, the bear shuffled backward. Tiana pressed ahead and pierced his shoulder with her lance, just enough to cause him pain. She backed near the entrance and stood still, waiting. It could go either way. He could become angered or give up and go back to his long sleep.

Her heart raced, blood sang in her veins as she felt the hunter in her long to do battle against all odds.

The bear opened his mouth and roared, the stench of his breath nearly made her stumble back and lose her footing. Clumps of snow fell from the entrance. Tiana held her head high, her back straight, the lance pointed outward, waiting.

The giant grizzly lowered his head and in a blink of an eyelid he rammed into her, hitting her hard with his body, his roar deafening, close to her ear. Too close for the lance, she dropped it and held her hands up over her head to keep her scalp from being torn off. He swiped with his paw, the black claws looking like large black stones and time stood still as the claws descended on her shoulder. She didn't feel the pain, the shock of the impact was too great. She fell to her knees and grabbed at the bird bolo, instinctively flinging it around the bear's back legs.

The bear stumbled and fell back on his hind quarters. Before he could recover, she grabbed the lance and tucking it against her body, threw herself off the edge of the cave and rolled down the hill. The weapon could turn in her hands and stab into her but she held it as close as she could with one shoulder throbbing. Part way down something caught on her ankle but she didn't have strength left to kick it away.

Had the bear followed to grab one last hold on her? Bile rose in her throat, but she gathered her last reserves, determined to leap to her feet at the bottom of the hill and face the bear with her lance. Her head bounced off raised parts of the hill and her body gathered momentum as she neared the bottom. The pain disappeared with the thought of the bear making a headlong run behind her and landing at the bottom the same time she did.

When she finally bounced to the bottom, she didn't have a leap left in her, but struggling to her feet, she turned toward the cave and

TIANA

felt her breath return. That was when she realized she'd been holding herself in place by sheer willpower. As relief thrummed through her heart and blood, her legs trembled, not able to hold her up. She had to leave! He was probably tearing at the bird and when he finished he might remember that he was hungry, and the bird was not enough.

She bent to look at her feet and found the sack with the slain birds entangled with her boots. That was what had made her think the bear grabbed her. Her shoulder hurt and throbbed but she didn't think he'd penetrated her clothing. Instead there would be a great bruise on her flesh. She slung the sack of birds and the lance over her other shoulder and paused for a look back at the cave.

The bear raised on his hind legs, front feet moving as if to balance him. He let out a mighty roar that shook icicles from the roof of the cave, which fell all around him, catching light in the faint sun that shone in the lip of the cavern. She stopped in stunned disbelief, the sight too magically breathtaking to turn away from.

She had found her spirit guide.

Tiana turned and walked away, not hurrying now, unafraid of being pursued. The bear signified all that had terrorized her in her lifetime, and she met it head-on and won. She was not supposed to go off alone. She would only find her daughter through the Inuits.

The problem now was finding them again.

Pinkie Paranya

TIANA

FIFTEEN

TIANA slogged through the new fallen snow with its soft sponginess clinging to every step and sinking her feet down into holes she had just made in the pristine whiteness. Every movement jogged her shoulder, causing a swift current of pain to jolt from her shoulder up the back of her neck to her head. It had been a long while since she'd eaten, and she rubbed her middle from time to time to try and soothe the gnawing hunger away. The noise of her complaining stomach reminded her of the bear's growls, and she managed a smile at the idea.

When she stopped far enough away to rest and take some breaths, she felt for her pouch of the precious fire starter she kept around her neck. Frantically she pulled open her furs to see if it had tucked in somewhere in her furs. What a terrible omen! The fire starter pouch is given to a woman after her bleeding time, and she is never without it. Kania had given it to her at that time, a precious memory of her past. Without it she could not melt snow to drink and light a fire to cook the birds she carried in her pouch. The birds were frozen stiff and covered with feathers. She wouldn't be able to eat them.

Did she dare retrace her steps toward the bear again? If she didn't, he would have won the battle after all.

She pulled her hood up over her ears, trying to keep out the now buffeting ice-cold wind and began to walk in her steps back toward the cave. Once she heard a mighty roar and stopped, heart thudding in her chest. The bear had not gone back to sleep. She was thirsty and exhausted from pulling up her feet and putting them back down again in the thick, mushy snow but pushed herself onward. The belt around her middle sent out warmth that traveled throughout her body. Was it telling her to go back or turn around again and try to find her first trail?

A shriek tore from her throat when a large bird exploded from behind an outcropping of rocks and flapped across her vision before it disappeared. A white ptarmigan. Before she could wonder what that signified, she looked ahead to something lying on the snow. It was her pouch!

She had no strength to run, but she hurried as fast as she could and swooped down to pick it up, thanking her spirits. That might signify that she was now kin to the bear spirit, since she had the courage to go all the way back to his cave if she had needed to.

Holding the precious square of hide close, she turned back and retraced her steps again. The cold wind was helping to form a crust on the snow, making it easier to walk now.

Going toward the cave, the light had appeared from low on the horizon, blinding her as it slanted off the prisms in the snow. Now it was at her back. The wind ceased and she felt a sudden drop in temperature and noticed that the land surrounding her had became quiet and still. But it was not a peaceful silence and was suddenly broken by the air crackling with the sharp cold.

Ahead lay the glacier the Inuit had skirted around.

Tiana stared long and hard at the vision. Is this what the giant bear was guarding? Was it the glacier that the Raven Mother spoke of? Relief at heading in the right direction to find the Inuits warred with her remembrance of how they had described the glacier, how they had feared it. She laid down her burdens and walked toward the towering majesty of the crystal ice, her thirst and hunger forgotten. Parts of the mammoth piece of ice glistened near the bottom with an iridescent sky-blue terminating deeper inside the ice in a bright color she couldn't describe. In the shadows it showed dark blue, like the sea. It exceeded anything Tiana had ever imagined. She understood why the Inuit might dread going near it. She wondered that she had no fear and felt her aches and hunger disappear in the face of the magical place.

Letting her breath out slowly, Tiana touched her earrings. She closed her eyes and tilted her face up to receive the faint sunglow.

TIANA

She had no thought of where to look for the Raven Mother. Tulunixiraq must know she was here. Tiana stood for a long time, chanting softly, her mind turning back inside itself. She no longer felt the strain of standing or the bitter sharp cold on her face. In the middle of her chant a billow of fog arose and in the midst of it, the faint outline of a form on the lip of the glacier.

Tiana's heart sang out a greeting. A welcoming look mirrored in the Raven Mother's expression as the mist gradually cleared. She beckoned, and Tiana followed without hesitation, not even glancing down as her boots trod a precarious path skirting high on the slippery ice. Her legs felt as if they floated forward, her boots barely touching the surface. When Tiana came closer and closer the sun faded away, unable to compete with the brightness of the mound of crystal. Just as Tiana thought she might float off the face of the glacier, she felt herself turning and saw a large flaw in the perfection of the smooth surface.

Completely lacking in fear, she crossed the slippery ice and bent to enter the crack. It was dark inside, but ahead a familiar pale green light whispered from the center of the glacier. Lethargy took hold of Tiana, recognizable as the feeling which always came at the beginning of a vision or a séance. This time she was wide awake and alert – her senses sharpened to exquisite heights. The only sound was the continuous creak and groan of the ice as it moved constantly with a trembling she felt sweep upward through her boots. No wonder the Inuit thought the strange noises came from demons in *ekoavik*, a place where people are afraid.

Tiana was certain it was true, that demons and awful spirits inhabited this place, but Tulunixiraq would protect her.

She walked toward something lying on the floor of the glacier in the center of the pale light. Kneeling, she carefully pulled aside the heavy fur. Her mouth worked to speak, but no words came forth. Tulunixiraq lay on a bed of piled furs, her eyes closed as if in peaceful sleep.

At first Tiana examined the thick fur surrounding the Raven Mother. Her eyes had never beheld anything like it. What sort of animal might it have come from? Her fingers pushed tentatively into the thick, luxurious fur. The long, coarse reddish-brown fur gave way to a downy softness underneath of dense, fine hair. She marveled at its strangeness.

As her eyes became more accustomed to the ethereal green light, she saw strange objects against the side of the wall. She recalled stories of ancient animals that roamed the ice when the Raven first created the earth.

There were some very old men in her first village who told about their ancestor's journey to the top of the earth where it was all ice and snow, and finding a treasure pile of ivory tusks under huge boulders that had shifted in time. From these, they made many carvings and fashioned wonderful tools, as well as toys for children. These stories had been passed down since their youth and they still talked about it as if they had been there too. Ancient stories told of the immensity of the animals – larger than the largest grizzly the people had ever seen, with tusks of ivory as big as three giant grizzly bears.

Her attention turned back to the Raven Mother. By now Tiana felt surer of herself. Her hand barely trembled when she pulled away the rest of the furs to reveal the entire length of Tulunixiraq. She was wrapped in a soft mantle of animal skin, tawny of color with slashes of black against the gold. An ivory belt of intricate carvings encircled her waist.

Tiana recognized the belt the Raven Mother wore as an exact copy of the one around her own waist. When she reached to touch it, the belt disappeared beneath her fingers like smoke.

Tulunixiraq's face was pale, her eyes closed, and her long, full lips relaxed in a slight smile. She was taller and larger than Tiana, but this was not surprising. The first women put on earth by the Raven were said to be very powerful. Men were created to serve as their slaves. Only when the first Raven Woman refused to give up her male child, as tradition demanded, was she punished by her creator, losing her status and becoming subservient to man. From that time forward, it was ever to be thus. Had Tulunixiraq been the first Raven Woman to give up her son?

Tiana had heard the story many times in her youth, from her grandfather and other old ones. It had been one of her first tribe's favorite legends.

TIANA

"What must I do now?" The sound of her own voice startled her as it echoed up and down the narrow chamber into the depths beyond. She waited for the Raven Mother to respond, but she lay still and waxen as if frozen. Frozen! The thought suddenly came to Tiana, and she touched the large, shapely hand, pulling back in alarm. The hand felt as hard and cold as a piece of ice. Tiana sank back in a crouch, never taking her gaze from the woman lying in front of her.

Had it all been a dream then? Had Tulunixiraq come to her in a vision? If this was true, then their souls had found one another, but the Raven Mother's body could not have moved from this resting place. Tiana closed her eyes and began a soft chant, her voice barely rising above the creaking sound of the constantly changing pressure of the ice. Her body began to relax, and her eyes turned upward as her lips moved. She did not open her eyes even when something soft brushed against her elbow and fanned the hair on her neck.

"Tulunixiraq?" She asked softly.

Daughter of the Raven. It is I. Do not be afraid, No harm will come to you here.

Tiana had lost all thought of fear.

I have waited long for you. You are not the first of our line since my world ended, but you are the first of your tribe to be chosen.

"Raven Mother, was your life so different from ours?" Tiana's thoughts centered on the giant furry creature with the huge tusks and knew it must have been.

Yes, Daughter. Our people came in great numbers, following the kilivaciaq, the giant hairy beasts. At first we saw only ice, but then we came to deep valleys with green forests and more animals than we had ever seen in one place. Not only did we find the hairy ones, but also encountered giant bison with horns as wide as I am tall, and huge sloths that fed us well, for they were the easiest to slay. We were the hunters of the tribe. Our men did the work and took care of our children.

Tiana listened, her eyes tightly closed, afraid to move for fear of breaking the spell. In her mind, she saw the tall, graceful huntress, standing in a long green valley. Her shoulders thrown back, she looked magnificent with lance poised, choosing her prey from the multitude of bison and mammoths grazing peacefully close by.

We pursued the giant beasts when they moved farther into the valley. One morning we awoke, and they had disappeared. We thought to return to our land, but the narrow bridge had gone. There was no crossing back, so we continued forward.

Tiana's eyes opened to stare at the shiny wall of the glacier, thinking and seeing how it must have been to come to a strange place and then not be able to go back. She saw the icy whiteness surrounding the lush green valley, the huge animals threading through a pass into the next frozen expanse of land beyond.

Tulunixiraq's lips parted in a slight smile, and she nodded with approval. *Your vision is good. It happened just so. We followed them, and they led us toward beautiful, treacherous glaciers such as this one, and over mountains of ice and into more green valleys.*

"And then?" The story fascinated Tiana. Huddled on a scrap of fur, she hugged her knees to her chest, unmindful of the bone-snapping, icy air in the center of the glacier.

We crossed treeless, rolling tundra, and there were animals as far as the eye could see. We made our camp, staying for the time it takes a small child to grow to the age of mating, but again the way was blocked for us. When we decided to return, the mountain pass had closed with ice. Where the animals moved, we followed. Some of our people continued to move ahead, leaving others behind. My own people stayed with me until one terrible night a giant wall of water came across the tundra and Sednah, the sea goddess, claimed us. That was the beginning of the salt ocean and the ice pack as you see it now.

Tulunixiraq's spirit floated upward, out of her body. The apparition folded her hands across her chest and stared down at Tiana as if seeing inside her mind and soul. Her expression was one of satisfaction. She turned back to regard her own body, lying stretched out in the fur robes.

You have survived and will continue to survive many hardships and sorrows through your own inner strength. The future will never be an easy one. Many adversities are still to come in the life you have chosen for yourself and your daughter. You may call on me, you may curse me at times, yet I cannot come to your aid. You think I am there, but you will find the strength within yourself.

The magical Raven Belt was my gift to the first Raven Woman as it was your ice sister's gift to you. The belt is a symbol of the bridge that binds you and your descendants together through the centuries — to fortify and multiply the strengths you possess. The belt has become a part of you, as much as your own skin or heart beat. It is there to make certain that the last Raven Woman does

TIANA

not perish.

Tiana reached for the belt around her waist and pulled it off to hold it up for Tulunixiraq to see. The Raven Mother touched it and smiled her sad, secret smile as Tiana felt the coldness of the ivory links transfer from the Raven Mother's hand to her own.

We learned our carving from the priests and shaman in our land across the ice bridge. Each Raven Woman who wears the belt must carve one of the ivory pieces as a symbolic bridge before giving it to the next. When the last ivory carving is done – that could signify the finish of our line. It will be time.

Tiana fingered the belt and tried to imagine the many Raven Women who had worn it after Umiak and Oolik. Their stories had become lost in the mists of time and their courage and strength of purpose only remembered by the squares they had carved and left behind.

As if in answer to her unasked question, a panorama of motion and color spread across the side of the cave. Tiana saw pictures her mind was unable to understand. One young woman appeared in the midst of a thick forest of trees. She was not Inuit, yet had tawny skin and black hair. Tiana's eyes widened at the spectacle of long vessels skimming over the water like terrible sea creatures with many legs. The boats carried huge, fierce-looking men with hair the color of the sun. The scene shifted and she saw a slight girl wearing the Raven Belt and leading a group of what appeared to be wolves tied together as they crossed a frozen plain of ice. Men walked with her, men with strange bloodless color to their skin. A woman wearing a headband and the Raven belt stood at the prow of a ship holding out her arms toward the sea, as if in a gesture of thanksgiving. Huge fish monsters beyond anything Tiana could imagine broke the surface of the water around the ship. Then the panorama faded, and the walls were as before.

"The Raven Woman will not be from the forest?" Tiana's thoughts were jumbled in her head from the wonders she had just seen.

Tulunixiraq shook her head. The Northland holds no boundaries for Raven Women. You will come from many clans and from every time. The Raven spirit will embrace all the people of the Northland. Through your strength and love you will help your people survive.

Tiana closed her eyes, her senses unable to accept more marvels.

Open your eyes, Daughter of the Raven. I offer a gift of my headband. Some day you must pass the belt on to your daughter, but the headband is your own.

I am a part of the belt always, as will be every Raven Woman who possesses it. The belt serves each of you at that time when you need it most. Not every generation will put forth a Raven Woman, but the belt will find them, as I found you. Your daughter will serve as a bridge between the people of the woodland and the people of the ice. We are all of the same origin and are a part of the Raven.

Tiana watched the Raven Mother fading, the soft green mist around her growing denser. She touched her hand to her forehead and felt the delicate feathers of the headband. It warmed her from her head down to the soles of her feet. Tulunixiraq's forehead was bare. Tiana no longer saw the specter above the body, they had reunited.

You must go! Tulunixiraq spoke again, her voice charged with urgent intensity. When my spirit returns to my body, nothing remains to protect you.

Tiana lifted her top fur and draped the belt around her waist. Unmindful of the cold, which had swept in like some live being after the green haze faded, she knelt at the side of Tulunixiraq's body and touched her hand. "Do not fear, Raven Mother. I have always treasured the belt and guard it with my life until I hand it to my daughter, Nikota."

She bowed her head to touch the band on her forehead to the cold hand of the Raven Mother a long moment. When Tiana arose, the green light had diminished to a dull glow hovering just over the body. Tiana gently restored the furs around the Raven Mother, and over her face as they had been before.

Go! Now! A voice whispered in her ear, urging her forward. Suddenly Tiana felt a compulsive need to rush toward the crack and the faint light of day beyond. She took one more look back. The tusk of the giant *kilivaciaq*! A treasure for Kivisik to use for carving. He would be overjoyed.

She ran toward the heaped pile of bones.

But now the voice of warning filled the inside of the glacier; the eerie whisper echoed and bounced off the walls and the dark ceiling. *Go! Hurry!*

TIANA

The glacier boomed, cracked, and groaned – loud noises that terrified her, chilling her from inside out.

Dragging the heavy tusk behind her, Tiana's legs trembled as she ran toward the crack in the glacier. Looking down at her feet, she noticed that her boots fit into faint green imprints which accompanied her through the crack and out onto the icy apron of the glacier front. Instead of making her way carefully alongside the solid ice, a sense of urgency overcame her fear of falling. She clutched the heavy piece of tusk, and slid down the slope of the ice skirting. Tiana fell at a heap at the bottom, but the whisper continued in her ear – unrelenting.

Go! Go!

She ran forward, dragging the tusk, panic pressing her heart up against her throat. When Tiana crossed the ice pack, disconnecting herself from the glacier completely, she stopped for one last look.

Her throat tightened in awe as the mighty edifice of ice shuddered and twisted on the base, roaring like some gigantic live creature in its last throes of agony. She watched as the long, narrow crack folded together, and the glacier collapsed in upon itself, covering the place where she had just stood. She looked down at her boots and the soft green glow beneath her footsteps had disappeared.

The Raven Mother, Tulunixiraq, rested peacefully.

Pinkie Paranya

TIANA

SIXTEEN

INVIGORATED and ignoring her hurting shoulder, Tiana moved away from the glacier's frigid air and walked until she found an outcropping of rocks only partially covered by snow and ice. She laid down her lance and the huge tusk, wondering how she was going to drag it much further, but the thought of Kivisik's wonder when he saw it would give her strength. She dumped the pack she carried and took out several small, precious pieces of tree branches from those the Inuit had collected on their sleds. With her woman's knife, she scratched a surface free from snow on the rock

Sparing a moment to look at the stark, serene beauty of the continual whiteness, Tiana wondered how these people survived without the protection of trees and brush to keep away the wind and offer protection from some of the snowfall. The land was barren and bleak, the whiteness broken only in places by outcroppings of huge rocks scattered here and there across the landscape. No birds appeared in the sky, which was so blue it almost hurt to look upward.

In spite of her dour thoughts, she had a feeling of homecoming. That sudden idea was so strange, she swept it away and taking the pouch from around her neck, stooped to start a small fire. She was hungry, her stomach growled. Before she could take a bird from her pouch, exhaustion caught up with her, and she dropped to her knees near a large tussock. Just a little rest and she'd start the fire and thaw out some snow in a little dipper she carried, and maybe thaw out part of a bird. She pulled the furs around her tighter and the hood down around her face, curling in the snow to sleep.

"Woman-who-walks-alone!" A voice intruded harshly into her

pleasant lassitude.

"Go away! I wish to sleep," she whispered, too weary to open her eyes. It felt so good to rest here in the warm spot melting around her body. She was so tired.

Rude hands shook her shoulders, prodding her to her feet. Her loud protests were ignored.

"Woman of the *itkiyyiq*, open your eyes and look at us."

She recognized the voice of Kivisik and heard mumbling from others who must have come with him. "Leave me alone!" She struck at their hands and tried to brush them aside, wanting more than anything else to stay in the dream she had just left.

"No! You must not sleep. Your hands and feet will freeze if you do not move." Kivisik motioned for another man to help him. They grabbed under her arms and pulled her along. At first her feet dragged, but as the feeling gradually inched back, she tried to walk, clenching her teeth against the exquisite pain of gradually returning feeling.

"No more! Please leave me!"

Kivisik shot a look at the man helping him and then laid her on a fur he threw down on the snow. He opened his tunic and stripping off her boots, stuck her icy feet next to his chest. His big hands enveloped hers which trembled so as he moved his slightly to create a small amount of friction.

When she gradually thawed, tears of pain trickled down her cheeks, but she made no more outcry.

"Don't forget the giant tusk," she managed, pointing to the half buried ivory next to her pouch and lance. The men's indrawn breaths cheered her. They would know her powers now, if they hadn't quite believed her before.

When she no longer felt cold to Kivisik's touch, he wrapped her in a heavy robe of musk-ox fur. She murmured protests to no avail as Kivisik tucked her in the empty sled they pulled behind them. When they finally reached the camp, he lifted her from the sled, threw her over his shoulder and carried her into the tent.

Inside she barely heard Igigik exclaim as they stripped off her damp, icy clothing down to her bird-skin undergarments. It was then they saw the large ugly bruise on her shoulder and half way down her

TIANA

back.

"Tell us. How did you come upon this injury?" Igigik went outside and brought in a bowl of snow to rub on the bruise.

Tiana winced at the cold but it began to feel better. She soaked up their solemn regard – saw the worry lines on their foreheads. They cared about her and this brought tears to her eyes. She brushed them away, not wanting to appear weak in their eyes. "A giant bear struck out at a woman alone when she fell asleep in his den during a snow storm. It appears he did not welcome visitors," she tried to make light of it. The cold snow on her burning shoulder felt good, and she closed her eyes to receive the sense of Igigik's healing hands.

"Naanuk does not venture far from the sea," Kivisik said.

She knew he referred to the white bear that swam in the ocean and lived on the ice. "No, it was not that bear. It was the grizzly, the sun touched bear of many dreams."

"The bear might have pulled your arm loose," Kivisik observed, frowning.

"Yes, a woman thought of that afterward, but she challenged him and survived." She told how it felt to roll down the hill out of his cave after entangling his back feet in the bola.

Igigik giggled, unfolding clean, dry clothing from a pile in a corner of the tent. "You are slender but too tall to wear a wife's clothing," she said. "You will have to wear a husband's trousers until we make you a fitting garment."

Tiana smiled and reached to take Igigik's hand. "Thank you, my sister. You both have done much for a stranger."

To hide her pleasure at Tiana's words, Igigik busied herself around the fire, stirring the pot with a long piece of carved wood.

After Tiana warmed and showed no evidence of the dreaded white skin indicating frostbite, the others in the group crowded around her in Kivisik's tent to hear of her adventures. Everyone wanted to know what manner of magic she used to get the bird-people to come to her. None of their women ever hunted or trapped. They were permitted to fish, but anything else was forbidden in the event it offended the animals.

No one waited for her to tell them how to prepare the ptarmigan. She struggled to keep the look of dismay from her face when they brought out the birds, boiled whole in their feathers. Everyone sat or stood packed together in the small tent, enjoying the fine feast. They spoke around the feathers as they carefully separated them from the meat and bones in their mouth, then spat them politely on the ground at their feet.

"The owls – have you prepared the owls?" Now that she was no longer under the dominion of the shaman in her tribe, it was not forbidden to partake of owl meat. She hoped they had let them be and not cooked them.

Igigik looked shyly at her and shook her head with obvious regret. "An ignorant woman is sorry – there was no time, but . . ."

"No!" Tiana held up her hand to silence her. "Permit me to prepare them for you, in the manner of my people. It will be a surprise for your many kindnesses."

"The owl is a brother to the fox of our totem," one of the men spoke up. "We prize his meat as we do the fox, for if a man partook of both with his eyes closed, he would not know the difference. They taste like brothers also."

"The man of the Inuit speaks the truth. It was never noticed before." Her people had killed fox but of course were not permitted owl as long as it was the shaman's totem.

"There is something that woman-who-walks-alone wishes to say." When she had their attention, she continued. "I respect your traditions and the way you speak. But on this journey my spirit guide, the bear, came to me and I found the Raven Mother in her glacier abode."

In the way of these people, they drew breaths between their teeth to indicate their astonishment, and waited to hear her story.

"I need no other sign that I will be shaman through my lifetime and do not wish to mold my speech into your way of speaking. It is enough, for now, that we have the ability to understand each other. Will this be a large stone in front of our friendship?" She wasn't comfortable with replacing all her I's and didn't want to spend her time trying to conform to their ways. Unless they insisted. Then she might have to in order to continue with them to find Nikota.

Kivisik looked around at the gathering in his tent and folded his arms across his chest. "If woman-who-walks-alone wishes to keep

TIANA

her speech unchanged, who are we to insist? She is, after all, not one of us."

Silence met his words for a long moment, and then all nodded and murmured their agreement.

They had never asked what she carried in her pack. After showing her lance when they first met on the trail, she had kept her bird bolas and throwing boards hidden, knowing they didn't approve of women hunting. With the renewed strength of purpose since she'd returned from the glacier and the bear cave, she no longer felt the need to blend in. She was Tiana, Raven Woman.

She felt too weak to walk and asked Kivisik to bring the extra pack still tied on her little sled. He brought it inside. The men and women who gathered inside had not moved nor spoken. By the pleased expressions they wore, she knew they patiently waited for either a good story or something to entertain them.

She lay her pack down and took out the carved throwing board. She showed them how a woman wore it on her arm to give her more strength and better aim. The hunters in her tribe used the same sort of boards, but wider and longer, for large game. She spread out the bird bola to indicate how she threw it to entangle the legs and wings of birds. It was a good omen to have brought two, for she had used one to ensnare the bear and left it behind in the cave.

One of the Inuit went outside and returned to show her a similar bird bola weapon although it had fewer corded sinew strips, and bones were tied on the end instead of small rocks. "We do not use this in the time of the snow, but only when birds nest on rocks near the big water," he explained.

What a strange custom. There were ptarmigans and winter birds to catch also, but perhaps she could show them later if it was not taboo for them to hunt birds in winter.

She considered giving the bark vest to Kivisik as a gift, for he had saved her life once again. She watched him as he spoke to the others and was not aware of her scrutiny. His gentleness, his concern puzzled her. Suddenly, as if he felt her speculation, their glances collided and froze in a moment of time. She was the first to look down, in utter confusion. She forgot about the arrow-stopping garment.

"I do not understand your custom that does not permit women to hunt." She spoke to avoid the tumult of her emotions.

One older man sitting on the edge of the group opened his mouth to answer, but his wife nudged him in the ribs before he could speak. None of the others said anything, and Tiana supposed it was because they had no wish to offend a guest who had captured the meat which now bulged in their cheeks as they chewed. They turned toward Kivisik.

He looked uncomfortable. "It is not a question of our giving permission. The shaman say women are weaker and thereby offensive to animals in general. None wish to be slain by them. Since you are woman and shaman it has become a problem a poor, foolish man does not understand. Perhaps birds do not object to being caught by a woman," he hedged. It was obvious he had no wish to insult her or incur the ire of a shaman, even one from another clan.

"I have also shot a caribou with arrows," Tiana stated quietly. This was untrue, and she hoped no malignant spirits hovered nearby to hear her lie. When she caught up with her daughter there might be no other way to claim her but to leave these people and strike out on her own. She needed to be able to practice with the lance and the bow for them to survive alone. Tiana felt certain these strange ideas came to her from the Raven belt.

The packed group in the tent hushed at her brave declaration. Some sucked in their breath through their teeth, shocked.

Kivisik regarded her, the expression of his black eyes unfathomable beneath the thick, short eyelashes. "Did a woman's clan permit this? Did your shaman not question the correctness of a woman slaying a large animal? It would seem a husband might think a wife wanted to exchange places with him."

The groups snickered politely behind their mittened hands.

It was Tiana's turn to look uncomfortable. She imagined Namanet receiving such a notion. He was so proud, and always feared being thought unmanly. He would have starved, and let her starve also, before he suffered her to hunt. "A man – even a husband – knows a Raven Woman is not the same as other women," she edged away from his question with quiet dignity.

"It is rude to ask, but we have a hard time to wait for you to

TIANA

think of it. You have a headband that you did not wear before. And what of the giant ivory tusk we found in the snow beside you?" A man she recognized as Apyuk spoke.

It took all this while for the memory of her visit to Tulunixiraq to fully return although it had been coming back in bits and pieces. She was still weak from her long journey without food. Her shoulder had begun to throb again. She gestured toward Kivisik and waited while he and Apyuk dragged in the tusk.

"It must be from the ancient *kilivaciaq*," an old man exclaimed." Our storytellers have long told about these giant beasts. Many songs have been sung about them and the huge creatures who roamed the ice."

Tiana touched her headband. It was so comfortable she'd forgotten it was there. The Inuit had been too polite to ask her about it before, but they must have been longing to hear her story.

"When I was near to dying from the cold, I made a mind journey to see the Raven Mother in the glacier."

They all sighed, some shivered, rubbing their arms as if each imagined going close to the forbidden place.

"The Raven Mother called me inside the glacier and told of amazing things. How our Raven belt was first given to your ancestors, Umiak and her daughter Oolik, a story we all knew. How your people first came here, over a bridge of ice and snow from another land far away."

All eyes were wide with astonishment, mouths agape in wonder. When Tiana paused for breath, an old man whispered, "It is so. Our stories tell us the same legend."

In one of their many conversations, Igigik had told her that the Inuit passed down their stories from generation to generation without one word being changed. The stories were sacred to the clans and exchanging them helped them survive long winter's isolation.

Tiana continued. "In front of me lay the Raven Mother, Tulunixiraq, and she told me I would regain my daughter. That Nikota would be the bridge between the woodland people and the people of the ice. Just before leaving the glacier, I took the tusk for Kivisik to carve. You both have been like my own family. Kivisik saved my life twice. No one could have offered more to a stranger than you two." She touched Igigik's hand.

Igigik dipped her head, her eyes were suspiciously moist and Tiana thought she saw tears on her cheeks, which the woman quickly wiped with her sleeve.

After the people had each touched the ivory and remarked and admired it, Kivisik spoke.

"Woman-who-walks-alone, a simple man cannot accept such a rare gift. It is a certain woman and man who are blessed with your company."

Tiana smiled at Kivisik's protest. He was bursting with pride that she'd given it to him. Some of the men slapped his back in good-natured joviality. A few looked envious.

Soon the guests drifted back to their own tents. When the three were alone again, Kivisik spoke. "A man gives thanks for the generous gift, but it may be better to present this to the shaman when we reach the village. It is too important an object for just one man to hold all to himself."

"Yes, that would be best," Igigik said. "The shaman cannot help but be impressed."

Tiana thought of the marvelous work Kivisik could do with the ancient ivory. She had seen carvings he'd done on wood, and he admired her ivory belt. She had risked her life to bring the tusk out of the glacier; the mammoth ice had nearly closed with her inside. It made her sad to think of giving the wonderful gift to a stranger, possibly a hostile shaman. "Allow me to think on it overnight," she asked. "I know how much Kivisik would appreciate working with the ivory."

"Yes, he would," Igigik agreed, surprising Tiana and Kivisik by her seriousness. "But if you are determined to get your child back, it may be a good way to begin. Only promise that you will think on it tonight." She passed each a bowl of broth to sip on before they rolled up in their sleeping furs.

"You are a good wife, Igigik, this is wonderful and fills an empty place." Tiana rubbed her middle. She had to ask the question puzzling her for so long. "Kivisik, how did you find me?" In that frozen wasteland, scattered as it was with harsh outcropping of rock and ridges which she had climbed over and around, and with new

TIANA

snow falling, he could not have tracked her.

He didn't answer immediately. When Igigik saw he might not, politeness forced her to speak for him.

"A husband told me a raven flew over him and screeched for him to follow."

Tiana looked at the man who had saved her life, feeling a bond flowing between them. "Is this true? Did a raven spirit come to you on my behalf?"

Kivisik frowned; his dark eyes regarded her as if they might peer into her soul. "Yes, a woman speaks the truth. It was clear you had gone away, but after much searching, no one could agree upon your direction. Then a raven came down and landed on the tent, and we followed it to you." His expression was still one of wonder when he spoke of it, and she knew that was the reason everyone had crowded into their tent and partook of her birds. They first had welcomed her as a stranger, woman-who-walks-alone, but now they knew she was shaman.

Tiana thought they might tell this new story over and over of how Kivisik saved woman-who-walks-alone with the help of a raven, and how she gave him a giant tusk in return. Would the tale grow with each telling, as it might back in her village, or would the Inuit keep every word the same each time as Igigik claimed they did?

Even if she agreed to give the tusk to another, she thought the story would be told just so. When they finally reached the village, perhaps the story might protect her from the jealousy of the Inuit shaman. No shaman wanted to share his power, and Kivisik had expressed his worry that she would not be welcome.

After that, the Inuits respected her need to hunt alone and no one mentioned her forays for birds and small animals. The subject of her hunting was not discussed. She showed the women how she removed the feathers and roasted the owls on a spit over the coals. None of the Inuits had ever eaten them cooked in this manner and they pronounced them delicious. From that time on, the women stripped birds of their feathers and roasted them.

The days grew shorter. When the sun lay in a huge puffball on the edge of the horizon in the middle of the day, Kivisik proclaimed they should stop until the moon came to visit the land. The earth lay in wait with potential hazards. Enormous ridges shoved up unexpectedly with sharp, jagged rocks littering the usually flat tundra. The people either had to pull the heavily loaded sleds over the obstructions or around them, a nearly impossible task without sun or moon to guide their steps.

The Inuit spent most of their time sleeping now, rolled up tightly in their furs like hibernating bears. Tiana once again considered leaving their company and striking out alone. When thoughts such as these came to trouble her, the Raven belt consoled her with its warmth and something else – some indefinable warning not to go alone.

One day, while Kivisik slept in his corner of the tent, Tiana sat on her furs across from Igigik.

"A mother knows that something is being held back. What is it that your husband does not wish me to know?"

Igigik looked anxiously toward the sleeping man and then down at the boots she mended. She shook her head in flat denial. She would not speak of it.

Tiana knew then that she must find out what they kept from her. She knew it had to do with her baby. "If you do not tell me, I will pack and be gone at the time of the full moon," she threatened. Since her journey, she had never again gone back to the Inuit way of speaking. She did not need to obey the edicts that ancient men in this stranger clan had set forth. Tulunixiraq had proclaimed her the Raven Woman, and she was destined to be a powerful shaman in her own right. She would not bend her will to others.

Not daring to let herself feel pity for the frightened woman who had been her companion and friend for so many changes of the new moons, Tiana had to know the truth. She folded her arms across her chest and waited, sitting quietly.

Igigik swallowed and shook her head in determination.

Tiana held her balled fist tightly against her mouth to keep the sound of weeping inside. Something was wrong, terribly wrong, and no one would tell her. She folded her upper body down over her crossed legs, in the age-old womanly gesture of mourning.

Igigik could not bear her distress. She crawled over to where Tiana lay bent and touched her hair gently. Tiana raised and they held

TIANA

one another, both crying loudly now.

Kivisik awoke and sat up, looking at the pair of sobbing women with a dazed expression on his face. One look at his wife, and he knew what it was about.

"Must we tell her?" He looked at Igigik. She nodded.

Kivisik refused to meet Tiana's steady gaze and instead, looked at his boots as if suddenly discovering something extraordinary about them. "The people of the beaver have a custom." He hesitated again before he continued. "When a visitor comes into their midst wishing to reside with them, the stranger must be tested to see if the spirits approve."

"Tested?" Tiana knew he meant her daughter. "Even a baby?"

He nodded. "It is the tradition and has protected them against sickness and evil spirits for as long as the oldest person can remember. We do not have such an unusual test among the fox people, but then every shaman knows what is good for his community."

"What is the test – and why have you not told me?"

Kivisik shifted uncomfortably. "The trial takes place on the first night of the full moon after the stranger arrives. Since our cousins are ahead of us on the trail we cannot be certain if we may arrive at our village before them. It does not matter, we dare not interfere."

"But . . ." Tiana leaped to her feet, clenching her fists against the urge to shake this quiet, calm man who took so long to tell her something so important.

Kivisik stood to face her, and they looked at one another a long moment before he sighed. "Strangers are sewn in beaver's skins and put into water – not too deep," he hastened to inject at the sudden alarm in her expression. "If they swim and flap their tail as does the beaver, the people welcome them with open arms."

"But a baby cannot swim!"

He shrugged. "Perhaps it can. How could we know for certain? A man has never recalled such a small person being brought to their village before. If you are shaman, it follows that your daughter is also. Will she not be protected?"

Tiana sank down to the floor, her energy suddenly dissipated. "No. She does not own a helping spirit yet. I must be there to prevent this test. You have to help me!" She looked up at Igigik and Kivisik, her eyes filled with torment.

Both of them knelt in front of her and took her hands. Kivisik spoke first.

"There is still a chance we may catch up to them or even pass them. Our kinsmen have a special place they must stop for a time to bury the heads of the beaver so that the spirits are at peace. Like us, they have to wait until they can see to walk across the tundra."

"You are shaman. If you wish to chance a dispute with their shaman, we can take you to their village. He will have to judge whether you have a claim to the child or not." Igigik rubbed her calloused fingers across Tiana's arm.

"We may not be in time. My baby will die."

Kivisik looked pointedly at the ivory belt around her waist. "Do you not have the protection of your *tunarak* – your helping spirit?"

Tiana touched her belt and then looked at them. Anger – at herself – welled up inside, choking her with the bitter taste. Why had she forgotten Tulunixiraq? She had just been thinking wasteful thoughts about not being forced to speak in their manner and neglected what was important. Yet, she hadn't known about the test, but she had suspected something was wrong since she came to reside with these people.

"I must make council with the Raven Mother. I need to speak to her. She told me not to ask for her help, but she also told me my daughter would be a Raven Woman." What if she meant other daughters? Tiana did not want other daughters, her heart and soul had been entwined with Nikota from the first time she looked upon the baby.

Tiana readied her drum and all her Raven totems in preparation of creating the proper atmosphere. "Will you ask the others to come inside?" she spoke to Kivisik who nodded and left the tent.

Outside, she heard the buzz of excitement that rushed through the camp as Igigik and Kivisik hurried around to the other tents to notify the group about the coming séance. Tiana did not have to explain to these people that the more who attended a seeing, the better a shaman was able to communicate with the spirits. All people must know this. It had to do with the combined energy and the belief

TIANA

of those who listened.

By the time Tiana began stroking her fingers on the drum in her lap, the entire band sifted into the tent and settled comfortably down on furs. The fire was banked so that it should not go out, but if it did, with so many packed so close together no one would be cold.

"Aya-ya-ya," she began slowly, steadily. Her fingers and heel of her palm alternated on the drum, changing the sound just slightly each time. The dark, shiny crescent of her hair drooped gracefully, hiding part of her face as she concentrated on her belt lying stretched out across her pant legs. The chant and monotonous beating of the drum intertwined until, when she finally looked up into the faces surrounding her, all eyes were closed. All heads nodded gently to the cadence of her music.

She continued far longer than usual, for she felt no vibration of movement inside the tent telling her the spirits listened. The small fire crackled and snapped occasionally in the stillness. It was the only sound, except for her voice and drum.

Even if she did not have the power to stop these events from happening, the spirit of Tulunixiraq could delay the ordeal until Tiana reached her daughter.

Tears coursed down Tiana's cheeks as she pictured her tiny, fragile daughter wrapped in beaver skins and thrown into icy water. It reminded her of the water trial she went through to save herself from the tribe's anger when Sarnat nearly drowned and then gave birth to a dead baby.

Through a curtain of tears, her belt shimmered and wavered in front of her studied gaze. Suddenly the soft ivory color blended into a pale green shadow.

She felt the Raven Mother's presence.

"Mother of the Ravens . . . Sister to Sednah,
goddess of the water . . .
I entreat you.
A husband is lost, a son perishes,
and now a daughter must also
join the spirits
before she has time to live.

Pinkie Paranya

*A shaman — nay, a woman, mourns
these tragedies.
She desires to know if a life can be traded.
A daughter must live to see
Sister Sun spread her pale,
delicate skirt across the harsh
land.
A daughter must live to see
Brother Moon as he journeys across
the sky — losing his fullness to the
darkness of time.
A daughter must live
to become Raven Woman
after I am gone."*

A low moan broke into her song, and she paused, letting a man speak if he wished. He moaned again and then broke into wild, uninhibited laughter. Relief coursed through his voice, and at first she was surprised and angered, but then guessed he had made a mind-journey to visit his family in the village of the fox people, where Kivisik and Igigik lived. She did not have to open her own eyes to tell the man was still asleep. She felt pleased that someone had been worried and now knew his family fared well.

Tiana waited, but no one else tried to speak. She began her low chanting again as she picked up the belt and held it to her cheek. The ivory felt warm, nearly hot to the touch. The green shadow still clung to the belt and now surrounded her body, giving her a sensation of warmth and protection. She slumped over and knew no more until much later, when she awoke to hear Igigik preparing their food.

"A woman became worried, you were away so long." Igigik spoke as she stirred broth and cracked bones with her cudgel to add to the pot.

Tiana looked at Kivisik, but he sat on his furs, not speaking. His usual pleasant expression hid beneath a taut apprehension.

"Is something wrong with your husband? He looks as if he slept too long." Both she and Igigik delighted in teasing poor Kivisik the few times he found a comfortably somber mood and floundered in it a while. She noticed this about the usual laughing, teasing people. Sometimes without warning and for no reason she could see, they shifted into bleak despair. Fortunately, the moods never lasted long. Now Kivisik did not respond as he usually did, with a shamefaced grin.

"Ugaruk journeyed to the village," Igigik interjected.

"I heard someone speak and laugh," Tiana said.

"He is very happy to know his family is well and misses him. From that we supposed all our people were well, or his family would have given warning. They are pleased with your mind-journey."

Kivisik cleared his throat, letting his wife know he wished her to be quiet so he could think. The women waited patiently, until at last he spoke.

"A man cannot regret helping woman-who-walks-alone, for it is believed she would have joined the spirits by now. No one, not even a shaman, can make this journey alone." He looked at Tiana, his dark eyes filled with compassion which temporarily crowded out his worry. "Yet you will cause great trouble when we return to our village, that is certain. And it is on the head of a man who seeks no trouble."

Tiana lowered her gaze, unable to meet the concern in his expression. These people thought as one body, felt pain and sorrow and happiness as one. She finally understood, although it was a concept foreign to her upbringing. In her experience with the two tribes she had been a part of, while her clansmen were together to offer support and company, yet they lived as individuals, doing as they pleased with no one to tell them otherwise. They shared when the spirit moved them to share, but sometimes they refused and this was accepted.

To the Inuits – who shared everything down to their wives and children, if need be – family was everything. Kivisik told her each village was almost entirely made up of kinsmen. A man or woman had to go to another village to find a mate.

Tiana reflected upon what must have been Kivisik's torment since the beginning, when he learned why she headed north to the land of the ice.

"My friends, I have grown to care for you both very much. You are closer than my own family to me now. I have no one else." Tiana looked at the pairs of black eyes regarding her every word, as if she might come up with a miracle. "I cannot change what has been set in motion. In the mind-journey, I did not seek the Raven Mother, but she came to me. She told me I have to trust my own judgment, that my resolution must not falter at any time. You, in turn, must trust me."

She took their hands in her own, pressing them to her face. The three stood still, silently wrapped in the strength of this one woman's determination.

Finally Kivisik pulled away and grumped a masculine denial of sentiment. He fooled neither his wife nor Tiana, for his eyes were moist with unshed tears.

"So be it," he pronounced. "We embrace you as one of us. You will be of our kin, and when you find your daughter we welcome her also into our family."

The next day they awoke to the white-darkness, with ice crystals as fine as dust particles enveloping everything in a deceptively delicate shroud of pristine white. Everyone stayed inside his own tent, sleeping and eating. During the next days and nights the wind blew fearfully, like a live, tormented spirit, angry at the world it rushed across.

Tiana sympathized with the wind, feeling the same tormented frenzy as she chafed at the forced wait. The Inuits could not be budged when they thought it dangerous to travel. She held other séances so that the people who wished might see and hear of the families they left behind. Often a tribesman would encounter his or her family and delighted laughter ensued. Once the old man burst out in sobs and weeping. His old wife had died in his absence, but her spirit came to tell him she knew he had to make one last journey. She was at peace with that and so should he be. But the face and form of Nikota never appeared to offer solace to Tiana, no matter how hard she tried to visualize it.

With all the leisurely stops for inclement weather and various fishing spots along the way, the Inuit suddenly awoke to the realization that their food supply was running low.

Kivisik refused to let them eat any fox meat. They had made the

TIANA

long journey to obtain the skins, tails and meat for the villagers to bring them good fortune for years to come. How might they explain it if they arrived with nothing but skins and tails? They would all suffer disgrace.

Wolves howled ever closer at night, sometimes just outside their tents. Each time the group completed a day's journey, they were forced to unload their sleds and bring everything inside so the creatures would not get at the packed foxes and the little bit of dried fish they had left. Finally, when the wolves came into their camp scratching against the tents, the men began to set traps for them.

Tiana watched as they smeared sharpened bone knives with blood and fat from the little bit of hoarded seal meat and set them points up embedded in the snow. A little stored urine or melted snow water around the base secured it against movement. When an *amawk*, as they called the wolf, licked the knives, he cut his tongue and bled to death. They found the bloodless bodies the next day, usually not far away. Sometimes they heard dreadful fights and knew the wolves were eating one of their own.

The Inuit also had a long, sharpened piece of something they named baleen and claimed came from a *sisuaq*, a whale. Tiana watched as they wound this thin piece of bony material into a tight circle and molded caribou suet around it. The men placed it outside, under a heavy object, until it froze solid. When the wolf came to gulp it down, it gradually melted within its stomach; the baleen sprang open, tearing the animal's insides. The hunters could follow its progress by the howls of pain and bloody droppings as it struggled to reach its den.

Except in dire necessity, they were not permitted to eat wolf meat. Igigik explained this to Tiana as they sat in the pale sun and waited for the men to return from hunting.

"The *amawk* is all-powerful, not like the generous fox who begs the people to partake of his flesh."

"Then how do you dare to slay him?" she asked.

"When the hunters slay a wolf, they attach a knife or weapon if it is a male, or parts of a woman's sewing kit if a female. They must skin it whole and cut off its head where they find him, to free the spirit. This way the animal could tell the others it was not treated disrespectfully or dragged back to a man's camp like an ordinary beast."

"But the fox is treated the same, except for leaving the skin on the tundra."

Igigik shook her head in denial. "No. The hunters must sacrifice their weapons and we our sewing necessities, not the little carved ones we put on the fox, but ones we use. This is the only way to appease the spirit of brother wolf. Therefore the slaying of this creature is not done without consideration and only in time of terrible need."

One day in their travels, fierce sounds of violence ruptured the peaceful silence. At first the Inuits hung back, fearful of the noise. They made as if to go around the fight, but Tiana closed her eyes tight to look ahead. She held up her hand. "We must move forward. No harm will come to us," she pronounced.

Trusting her and curious, the group continued to travel toward the noise until the lead sled stopped abruptly, bumping them all together. They looked ahead and saw a band of musk-ox. All the beasts appeared paralyzed in fright by two black bears. Their noise had been so fearsome, the bawls of frightened animals so loud, the bears did not hear the Inuit approach.

Tiana began a hushed chant of thanksgiving to the souls of the bears and the musk-ox, while the hunters crept closer and closer. She felt relieved it was only black bears and not the awesome grizzly of her dreams even though she had accepted the grizzly as her spirit guide.

With a loud cry, Kivisik who was in the lead, shouted to stop the hunters from slaying the bears. "These creatures must not be harmed. They found food for us."

The women shouted and shrieked. The men banged their lances together. Finally the bears ran away. The musk-ox stood in a circle, not unduly alarmed by this new threat. Their large, dangerous-looking horns all pointed outward in defense of the females and smaller animals inside the ring. The hunter's arrows brought down several of the shaggy animals and the men rushed in to finish them off by thrusts of their lances.

Kivisik stopped the slaughter before the men took more meat

TIANA

than they needed or than they could carry. The women rushed out and shooed the remaining beasts away by snapping flaps of hides in the frigid air.

"What do you call these creatures?" Tiana asked as she knelt in the snow to help skin the animals. Was this a present from her old grandfather, whose death she had caused by trading with the white bear's spirit? That had happened so long ago it was like a faint dream, and she had to brush away the edges to remember it.

"We call them *umingmaks*, the bearded ones," Igigik replied. "Have you not seen them before?"

Tiana smiled. "Once, in a dream with my grandfather and my father, Quaanta." She did not elaborate; it was not the time for a lengthy story. "Sometimes our hunters brought back the meat and fur. Our food came most from the deer, the caribou and the moose."

"Waugh! This will provide us meat until we reach our journey's end," Kivisik pronounced. "A certain woman who is also shaman has brought us much good fortune." He looked at Tiana, and the others nodded and stomped their boots on the snow to indicate agreement.

Unable to answer, Tiana had a lump in her throat, along with a feeling of humble pride. These people accepted her presence, even if it might bring dissension and conflict into two villages which could last for generations to come.

More than merely accepting her, they now welcomed her into their midst. If only they could be persuaded to quicken their pace.

Tiana's fingers played over her raven earrings as she silently voiced her thanksgiving for the fresh meat and the support from these people. Perhaps there would be no welcome in the new village when the others learned of her reason for being there. Perhaps her daughter even now was lying on the tundra, her living spirit expired from her fragile body.

If she found her alive, there may be no way to remove Nikota from the people of the beaver tribe. These thoughts, which had tormented and driven her for so many moons, Tiana realized had begun to lack their usual frustrating urgency. Was she gradually learning patience from the sturdy Inuit without knowing when this happened? She hoped it was possible, for she admired them with all her heart.

Pinkie Paranya

She didn't notice until thinking upon it afterward that Kivisik for the first time, did not refer to her as woman-who-walks-alone.

TIANA

SEVENTEEN

THE days grew longer and longer, and Tiana knew that soon signs of the approaching warm days would creep upon the land. In the forest, trees grew new leaves, and the pines would sprout shoots of lighter green on the ends of their branches. Creeks and small rivers would start to melt from the shoreline toward the centers, and the large rivers refused to thaw until the sun shone everyday.

This land was so different, the ground beneath her feet turned soggy and treacherous with tussocks which protruded from the earth, jiggling and wobbling in their pathway. The Inuit wanted to stop at every thawing stream to fish. Tiana felt a rush of frustration each time that she tried to hide.

One morning a woman twisted her ankle in the bog, but didn't mention it until they stopped to eat later in the day. The sealskin boot had to be cut from her swollen foot. She apologized for her clumsiness. Tiana had not thought of Kania for many moons, but she tried to recall some of her tender ministrations and how she would have helped the woman. She did not think this a time for shaman works as much as help to ease the swollen foot. She instructed Kivisik and the other men to find branches as flat as possible and shave off the protruding buds and twigs. When they brought her several good pieces, she bid the woman sit and then placed the branches just so, with help holding them steady. She wrapped the protruding bone back into place with a tight bandage of stretched hide. If it had been in the summer, she would have soaked the hide in water and then wrapped it, but it was still too cold. If she did that now it would freeze to the leg.

Kivisik, without being told, had fashioned her a carved cane from a birch tree which delighted the woman and seemed to make her forget the pain.

The hunter with a name Tiana could not pronounce, but which meant *one who speaks little*, shot himself through the foot with an arrow. After the men cut off the head of the arrow and pulled it out, Tiana made him soak the foot in hot water that she'd instructed the women to heat.

Both of these incidents served for much teasing and hilarity among the people, something Tiana found hard to understand. It seemed to her that the Inuits smoothed the harshest reality by their constant humor and rough joking. Even the ones who were the butt of the teasing laughed at themselves with good-natured unconcern.

"Where did you learn to do this?" Kivisik wanted to know.

"We leave a bone that goes awry alone, maybe it will turn back the way it is supposed to go," Igigik suggested politely.

Tiana thought again of Kania, and how much she had learned from her. She had been so good at mending hurts. Many had come to her for help when an accident occurred. The pain of missing her had not yet healed, and Tiana closed her eyes to find another thought to replace the painful ones.

Gradually the landscape changed until, without her knowing exactly when it happened, the group had traveled away from the tundra and out onto the ice. Her thoughts dwelt more and more on her daughter, Nikota. The sharp hurt of her loss was undimmed by the passing months. Soon – soon, her crunchy steps in the snow called out to her – soon – soon.

The travelers stopped, set up their tents, and soon the three ate their meal before retiring after the long day's walk. Kivisik spoke into the companionable silence. "A man has been thinking."

Tiana and Igigik waited, knowing he would eventually finish his speech when his thoughts found their way out of his mouth.

"A man supposes that two wives are better than one. A man also thinks that when a certain handsome woman enters a village, many hunters will desire her. It is not uncommon for her to be taken away for a wife if she does not already belong to another."

He looked at Igigik, and a large grin spread across her round

TIANA

face. Her little nose disappeared into the folds of her cheeks. She had been thinking of this too – their eyes conveyed their thoughts without needing speech, so long had they been together.

Tiana swallowed. She felt attracted to Kivisik. His quiet strength, the generous, open quality of his disposition, his many thoughtful kindnesses were flattering, and indeed, caused her memory of Namanet to recede with improper haste. But there was the problem of her daughter. How would it affect Nikota if she became part of their family and wife to Kivisik?

She pointed this out to them.

No one spoke, as the Inuit couple gravely considered the situation. It was apparent by their expressions that they assumed she had discarded the impractical idea of finding her daughter by now.

"There could be other daughters . . . and sons," Kivisik said.

Igigik ducked her head, and then kicked at the campfire with her boot in a paroxysm of giggles which did not subside until her husband threw her a glance.

"No! The Raven Mother came to me in a dream long ago and commanded that I follow my daughter and claim her for our Raven line. I will find her. I – I had hoped that you would help me."

"So be it," Kivisik said with quiet resignation. "If that is your wish, when we find your daughter, it can be decided then how to proceed. Perhaps something can be exchanged for the girl. Still, we would welcome you both into our family, and you will not be alone."

"But what if we do not arrive before their ceremony? My daughter will not survive that."

He shrugged his broad shoulders. "A man thinks our cousins are in no more of a hurry as travelers than we are. There are many ceremonies the beaver people must perform while out on the tundra and although they are terrible fishermen, they enjoy fishing even more than we do," he offered.

So it was settled. Becoming wife to Kivisik was not a displeasing prospect to Tiana. Indeed secretly she had wondered how it might be. He had saved her life twice. Wasn't this a sign? That Igigik approved and longed for her to become as a sister was also a sign. A woman alone was not good. Perhaps her ancient ancestors, Umiak and Oolik, could survive on their own without a man, but times changed. She knew any hunter might claim an unattached woman for as long as he liked and then trade her to another when she no longer pleased him. Many wives were gambled away among her own people by games of luck the men played or wrestling matches to test their strength.

Would Kivisik or Igigik tell the others? What would be the reaction? She was determined not to bow down to all of their customs. She was weary of seeing things in the future that only she could see. If they chose not to accept this or her as Kivisik's second wife, what would happen to her? As much as she felt Kivisik cared for her, he would not go against the good of the tribe. The thought of leaving these people and finding another tribe to live with filled her with sadness. She'd had so many homes, this one, she hoped, might be the last. So many questions. She would have to work on her newly discovered patience and wait and see.

As they moved along the next day, the landscape continued to change. Each day was a new marvel. Rocky ridges erupted in the glaring whiteness of the snow as they crossed from ice to land and back again. White hare as large as wolf cubs startled from their resting places, and fled before them. Ptarmigan, still in their feathers of concealing white, rattled up from nests when they passed. The Inuit's pace suddenly dropped to a slowness hard to understand. It was as if they were feeling their way along blindly. Were they getting ready to stop and hunt again? Since they seldom spoke as they traveled, Tiana made no comment and held her questions until later.

Just at that moment she heard a loud shriek as the first sled disappeared into nothingness. Everyone ran forward and looked down. Two men pummeled the surface of the water with open palms, in ineffectual terror. Their robes tangled about them, dragging them down. Only the back runners of the sled were visible, protruding from the black water.

Kivisik uncoiled a length of braided sinew he had lately carried in a circle over his shoulder and tossed the end to one of the men in the water. The man ceased flailing in blind panic and looked up at the surrounding crowd of people with calm, resigned expression. Kivisik grasped the rope when the man held on to his end. The other man grabbed hold of his companion's shoulder as the entire group of men and women took hold of the rope and began to slowly pull back on it.

The older women stepped from foot to foot to show their concern. One sobbed, looking down at her husband in the water.

"If they do not come out soon, they will not be able to hold the rope. Their hands will freeze," Igigik whispered to Tiana. The men chanted as they pulled on the rope, the women made little sobbing noises deep in their throats.

"Then what will happen to them?" Tiana whispered back.

Igigik grunted with the strain of her pulling. "We must leave them, for the spirits of the water, perhaps even Sednah the sea creature, desires to keep them."

A hoarse shout came from the broken ice, but Tiana could not see over the men who pulled in front of her.

Suddenly the taut rope went slack. The people holding the line fell to the snow in uneven heaps like overstuffed dolls flung down by an unruly child.

Tiana watched in fear as they pulled one man from the water. Where was the other? She ran to the edge of the broken ice and saw the man sinking out of sight in the water. His jacket hood lay against his head and only his eyes were above water. Even when she was an old woman, she would not forget the look of stark terror and the resigned hopelessness in those eyes.

"Can nothing be done for him?" she cried out.

The people had all turned away, to give the man privacy in his last moments. Only his woman shrieked and tore at her hair in sorrow and pity.

Without stopping to consider the consequences of her actions, Tiana grabbed the rope lying frozen on the ground and raced lightly across the snow to leap on the overturned sled which had not yet sunk. It wobbled precariously under her slight weight, but did not sink any lower into the icy sludge.

From the corner of her eye she saw a blur and knew someone, probably Kivisik, had reached out to try and stop her. She grasped the curved ends of the sled for support and felt an odd warmth of the water seep into her lower clothing. Soft tendrils of fog escaped from the warmer liquid below and began to sift upward, giving the shattered ice a placid look.

Tiana projected an image of her Raven belt on the inside of her closed lids and then looked down at the man below. He stared up at her with wide-eyed wonder. His look of resignation was replaced by an expression of hope. He stretched his arm toward her with his last remaining strength. She knew his fingers were numb, and he could not grasp hold of the line.

She paused to tie the hardening sinew in a loop as her people had once done to hold a bear cub when they hoped to tame it. Tiana leaned far out across the edge of the sled, teetering precariously.

> *"Raven Mother, do not desert me now.*
> *A man who has fathered children,*
> *a wife who sorrows*
> *need someone's help."*

Her chant was soft, barely audible, but it seemed to provide the courage needed to ignore the increasing tilt of the sled and to reach out with the loop. She draped it around the man's shoulders.

Weakened from the cold, with his last energy, he managed to wriggle his arms above it. Tiana called to the watchers on the shore line. "Pull! Pull the line now!" she shouted, galvanizing them to action.

The chunks of slush ice parted when the crowd towed the man toward the firmer area. No one noticed the shifting ice until Kivisik shouted a warning. The floe on which Tiana stood began to move away from the shore, the current taking it away toward the sea. Fear clutched at her heart. Her throat filled with it so that she could not move. Since Tiana had been with the Inuits she heard stories of the many hunters – entire families – who had been lost forever, falling over the ends of the earth when they were caught out on moving ice floes.

Kivisik, poised on the edge of the ice with Igigik and several others holding to his jacket, looked as if he meant to jump in the water and swim to her rescue. Tiana held up her hand to warn him away. When her weight shifted, her thigh pressed against something hard. She looked down at a lance of carved wood.

TIANA

Something urged her to use it. But how?

Her headlong rush into the main current slowed as her ice floe bumped into another, larger one, and held firm. The lance had a rawhide string and inflated bladder attached to the toggle end; the hunters had been preparing their gear for the coming seal hunts. She used this time to unleash the lance and hold it, bouncing it lightly in her hands.

When Tiana grasped the lance it was clear from the warmth of the belt that this was what she needed. She took careful aim at a piece of floe closer toward shore and heaved the shaft with all her might.

The weapon stood quivering, point down on the ice. She pulled the rawhide rope slowly, bringing her chunk of ice closer and closer. At the last possible moment it gave a lurch, and swerved around in the water like a canoe, putting her on the other side of the ice mass, much closer to shore. Tiana gauged her chances for leaping to shore. It might have been possible – if she were willing to do it.

But now another idea came to her. This sled was the most laden with fox pelts and musk-ox meat. What a terrible waste, towing it so far, only to lose it now. She heard a cry from the bank. The Inuit beckoned frantically. Igigik had her hood down over her eyes, refusing to look. Kivisik cried out, motioning for her to jump across the chunks.

Tiana pretended not to hear and began reeling in the rope attached to the lance. The lance stayed embedded. Her idea was going to work! Suddenly the lance released. She almost fell backward, but regained her balance. Her feet had no feeling, soaking so long in icy water. That made her footing precarious now.

She took aim to throw again, this time to a large ice floe close to the shoreline. If the shot missed, she would have no more chances. The open water lay just beyond and nothing could stop her headlong passage once the floe she stood upon entered into the current.

Tiana sighted down the long, thin pike grasped in her hands, closed her eyes to imagine her arm shielded by her throwing board the Inuit thought so magical. The Raven belt sent shivers of warming vigor radiating from her waist to her drawn-back arm.

She threw the lance with all her strength. It barely landed on the edge, stuck, quivering, in the ice. Breathing a deep breath of thanksgiving she began to reel in the sinew carefully so that it would not jerk loose.

The people on the shore watched silently now. The only sound came from the creaks and groans of the ice field constantly in motion. The spring thaw was close at hand, but the ice was still restrained and sluggish in its movements.

This time she moved close enough so that Kivisik raced over to the large floe, leaped upon it and held the lance still so she could pull against the rope. Slowly, painfully slowly, she reeled toward him and safety. Even through her numbed feet, she felt the lapping water rising higher and higher against her legs.

Her ice floe began to sink as parts of it chipped and dropped off the edges from the friction of the water against the sides. She was close enough to Kivisik to see his mouth clenched in grim determination as he held on to the wavering pole with all his strength.

A cry arose from the group crowded together as she came within four or five canoe lengths and then so close she leaped up into Kivisik's waiting arms.

"Put me down, Kivisik. See to the sled. You can pull it here." He had forgotten all about the sled in his anxiety for her.

Tiana pushed him away just as several men jumped over to help them. They managed to pull the sled across the small inlet of water not a moment too soon. The entire chunk which had held her and the sled collapsed and sank with only a faint gurgle and a heap of bubbles to show where it had been.

Many rushed forward to envelope Tiana in fur robes. Since she was unable to walk, Kivisik, refusing help from the other men, picked her up and carried her to the sled, until they could set up tents.

For several sleeps Tiana was grateful that they made camp with roaring fires, using up their precious store of wood to warm the frostbite from her and the two men. The first man seemed to be unharmed, but the unlucky one had two feet which did not turn back again to their normal color and had no feeling at all. Nevertheless, he was happy to be alive, and beamed upon everyone who came into the tent, showing off the blackened areas as if it was some magnificent joke.

TIANA

Igigik watched over Tiana lying wrapped in fur robes next to the men in front of the fire. She manipulated Tiana's feet to keep them from going to sleep forever. By her constant smiles, Tiana could tell she did this lovingly, and with much pride in her heart for the bravery of her new sister.

Tiana knew Kivisik admired her greatly, yet he was still angry that she took such a chance. He did not speak of it since they were never alone now, sharing the tent so that the two men could have use of the fire. Yet the tribe must have known his feelings for her by now, he was very protective and watchful that she be made comfortable.

When she was able to sit up, the entire tribe came to stand in front of her, shyly thanking her for rescuing their sled with the precious cargo. The wife of Iliak insisted she accept the new pair of boots that she had saved for homecoming. Everyone laughed and complimented the wife on such a good joke when she remarked that her husband may never wear boots again.

One night while they all sat huddled around the campfire, watching the brilliant stars overhead close enough to touch, Kivisik took Tiana and Igigik's hands and pulled them to their feet.

"Friends and kinsmen of the fox. A man wishes to speak."

Everyone looked up, pleased at an interruption of the quiet night.

For once Igigik forgot to giggle, and Tiana's heart beat strong in her breast. She sensed what Kivisik was about to say. Since his speech to her about being in danger as woman-who-walks-alone, she had talked to Igigik, who was more than agreeable to the idea of Tiana joining their family.

"Woman-who-walks-alone wishes to become a part of a poor man's family, and the man and his old wife agree it would be a splendid thing."

Some of the people stood, stamping their feet and making noises of approval. Several women ran up to Igigik and Tiana and hugged them.

Kivisik tried to maintain his dignity, but his grin showed he was pleased. "From this time, she will no longer be known as woman-who-walks-alone. Her name is Tiana which means *gift of the moon*.

Since she is a shaman and not of our people, she need not speak in the manner of the Inuit, and we may use her name without facing disapproval from evil spirits."

Amidst much back slapping and joking, the men gathered around Kivisik and took him off to the side, presumably to offer him their advice on taking a young wife. The women rubbed noses and cheeks with Igigik and Tiana. Someone brought out a drum and made music while the men danced around the fire in their winter leggings and parkas, looking like clumsy bears dancing on hind legs. Everyone had such a good time and without saying it in words, offered Tiana much love and affection. For the first time since she'd left Kania and her village, she felt as if she'd found a people who could be her family again.

After they had rested and all the wet clothing dried on racks, the Inuit began the last part of their journey. The man they now called *No Feet* never again stepped upon the earth. He had to be carried. Tiana was surprised at his continuing joy at being alive. Had this happened to one of the hunters in her clan, he would have cut off his own offending feet, preferring to die. No man wished to live his life as a cripple, and no one would have offered pity or sympathy for a man unable to hunt.

But the other Inuits considered Iliak a living legend, having been wrenched from the arms of Sednah herself. They would tell the story over and over, exactly as it happened. Iliak was forevermore a hero.

Tiana watched and listened, trying hard to fathom the meaning of what she was learning. The image of her baby daughter intruded on her thoughts. The thick, spiky hair sticking out of her head at all directions, her tiny fist clutching the Raven belt – all of these things had wrapped around the heart of Tiana and would not let go.

Also she thought sadly of the poor doomed little boy child. Why was he put inside her body at the same time as her daughter? Was it something she had to learn? Did he have a quick death without suffering? She hoped the little man did not feel pain. Perhaps he had been too fragile to last long on the journey. Nikota claimed the strength of her mother's body, as if it were her birthright, leaving the boy what was left.

Although thoughts of him often entered her head, it was the first

TIANA

time Tiana had allowed her thoughts to dwell on the boy child since joining the Inuits. The image of her tiny, helpless son dying without her to hold him and love him was a tragedy she still was incapable of examining too closely.

More than that, she put away entirely the idea of Nikota as the one who might have died on the trail.

In the days that followed, Tiana learned much from the people, for they finally opened up to her without reservation. They sang old songs of the days when huge, furry animals roamed the earth, much larger than even the giant white bear they called *naanuk*.

Tiana was certain they made up this terrible white bear to tease her, for they all knew of her respect of bears by now.

Her nights with Kivisik warmed her just thinking about them. While Igigik stayed with friends in another tent for several nights, Kivisik proved a gentle, thorough lover. The first night they undressed in the dark tent with only the tiny glow of an oil lamp spreading a soft light over the tent sides. They lay down on furs and he gathered her into his arms. They lay together under the furs for a long time, holding each other close. She felt his uneven breath on her hair and knew he wasn't as confident as she'd thought at first. She fluttered her eyelashes against his cheek in a loving gesture she'd seen the Inuit use. He grasped her hands between his and brought them to his lips.

He left no part of her body untouched as he explored, moving his hand across her stomach down to the swell of her thighs. At first she was hesitant, since Namanet always initiated their coming together and except for their first time in the woods, she had always remained passive and accepting. But now Kivisik whispered encouraging words to her, which moved her to touch him in places that made him gasp with pleasure. His body was sturdy and strong, the taut muscles felt good beneath her fingers and she played them along his back and down to his buttocks.

When she took a deep breath and reached to hold his male hardness he groaned and almost stopped in his touching and kissing, but then moved his hands to more intimate parts of her body. She'd only felt the earth and sky blend together once with Namanet in their first lying together in the woods, but now if she closed her eyes it was like the sky throwing colors against her eyelids time and again.

When she thought she could bear it no longer, he moved on top of her and she welcomed him into her body. She knew when his rapture came by his low moan. He slowly relaxed his body, and she pulled the furs back over them. They slept entwined most of the long night, only waking now and again to touch and kiss sleepily.

She enjoyed looking at him when he was unaware of her observation. His bulky sealskin jacket hid his well-formed, muscular body, so familiar to her by now. It was good to look forward to their lovemaking. Tiana had anticipated at the beginning with Namanet too, but after the courting period, he sometimes took her as if angry at his need for her.

After the first night she and Kivisik spent the night alone together, Igigik giggled and teased her shyly about it the next day. Igigik had been with him so long, the thought of sleeping in his furs held no mystery or wonder for her. She indicated she was happy to relinquish her place to Tiana.

They were sisters now. Igigik was the sister Tiana never had.

When Igigik moved back into the tent, their time together was spent with cooking and eating and visiting with the people who wandered in and out of their tent. Tiana felt grateful that they would share their songs with her. She knew it as a great honor. To the Inuit, songs were sometimes the only personal property they owned and were passed down within the family, unless given away or traded.

Still, a deep, gnawing sadness continued to bother her. Would she have to leave these people when she found Nikota? A woman craved a family and familiar surroundings. She had deep feelings for Kivisik and her new sister. Yet she did not wish to cause these gentle people trouble.

One morning they started their journey again, and Tiana noticed the group had become more talkative, more eager than ever before. It was not long before she knew why. In the distance, she saw long rows of piled stones, the summerhouses they spoke of in their songs and chants.

Tiana thought everyone in the village must have turned out to

TIANA

greet the trail-weary travelers. Men and women talked all at once and shouted greetings while the children hung back with shy dark eyes, watching. Men thumped one another on the back and hugged, women wept and laughed.

Igigik and Kivisik knelt to greet their children who moved as close to their parents as they could with the bulky clothes they wore. They all touched hands to faces and nudged noses into cheeks. Tiana felt tears cloud her eyes when she saw the love and affection that centered around the little family.

Kivisik moved off to join a group of men. Tiana looked around in wide-eyed amazement. She had never seen tents made of piled stone. Sometimes her people used brush and mud to make a more permanent dwelling, but they usually preferred deerskin tents.

Tiana dressed like the other women now, but she was taller than most of the hunters and her slenderness showed even covered with furs as she was. Soon she felt overwhelmed at their obliquely courteous stares. Igigik had been laughing and rubbing faces with her children who now peeped shyly at Tiana from the safety of their mother's sturdy legs. Igigik suddenly remembered her new sister, and turned smiling to face the ring of people watching.

"My old husband, Kivisik, has become young again with the wish that he have another wife. A woman welcomes Tiana as a new sister."

Kivisik must have heard her and left the other men to walk to Tiana's side, taking her arm with possessive familiarity. "A man saw a woman who pleased him and also pleased his worthless old wife, who is good for nothing else but to tease and gossip." He put a stern look upon his face which fooled no one. Igigik giggled all the harder. He made it plain he wanted the other men to know this stranger was not open to their attentions.

For that Tiana was grateful. The men, in spite of their jokes and wild laughter, had an aggressiveness about them which bothered her. They were short, compact men, some dressed in leggings of long, white hair which she knew came from the giant white bear. Some wore sealskin. Most bared their torsos in the spring warmth. The women wore their leggings shorter, with bird-skin tunics to cover their chests.

The group began whispering excitedly. The shaman was approaching, she could feel the vibrations from his fierce presence. Tiana's heart beat so hard in her breast she thought he must be able to hear it

As if conjured up by her thoughts, he darted into the center of the crowd. It was easy to recognize him. He was the dirtiest, shaggiest, most intimidating man among them. The people stepped back in unison, to make room for him.

He leaped forward to confront the three who stood close together.

"What say you, son of the great hunter Ayaiak. Are there not worthless women enough among our own? Did you have to bring one of the *itkiyyiq* back with you?"

Tiana forgot her first thoughts of fear which were replaced by anger at his tone of mockery and the word he used for her tribe. *Those who mate with wolves* was a description her Inuit friends and family had stopped using almost from the first day she came to them.

The shaman shook his fist in the air and danced around the three. His hair stood up in spikes molded by rancid grease, the smell of which followed his body as he moved. His bottom lip was pierced by the largest labret she had ever seen, causing a grotesque smile which merged with the malice in his eyes. His torso was covered with tattoo marks, some of which had healed poorly, scarring him with barely-healed sores.

"Someone desires to call a feast for our safe return," Kivisik reminded him mildly. "There may be some hunters who have traveled far and suffered many hardships to bring back magical fox tails and hides for many jackets, and fresh meat."

For the first time the villagers seemed to notice the high-piled sleds. Some of them rushed over to throw off the coverings. Soft, sibilant exclamations of delight broke the silence as they regarded the treasures spread out now on the ground.

But Tiana knew the shaman would not to be deterred from his examination and questions for long. "Can this woman speak, or have you removed her tongue, the better to serve you?"

Kivisik laughed at the idea of Tiana not being able to speak.

Tiana turned her smile to him, knowing he was thinking she was seldom at a loss for words. He'd already teased her and mentioned that her sharp tongue even exceeded the nagging of Igigik. His look told her she was free to speak when she wished.

Before Tiana said a word, she walked back to the sled and removed the giant tusk, dragging it back and setting it in front of the shaman. She looked down on him from her superior height, keeping an expression of defiance on her face, where he had probably expected deference and submissiveness.

"I am Tiana, Woman of the Raven," she said proudly. Her clear voice carried above the murmur of the crowd.

Suddenly everyone gave up inspecting the bounty spread upon the ground. Their attention was caught by the tension which surrounded them. The villagers fell silent, even the little children, as they stared at Tiana.

"I am woodland shaman from the Raven Mother, descendent of Umiak and Oolik." She reached beneath her jacket and slipped off her belt, holding it high for everyone to see. "I wear the ancient, magical belt that only a Raven Woman may possess." She knew her speech, different from theirs, set her apart and told them all that she need not obey their edicts, nor mold to their ways if she did not wish to.

During the past sleeps, her dreams had warned her this was the only way possible to retain the power and the right to claim Nikota. If she showed her underbelly, Tiana would be slain.

"I have been given the giant tusk of the ancient *kilivaciaq* to bring to the fox clan as a gift to show the Raven Woman's influence on our lives." It had been so wise of Kivisik to advise her to present it to the people when she arrived.

"Ay yaa!" Someone behind her shouted into the shocked silence following her brave words. "This person we used to call woman-who-walks-alone saved our hunters by reaching down into the water and plucking them from Sednah's grasp!" At this statement, everyone began to speak at once.

Then another person from the band she had traveled with spoke up, not wanting to be outdone in the importance of his message. "True! He speaks the truth! What a grand battle that was! The Raven Woman against the sea goddess. We must make a song and tell of it properly so that our children will always remember it."

Iliak's shrill voice, filled with self-importance, penetrated the confusion as his wife made room for him to come to the front of the crowd. "You see before you a man who is among you today because of this woman's strong magic. Sednah had bitten off a man's feet, and began to gnaw on his legs when the Raven Woman's magic fought the sea for my worthless person." He hitched forward on the sled he had been riding on and flung off his covers with a dramatic flair. The collective intake of breath was loud as everyone stared at the stumps of his legs, the feet missing.

Tiana also was shocked. When had the black, ugly mass at the ends of his legs been removed? It was not unlikely that he cut them off himself, for the feet and lower legs had never regained feeling. She had seen brave hunters do this before, in her village, when the snow-hurt did not go away. Usually they went off alone, never again to be seen rather than be thought of as useless as a hunter.

The Inuits did not seem to regard Iliak the same way. They looked upon him with awe and envy for the role he played in the heroic battle of the two powerful forces, the Raven Woman and Sednah, the Sea Goddess.

Tiana's long earrings scratched lightly against her cheek as she swerved to face the shaman. "We need not be enemies. It is told that your people were once mine, and that I was born among the *people of the woodlands*, so the Raven Mother's line will belong to all the people of the Northlands. I came back to the *eaters of raw meat* even as the moon melts into the warmth of the sun, and then changes back to the moon again." It was then she knew why she had given birth to two babies and why her son had to be sacrificed in the process. It would have been the only way for her to bring her daughter, the future Raven Woman, back to the Inuits.

The shaman regarded her through eyebrows that grew between his eyes. He reminded her of the spiny porcupine, but there was no amusement in this thought. She held her breath, waiting. If he chose not to be impressed, if he challenged her power, she had lost. In spite of Kivisik's strong feeling for her, he would never dare go against the will of his own shaman.

The magic man had the power to make game avoid the people

until everyone died of hunger. He could make women give birth to stillborn babies. A powerful, vengeful shaman was capable of anything.

The crowd watched in silence – waiting.

Tiana clutched her Raven belt. She felt Nikota so close – only a village away. Was her quest hopeless? Would it end so soon? Was her journey to the Raven Mother only a dream?

Her questions were not answered when the shaman turned without a word and walked away.

Kivisik took hold of her hand, and she walked between him and Igigik with the children darting between their legs as they moved to her new home.

Pinkie Paranya

TIANA

 **EIGHTEEN**

TIANA'S dramatic entrance to the village of the fox people was always spoken of thereafter by the Inuit as *the day the Raven came to abide with us.* Everyone but the shaman appeared pleased that Tiana had become part of their clan.

She understood that although the shaman grudgingly accepted her gift of the tusk, impressed in spite of himself, he was wise enough to avoid making any overtly aggressive moves toward her. She knew he was not finished nor was he convinced of her powers. Someday soon they must lock horns, as the bull moose defends his position in the herd.

During the days to follow, Tiana absorbed much of the newness in her surroundings. The stone and mud huts were ugly but comfortable and warm inside. When she ventured down to the water's edge, it was hard to tell her abode from the identical ones nearby except for Kivisk's distinctive sled propped against the side. He had tied a foxtail to the front of the sled on the pulling sinews, and carved a fox totem from light driftwood and attached it to the side. She understood now about the strange gray wood they made theirs sleds from, when she saw pieces of it strewn along the shoreline.

The travelers had brought in their bounty of fox meat and skins and frozen fish. Tiana watched as they divided it up. The warm chinook winds brought spring-like weather. They had to hurry to store the meat in caches beneath stones, next to the permafrost.

The old women manipulated and chewed the cleaned and scraped hides which had been tanned with urine. Tiana observed with amazement the cooperative spirit of the community. Everyone worked together, and every scrap and morsel was shared. If a man decided he preferred to eat seal meat and his neighbor had some, he had only to mention it.

One day Tiana overheard such an exchange.

"A man who tires of fox flesh desires a taste of seal."

The one whose treasured store of seal meat was in question raised his eyebrows in exaggerated surprise. "A worthless hunter is honored that his maggot-infested meat taken from a seal well over his prime would be of interest. Please, share if you do not mind eating poor, skinny seal meat."

She thought how inconceivable this conversation would have been in her tribes. If a man dared ask another for his stored meat he would have been met by a harsh laugh and a resounding "No!" If a hunter was unable to care for himself or his family, that was his problem. Only immediate family members looked after one another.

It did not take her long to learn that honesty, humility and a desire to be exactly like everyone else were values most esteemed by these Inuit. The shaman was the only person permitted any leeway when it came to outrageous behavior. Children were not punished, other than by gentle, persistent teasing. She noticed it worked very well. No one desired to be set apart as different.

She thought of how strange the village had looked when she first came, and now how ordinary it was since she'd accepted her surroundings. Everywhere she looked she saw long rows of shelters made by waist-high river-washed stones stuck together with mud and debris lining the beachfront. From the point where the stones left off, the people used caribou, deer and musk ox hides as tenting to form walls and a ceiling. All the enclosures led into one another, and communal fireplaces lined the beach in front of the houses. The women cooked, and the people ate when they were hungry, any time of the night or day. Some, especially the men, stuffed themselves to satiety and then did not eat again for several sleeps.

Women crouched in front of their fires, poking and stirring, alike in their summer tunics of bird skin. When Tiana showed them her throwing board and they mastered it, there would be plenty of birds to eat and skins to wear.

TIANA

Tiana's hair had grown longer, but she refrained from wearing it in the fashion of other married women, pulled back and up into a firm knot that drew the hair toward the top of their heads. She decided to wear it in one long braid to show her difference. Unmarried Inuit girls wore their hair hanging loose and Tiana privately thought it unattractive. The men in her tribe had worn theirs that way when in mourning. It used to frighten her to see them with their black hair in disarray around their heads.

She corrected her thoughts. Her old tribes were in the past, and she had only one family now, and that was with Kivisik. Until she found her daughter. Then she would see.

"Kivisik, a woman wonders when you will take her to the village to see her daughter." It had been a while since Tiana had mentioned this subject. According to the gossip around the village, the beaver people had not yet returned from their journey.

Kivisik frowned his disapproval, for the first time since Tiana joined them. "It appears a woman has not enough to keep her busy and so must ask foolish questions. Did a husband not promise to take her to the village of his cousins when the time is proper?" He walked out of the house and wandered off for a day and a night alone. This upset Igigik and brought tension into the close family relationship.

Tiana struggled to hide her anger and frustration. Little Nikota would be nearly two summers in age by now. Tiana had kept track of the passing time by marks on her Raven belt and felt an urgency no longer to be denied. She must be there when the travelers arrived at their village or soon after, before the test.

When Kivisik returned, he relented. "A man will decide to make the journey soon. We must first cover an *umiak* with new skin, so that a family can arrive without embarrassment and shame. A husband has learned that the travelers of the beaver clan have just returned and rest from their journey."

Did Kivisik delay because of his natural aversion toward *maqurauq*, trouble making, or was it just normal for a hunter, since the men had been having such good luck hunting seals?

From the first day at the new village, Igigik had sent her children to follow Tiana when she went out to walk along the shore, so certain was she that her new sister couldn't find her way home again. Having the children run along with her brought other village children and made Tiana's heart soar and plummet at the same time, with the giggling happiness of the Inuit children and the worry about Nikota's fate.

"I must go alone to the water, my sister," Tiana told Igigik one morning after Kivisik and the older boy had left to fish with the men. "Our husband will not speak of making the journey to the people of the beaver. I feel so much pain and anguish about my daughter, wondering where she is. I need to speak with my spirits."

Igigik shook her head at the children who came inside and they obediently ran out again. "A man may hear and a man knows when it is proper to visit another village. If we are not welcome, it will be worse than for nothing. A husband feels much of your pain and sorrow as does his old woman, and will know when the time is right." She smiled the endearing way Tiana thought must have captured Kivisik's heart when they first met. Since it was so crowded in the little hut, she and Igigik no longer slept in Kivisik's furs, but there were times when he looked at her from across a space, and Tiana felt the bond between them which for now was sufficient.

The children came back inside and Igigik motioned for them to sit. Tiana knelt and took their little hands in hers, happy that they were no longer afraid of her. "A woman gives thanks for such beautiful children who wish to show her their village. We are not finished with looking at the special treasures you have to show me, and we will go together another time, perhaps when the sun comes up again. But I must speak with my spirits. Alone."

It was hard telling them apart, and she didn't have their names straight in her head yet so she refrained from saying them out loud. The little boy was the shyest, but the girls, who looked almost the same size and age but were not, were bolder and hugged her.

"May I help you prepare the food before I go out?" Tiana asked politely.

Igigik shook her head. Since she returned from the journey, she wore her hair in a matronly knot on top of her head. Tiana often wondered if it hurt to pull it so tightly back, but decided that might be considered a criticism. In spite of their continual teasing and

TIANA

making fun of each other, Tiana thought the Inuits extremely sensitive. She watched Igigik while she threw pieces of chopped seal into the stew. They had a small fire inside to keep them warm and a larger fireplace outdoors to cook with. She thought the people of the woodland tribes could learn from those they considered ignorant and barbaric and said the same to Igigik who smiled, her eyes showing pleasure.

Tiana left the family behind and walked along the shoreline, looking out over the frozen water. Piles of gray-white ice lay scattered over the landscape reminding Tiana of giant bird droppings. Thinking of birds, she looked up in the sky which sometimes was so blue it hurt to look upward. The birds had not returned yet, Igigik told her. On an almost sheer rock formation across from the village along the shoreline, she saw traces of nests and bird droppings which told her in the warmer months birds nested nearby and the Inuits had plenty of birds to eat.

Her eyes could not become accustomed to so much flatness and no trees. She had walked around the shore and paused to look back at the village. Smoke came out of most of the huts. Some women squatted at their outdoors fire to stir a pot. Little girls usually had that chore and they hovered around their mothers, trying to help.

Drying racks, looking like children's toys from far away, built from pieces of driftwood and tied with sinew, stood in back of every dwelling. Though she could not see all of them from where she stood, she knew each dwelling had a refuse pile behind their hut, a hole dug in the snow, where human and animal waste was left to freeze until summer when it would be buried and another hole dug.

She turned back to the empty shoreline and moved ahead, putting the fur she had wrapped around her shoulders down on a large rock that jutted out from the sea onto land. She climbed up and sat on it. The wind, usually blowing so fiercely, had calmed and the sky looked overcast, as if it might snow again soon. She took off her belt and held it against her cheek. As usual, when she thought the ivory would be cool, it felt warm and soothing against her skin.

"Raven Mother, my heart is worn away by the waiting.
What if my daughter has been tested in a ritual

Pinkie Paranya

and is now gone from me forever?
You promised I would mother a Raven Woman
but I do not wish another.
My being cries out for Nikota.
From the first time I saw her, wet with my blood
and screaming her anger at the forces
that tore her from my belly,
I knew she was the one.
And so did you."

Would she always be tormented by indecision? Should she strike off on her own to find the people of the beaver? Was her inactivity the wrong way?

The sky cleared in places momentarily and the pale, wispy sun appeared low on the horizon. A flash of colors leapt into the air in front of her and she heard the snapping of the lights.

Patience . . . patience. The time will come to you.

She cocked her head, listening. Had the whisper come from outside her head or within? Tears fell, burning hot trails down her cheeks. She bent her head, too moved by the answer to understand exactly what she'd heard. The Raven Mother had not abandoned her. Her daughter was alive; she felt it in every bone in her body. Tiana closed her eyes and when she opened them, the lights had gone, the sky had closed up again with a dark gray covering that blended with the ice horizon and everything looked different, new again.

Slowly she started back toward the village. She vowed to practice patience, feeling strongly that the Raven Mother was with her and her daughter was safe for now.

As if in answer to her thoughts, Kivisik greeted her. "When the sun comes upon us, a man wishes to take his wife hunting. The shaman spoke of it to the men when we met and said a shaman who also happens to be a woman should be permitted to hunt. No one has slain a seal in many turns of the moon."

Tiana felt excitement warm her insides, and she wanted to jump up and down for joy. It felt like more answers to the question she'd asked the Raven Mother. She wanted to learn to hunt because she had no way of knowing what the future held for her and Nikota. If

TIANA

they were alone, she would have to provide food for them as did her ancient ancestor Umiak provide for her daughter Oolik and old Grandmother.

In the morning, while the children still slept, Igigik saw them off for their hunting.

Tiana and Kivisik waited for four men to join them on the beach, and they set out to walk across the ice. The men didn't speak to her, but their looks were accepting. They carried rolled up sealskins on their backs, and she wondered why but didn't ask Kivisik for fear of embarrassing him. They walked past several *umiaks,* which Tiana knew meant woman's boat. The men had left them there, waiting for the ice to melt. Igigik had explained that it was called a woman's boat mostly because they were always the ones who navigated and paddled it, while the hunters searched for game upon the water.

Walking on the ice made Tiana very nervous and at first she almost tiptoed, much to the amusement of the hunters who sneaked looks back at her. She looked back toward the shore, such a long way back to land. If the ice broke beneath their feet what would they do? But the men didn't seem concerned and walked along normally as they would have on land. Finally Tiana had to give up wincing at every step they took and began to look ahead more.

Kivisik held up his hand to stop. At first she didn't see anything but piles of ice until he touched her shoulder and pointed toward a dark shape way out on the ice, near a point where open water lay. He handed her a sealskin and motioned for her to drape it over her head. The men did the same and now she understood why they had brought them. Following the men's lead, she bent low with the covering over her head and they crept toward the sleeping animal.

Kivisik put up his hand again, and motioned them close to whisper. "It is no seal, it is an *ayvuq,* a walrus."

The men looked at Tiana, wide smiles on their faces. What did that mean? It must be good, although it was clear they had no intention of letting her join them in the kill. Kivisik motioned for her to stay back. The hunters crouched low and began their slow movement toward the animal. Tiana watched as they moved forward step-by-step, stopping whenever the animal looked up or sniffed the air. Finally when he was close enough, Kivisik leaped out from behind his covering and plunged the lance into the dozing walrus.

Quick as the blink of an eye, the creature tried to slide into the nearby water. Another hunter let go his lance and this time the animal splashed into the water, diving toward the bottom. Each lance held an inflated seal bladder float preventing it from staying down. Several times the walrus surfaced, bellowing in anger and pain that shook the ice. Tiana felt elation and sadness at the same time. They would have plenty to eat and share with the villagers, but she wanted the animal to leave his life behind without pain and fear. It wasn't long before the walrus drowned and the hunters pulled in the lances by the attached sinew.

She ran to help them drag in the beast, and gasped when she saw the size of it. A walrus was as big as a moose!

Kivisik, as leader of the little band of hunters, took a skin container from around his waist and poured some of the contents in the mouth of the walrus and gently over its head. "We honor you, brave and foolish ayvuq, for allowing us to slay you to feed and clothe our people."

He turned to Tiana to explain. "We bring fresh water to offer him, they prefer it above all else and will tell the others that he must die so that we might live."

"You showed us the ayvuq; you brought us good luck," Kivisik said, "But a man could not allow you to approach the beast, it is too dangerous for a new hunter to help slay a walrus – even as a shaman who is also a woman." He touched his foot against the huge tusks of the dead creature which lay on the ice as if peacefully sleeping. "These creatures have slain many an experienced hunter. A husband would never chance danger to a wife, even if he lost the bounty." This last he whispered to her alone, since the men were busy kneeling over the carcass and exclaiming about their good luck.

She felt pride at his gentle caring and exulted in the food they would have to share.

"This will feed us for many full moons and provide skins for umiaks," one of the hunters exclaimed, looking up at her. They began to skin the animal. One man went back to the village for help.

When the triumphant hunters returned to the village the shaman

TIANA

proclaimed Tiana as good luck to hunters.

She did not always accompany them on their hunting expeditions, and for that she was grateful. It was cold and sometimes snowed, and they walked long ways. But she gave Kivisik one of her earrings to keep in his pack to give them luck.

Tiana privately thought their luck was not so much from her as it was in Kivisik's own prowess. She noticed the people of the fox highly respected her husband for his ability to hunt. That was the reason the shaman had sent Kivisik as leader of the group who journeyed to the woodlands for fox skins and meat.

Now, on occasion, the shaman permitted Tiana to help him when he made chants to appease the weather spirits. She also helped him make songs when the hunters brought home their kill.

The animal's head must be cut off to release its soul, otherwise the creature would be trapped forever inside its dead body, and eventually inside the Inuits who ate him. When she questioned this once, the shaman told a story.

"Once, long ago, this happened with lazy hunters who failed to perform this ritual. For one entire season of the cold, they caught no game of any kind and many children and old people died. The people even ate the soles of their boots and, finally, the bodies of the dead. This made them all a little crazy, *wittiko*. Ever after, the spirits of these unfortunates turned themselves into the ancient giant who devoured human flesh. Even now some of us have heard the giant on moonless nights, wandering along with the north wind."

The people shivered with delight mixed with fear at his story, and it sent chills up and down Tiana's arms. When she rubbed them quickly with her mittened hands, she noticed others doing the same.

Sometimes the people came to her with complaints of aches, pains and wounds. However this tribe was normally very reserved and complained little even of the most terrible accidents that befell them. Only when they feared an evil spirit was causing trouble, did they come to ask her interference. At first she thought the shaman would protest, but he seemed to be in a world of his own most of the time, off visiting Brother Moon and the bright lights in the sky which no one but him could see in the daylight.

Tiana helped Igigik and the other women prepare skins for the *umiak*. They first dried and scraped the walrus hide and then soaked the pieces again to stretch them out between heavy rocks that the men rolled onto the corners. They let the skins dry, then measured and cut and sewed the parts together with tight sinew so that water could not penetrate. It was an exacting, time-consuming work and for the most part Tiana felt grateful to keep her thoughts together. But sometimes they strayed away toward her daughter. The ache inside her breast was always there; it seemed a permanent part of her now. A hole within her that could only be filled when she saw Nikota safe and unharmed again. Nothing else mattered to her now, not Kivisik, not Igigik or the children playing around her feet at night. She feared they would be too late. Perhaps the trial had begun in spite of Kivisik's promise that it would not happen until the next full moon.

The children of Igigik did help to soothe her sadness. They were shy at first but soon became used to the new woman in their midst and their usual happy, boisterous manner came back to them. When Tiana reached to smooth back a stray lock of hair from a forehead the child responded with a wide, toothy smile, eyes almost disappearing in a round face. In spite of wanting to be happy for the little family, remorse settled about her as she wondered if this would be her family always, or if she would have to exchange them for Nikota when that chance came to her.

Finally, just as she was about to give up in despair and try to find the village of the beaver people on her own, Kivisik announced one morning that he was ready.

"A family goes to visit some cousins. Hurry now, or someone will be left behind."

Excitement filled the little enclosure, as everyone scrambled to get ready.

"A man does not leave on a journey in an *umiak* without women to do the work," Igigik laughed at the idea of them all hurrying so. "He cannot leave any of us behind."

Chastened somewhat, Kivisik sat and waited until the two women and the children were ready. They loaded gifts – pungent smelling little auks fermented in a tightly sewn skin with melted seal blubber. These they stacked on musk-ox intestines rich with half digested vegetation. A good woman always saved the delicacies for

TIANA

such an occasion by burying them under rocks where the temperature stayed just a little above freezing.

Since the beginning of her travels, Tiana had been collecting raven feathers of various sizes and shapes, from the downy under feathers to the hard top wing feathers. She had been painstakingly fashioning them into a tiny cape for Nikota which she'd finished. When Kivisik saw her putting the cape in her baggage, he frowned.

"A husband has told a woman without ears that it will not be proper to speak to the girl directly."

Tiana nodded. She had pulled her hair back into a matronly knot, in deference to her new family's custom, but she knew everything about her looked different from the Inuit females. Her skin was the same russet color, but her nose was slender, with a delicate arch. Her small breasts pushed through the thin bird-skin material, and her long waist and long legs betrayed her origin as different. She caught Kivisik watching her sometimes with a look of passionate wonder which always made her heart beat faster.

Once he told her that she did not need to appear calm and placid, like the other Inuit women. He reveled in her difference, and admitted to provoking her sometimes to watch her black eyes snap and sparkle when she grew angry. He said her expression was never one of compliant patience, but instead, impulsive eagerness. Tiana realized there were times when she knew she confused this dear, imperturbable man beyond reason. At these times he retreated out to the ice to fish or hunt alone, with only his thoughts to accompany him.

Jerked back into the present by the children shouting outside, Tiana thought of his warning words and answered him. "A woman knows and remembers your counsel," she answered. "But a mother's eyes hunger to see – her hands hurt to touch. It will be hard. You ask much of me." She understood his concern. Having lived with these people nearly two winters, she knew their ways. If a blood feud developed between the fox and the beaver clans over Nikota, nothing would end it but the last death, extending through generations to come.

It was not a price Tiana was willing to ask Kivisik to pay. Not yet. What if her daughter was content with her now-mother? What then?

While the others readied the boat, Tiana packed away the little garment and at the last minute thought of the bark vest. Maybe sometime in the journey she would give it to Kivisik for his generous spirit in taking her to see Nikota. She laid it in her pack. Rubbing her fingers along the smooth ivory belt, she sighed. It was too much to think about sometimes. Better to move ahead slowly, with care and patience, as in stalking a seal. But she didn't want to do that! She felt a singing in her heart, her step lightened, and it was such a good feeling to at last be going toward Nikota. She hurried to join them on the beach.

The trip skirting around and through the ice floes was filled with wonder for the children. They chattered shrilly like the many birds that filled the skies in the warm months.

Tiana normally would have felt the same wonder and excitement, if she had been able to concentrate on the passing scenery. She bent her back to the rowing of the boat, alongside Igigik. The heavily-laden skin boat shoved through the water lightly, easily pushing aside the smaller chunks of ice.

Kivisik stood at the prow, fending off chunks of ice with a long pole especially made for this task.

"Is it not possible to visit your cousins by land?" Tiana's back felt near to breaking from the unfamiliar strain of rowing, while Igigik blithely paddled along.

Kivisik grinned, his teeth white against the tan of his face. "Of course, but it takes longer and there is always the danger of *naanuk*. When a hunter searches for the giant bear it is one thing, but when he takes his family with him, caution is expected."

As if the name created up the form, the children began to shout. "Look! Look!" They popped up and down until Igigik had to forcibly restrain them, fearing they would go through the bottom of the boat.

They all turned to look. Tiana's heart skipped many beats as she stared at the apparition.

The largest creature she had ever seen looked down from an ice ledge in front of them. It was more immense than two grizzly bears together. Fear coursed through her body, icy chills swept up her arms and the back of her neck when she stared at the formidable beast.

TIANA

Her dreams had been of the golden bear, and she had understood that had been settled on her journey to the glacier, although she still didn't remember everything about their meeting. This creature was different, not the spirit guide she'd finally accepted.

Kivisik raised his hand for silence. The little family waited while *naanuk* decided if he should dive into the water and swim to this strange looking fish or ignore it. To his nearsighted, squinty eyes they might even appear to be a whale. He licked his long yellow teeth as if at the thought of whale meat.

Igigik motioned for the children to come close to her. She pulled them under her furs like a mother ptarmigan would nestle her chicks close in danger.

Kivisik grasped his hunting harpoon and removed his jacket, in spite of the chill wind over the water. He needed to fight unhampered and be able to reach the knife attached to his trousers.

Tiana wondered at the family's strange silence. The children of the woodlands were taught from early on to carry rattles made of small animal's knucklebones inside the dried, inflated skin of a rabbit stomach. When the women went berry picking, this was the task of the children, to make noise to frighten bears away. It didn't always work with a grizzly, but they never saw black or brown bears. Everyone knew bears respected humans and did not wish to challenge them intentionally.

They watched in stunned fascination as *naanuk* readied himself to slide into the water. Acting on sheer impulse, Tiana leaped to her feet, holding the raven belt in her hands and swung it around her head in wide circles.

"Yi yi yi! Eeeeeeah!" Tiana shrieked at the astonished animal poised with a foot already in the water. She leaped up and down, remembering not to sway the boat too severely, swinging the belt and yelling all manner of the strangest sounds her tongue could produce.

The family drew away from her, more afraid of this sudden outbreak of *wittiko* from her than the horror of being torn apart by the bear, or drowning in the icy water when he turned the boat over.

Tiana wished the family would make a commotion also, but even Kivisik sat stunned, staring at her. Their minds had been fixed on the inevitable. They knew the bear would have them. She could tell by the grim set to Kivisik's mouth and the way Igigik clutched her children close.

Not daring to lose her concentration, Tiana leaped and shrieked as she clutched her belt in one hand and Kivisik's jacket in the other and waved them in frantic desperation.

Suddenly the giant creature reared on hind legs and gave a mighty roar of challenge. That done, he ambled away as if unconcerned by the strange objects that had just made him so curious. The sight of his giant rump, hips moving up and down like two children playing in a large white fur, stunned them briefly and then they all burst into happy laughter, clutching each other, tears streaming down their cheeks.

Tiana swayed, struggling to keep her footing as the cluster of small bodies flung themselves against her. The children, their eyes no longer round and frightened, laughed and giggled, pushing to get close to her.

Kivisik recovered his dignity and stared at this woman he had so casually taken as wife. "Your magic is powerful – more powerful than the mighty *naanuk*." He put his knife back in his belt under his tunic.

Tiana shook her head in denial, wanting to tell them about how the woodland people kept most bears away, but gave up. There was no use explaining to this strong, gentle man that she only did what any child of the forest would have. He would not understand. She was different from these people and always would be. Hadn't the Raven Mother promised that Nikota was to be the bridge between the ice people and the people of the woodlands?

They pushed ahead, nibbling on dried fish and strips of smoked musk-ox when hungry, careful not to touch any of the gift food.

"My sister will be surprised when she meets Iliaauq's woman," Igigik said.

Tiana smiled and turned to look at Igigik. Sometimes she said things as if she'd been speaking of them all along. At first that had been confusing but Tiana was used to it now. "Why?" she asked, knowing Igigik wished to gossip.

"She does her husband proud, she is as large as this umiak and is very hospitable. But sometimes when a person looks into her eyes, they may see a mean spirit and angry."

TIANA

"Woman, what are you babbling about?" Kivisik said, letting her know he didn't like gossip.

"She is a stranger and should be warned," Igigik retorted mildly.

Tiana thought her sister sounded envious. "Do you wish to be as large as an umiak?" she asked.

"Of course! Every woman wishes this. It is a sign a husband is a good provider and much to be proud of."

This little woman would never reach that status then, Tiana decided. Igigik was small and round but no amount of seal blubber would ever make her fat. "You do Kivisik proud as a wife, my sister, do not fret that you are not as big as three women."

Igigik giggled and bent to push away a piece of ice, ending the conversation.

When they turned a bend in the shoreline Tiana saw the village spread out all along the beach. Pale, blue sky sucked up trailing smoke from many fires.

"Ho ho! A family comes to visit. Is everyone lazy and asleep?" Kivisik called out in a booming voice. As if by magic, children tumbled out of shelters, women ran toward the beach, and the men came also, holding their weapons prominently displayed.

Kivisik held his palms up to show empty hands. "People of the beaver, a man of the fox comes without a knife. Someone journeys to visit friends and kinsmen. Where is my cousin, the mighty hunter Iliaauq?"

A man leaped from the crowd lining the shore and waded through the icy water to pull the umiak forward. "A poor man is happy to see the face of such a superior kinsman!" Kivisik's cousin shouted, that the entire village might hear. "It has been two turnings of the warm moons since a family saw your family in the land of the forest. Our shamefully inadequate home is open to you; a useless wife will prepare a feast, with the thin, pitiful creatures a hunter was able to provide."

Igigik and Kivisik's faces broke into wide grins, their eyes almost hidden by their cheeks. The children whooped for joy and jumped from the boat, unmindful of the splashing water. It was sure to be a good visit. Iliaauq's modesty meant he had much wonderful eating to share.

Tiana felt the curious stares as she stepped off the boat beside Igigik. Then the villagers looked away, as if ashamed of their discourteous behavior in staring.

Holding her breath, Tiana struggled to quiet her thudding heart, as she looked at the children on the beach. Was one of them her daughter?

Kivisik and his cousin walked away from the boat, arms around one another's shoulders. The women were temporarily forgotten. They were supposed to unload the boat, as was proper, while Kivisik and the men entered the *karigi*, the meeting house, to catch up on all the gossip and news of the villages.

Word sped and Aalik, the woman of Iliaauq, waddled toward them, a beauty according to Inuit standards. She was almost as round as she was tall, the mark of her husband's great prowess as a provider. Her eyes were slits of black obsidian in a wealth of soft skin and fat that formed her face. She held out her arms to Igigik and they touched cheeks and noses briefly.

"This also is the wife of Kivisik? We have heard of him taking another to his sleeping furs." She giggled behind a fat hand. "He must be very wealthy to need two women to chew his boots and keep his furs warm. You must be so grateful to have someone to help you – although she does not look too strong."

"No indeed, a husband has no wealth," Igigik murmured politely, as was expected of her. "This old wife is so useless a husband had to have another to do the work properly. A young woman named Tiana has become a worthless woman's sister, although no one knows why. She is very sturdy in spite of her slenderness. Her slender body holds many secrets." Igigik needed to tantalize this woman with a teasing about Tiana's shaman status and her position as Raven Woman, but her husband had forbidden her to mention it outright.

Igigik bent and took one of the wrapped packages. "A family is so poor to only bring these few detestable gifts which heap shame upon our heads." She handed over the food wrapped in a beautifully cured sealskin.

Aalik slanted a questioning look toward Tiana but made no further comment. She helped them unload, surprisingly agile for her

TIANA

bulk. The children had disappeared to play with the others the moment the boat touched shore. As the women walked toward the center of the community, Tiana looked around.

The village was not very different from the one she now lived in. Fish dried on hangers made of driftwood pieces tied together. Several women knelt on the rocky shore to flense out a seal carcass. Piles of bones lay strewn about everywhere, thrown in the pathway and outside the huts.

"Permit a woman to show her guests our village," Aalik said politely. They moved across the bone-littered ground and dipped their heads to enter one of the structures with the stone base. In each structure, the woman of the house had hurried to get inside first to be able to greet the two women. Each time they were asked politely to sit and talk. Even if the hostess was too shy to speak more than a few words, Tiana and Igigik sat obediently and smiled.

After the third visit, Tiana's nerves were spilling out of her skin. When would she see Nikota? Maybe not for a long time if the child was with the children playing outside in the center of the camp. Sometimes the children who lived in the hut they were entering came up shyly, filled with curiosity. Tiana searched the faces of each. What did she look for? How could she know which child was her daughter? From afar, the children looked so much alike with their snapping black eyes, round cheeks, white teeth – happy children. They all wore furs with long sleeves, so she would not be able to see if Nikota wore the mark of the Raven feather.

The time dragged on. They were offered food, which often they had to eat so as to not offend the woman whose abode they visited. Each time Tiana put a bit of food on her tongue, she hoped not to choke. Her throat felt dry and parched with the waiting. How would she know Nikota if she couldn't see her eyes first?

Finally they came upon the last hut in the village.

"Welcome to the poor home of Iliaauq, the hunter of beaver," Aalik said. As their eyes adjusted to the semi-gloom indoors, Aalik spoke again.

"Someone's daughter, Suloq, greets you."

They looked down at the tiny girl child playing on the floor of strewn pelts.

Tiana's heart leaped into her throat, the pulse thudded alarmingly in her neck. She clenched her hands tight to avoid crying out as the child looked up at them with Namanet's smoke-gray eyes.

Igigik heard Tiana's indrawn breath. The older woman's brow wrinkled in a worried frown. Igigik took Tiana's arm and pulled her aside, out of the way, while she busied herself setting out the gifts of food they had brought. "You may help your old sister if you have time," she said a bit sharply, to break Tiana's glazed stare.

By now the children had tired of running up and down the beach and crowded in to watch the opening of the gifts. They giggled shyly and hovered in the doorway, well out of their mother's way. They licked their lips in anticipation of the feasting to come.

Tiana struggled to behave normally, but her gaze kept returning to the little girl. Finally she could stand it no longer. She must speak.

"My husband, your kinsman, said your small son perished on your journey to the woodlands." Everyone sucked in air loudly through their teeth at this affront to polite conversation. By now Tiana knew the Inuit considered it unforgivably rude to ask even a close friend a personal question, but of a stranger, it was never done.

The air between Tiana and Aalik seemed to bristle with animosity.

Finally Aalik smiled with stiff politeness. Her look said she was determined not to insult a guest, even a stupid one, by behaving inconsiderately. "A woman's child was lost on a journey, that is true. But the mighty beaver, who is our totem, brought us Suloq. She came to us in the night, on the back of a giant animal with a flat tail so huge he could have slain us all with one blow."

No! That is a lie! Tiana closed her eyes and put her hand over her mouth, not certain if she had said the terrible words out loud. Once spilled, they would be like blood, never to be retracted. She turned away, hands against her belt, as if to hold in the pain. She couldn't hold back any longer, she had to speak no matter the consequences. "This is my daughter, the one you call Suloq. Her name is Nikota and I have come a long way to find her. Two seasons have passed since the milk in my breasts dried. My husband stole my two — my babe from me while I lay in the birthing lodge."

"You lie!" Aalik shrieked. The little girl began to cry and crawled

TIANA

toward the woman she thought of as mother. Aalik picked her up and comforted her a moment before turning her rage on Tiana. "Leave! We do not wish liars in our presence." The mound of trembling flesh pointed toward the doorway.

Unable to bear looking at her child held so possessively by Aalik, Tiana stumbled toward the door, waving Igigik away. Children parted in front of her as she ran outside into the pale sunlight.

At the edge of the ice she knelt and splashed some cold water across her flushed face. Time blurred. The agony of losing her two babies flooded back to haunt her. Perhaps it would be best for everyone if she went away from here – alone. She had no life without Nikota, and this woman would fight to the death to keep her. What if she just lay face down in the water and let the waves lap over her body, floating her away, far away. That would cause no one harm.

A gentle, firm hand gripped her shoulder, startling her from the hypnotic stare beconing ice floating in and out with the lapping waves.

"Tiana, a man must speak with you."

She stood and faced Kivisik, expecting to be chastised and humiliated for her rudeness to Aalik. His eyes were filled only with concern for her.

"A husband has told everyone in the *karigi* about your fearlessness against the mighty *naanuk* and how you called upon the Raven to help you save the lives of our kinsmen on our journey back from the woodlands. Even so – it will not be a simple deed to take this child from my cousin and his wife."

"Take?" Her voice rose in near-hysteria. "I did not come here to take her. She is mine. She is mine!" She hit her fists against his chest, trying to make him understand.

Kivisik nodded and pulled her close to touch his cheek to hers. It was the first time he had acknowledged their affection in public. She stopped her outburst, looking in surprise at this person she called husband.

"Do not find offense in a woman's sharp tongue," she said, smiling sadly. "If they will not let me have my daughter, I must come here alone and take her away. It would not be truthful to have you think otherwise."

255

"They will regard you as an intruder. You would be slain," he stated matter-of-factly.

"My life is of no importance if I do not have Nikota. She is the Raven line and must be given the belt and taught the legends. Otherwise the line will perish with me." Somehow it had come to her she would have no other births.

His eyes told her he understood, but was unsure of how to comfort her.

"Did Kivisik hear of another child? A baby brought to your kinsmen the same time as Nikota?" She must speak of the boy now. She had to know what became of him.

He looked surprised that she should know of a second child. "It is said that when the giant beaver brought Suloq, or Nikota as you call her, he also brought a male child. The little one's spirit was already gone. My kinsmen laid him out in the snow with many gifts and chants to take with him on his journey."

Kivisik stepped back in alarm at her cry of pain.

Tiana remembered her dream – of huddling weeping over a small bundle lying on a cold snow-bed. But at least he had not made the journey alone, for Kivisik said the Inuit mourned him and sang over his tiny body. She sank down on a large stone, not feeling its round, smooth coldness through her doeskin shift.

"My husband, these two babies were mine, of my body. The ones Namanet, my husband, took from me while I was yet in the birthing lodge. I did not speak of them before because I feared you would think two babies would summon bad spirits."

He shook his head. "What manner of ignorance do you speak, woman?"

It sounded to Tiana as if his patience was wearing thin. All this talk must be tiresome, and he wanted to be done with it.

"You did not tell us of another babe when we found you in the snow."

She pulled him down to sit beside her. "I am Raven Woman, do you forget so easily? This signifies that I may do things differently from other women. I gave life to more than Nikota. There was a son born at the same time. One boy and one girl child." She waited, wondering what his next words would be.

TIANA

Surely these Inuit must feel the same way about twins, harbingers of affliction and disaster. Now he would turn her away, no longer wanting her as his wife.

His wide grin startled Tiana.

"You are like us, you never lie. Therefore what you say to me is true. We must tell my kinsmen. The Inuit regard two little ones born at the same time with great joy. They signify bountiful hunting seasons – the promise that no babies or old people have to be put out on the ice for lack of food." His expression turned grim. "This may make it even harder to lay claim to your daughter. The people of the beaver will want to keep her to insure good hunting."

Kivisik pulled her to her feet. "A husband will ask his cousin to call a meeting. The shaman, Auqauq, will be there," he warned. "He is unpredictable when angry, and is greatly feared and respected in all our villages. His reputation has spread as far as the tundra. The shaman in our village is not to be compared with Auqauq's ferocity when opposed."

She sighed. Always the shaman. But there was no turning back.

Pinkie Paranya

TIANA

 **NINETEEN**

WHEN Tiana, along with Kivisik and his family, arrived at the *karigi*, it was packed with Inuit. The air was stuffy and close. With shoulder touching shoulder, there was hardly space to move. Children played beneath the adult's feet, everywhere.

Kivisik pushed a way through and into the center of the large structure, where he found a little space to move and motioned to Tiana and Igigik. They stood waiting, along with the other people of the beaver clan.

Suddenly a shriek emanated from the ceiling as a wild-eyed shaman made a dramatic entrance. It seemed as if he had dropped down from the sky. A handful of men who had been outside saw Auqauq throw himself forward from a long pole, vault upward and through the skylight in the tent top. This did nothing to diminish the grandness of his tactic, that of intimidation.

Tiana had to admit it was a very effective strategy. The shaman from her first village of her birth parents was kindly and strict but not strange. In her second village with Kania and Namanet, the shaman had been cruel and savage, but also old and beyond tricks and much magic. The shaman from Kivisik's clan which was now hers also seemed as ordinary as anyone else in their village except for the fox tail he wore around his waist and the skinned and dried head of the fox that he wore on top of his own head for special occasions. Auqauq, the shaman of the beaver people, seemed to personify all the shamans she had met with his eccentric and strange behavior. Did shaman need to go to elaborate measures to insure the people listened to them, she wondered.

From the first, Raven Mother had let her know that this was not the essence of becoming a true shaman. Tiana wanted to be a person who had been given mystical, magical powers to heal and perform wonderful miracles for the benefit of others. So far, this had worked well enough for her.

After a brief explosion of cries and talking, the noise subsided into furtive whispers. All stares focused on Auqauq in the center of the floor. The children sat subdued, close to their parents.

Tiana watched as the shaman strutted around in his astonishing garb of beaver pelts sewn together with the tails attached. The tails dangling around his thighs had no hair and were a darker color than the surrounding fur. He wore a necklace of long, curved yellow beaver teeth which clashed together as he moved in jerky spasms. The back webbed claws of the animal encircled the drum he carried. Auqauq's coarse, bushy hair was greased until it spiked in many directions, with little carved ivory beavers tied to each spike. His ears were pierced with labrets of ivory similar to those of Kivisik's group who wore them in their bottom lips. Long, black beaver claws clicked against his waist as he moved.

When Tiana saw the family of Kivisik's cousin surge forward, she caught her breath, hardly daring to swallow through her dry throat. The woman pushed Nikota ahead of her, while the husband swaggered with head-high arrogance.

He and Kivisik did not look at one another, and Tiana felt a jolt of sorrow for the trouble she caused. Kivisik had warned her this would happen, but she could no more stop her actions than try to stop the North wind from blowing. Her heart went out to her daughter. She closed her eyes, concentrating on thoughts of peace and tranquility that she wanted to go to the little girl standing so forlorn in the midst of the crowd of people. *Be brave, my daughter, the next Raven Woman. Be full of spirit and strong for you have me and the Raven Mother on your side.*

Tiana opened her eyes and saw the child they called Suloq turn fully toward her. Their eyes met and held for a long moment. It was as if the girl understood, for she lifted her chin and straightened her back before turning away. Such a tiny child, Tiana longed to hold and comfort her, but she dared not look at her overlong again or they might accuse her of placing a spell on her.

TIANA

Auqauq began speaking and the whispers ceased. "A question has been put forth among us, by our kinsmen, brother of the fox. A shaman wishes the family of Iliaauq to come forward with their daughter." He spoke the words 'their daughter' with defiant emphasis, slanting a look at Tiana from beneath his thick brows.

The couple pulled the little girl along, moving into the center. They stood self-consciously waiting for the shaman's next command. He held up his hand for quiet, although it was unnecessary. Everyone had subsided into subdued silence.

"There is a person among us, a stranger, who claims to know a child of the beaver." He motioned for Aalik and her husband to come closer with the child. Both pushed the little girl forward with obvious hesitation. A shaman was capable of working in unexpectedly outrageous ways and they were wary, but obedient.

Auqauq took Suloq's hand and signaled for Aalik to move away. He bent and picked up the child, scrutinizing her carefully as he ran his hand with long, dirt-packed nails across the tiny face.

Tiana felt pride that the little one barely flinched, but gazed back unperturbed by his closeness.

He put the child down and curled his fingers for Tiana to come forward.

Kivisik made a move to come with her but the shaman shook his head.

Tiana touched her belt one last time for support and walked across the floor to stand near Auqauq and the girl. Her heart felt near to bursting as she looked down upon her daughter, Nikota, flesh of her flesh, bone of her bones. It felt so good to be this close, almost touching her.

Ignoring everyone, Tiana knelt in front of the child, searching her face with greedy eyes, as if she could never have enough of looking at her. Wolf-gray eyes stared back into hers, unflinching.

"Rise, woman of Kivisik. Tell everyone here what is in your heart. Those who lie often find themselves without speech."

Swallowing through a throat suddenly gone dry, Tiana knew what his threat meant. Igigik showed her a young girl back in their village who had been known for her lies and gossiping tongue. When her father had his fill of it, he cut her mouth open from ear to ear so that now the scar drew her lower face up into a perpetual hideous grin.

Tiana shivered inside, but steadied herself. She did not lie.

She closed her eyes a moment, calling upon her Raven spirits to give her the proper words to say. She began by telling of the birth of two instead of one.

At this juncture, the crowd started talking excitedly among themselves, and Tiana felt a more favorable attitude surrounding her. Strange how this revelation would have doomed her cause forever with her woodland clan.

The shaman held up his hand for silence, and the people obeyed.

"In my clan – in the woodland tribe I belonged to when I gave birth – people looked upon the birth of two babies as unlucky, even harmful. My husband asked me to choose between the babes, and I had to choose the female. He wanted his son and in anger, took both of my children away while I lay helpless in the birthing lodge. I am shaman, that is true, but everyone knows that while a woman is birthing, the shaman part of her must be suspended so that the powers will not be harmed."

"Ayii!" The people spoke in one exhalation of breath.

"Are we to believe a tribe, even a woodland tribe, could be so barbaric?" The shaman spoke. "We know two babies born at the same time are special. It is very rare, and it is said when they are born they are small enough to drink from the skulls of chickadees. Many time they do not stay long on this land before they return to the spirits. Does this not signify their magical qualities?" Auqauq turned to the crowd. "What fools this stranger imagines us to be – to believe her people's thoughts could twist so?"

Tiana held her breath and waited for a wave of excited chattering to abate. "I cannot hate my husband for this terrible thing he did. Our village was near to starvation, and two new mouths to feed was too much."

At this, most of the people nodded in agreement, for they might have felt the same, except that these were sacred twins.

Tiana whipped off her belt, holding it high for everyone to see the carvings. "I am a descendant of the Raven Women. My beginnings are here on the ice. Each of you has heard the legend of

TIANA

the Raven Women many times – of Umiak and her daughter, Oolik and those who followed over time. The destiny of my daughter is to live with the Inuit – to complete the circle between the clans of the woodland and those of the ice land. I did not come here to take her away from the Inuit, but she does not belong to this village, to this family who have cared so lovingly for her. You must not interfere with the Raven Mother's wishes."

Tiana knew the stories had already circulated over and over about her deeds, and that her ancestors came originally from the land of the ice. Yet the people hung on her every word as if it were the first time any of them had ever heard it.

"If this is true, why are you here? The girl is now of the Inuit. With the coming full moon we will conduct the test to prove it. Leave us alone." The shaman spoke loudly, gesturing with expansive movements of his body and hands to regain his control over the emotions of the spectators.

"No! Nikota is blood of my blood and must come with me – to be taught by me – so that she learns of her origins and can become a shaman. This is her destiny. If you defy the will of the Raven, the spirits will punish every one of you!" Tiana looked over the crowd and then subsided, breathless and spent.

The people broke from their restraint of silence, and the excited talking seemed to swell the sides of the tent.

Auqauq looked pensive, deep in thought.

Aalik, the woman of Iliaauq cried and wrung her hands while her husband stared at the floor in sullen resentment.

Tiana felt such pity for these two who had cared for her daughter as if she were their own. She longed to offer comfort in their torment, but dared not show any weakness at this crucial time.

But the shaman was not yet finished with her.

"Kivisik, your husband and our kinsman from the fox people, has told us of your powers. He brought us stories of your long journey. He told us how you encountered Tulunixiraq in the forbidden glacier and brought a magnificent tusk as a gift to the shaman of his village. He told how you invoked the Raven to battle with the sea goddess, Sednah, to save the lives of two men and a valuable sled full of precious fox spirits. He told us of your confrontation with naanuk, and that your Raven power defeated the dominion of the bear." The shaman ran his hand through his spiky hair, careful not to dislodge the ivory trinkets.

Tiana wrinkled her nose and tried not to be reminded of Ikgat, her old enemy. Perhaps these two were brothers in spirit and journeyed through the sky to be here, inside Auqauq. She shook the idea away as being too frightening.

"Now that we know of your great powers . . ." his voice underlined with heavy sarcasm made the people draw in their breaths, ". . . what is it you want of us?"

Tiana could understand that never in the memory of the oldest person in the village had there ever been a battle between shamans. The idea had to be both ominous and exciting to them. She looked down at Nikota who had never taken her wide-eyed gaze from Tiana's face. "A shaman who is also a mother has made a long, hazardous journey to find her daughter. More than that, this girl is not an ordinary person. It is foretold that she will also be shaman. She has a destiny to fulfill, and we must be together."

A cry of pain issued from the Aalik, but she did not move. Obedience and fear of the shaman were too strong.

Auqauq looked from Tiana to the girl. "How do we know this is not one of the Raven's perverse tricks? He is well known for jokes played on the Inuit. How do we know this child was first yours?"

"Look at her eyes!" Tiana exclaimed. "They are the color of smoke rising from the mountains, the color of the underside of a Raven's wing. Do you not find this strange? My husband has eyes the same color, and the men of the beaver must remember this."

Auqauq picked up the child and peered closely into her face. He turned to stare with malice at the hapless parents.

"Where is the woman who suckled this one?"

Iliaauq stepped forward dragging his wife. "My worthless wife did this, only thinking to save an innocent life. It is true, she did not enter the birthing lodge for the baby. We thought it a gift from the spirits, since we had just lost our only son on the trail. Someone was certain he saw a giant beaver bring her to our camp during the night."

Aalik was far too intimidated to speak out in her own defense. She trembled as the shaman glared at her from narrowed eyes.

TIANA

Tiana's voice remained calm and steady, in spite of her inner turmoil. "The giant beaver you speak of did not bring my daughter. My husband, with eyes the same as hers, gave away my children." Tiana reached to pull back the sleeve of the girl and held her arm for all to see. "The mark of the Raven is on her arm."

She was saving this disclosure for last, hoping the mark had not faded away. She noticed Aalik had wrapped the girl's arms up to the elbow in bird skin. She had probably never let anyone outside the family know about the strange mark. It was hard not to feel a twist of compassion for Aalik as the woman emitted a pitiful little gasp.

"There is no need to look." Aalik rushed to stand in front of the child she called Suloq. "This strange shaman speaks the truth. The mark is there, and her eyes are like smoke, anyone can see."

"Then how came the girl to be with you and Iliaauq?" Auqauq looked at her under his fierce, puckered brows.

This time Aalik did not flinch away. "The *itkiyyiq*, the woodland man who gave the babies to us said two women in his village died giving birth. He told us a pitiful story of starvation and how his village elders commanded he get rid of the babies. One – the little boy – was weak and puny, already near death. He died before the next sunrise."

Tiana put her hand to her cheek and with all her might, held back tears. So this was how Namanet gave away her children. It was as if she were back there on the snow trail so long ago, inside Namanet's thoughts. She knew the agony of his rage mixed with sorrow for what he felt he had to do. Tiana knew that he was not an uncaring, spiteful person. She sent a small song of thankfulness toward his spirit for trying to save the children, not leaving them in the snow to die.

"She speaks the truth. I see it in a vision as it happened." Tiana spoke, her voice strong and clear.

Auqauq looked from Tiana back to Aalik. "A decision must be made here. A séance is called for. Calm yourselves, and be still while I prepare."

The assemblage murmured with excitement. Everyone but the participants enjoyed the drama, knowing they were now a part of a legend that they would pass in story to their children's children.

Tiana began to worry anew. This shaman had not given up yet. He played with her as a fox teases a lemming before he pounces and devours it. It was not the first time the thought came to her that Auqauq should have been born into Kivisik's fox totem rather than that of the docile beaver.

Some of Auqauq's helpers went outside and put skins over the openings covered with walrus intestines that let in light. A somber murkiness crept into the area. Only the burning fire in the center gave off light. The sour smell of sweating bodies packed closely together combined with the sharp odor of burning pitch. The people stopped whispering. Even the babies did not fret, but stayed still in their wrappings.

The shaman's helpers carefully placed the green wood just so; a fire was not wanted, but clouds of smoke.

Tiana waited. When Auqauq finished his magic, it would be her turn.

"Ayya ya ya, ayya ya ya," Auqauq began his chant, beating on the flat, round drum between his legs.

Tiana had not thought to bring her drum, a serious handicap. Behind her, Igigik made a hissing sound. When Tiana turned, Igigik's round face split with a broad smile as she handed Tiana her drum. Her new sister had remembered to pack it, thinking it might be needed.

Love and gratitude for this family swelled within her and gave Tiana the strength needed to overcome her apprehension. What magic had she to use against this determined, aggressive shaman?

She stared at her meager pack of possessions beside Igigik. Was there anything there she could use to make a serious impression upon the people and Auqauq?

The monotonous, steady chants continued as the drumbeat maintained a steady cadence. The space around them seemed to grow smaller and the shaman larger as he stood in the center, alone. Soon the spectators seated on the floor began to sway gently from side to side, shoulders touching – in time to the steady beat of the drum.

The enclosure grew hotter, making it hard to take a full breath. Only a small aperture in the ceiling permitted any of the stale, overused air to escape.

TIANA

Abruptly Tiana's wandering thoughts jerked to attention as the shaman leaped into the center of the fire pit filled with smoke and out again. His head swung loose on his neck, around and around, reminding her of a snow goose once, which had its throat slit and yet its spirit refused to leave the body for a long time.

The beaver pelt covering his shoulders shifted and moved on his back, as if it had a life of its own. Every miniature carved beaver on his head danced maniacally, in individual abandon. He jumped in and out of the billowing smoke and then fell to the ground and began rolling, obviously wrestling with a powerful enemy spirit.

The people watched in rapt fascination as he rolled in and out of the fire pit, seeming not to notice any discomfort. He suddenly leaped to his feet. A deep voice rose from somewhere behind the gathering, near the shadowy rear of the tent.

"People of the beaver, a stranger comes who wishes to steal what belongs to you," the voice intoned with slow solemnity.

"A worthless girl is of no value. What care we?" the shaman answered in his own thin voice.

"A magic beaver delivered her to your people. Thus she must be of some importance," the deep, sonorous voice insisted.

The drumbeat continued. The shaman did not speak for a brief period, as if listening to voices only he could hear. He gnashed his teeth, the sound causing hair to rise on Tiana's arms. Before the ceremony began she made certain to hide a sharp stone in her palm. When she pressed this stone into her hand, she did not fall into a stupor as did the others in the tent – an old trick taught to her by the beloved shaman of her first parents.

Below Tiana's level of concentration, she felt heartsick, as if Nikota were already lost. Never in her experience with shaman had she ever crossed such a formidable opponent. The trifling magic of Ikgat was childlike and silly compared with the overwhelming presence of Auqauq.

She never was certain where the idea came to her of how she might best him. She cautiously reached for her pack so as not to disturb Kivisik and Igigik.

When the shaman finished his drumming and collapsed dramatically in a crumpled, exhausted heap, the smoke disappeared and the fire pit extinguished itself. Nearby people began to stir and waken from their trance. They sent challenging looks in Tiana's direction – polite, yet insistent questioning.

Tiana decided it was time. She walked to the center to stand next to the shaman.

"People of the great beaver spirit. I have come to you with palms open, carrying no weapon," Tiana began. She stood before them, already at a disadvantage for lack of the elements of shock – the frenetic outrageousness that male shaman regarded as important. She moved her fingers on her drum, to begin the monotonous resonance she needed. She swung her gaze slowly around the spectators, not missing a man, woman or child. They all must be brought under her spell if her magic was to work.

Judging her timing, Tiana began to sway her body and head, from side to side. When the crowd started to move along with her as one unit, she knew they were ready.

O Tulunixiraq . . . a woman of the Raven beseeches you. Come forth permitting these strangers to hear your voice and heed your words. In the cave of the glacier . . . in the spirits of your children Umiak and Oolik. and the others who followed through the mists of time . . . in the heart of Nikvik who rode to the woodlands on the backs of two giant Ravens . . . wherever you dwell . . . come to me.

Tiana waited, hardly breathing, playing slowly on the drum. Perhaps the Raven Mother would not come. Perhaps she had committed a grave offense to ask her to appear before others.

Time crept slowly by. Now and again someone coughed, a child whimpered restlessly, but Tiana sensed they were still with her, bound to her spirit until she or time released them.

The fire erupted again and then died away. From the faint, clogging wisps of smoke which rose to the roof, a form appeared in the center. It hovered halfway between the ceiling and the ground. Tiana could see it was the woman clad in a russet colored cloak. The long hairs of the garment glinted in the light from the glowing coals. Her hair, secured by an intricate headband of woven Raven feathers, was nearly the shade of her furs.

Tiana continued to touch on the drum, her own heartbeats matching each beat. She felt if the drum stopped, so would her heart.

TIANA

Beads of sweat covered her forehead. Her fingers on the taut drum skin seemed to barely touch, they flew so fast to match the blood thrumming through her body.

Woman of the Raven – you rightly called me from my resting place. These Inuit who will be part of your daughter's heritage, need to know of me. They need to remember Raven Women before you – Umiak and Oolik and the others and of their passage into the spirit world. The knowledge will serve as your source of courage for what you must do.

Tiana forgot the onlookers as her eyes turned inward and time lost all meaning.

Pinkie Paranya

TIANA

 **TWENTY**

TIANA'S fingers and the heel of her hand continued to make steady contact with the drum without conscious effort.

An icy blast of fresh air had entered with the Raven Mother. Tiana could see the light wind, with a pale hint of green, visibly hovering over – dancing playfully in and around the people, teasing and taunting. She had seen this green mist in the place of the glacier where she found Tulunixiraq.

The Raven Mother's voice came from the whirling center of the mist. You searched for me in my sacred burial ground, the sermersiraq. It was your passion for living that woke me from my endless sleep. You are filled with an intensity of feeling, of unselfish love. I knew it was time for the Raven to live again.

The voice of Tulunixiraq was rich and full, carrying to the very edges of the tent, yet she seemed to be speaking only to Tiana.

The belt you wear is not of this world. It protects your spirit in the afterlife, so that your thoughts, your deeds will never die. You live forever in the soul of your daughter and she lives in the coming Raven Women.

"The legend tells of Umiak's sacrifice so that her daughter might survive and return to the people," Tiana ventured, needing to be a part of the interchange.

The legend is true. Umiak came from the woodland to the ice people. Her daughter Oolik in turn found the people she searched for. She and her daughter had a long life, filled with contentment. After them there were many other Raven Women, some who are lost in time and will only be counted through their carvings on the belt. Nikvik, the one who brought the belt to your clan, was destined to begin the blending of the blood with the woodland people again. Your daughter Nikota brings the circle full around, back to the people of the ice. It must be a never-ending circle uniting the women of the Northland.

Tiana could not speak. The magnificent apparition of the Raven Mother filled her eyes and ears, giving her a sense of serenity she had never known. Her eyes closed, and she saw visions of a future, some of which were only hinted at when she found Tulunixiraq in the glacier.

She saw a shoreline with small, round subterranean houses made of rock. Russet-skinned, compact people dressed in furs gazed across an expanse of ice-choked water at a distant shore. What Tiana saw on the other side caused her to gasp with disbelief.

A structure of imposing proportions loomed on the horizon. Smaller buildings lay scattered around close with tame, deer-like animals emerging from them. The valley on that side of the water was green and lush, with no snow. The earth was scratched bare in places with shoots of new plants emerging from the dark brown soil.

Men walked on the land, men of giant stature with fiery hair growing on their faces.

Another vision came on the fringes of the first. Huge vessels, higher than the forest trees, cut through the seas, their prows curved and graceful with strange, beautiful carvings. A tall, full-bodied woman stood proudly, gazing out over the water. Her long thick braids, the color of fox fur, caught fire in the pale arctic sun, as did the shiny-bright weapon in her hand. The ends of her braids which lay across her breasts were tied with Raven feathers.

The vision changed as the valley disappeared. More ships of a different kind sailed into her vision. These vessels traveled in pairs, stopping only when the men saw huge fish swimming the seas, with great gushes of water spurting from their heads. A dark-haired girl – small, with a regal beauty – stood in the midst of scurrying men as she directed their movements. Her demeanor was proud and imperious. The Raven belt wrapped around her slender waist, and she wore the Raven headband.

This sight barely disintegrated before another assailed her senses. A woman ran behind a strange sled tied to animals resembling wolves. As she turned to look back over her shoulder, Tiana saw men following behind, men with faces the color of snow. There was the sense of the woman leading them across the treacherous ice on an

TIANA

important journey.

"I am afraid to see more," Tiana protested. Her mind overflowed with the strange visions, she could comprehend no more.

There is no need. What you envision is the future of the Raven Women. I showed you a portion of it before and it is beyond your understanding, in a time and place you could not imagine. But know this. You and your daughter are a vital part of this future. You must win her back to us. Without her, none of this will come to pass.

Tiana remained silent, thinking of the miracle she just witnessed. Finally she spoke. "Do the people here see you as I do? That would help my cause." Her fingers trembled and faltered on the drum when the Raven Mother shook her head.

No, my daughter. No one sees me but you. In their hearts they hear my words and know that I come to you, but they cannot see me.

"Then what magic have I to win Nikota?"

The figure of the Raven Mother did not move, but Tiana felt a firm, gentle pressure on her shoulder.

I think you already know the answer. Trust your instincts. The answer comes from within you. The spirits of Umiak and all the others are nearby, waiting. We will take pride in your decision.

The haze surrounding Tulunixiraq gradually changed from pale green back to ordinary smoke as she began to fade.

"Oh, wait! Please do not go! When will you come back?" Tiana cried out. The belt oozed warmth into her skin as if a farewell had been given.

Suddenly the Raven Mother was no more.

Tiana's neck drooped as her body relaxed into a deep, dreamless sleep. She awakened abruptly at the same time the sound of people talking began. A glance toward Nikota insured her that the child was still there and not a dream also.

She drew in a gulp of air to quiet the pounding of her heart. The little girl held a handful of feathers clutched in her tiny hand. Tiana put her fingers up to her ear and felt one of her earrings was gone. Those close by noticed immediately and gasped.

Tiana rose to her feet. She must speak, to gain control of their thoughts. "People of the beaver, you have listened to Tulunixiraq, the Raven Mother. As my helping spirit, she commands me to claim my

273

daughter without bad blood between the beaver and the fox."

"Paugh!" The shaman had fully recovered from his trance, and the glob of spit he let fly landed on the hard-packed earth between her boots.

Tiana's cheeks burned at the deliberate insult; her back stiffened as she glared at his ugly face. "I will show you my powers. When you witness how the Raven helps me, you will have to let my daughter come with me." She turned to Kivisik who stood nearby.

"Husband, a woman needs your help. Bring your bow and arrow and place yourself in front of me." Kivisik did as she bid, reluctance plain in his actions. She wished there had been time to prepare him for this idea. What if it did not work?

While the people slept she had slipped on the tightly-woven bark vest. It lay next to her skin, hidden by her light jacket of rabbit fur. She had never actually seen the vest prevent arrows from killing; there were only the stories told by Namanet and the other hunters who returned after a battle with hostile tribes.

Perhaps it was a magical garment made only to protect warriors, or perhaps it was nothing more than flimsy bits of worthless wood she had woven together to sustain a brave's courage.

Something else nagged at her thoughts. How far back should Kivisik stand and would his aim be true? She flashed a look at the shaman and then turned her gaze to her daughter, still playing with the Raven feathers.

"My husband will shoot his arrow into my breast. In so doing, he appeases your spirit of anger, your desire for revenge. After this I will come to life again and rightfully claim my daughter and in the future there will be no bad blood between the beaver and the fox clans."

At her bold words, Auqauq looked smug. The crowd gasped its disbelief. The shaman demanded to examine Kivisik's arrow and looked even more triumphant as he finished.

Igigik cried out in protest. Kivisik frowned, stamping his feet in the gesture she now knew was the Inuit way of refusal. He moved his mouth as if he found the words impossible to speak.

Tiana looked into his eyes, begging him to believe in her. "You must trust me, husband. I will not permit myself to die by your

TIANA

hands." Would she die? She thought of how terrible for Kivisik if that happened. He cared more for her than a man was supposed to care for a woman, and well she knew it. He had rescued her twice from certain death and defied the shaman for her. He had accepted and gloried in her strangeness although knowing it would upset their lives when they returned to their village. He was a good man and would be devastated if the bark vest did not work and he killed her. But she couldn't go back now. It was too late to try anything else to save her child.

She stepped closer. A sixth sense warned her that the farther away he stood, the more power his arrow would have. "Kivisik, look at me." She balled up her fist and hit the middle of her chest where the bark felt the tightest. "Make your arrow strike true, just here."

His eyes pleaded with her not to do this foolish thing. Unflinchingly, Tiana returned his gaze until he sighed and raised the bow to his shoulder.

The tent was filled with complete silence. As if all the people held their breath.

Tiana closed her eyes, bracing her body for the impact. The sinew twanged loudly in the silence. The arrow whistled toward her, and she had a hard time not to duck or flinch. The stone point struck, leaving her breathless as she plummeted backward, her feet rising off the ground. Lights of the borealis exploded in her head.

Certain her life was over, she felt blood trickle down between her breasts.

"Woman! What has a husband done to you?" Kivisik ran to lift her in his arms, holding her close in a crushing grip. With a hard wrench, he pulled the arrow out and bent his head to the site of the injury. In the background she heard Igigik sobbing and the voices of people.

Tiana struggled in his arms. The shock of her unexpected movement sent him reeling back, stumbling against the crowd that had pushed forward to see.

Dizzy, chest hurting so that it was painful to breathe, Tiana rose unsteadily to her feet, striving for normalcy. She took the arrow from Kivisik in her clenched fist and looked at the trembling shaman. His eyes were wild with surprise and awe. He struggled to speak, but no words came.

"Does a Raven Woman lie? Is my spirit indeed powerful?" She stared into the stunned, disbelieving eyes of Auqauq. His expression made her want to shout for joy, but she kept her voice steady.

"I have journeyed to the land you call *tununirn*, the place where your wiivaksaat dwell." She heard the indrawn breaths of everyone, and the shaman's eyes widened. Knowing that they feared the wiivaksaat, or dead people who come around again gave her the surprise edge she needed. "I hereby claim my daughter – the future Raven Woman."

The shaman recovered enough to motion for Aalik and the girl. Reluctantly, the woman took Nikota's hand and pulled her forward.

Tiana reached out and touched a hand gently to Aalik's cheek. "This is a time of great sorrow for you and your husband, but a shaman who is also a mother has looked into your future. I promise you will bear another son, blood of your blood."

She spoke the truth, for it came to her that Aalik would indeed bear another child – the son they truly wanted.

"Thank you for caring for the child you called Suloq – for saving her life and keeping her well. I need not ask my family, I know they wish it too. You will always be welcome to come to our tribe, to see her any time you wish."

Tiana was moved to tears when Aalik knelt, taking the little girl's hand and reaching for Tiana's, holding them together tightly before bringing them up to her tear-stained cheek. When she stood, Tiana knelt by Nikota and gazed into her face. The little girl did not want to part with the one she knew as her mother, but this would change in time. Her daughter had spirit and wisdom beyond her years, it shone from behind her wide, gray eyes and in her expression.

"I have a song for you, my daughter. One you will pass on to your daughter and hers. A healing song." Tiana turned to face the people, absorbing the impact of the sea of black eyes staring at her in rapt attention.

"Each of us has within a little bird-spirit
to fly free.
Some of us have a hole

TIANA

*in the heart of our little bird-spirit
so we cannot soar and flap our wings.
The hole in our heart is an opening to
call in bad thoughts of anger and fear.*

*Sometimes our beaks get hurt or broken
and it is hard to
make a sound out loud
so we grow silent and still —
forgetting how to sing.
Often we live with broken beaks, only knowing
how to peck so that we hurt ourselves and others.*

*We must learn to heal our little bird spirits —
to heal our beaks and hearts by sitting in the
moonlight and soaking up the soft, warm essence —
by trusting enough to let a healing power come
close and touch our little bird spirit
to bring us comfort, courage, and peace.*

*When we close the hole in our heart and make
it well, fill the emptiness with joy and harmony,
we learn to fly again."*

Tiana extended her hand toward her daughter. With only a moment's hesitation, the little girl took hold of her hand. Tiana turned to the waiting Kivisik and Igigik. "Come. You are my people now. We are a family. It is time to go home."

Pinkie Paranya

TIANA

TWENTY-ONE

HIDDEN away in the empty abode offered to them during their visit, Igigik helped Tiana slip from her outer furs to check what she must have thought a terrible wound. Kivisik stood helpless, watching. When it came to the bark vest, Tiana enjoyed their identical looks of amazement before holding Igigik's hand to her cheek. "My husband and sister, I could not have warned you because I did not know until the last what I had to do. And heart of my heart," she took Kivisik's hand, "it was a test of faith from you and for your pain I am heartily sorry."

She let go of their hands and shrugged carefully out of the tight fitting vest, handing it to Kivisik. Her blood was still in the middle of the vest where his arrow struck, and when she bared her breasts, between them a large bruise already formed. They both reached to touch it gently, as if they could make it go away.

"Do not trouble yourselves. It will heal as is my heart healing now with my daughter nearby."

Igigik helped her into her bird-skin vest and wrapped her in furs again. "The bark vest is yours, my husband. I hope it serves you well." She took pleasure in the look of excitement lighting his eyes.

When they went outside, Tiana thought she would never tire of feasting her eyes on Nikota playing nearby, with Igigik's children. Her heart swelled to near bursting when she beheld her family around her and the people of the beaver bringing them gifts and food to take back to their village.

Kivisik's cousin, recovered from losing what he'd thought of as his daughter, seemed delighted by the frenzy of attention paid to him and his wife and begged Kivisik to stay longer.

"Husband, if it is well with you, I am weary and think we should go home. I want to take Nikota away before there is a change of heart or we wound your cousins more with seeing her here."

Igigik spoke, nodding her head in agreement. "Yes, it is time we leave. The children are weary from new sights and sounds, and we should return to our people who await us with questions."

After the beaver tribe loaded them down with food gifts for their village, amid hugs, nose rubbings and shouts of farewells, Tiana watched the people on the shore become smaller and smaller as they poled the umiak away. The older boy manfully took a pole to help his mother, since Tiana could barely raise her arm now with the pain radiating out from her chest.

She enjoyed the trip back, with naanuk not in sight and the ice melting more so there was not so much work to dodge the floes. She rested and dozed and watched the children. At first Nikota seemed afraid, especially when she saw the figures on the beach diminishing in size as they pulled away from the village of the beaver. Tiana and Igigik held her hands, and Tiana murmured her name over and over to her, telling her how much she would be loved in her new home. After a little time had passed, the child adjusted to her new fate as a typical Inuit would have done and began playing a game of little carved pegs with the other children.

Tiana took off her belt and felt the squares beneath her fingers; she'd memorized each carving. When it came to the ivory square that would be hers, she paused and let her mind wander back to her beginnings and all the changes she'd been through. She would carve a portion of a glacier as a remembrance where she saw the Raven Mother, a giant sun-touched bear, her spirit guide, would be there and in the sky, a raven in flight.

Her daughter looked up from playing just then and their eyes met. Tiana felt understanding beyond her years come from Nikota, the next Raven Woman who would be the bridge between the people of the ice and the people of the woodland. From their blood, the Raven Woman line would continue forever.

THE RAVEN WOMEN ANCESTRY LINE

BOOK I

DENBIGH FLINT
Tulunixiraq
Alaska – 2000 B.C.

OLD BERING SEA
Umiak and Oolik
Alaska – A.D. 300

BOOK II

ATHABASCAN INDIAN
Tiana and Nikota
Canada - A.D. 500

BOOK III

DORSET (Thule)
TuluGreenland – A.D. 900

MEDIEVAL NORSE
Eric the Red's son, Rolv
Greenland – 975 to 1500

WOMEN OF THE NORTHLANDS
Sedna
Mainland U. S./Alaska-contemporary

GLOSSARY OF INUIT AND INDIAN WORDS OR PHRASES

AAKLUQ	Brown bear, possibly the grizzly
AMAWK	The wolf
AYVUQ	Walrus
BABICHE -(Indian)	Braided moose hides
BALEEN	Springy material from the whale's mouth
EKOAVI	The place where people are afraid
INUIT	The People, as they called themselves – Eskimo
ITIKIYYIQ	Inuits applied this term to Indians because of their more aggressive nature – "The men who mate with wolves"
KASLIM (Indian)	Meeting place, usually a large tent
KARIGI	Place of gathering for winter games, feasts or men's doings
KAVAKTUQ	Red fox
KILIVACIAQ	The wooly mammoth
MAKARAUQ	Fighting – dissension – trouble making
MITKOSARRET	Five skins – enough for a jacket
MUKTUK	Whale skin, very much desired by Inuits
NAANUK	Polar bear

SEDNAH	Goddess of the sea, provider of food from the water
SERMISIRAQ	Name Inuits gave to glaciers – a place to avoid because of evil spirits
SHAMAN	Male or female wizard – served as buffer between the people and the supernatural
TULUGAAK	The raven – believed by aboriginal people to have created the earth
TULUNIXIRAQ	Name derives from "someone who can change forms from a person to a raven and back again" – in Women of the Northland series, the name refers to the Raven Mother who lived around 2,000BC
TUNARAK	Shaman's helping power – usually an animal, but sometimes ancestral spirits
TUNUNIRN	"The country beyond the back of something," probably where the WIIVASKAAT stay
ULU	Woman's curved, circular shaped knife, usually of bone or slate
UMIAK	Large skin-covered boat used in hunting or journeys
UMINGMAK	"The bearded one," meaning musk ox
WIIVAKSAAT	"Those who come around again" or "strangers in the sky" – dead people

SUGGESTED READING

Franz Boaz, *The Central Eskimo*, University of Nebraska Press, 1964

Fred Bruemmer, *The Arctic*, NY Times Book Company, 1974

Norman A. Chance, *The Eskimo of North Alaska*, Holt, Rinehart & Winston, NY, 1966

Robert Claiborne, *The First Americans*, Time Life Books, NY, 1973, pp1-33 and pp 88-109

Nelson Graburn, *Eskimos Without Igloos*, Little Brown, NY, 1969

June Helm, *The Indians of the Sub Arctic*, Indiana University Press, 1976

Hans Huesc, *Top of the World*, Simon & Schuster Pocket Books, NY, 1969

Diamond Jenness, *The People of the Twilight*, University of Chicago Press, 1959

Jesse D. Jennings, *Prehistory of North America*, McGraw-Hill, NY 1974

Geography of the North Lands, Kimble & Good, Editors, American Geographical Soc., 1955

North American Indians In Historical Perspective, Leacock & Lurin, Editors, Random House, NY, 1971

Wendell H. Oswalt, *This Land Was Theirs*, John Wiley & Sons, Inc., NY, 1966

Robert F. Spencer & Jesse D. Jennings, *The Native Americans*, Harper & Row, NY, 1965

Time Life Books, *The Poles*, Life Nature Library, NY, 1977

PERIODICALS

Douglas Chadwick, *Our Wildest Wilderness*, National Geographic, Dec 1979, pp. 740-769

Colin Irwin, *Trek Across Arctic America*, National Geographic, Mar 1974, pp. 295-321

David Jeffery, *Preserving America's Last Great Wilderness*, National Geographic, Jun 1975, pp. 769-791

Peoples of the Arctic, Joseph Judge, Editor, National Geographic, Feb 1983, pp. 144-223

Joseph Judge, *Alaska: Rising Northern Star*, National Geographic, Jun 1975, pp. 730-767

Thor Larsen, *Polar Bear: Lonely Nomad of the North*, National Geographic, Apr 1971, pp.574-590

Guy Mary-Rousseliere, *I Live With the Eskimos*, National Geographic, Feb 1971, pp. 189-217

About the Author . . .

Born and raised in Phoenix, Arizona, Pinkie Paranya soon discovered she was happiest when she allowed herself to put words on paper, or brush to canvas. After attending Northern Arizona University, she traveled on assignments in a motor home for many years in The United States, Canada and Mexico, with her professional photographer husband, Andy. Five of those years were spent in Alaska, where she developed a deep respect for the Inuit people.

After two years of concentrated research, she started the trilogy – WOMEN OF THE NORTHLAND. TIANA, Gift of the Moon, is the second of the trilogy. The first, RAVEN WOMAN, favored among critics, took silver historical in the prestigious BOOK OF THE YEAR award presented by FOREWORD Magazine.

In addition to the WOMEN OF THE NORTHLAND trilogy, Paranya has written 12 novels, some under the pseudonym, Carrie Peterson.

RAVEN WOMAN, first in the WOMEN OF THE NORTHLAND series, is available at amazon.com, bn.com, sandspublishing.com, most bookstores, or directly from the publisher.

To order toll-free by phone, dial 1 877 365 0241 ext 0342.

To order by mail, send 18.99 + 3.85 shipping & handling to:
   Book Orders
   SANDS Publishing, LLC
   PO Box 92
   Alpine, CA 91903

Watch for BOOK III in the series.